Edward Topol worked
the USSR before movi
prior to her emigratior
director. They now m
their daughter Sarah.

Topol's previous bestsellers include RED SQUARE, SUBMARINE U-137, DEADLY GAMES and RED GAS.

By Edward Topol in Futura:

RED GAS

THE RUSSIAN SEVEN

Emiliya and Edward Topol

translated by
Christopher Barnes and Roger Keys

Futura

A Futura Book

First published in Great Britain in 1990 by
Futura Publications, a Division of
Macdonald & Co (Publishers) Ltd
London & Sydney

ISBN 0 7088 4895 8

Reproduced, printed and bound in Great Britain by
BPCC Hazell Books
Aylesbury, Bucks, England
Member of BPCC Ltd.

Futura Publications
A Division of
Macdonald & Co (Publishers) Ltd
Orbit House
1 New Fetter Lane
London EC4A 1AR
A member of Maxwell Macmillan Pergamon Publishing Corporation

Dedicated to Olga Narodetsky and
the memory of Semyon Narodetsky

ISLAMABAD (Reuter) – Eighty Soviet troops were killed by guerrillas in northern Afghanistan in one of the worst death tolls for a single attack during the eight-year war, Western diplomats in Pakistan reported yesterday.

They quoted reports received from Afghanistan as saying two Soviets were also captured in the attack on the Salang highway, the main land link between Kabul and the Soviet border.

(1987)

PROLOGUE

Ulima was her name. U-li-ma . . .

At first Alexey didn't even get a proper look at her. A swarthy arm extended from the dark, cavern-like doorway of a claybuilt Afghan hut, and a slender hand beckoned him inside. With a furtive glance around him, Alexey ducked his head and dived into what half reminded him of a peasant hovel in the Caucasus, or a dog kennel. Two months before, he would have never been lured into an Afghan hut with a single wave of the hand: once inside you could as easily end up with a dagger between your shoulders as get a dressing-down from your commander. But at that time they had been up at Nanganhar, manning road blocks and outlying guard posts up in the mountains. It was their job to intercept any of the Mojahedin or their scouts, or any caravan consignment of weapons. And not only had they frozen to the marrow as they stood there on sentry duty, but at any moment one of the Mojahedin might jump you from the rear and rip your throat out with his knife. Down here, though, in the Lohar valley it was quite different. Compared with Nanganhar this was a real picnic. Of the eighty local villages more than half lay in ruins and were abandoned, and their inhabitants had fled to Pakistan. A further six villages were 'on trust'. This meant that the Soviet army command had reached an agreement with the local headman and the mullah: their village would not be bombed or fired on, and they would even be provided with kerosene fuel, so long as they did not allow the Mojahedin to use their area for launching attacks on Soviet forces. And of course, all around here there was greenery as cover, and kilometres of ravaged vineyards. There were also ancient underground irrigation canals called *kiriz* from which small bands of Mojahedin regularly emerged to mine the roads then disappear again, or else they attacked your columns and sniped at your guard posts ... Yet still these half dozen villages 'on trust' seemed like a paradise, a welcome oasis, after what they had experienced before.

When Alexey first came here and plunged into the darkness of that windowless hut, he merely caught a glimpse of her large dark eyes with dark lashes, a broad mouth, long nose and straight black hair. She was only a slip of a girl, perhaps no more than fifteen. Yet from the shadows by the wall an invisible figure could emerge at any moment, holding a dagger or a Kalashnikov rifle – even if this village was 'on trust'. How often had they been deceived! Only a week before, a Soviet team bringing a tanker-load of kerosene to one of these villages had been fired on by the Mojahedin. But here in Tapbil things were still quiet. Over the winter this large trading settlement (*tapbil* in Afghani meant 'barter') had changed hands several times, taken now by the Mojahedin, now by Afghan government troops, and now by the Soviets. The mosque was in ruins, and the terraces of clay and adobe huts had been gouged by missiles and tank tracks. It was hard to fathom how several dozen children and women had managed to survive. Probably they had hidden in the *kiriz*. And now they had found shelter in various howitzer shell craters roofed over with branches and straw, in hollows dug out of the hillside, and in a few adobe huts that had miraculously survived the artillery shelling. But how did they manage to keep alive? What did they eat? Where did they find pasture for their few mangy goats?

Alexey quickly thrust his hands into the bulging pockets of his army breeches and produced two tins of condensed milk and half a piece of black household soap.

But without taking her eyes off the tins, the girl shook her head and pointed a long slender finger with a dirty nail at his sleeveless army shirt, the edge of which showed under the open collar of his tunic. And she curled her finger a few times as a clear sign of what particular item of *tapbil* she had in mind.

Alexey hesitated – not because he begrudged her his shirt, but because he suddenly felt awkward at having to take off his tunic while this young Afghan girl stood watching. His eyes were getting used to the darkness, and he glanced around him. Here were all the signs of poverty and desolation. The one room contained neither table nor chairs. At the far end was a hearth and in the corner lay a straw-filled mattress.

'Where's the grass? The hashish?' he asked. And thinking she couldn't understand his Russian, he put his fingers to his lips and pretended to inhale deeply. The girl quickly took from inside her jacket a small package wrapped up in a dirty cloth. She drew back one edge of the wrapper and the air was immediately filled with the sweetish intoxicating odour of fresh hemp. Alexey's stomach churned and his hands and nostrils twitched impatiently. But the girl removed the package and held it with one hand behind her back as she pointed again at Alexey's shirt.

'You ... take off!' she suddenly said in Russian, but with a heavy Afghan accent.

He gave a start.

'What? ... Do you know Russian?'

'Leettle ... very leettle,' she answered slowly. 'Take off shirt.' Her accent gave her words a strange metallic ring.

'What? ... Right here?' Alexey was now even more hesitant. And the fact that the girl knew Russian made him feel even more awkward at stripping to the waist in front of her.

'Here! Yes! Here!' she insisted, still holding the package of hashish behind her back.

Alexey could no longer resist the tantalising heady

aroma. With a final glance around the bare walls of the hut, he quickly took the rifle from his shoulders, and holding it squeezed between his knees, he undid his belt with its heavy brass buckle and thrust it in the pocket of his breeches. Now all he had to do was pull off his tunic and shirt. But ... but the instant he pulled them over his head he would be unable to see around him. And at that moment it would be so easy to spike him – with a dagger, a knife, or whatever ...

'Not cowed! Not cowed!' the girl flashed with mocking impatience, and he guessed with difficulty that she meant he was not to be a coward.

In fact he did feel a certain shame at his fear. So with one jerk he pulled off both his tunic and shirt together. Then he tried awkwardly to extract the shirt from one of his jacket sleeves which had turned inside out. As he did so he felt the rifle slip from between his knees ...

'Give me! ..' The girl seized both his shirt and tunic. She quickly disentangled the shirt, then threw him his jacket together with the packet of hashish. She looked at Alexey's bare shoulders and chest intently. 'All Russians ... no hair!' she said. She gave a wry laugh and shook her head sadly.

'How do *you* know all Russians are like that?' he asked mockingly as he pushed his arms back through the tangled sleeves of his tunic.

'I know,' she said, and Alexey for some reason believed her.

Suddenly she turned away from him. In a single movement she flung off her own tattered dingy knitted jacket and quickly put on his shirt. For a second Alexey caught a glimpse of the girl's dark spine with its sharp shoulder-blades and tender narrow shoulders. He was dumbfounded that an Afghan girl should get undressed in front of a man – and a Russian soldier, a *shuravi*, at that!

'It's still warm.' She turned towards him with a sudden happy smile. Bending coquettishly, she tied the broad hem of the shirt in a knot at her hips and stroked the soft material. For a moment the shirt stretched tightly over her small pointed breasts with their large nipples.

Now he had his hashish, Alexey fumbled in his pockets for some paper to roll a joint.

'Dammit!' he swore aloud. He had no paper, there were only crumbs of tobacco in his pockets. 'Do you have paper? Newspaper?' he asked, still looking down in embarrassment as he did so.

The girl looked at him intently and said nothing. She probably hasn't understood, Alexey thought.

'Paper! I want to smoke ... hashish!' he said again, and pretended to roll a cigarette to show what he meant.

She continued staring. Then without a word she turned away and went to a shelf, her bare feet shuffling lightly on the earthen floor. She stood up on tiptoe, reached out and fumbled in a brass dish and produced several hand-rolled cigarettes. She motioned towards the two jars of condensed milk and the soap that still lay at his feet.

'*Tapbil?*' she asked.

'*Tapbil.* O.K. *Tapbil,*' he agreed quickly. He was now desperate for a smoke.

He took a few paces towards her and hastily held out a hand. He knew Afghan women hated Soviet soldiers ... they hated and feared them. And the girls often put on their ugliest tattered dresses, trying not to attract attention, covering their faces and going around only in groups. But this girl! ... She suddenly held out a little swarthy clenched fist. Racked by a yearning to inhale which gripped at his stomach and very bones, Alexey seized her hot little fist and carefully began straightening out the fingers. She gave a sudden tinkling laugh. Her palm was empty, and she playfully hid her other hand behind her back.

He felt himself blushing.

'What are you up to? ... Stop it! I want a smoke! Give me one!'

Still laughing she backed away and gently lay down on the bedding in the corner. She tucked her legs up under her and covered them with her broad dark skirt.

'Come,' she said. 'We smoke together.' She patted the mattress next to her. Then, from goodness knows where, from a pocket in her voluminous skirt, she suddenly produced a large brass lighter made from an empty cartridge. A lot of Russian soldiers made these lighters, not because there were no matches, but so as to bring home some memento of army life in Afghanistan. The flint rasped and she quickly lit up, then, taking it in turns, they inhaled several times in silence.

Blissfully Alexey stretched out his legs.

'How do you know Russian?' he asked.

'I know,' she said reluctantly, 'because I had friend ... he teach me. Now he not there. Allah call him.'

'Who was it? Someone from our unit?' He studied her intently. Even in this peaceful spot, twenty-three men of their regiment had been killed over the last two months. At one time, a year or more ago, everyone had felt a comrade's death almost as if it were his own. As they returned to camp from some sortie, or from guard duty on the road blocks and outlook posts, they had been unable to bear the sight of the empty bunks of the men who had been killed or gone to hospital. Several of the men had wept and howled, beating their heads on their pillows. And in the mornings you were scared to open your eyes: you knew you were bound to be sent on some dangerous new assignment, and by that evening it might be your own bunk that was empty. But later on they became numbed by it all and began looking for ways of escape – by smoking hashish, for instance. Or else they were worked into a frenzy and began seeking to avenge the deaths of their comrades.

'Who taught you Russian?' Alexey repeated his question after her first vague answer.

'You not know him,' she said brusquely and rather reluctantly. 'He was killed before you come. You not come a year ago.'

'How do you know when I came here?' Alexey said in surprise.

'Ulima know. Your friend you go with ... Ulima know him too.' She gave a quiet laugh. The hashish had made her slightly giggly.

Yury Shalygin was Alexey's bosom friend. He was number four in the crew of their reconnaissance vehicle. And he was somewhere in the vicinity right now. Yury's main occupation was bartering old army uniforms and supplies in exchange for hashish and goat's milk. But his main achievement was his idea of running a power-line down to the village from the generator in their unit. It provided the villagers with light and also made it possible to put them 'on trust'. It meant that in exchange for electricity the villagers were to keep the Mojahedin away from that area. So in the eyes of these locals Yury Shalygin was a hero, and the commander would happily release him to do minor repairs on the power-line and also to 'foster contacts with the local populace', as the official phrase had it. That meant repairing some old woman's wall or else teaching local children the letters of the Russian alphabet. In other words, their unit was behaving like true 'internationalist warriors'. And Yury in particular was someone who was never lost for words. He could pull the wool over anyone's eyes and talk the hind leg off any officer. And he could even hold his own in Afghani – unlike the rest of them who could just about manage 'Salaam aleikum' (How do you do?), 'Khosh amadyd' (welcome), and 'Tashakur' (thank you). And of course, whenever Yury went down to the village of Tapbil he took Alexey with him ...

'So they call you Ulima, do they?' Alexey held out a hand to take the hashish joint. 'My name's Alexey.'

'Ulima – she know you Alexey, Aliyosha,' she said. But she did not hand him the joint and held it away in her other hand. Then suddenly she knelt up and moved closer to him. The scent of her warm skin made him catch his breath. She embraced him about the neck with one arm, and with the other hand she placed the short stump of hashish to his lips. He was taken by surprise and choked and coughed. It took him some time to recover. Ulima waited patiently, still with her arm about his neck; her moist dark eyes looked down at him mockingly. Then, suddenly she lifted the shirt up to her shoulders and pressed a strong brown nipple to his lips. Alexey fastened on it hungrily and embraced her round the waist with both hands. She gave a soft moan and then laughed again.

Never before had Alexey known such excitement as he kissed the firm, salty nipples that filled half of Ulima's breasts. They reminded him of the large sun-dried plums which he used to stuff into his mouth as a boy, when nobody was looking. Grandma Masha used to scold him for it, and she kept making the sign of the cross over him for fear he might choke. But Alexey used to run away and hide in the bushes, his cheeks stuffed with black prunes. And like those prunes, he now relished the feel of Ulima's nipples in his mouth as he rolled them around with his tongue or nibbled them gently with his teeth.

Ulima lay beneath him and moaned softly. Now she drew up her legs beneath her, now she stretched them taut. She was inexhaustible and hugged him about the neck with her slender arms. This Afghan girl had given herself to him of her own accord ... to him, a Russian *shuravi*! And what a girl she was! In that small, fragile body he could sense an amazing energy. Her desire seemed to burn her from inside, tearing at her thighs. And then she cried out, as though seared by some pain – a wild, guttural cry.

She had a strange body: breasts, stomach and shoulders that were smooth and tender, while her arms and legs were hard and hairy, as though they belonged to another person. And Alexey liked this better, after the inert, flaccid bodies of the Russian girls he used to clutch in the bushes behind the dance-hall, or earlier under the stairs at the orphanage. But here was a girl whose body was pliant, full of life, and pulsing inside with waves of some animal energy. And now that same energy suddenly prompted the two of them to freeze and cling to one another. It was then that he felt her own furious internal pulsing, contracting and expanding, like small hot pincers that gently gripped him ... As they lay there on that straw mattress, it occurred to him that the dusky Oriental knows far more about love than any pallid Westerner. But he could not endure the ordeal of that motionless paradise for long. Her own fire flooded into him, and new stores of energy and strength which he never knew he had exploded within him, arched his back and hurled him into the assault, groaning and gasping with never a pause to recover. Again, again and again ... the imperious and impatient West melted and fused with the mystic steady fire of the Orient. Again, again ... as though for the first and very last time in life ...

The shadow of the nearby hill had fallen over the village before they heard the crunch of Yury Shalygin's boots upon the stones. Then there was the sound of him whistling uncertainly as he tried to summon his friend.

Alexey emerged from the hut, dragging his rifle by the strap. He still could not fathom why God, or Allah, had presented him with this crazy young Afghan girl. If the Mojahedin found out they would kill her – they would quarter her, hack her to pieces. But he did not think about that. His legs were trembling, and even his arms felt unusually feeble. And the whole of his body somehow seemed empty and transparent. If at that moment he had been blown up by a grenade he would scarcely have felt it. It was as though he had left the whole of his strength behind in the girl's now quiescent body, as she lay there on the mattress, on the floor of that clay-adobe hut ...

So Ulima was her name ... U-li-ma ...

PART ONE

1

'Well, ladies and gentlemen, we've just landed at Moscow Sheremetyevo. Moscow time is now 5.45 a.m. and there are twenty degrees of frost outside. Br-r-r-r! Well, I for one am not very fond of frost, and I'll be turning round right away and flying back to the US. But to those of you who are staying on, I wish you an enjoyable stay in Moscow ... And thank you once again for flying Pan Am!'

The captain of the Boeing had a gentle soothing baritone, and over the intercom it had a certain beguiling sincerity, like a priest at confession. As they rolled slowly towards the terminal, the passengers had their eyes glued to the aircraft windows. But in the blackness of that March night there was little to see apart from signal lights on the runway. At last, however, the engines were cut, and the 'no smoking' and seatbelt signs turned off. Then a fairly heavy jolt against the side of the Boeing signalled that the expanding bellows of the passenger gangway had docked with the aircraft.

'That's your first bit of rough Russian service,' one passenger commented loudly.

The others responded with a nervous laugh. They were now queuing in line for the aircraft exit and eagerly looking around them. Like all tourists, they immediately expected a host of new impressions, even before passing through Customs, and they were not disappointed: already in the disembarkation corridor there were two soldiers, or frontier guards, in green caps and with rifles held at the ready. One of them had an obviously oriental appearance, but to the tourists he was a Russian all the same. And at this first glimpse of a Russian, one of the jovial types one always encounters in a tourist group immediately turned his camera on him. But the other guard, who was fair-haired, severely raised a warning finger.

'*Nelzya*!' he said.

'*Nelzya* means "It's forbidden" in Russian,' said another tourist, who knew. 'That's a good word to start learning Russian with....'

Meanwhile the other passengers were already filing past the soldiers and trying not to look them in the eye.

As they entered the Customs Hall they were cheered to see on the wall a huge poster displaying an American Express credit card against a background of Moscow's Red Square. They formed queues at the glass passport control booths where young Russian border guards sat checking the new arrivals. The queue moved fairly rapidly. However, there was one blue passport embossed with 'United States of America' which aroused special interest in a young blue-eyed official: GOEHR, TANYA were the surname and forename of its bearer. Then came further details: Date of Birth – 19 July 1904; Sex – F, Place of Birth – RUSSIA.

The official looked up. Before him stood a tall, gaunt elderly woman with powerful features and dressed in a light cream leather coat with a fur lining. She was obviously nervous, although her bearing conveyed total self-confidence – her glance was severe and direct, somehow almost relentless. Her lips were pursed and she clutched one kid glove firmly in her left hand. The young officer had done a special course in psycho-physiognomy, and he was about to raise his left foot to press the special button warning the Customs Officers ahead to take special care in checking the luggage of this woman. But at that instant his glance fell on the ungloved right hand with which she had just handed him her passport. He had seen plenty of wealthy tourists before, but at this sight his eyes went wide with astonishment. On the woman's slender aristocratic fingers were three rings of exquisite beauty and obviously of immense worth. One was of white gold with a large, probably twelve-carat, brilliant in its centre, surrounded by a two-tier spanglement of smaller diamonds. The second ring was of antique dark gold set with a large emerald. And the third, like the first, was of white gold with a black agate on which was sculpted a complex coat of arms, round which ran a chain of small diamonds. All the rings together had a special air of antiquity about them. They were of a sort that one could normally see on display only in the Moscow Kremlin, where the tsars' crown jewels were kept.

'Have you included your rings in the Customs declaration?' the inspector asked her in English.

'*Da*', Tanya Goehr replied in Russian.

He glanced at her declaration form. In the section 'Items of jewelry and other valuables' was written: '2 (two) platinum and 1 (one) gold ring with brilliants and diamonds'. And in the section 'Approximate value' she had put the single word 'priceless'.

'Do you not want to leave them with the Customs for safe-keeping until you leave?' he asked her, switching to Russian.

'No,' she said sharply. 'I never take these rings off. I've worn them for sixty years. You'll have to cut my arm off if you want to remove them!'

'Oh, no, no! Good heavens, no!' he smiled in frightened protest. He had now removed his foot from the signal button. After all, an old woman openly wearing rings like that would not be trying to smuggle in narcotics, Bibles, or other anti-Soviet literature. Her entry visa was in order – she had got it in New York along with other members of her group. So she could be let in without further ado. But the young inspector's curiosity prompted him to one final question:

'You were born in the USSR, I see. Whereabouts?'

'I was not born in the USSR. I was born in Russia,' she announced sharply.

'Well, it's all one and the same,' he smiled. His sympathy for the elderly woman was growing and he wanted to demonstrate the fact to her.

But Tanya Goehr gave a shrewish smile and said haughtily, 'Oh, no, young man. Russia is Russia ... for Russians anyway, at least!'

His face became serious again and the two of them exchanged a hard glance.

'But you're an American now ...' he smiled again, deciding not to bother with her further. He raised his hand to stamp her declaration form.

'I'm an American citizen and a Russian princess!' she declared.

The young official looked at her again and his hand hovered, still holding the stamp above her declaration form.

'Goehr?' he puzzled. 'Is that the name of a family of princes?'

'It is my husband's surname. And he incidentally was also a nobleman. But my maiden name was Odalevskaya. One of my ancestors was prince Odalevsky, the nephew of General Kutuzov. Any more questions?'

Her steely tone and furious glance that blazed with the same inner fire as her diamonds might have incinerated the young official as he sat there in his dark-green tunic and Young Communist League badge. But he withstood her gaze.

'And how long is it since you were last in Russia?'

'Sixty-eight years. I left in February 1919.'

He banged his stamp down on her declaration form, then laid the form inside her passport and handed it back to her. With a smile he said in English again: 'Welcome home!'

'What an idiot! What a cretin I am! What an old fool! Thank God it turned out all right ... But what an old fool I am!' Tanya Goehr thought to herself. 'Fancy getting caught up with that young whippersnapper! What has he got to do with me? He wasn't around seventy years ago. You old cretin! ...'

Tanya continued to curse herself as she nervously drew on a cigarette. But she never lost her smile. For two reasons. First of all, she hadn't lost her nerve or let herself be put out by that young Bolshevik border guard. She had answered him in the way these communists deserved to be addressed by a Russian princess, even if he was only a boy. And secondly . . .

'Attention please! Those awaiting passengers due to arrive from Warsaw: flight number 113 has now landed and . . .'

All these public announcements were in Russian. . . . in *Russian*! And all these Russian signs everywhere: 'Departure Gate', 'Ticket Office', 'Information' . . . and all the people around her hurrying in various directions, laughing, greeting one another and saying their farewells – and all talking *Russian*! It set her heart and head spinning, in just the same way as dancing the mazurka had when she was a girl. She had prepared herself for this journey to Russia more carefully than even the most perceptive Soviet border guard could have suspected. Yet in all her mental preparations (which actually even allowed for some contretemps with the Customs) she had overlooked one thing: the simply wonderful, magical pleasure of hearing people around her speak Russian! For sixty-eight years she had been surrounded by other languages – like sailing in foreign waters. But now, here she was, back in her native element!

She turned this way and that, absorbing the sound of Russian speech and the notices. And in order to dispel the imbecile happy smile she knew she was wearing, she continued to reproach herself for the quite unnecessary discussion with the border official.

At last she caught sight of her friend Elizabeth, whose buxom figure could now be seen emerging from the Customs control area. Glancing myopically over her spectacles and hauling her little suitcase on wheels, Elizabeth came over to join Tanya and the other American tourists who were gathering by a window that was now letting in the first signs of wintery daylight.

As she joined Tanya, Elizabeth's cheeks puffed and blazed with righteous anger.

'Just imagine! It turns out that you can't bring in more than one Bible,' she said. 'And what's more, they've written on my declaration that I've got a Bible with me. So I can't leave it behind here! Can you imagine it?!'

'I can imagine it perfectly,' Tanya smiled. Meanwhile she was looking away over Elizabeth's grey head towards the remaining tourists who were moving through Customs with their baggage. The one she was interested in – a young girl with a drained appearance, evidently from lack of sleep – was still a long way off and still standing at the back of the queue.

'And you know that woman from New Jersey,' Elizabeth continued. 'The one with the outside pockets on her case? Well, she had those pockets stuffed with all sorts of oddments – chewing gum, razor blades, mascara, and eyeshadow. And do you know? The whole lot has vanished! Can you imagine?'

'It could have been stolen in Brussels ...' Tanya said dismissively.

'Do you think so?' Elizabeth adjusted her spectacles. 'Yes, maybe ... Well, it's not too bad at all here ... quite a decent terminal in fact. Just look how the ceiling is decorated. It looks like a set of organ pipes!'

The roof of the terminal hall was decorated with a pattern of sawn-off metal tubes, like cake tins, and only Elizabeth's feverish imagination could have seen any similarity with an organ. But that was Elizabeth's strong point: she could sense even the finest changes of mood in her friend Tanya and immediately adjusted to them. She quite readily therefore discarded her anti-Soviet views of earlier (which she had in fact acquired from Tanya), and she now began reflecting Tanya's own delighted view of her Russian surroundings ...

'Are you from the USA? With Golden Flight tours?' a voice called out.

The American tourists turned and saw a short man of between thirty-five and forty hurrying towards them. He wore a leather jacket and a mohair scarf, and on his head was a deerskin hat with earflaps. His fur-lined boots skidded on the marble flooring as he came to a halt half a yard in front of them.

'Is that right? Golden Flight tours? A party of twenty-eight? All correct?'

'Yes, sir!' Elizabeth announced.

'My name is Oleg – Oleg Petrov,' the man continued. 'I shall be your guide and interpreter. Welcome to Moscow. I hope you aren't too exhausted after your long flight?' He spoke with perfect fluency and had an English accent. When he smiled, his round face with its chubby, girlish chin lit up and had an air of quiet charm. A face like that seemed calculated to put one at one's ease and smooth out all conflict. Maybe that was why Elizabeth immediately proffered her hand in greeting.

'I'm Elizabeth Wollens,' she said, 'How nice of you to come and meet us! Here we were standing around and not knowing what to do or where to go! And I'm terribly nervous of strange places.'

'I should warn you straight away, Oleg,' said Tanya. 'My friend is always inclined to exaggerate her fears.'

'Oh, you've nothing to fear in this country!' Oleg smiled. But where are the rest of you?' He quickly glanced around the group. 'Are they still going through Customs? Surely not! I'll go and give them a hand. Please wait for me here. Don't go away. We'll be setting off for Moscow in about ten minutes!'

Tanya watched warily as he walked away. Two hours had now passed since they arrived, and it was now getting light outside. But barely half of the passengers from their plane had made it through Customs. The officials were X-raying every single suitcase, bundle and handbag with that apparatus of theirs which showed up every bit of metal right down to the last button and hatpin. But in addition they were also going through all the luggage by hand and pulling out objects like walkmen and other radio apparatus, copies of *Playboy* and *Penthouse*, Bibles and other books . . .

But once Oleg Petrov turned up things did start to move faster. He went through into the Customs area and called out in a commanding voice: 'All tourists on Golden Flight! Golden Flight. . . . Over here!' And he gathered in his eight remaining charges like a mother hen with her chicks. Among them was Judy Sanders, the girl Tanya Goehr had been looking out for. Petrov took his group to another Customs desk. It seemed not to be working, but he left them there for a moment and ran off into some inner room. Then he appeared again immediately with another Customs official, who quickly began checking the remaining Americans' things. And he did so in a manner that suggested he didn't care how many copies of the Bible or of *Penthouse* they were carrying. But even in this small queue Judy Sanders held back right to the end. Tanya smiled to herself. Judy was obeying her instructions down to the letter. Her pallid face and the inflammation around her eyes were not the result of make-up either. They were natural in someone who was playing her part for all it was worth: she was the very image of a sickly student who spent her days studying Russian and poring in libraries and language laboratories at New York University.

Back in New York Tanya had set things up precisely. At no time during the Moscow trip was Judy to reveal that they were already acquainted. She was to keep to herself the whole time. So that even if Tanya had trouble there because of her own Russian aristocratic origins, this would not prevent Judy from carrying out her part of the mission to Moscow. In fact, of course, it was a scheme that involved all three of them – not just Judy, but Tanya and Elizabeth as well.

'Tell me, are Russian women allowed to wear make-up? I'd heard it was forbidden . . .' came a voice from the front of the bus. It was the forty-year-old New Jersey woman who had lost the chewing gum and eyeshadow from her luggage. She was obviously now trying it on with the guide and holding forth about Russian winters as though she had never seen snow before back in New Jersey.

'Good heavens! What nonsense!' Oleg answered with a laugh. 'How could you stop a woman from using make-up, even if you tried?!' Then, more seriously, he announced over the loudspeaker system in the coach:

'Ladies and gentlemen, you have come to a country unlike any other which you may have visited. Nevertheless, it isn't a zoo full of wild animals. People here live just as people do everywhere. So I would ask you to try and forget all the cheap, false information you may have been fed on television and in the newspapers. Of course, there are plenty of things wrong here too, but we talk about them more openly and freely even than the *Washington Post*! In fact, you have come to a country full of life and interest, where amazing changes are now taking place. So keep your eyes open and come to your own conclusions. We've nothing to hide any more ...'

Tanya did not need such advice. Her eyes were already glued to the windows of the bus. And what she saw amazed her. She knew of course that a lot of new houses had been built in Moscow, and even whole new streets. But somehow she expected that would be only a superficial impression, and somehow irrelevant. Inwardly she was convinced she was flying back to visit the old Moscow she knew and loved. Although over the years the Bolsheviks had probably allowed it to go to rack and ruin – like some of those awful places in the Bronx, where a Puerto-Rican taxi driver had once taken her by mistake. And if things turned out to be not quite as bad as in the Bronx, even that was to be expected – after all, the Bolsheviks did have to keep the country going somehow or other!

However, as she looked out of the broad windows of their Czechoslovak-built motor coach, what she saw bore no relation to the communist concentration camp she had mentally pictured. On both sides of the straight six-lane motorway, as far as the eye could see, there were huge residential blocks rising up twelve and fifteen storeys. Tanya had seen suburban areas like that in Europe, in some areas of Paris. But even there, such tower blocks were usually clumped near together, whereas here there were broad, open spaces, snow-covered parks, houses, schools, trolleybuses, a stadium, another park, and after that the usual panorama of white buildings. And all this she saw framed in the frosty pink tremulous haze of a Moscow dawn. Everything sparkled in the sunshine, hoar-frost and clean air. Good heavens, so this was Russia!

'And now, ladies and gentlemen, if you all look to your right,' said the guide's voice over the speaker system, 'You'll see Moscow's Northern River Station. In the centre of this building with all its tracery, you can see the tower with its spire of stainless steel. On top of it there is a five-pointed star – one of those that used to decorate the Kremlin towers. Maybe it will strike you that the river station itself resembles a steamer lying at anchor? That was how the architect Rukhlyadyev planned it back in 1937 . . .'

Elizabeth held Tanya's hand in her own and squeezed it encouragingly. She sensed her friend's fingers grow numb, and saw her gaze riveted on the scene outside. Tanya seemed unaware of the conversations around her. Of course, Elizabeth felt like saying something to Tanya, either to cheer her, or else to express her own, weepy emotion at this solemn moment of Tanya's re-encounter with Russia. But she was afraid lest her friend might suddenly be annoyed with her, or – even worse – burst into tears herself. Although Elizabeth had never seen Princess Goehr weep – not even in the hospital in Sarasota, Florida, where they had met two years ago, on the day Tanya's husband died. And even then this austere and imperious princess had not given way to tears but had simply collapsed on the floor of the hospital foyer and then spent more than a week in a ward of the same hospital. Then she had got up, dry-eyed, and without a tear she had gone to the cemetery to visit her husband's grave ...

But now Elizabeth was convinced Tanya must be choking back tears. Yet this tight-reined Russian aristocrat seemed incapable of letting go, even at such a joyful moment as this.

Tanya meanwhile was grateful for Elizabeth's silence. Yet she could not understand herself. If she had seen what she secretly expected to see – old, half-ruined houses with peeling stucco, dirty streets and people dressed in rags – she might have felt a certain spiteful pleasure. But those newspaper reports of Russia having been enslaved or conquered by the Bolsheviks were simply not true. Say what people might, Tanya herself could remember how in 1917 and 1918 Moscow had seemed to go mad with its red Bolshevik flags and slogans. Everyone, even her father, had worn red ribbons; students on the streets had joined in a rousing chorus of the 'Marseillaise', and working families, intoxicated with their new status, were settled in the houses of aristocrats who had either fled or been executed. And if she could have seen these houses in ruins, maybe that would have been a form of historical retribution for her own parents' execution in 1919, and for the children which, thanks to the Bolsheviks, she herself had never borne. On the other hand, was it fair to wish ill upon the grandchildren of those who were once fooled by Lenin's slogans about 'All power to the workers!', 'Land for the peasants!', 'Peace to the people!'? And was that blue-eyed Russian border guard to blame for what had happened to Tanya sixty-eight years ago? Even so, as she looked at those fine new residential areas, Tanya could not help pursing her lips with a sense of embitterment.

As they stopped at a red traffic signal, the gleaming side of a tram pulled level with them. Its windows were brightly lit, and the seats inside were empty apart from one at the rear where a man of about fifty was asleep with his head slumped against the window. His mouth was wide open and his grey sunken cheeks were unshaven.

Tanya recoiled in horror. No! It couldn't be true!

Those soldiers who had raped her back in 1919 would have been about his age. Was she doomed to see those awful spectres from the past wherever she went in Russia?

The tram had by now already turned off into the depot, but Tanya could still not control a nervous shiver that ran through her.

'What is the matter? What has happened?' Elizabeth asked anxiously.

Meanwhile the guide continued:

'And now we are coming onto the famous Gorky Street. To the right you can see the Belorussian Station Square and the monument to the great proletarian writer Maxim Gorky . . .'

Tanya gazed out at the square and the station from which sixty-seven years ago she and her parents had left Russia. Good Lord, here it was at last, her Russia! They were the same station buildings, the freshly painted pink and green pilasters, domed towers and massive wooden doors. And – heavens! – the same yardmen in their aprons worn over black overcoats or quilted jackets were clearing snowdrifts with shovels and breaking up ice on the pavements with heavy metal crowbars. 'Good grief!' Tanya shuddered as though she had seen another ghost. Just as it was half a century ago – still wearing their felt boots! But where was the Triumphal Arch?! What was so wrong with an arch built to celebrate the defeat of Napoleon 175 years ago?

Before Tanya's gaze flashed the stencilled signs of shops and cafés: 'Tadzhikistan', 'Pioneer', 'Dynamo', 'Anchor', 'Men's suits'. Heavens! This was old Tverskaya Street! Garrulous and pulsating with life, bright and luxurious, this street was a place where sumptuous carriages had once bowled along, drawn by famous Kursk trotters; here in about 1915, the first car horns had honked; tradesmen had offered sweets, chocolate and hot rolls for sale from their trays, and newsboys had sold copies of the *Stock Exchange News*. So Tverskaya had now been turned into

Gorky Street. What a contrast! Occasional passers-by huddled in the cold; there were crudely uniform notices, plaster-casts or paper-maché mock-ups of food products in the shop windows, and the gigantic poster above a concert hall proclaimed that 'Art Belongs to the People!' ...

What about the English Club? Was that still there? Tanya had difficulty restraining a shriek. There it was! There was its famous metal fence, colonnade and familiar lions at the gate! It was here that her father had come – her beloved father who had been so successful and happy both in his work and family life. And it was here that Tanya had attended her very first ball. There was only one thing that now offended her gaze: on the wall of the Club, where all the leading figures of Moscow had once congregated, was a sign proclaiming it was now the 'Central Museum of the Revolution'.

Tanya turned away from the window and for the rest of the journey to their hotel she gazed stolidly at the back of the seat in front of her. No, it was not her country! Enough sentimentality! She had come here for a purpose, and it was for that that she had engaged the services of Judy Sanders, who was sitting at the far end of the bus. So she ought to cut out the emotion and be serious and practical. She should forget that she was back in her homeland: she was simply 'travelling abroad' on business ... How was Judy finding things? ... They had a mere fourteen days to carry out their operation ...

2

The elegant hand with its carefully pared nails rapped loudly and impatiently on the glass pane.

'For God's sake, Ivan Mikhailovich! Is it so hard to find someone in this lousy factory of yours?'

The owner of the hand – and of the voice – was a pale-eyed young man of thirty-five. He was clean-shaven and had fair hair and regular, handsome features. Over his white shirt and tie he wore a grey suit that was obviously of foreign cut. He sat on the sill by the window which commanded a view of the whole factory courtyard. But despite his casual pose with one leg crossed over the other, he was obviously annoyed and his foot in its immaculate black leather shoe kept twitching.

Next to him, by the wall, sat another man of sporting build, and of about the same age. But he was less handsome. Somehow his face did not match his physique: it was small-featured and stony, with prominent Tatar cheekbones and low forehead. He kept running a sinewy hand through his hair, which was cut short like a boxer's. And although he had the same well-polished shoes, his suit was less smart than his companion's. As he sat there, he was examining a file that was labelled:

PERSONAL FILE
Alexey ODALEVSKY
(Metal-worker 4th Grade)

'Now, you young men ... Oh, er, pardon me! Comrades, that is ... Don't get excited!'

The new speaker, who was trying to reassure the first man, was Ivan Mikhailovich Gushchin. Gushchin, who was party secretary of the Red Banner machine-construction plant at Mytishchi, near Moscow, was a thick-set, elderly man of at least sixty-five.

'They'll find him! He can't be far away ...' said Gushchin ingratiatingly as he got up and went over to the window.

Outside, the large factory yard lay under snow and its wintery desolation was emphasised by the dull windowless concrete-block workshops surrounding it, and by the sluggish movement of a tractor, forklift truck and three workmen who were sitting down below in the smoke-room. As Gushchin watched, one of them produced from inside his quilted jacket an object that was all too familiar in Russia – a little quarter-litre bottle of vodka. Pulling off the cap, he immediately put the bottle to his mouth.

'Well, I'll be damned!' Gushchin fumed. And to the ironic amusement of the fair-haired man, he rushed to open the window and find out the name of the alcoholic who was breaking all the work rules. But at that moment there was a cautious knock at the door.

'Yes?' Gushchin said in a voice now full of authority. 'Who's there?'

The door opened. On the threshold stood a young man of about twenty-two. He had black hair and a slight stoop. He was wearing a slightly crumpled quilted jacket and a checked shirt, and his thick flannel trousers were tucked into his military boots and caught in at the waist with a broad soldier's belt that had a metal fastener. He stopped in the doorway looking from under his brow and with his hands thrust in his jacket pockets.

'You sent for me?'

'Come in, Odalevsky!' Gushchin said imperiously. 'How is it that it took half an hour to find you? These comrades here have come all the way from Moscow ...'

'Well, if you must know, I've been on the john. I've had stomach cramps.' Odalevsky's thick parched lips parted in an ingenuous smile. 'So why have these people come from Moscow?'

'Never mind, come in ... come in! Let's have a look at you!' The fair-haired man sprang from the window-seat and came forward holding out a hand. 'My name is Igor. And this is my friend Stanislav – Stass for short,' he said, pointing to his companion. Then, turning to Gushchin, he added: 'Comrade Gushchin, could you possibly fix us some tea?'

Gushchin sprang to his feet and trundled towards the door.

'Of course, of course! Coming right away! I'll have it ready in a jiffy. And would the gentlemen like it with a little lemon, or without?'

'No hurry, comrade Gushchin. We've plenty of time. And we've got a thing or two to discuss with Alyosha here.' Igor beamed broadly at Odalevsky. 'Sit down, Alyosha.'*

Alexey looked round in surprise as Gushchin disappeared through the door. Cautiously he eyed the guests from Moscow. Who were they? How was it that even the party organiser fawned on them? Even to the point of fetching tea for them? ...

'When did you get back from Afghanistan?'

'In August of last year.'

'And which unit were you with?'

'I'm not entitled to talk about my army service. I've signed the form – the one about official secrets.'

Stass swapped glances with Igor. Then, opening the black leather attaché case on his knee, he produced a sheet of stiff paper and held it out to Alexey. It was a photocopy of an official letter with a printed heading across the top of the page:

* Alyosha – familiar form of Alexey – *Tr.*

MINISTRY OF DEFENCE OF THE USSR

Instruction No. 126/03 of 25 March 1981

TO ALL SOLDIERS, SERGEANTS AND OFFICERS OF THE RESERVE

engaged in service on the territory of Afghanistan, and to all signatories of the document concerning 'Non-Divulgence of Official Secrets':–

I thereby bring to your notice that in accordance with the CPSU Central Committee resolution of 24 March 1981 and in the interests of national security, the USSR Committee for State Security (KGB) has been permitted to conduct questioning of former servicemen in the Soviet Army.

Upon production of identification documents employees of the Committee for State Security are entitled to receive complete information on all questions concerning former servicemen's period of army service.

(Signed) P. Ustinov
Minister of Defence of the USSR
Marshal of the Soviet Union

Once he saw Alexey had read the instruction, Stass took the sheet from him and returned it to his case.

'This document entitles you to answer all our questions. Including any about Afghanistan. And here's my official identity card – just so you're not in doubt as to whom you are talking.' He thrust a folded red identification pass in front of Alexey, who spotted the small gold embossed letters 'State Security Committee'. Then, with a practised gesture Stass opened up the pass to show his own photograph and name marked in Indian ink: 'Senior Lieutenant of State Security, S.F. Koval'.

'Now why do you put the wind up a man by showing him that?' Igor frowned with displeasure. 'After all, we're talking to an Afghan war hero! And he was wounded out there, weren't you? How long were you in hospital, Alyosha?'

'Three months and six days. But what is it you want of me?'

'Out in Afghanistan you were friends with private Yury Shalygin.' Stass leaned back on his chair and looked Alexey straight in the eye. 'During the April advance in the Lohar valley private Shalygin disappeared. And since that time he has been regarded as "missing in action". Recently, though, we learned that he voluntarily gave himself up to the Mojahedin and has been granted political asylum in Britain. So we wanted to talk to you about this former mate of yours.'

'What do you expect me to tell you?' Alexey gave an embarrassed smile. 'I don't know anything ...'

'Wipe the grin off your face, Odalevsky!' Stass said sharply. 'If that scum Shalygin had merely deserted none of us would give a damn! Or even if he'd given a couple of anti-Soviet interviews to the papers or the BBC ... we'd have weathered that. But the bastard has gone back from England to Afghanistan – or else he makes regular trips there – and he's actually helping the other side! He's not doing any shooting, but he's turning out anti-Soviet literature. Have a look at this!'

Stass opened his attaché case again and produced what looked like a copy of *Pravda* and laid it on the table in front of Alexey. Alexey looked at it in bewilderment. It was a copy of *Pravda* all right ... slightly yellowed, probably it was one of last year's.

'Just read the headlines, Alyosha,' Igor said gently from the side.

Alexey took the paper and could not believe his eyes. On the front page was a heading that read: 'Russian soldiers – victims of Soviet Communist Party criminal policy'. Alexey held the newspaper out at arm's length in alarm.

'Just read some of the articles. Come on, read them!' said Stass in a commanding voice.

'Why?' asked Alexey.

'I think probably he's seen articles like these in those leaflets that sometimes get passed around in Afghanistan,' said Igor.

Alexey realised at once: this was one of the propaganda leaflets that the Mojahedin periodically scattered around at Soviet troop positions. Once in Nanganhar half the town was littered with them. They contained phrases about the 'fascist authorities in the Kremlin', the 'communist yoke', the 'barbarian Russian occupying force', and about Russian soldiers bringing shame on themselves by killing old men, women and children, and about how more than a hundred Russians had crossed to the Mojahedin side and were fighting for the Afghanistan National Islamic Front against the Soviet army. Probably it was those deserters who wrote the leaflets. But they had been written by hand and had spelling mistakes in them that made all the Russian soldiers laugh. But here was an actual newspaper – *Pravda*, set up in type! Yet what had all this to do with Yury Shalygin?

'Have you ever heard the surname Tverdysh?' Stass asked.

'No,' Alexei answered.

'Are you sure?'

'Yes.'

Stass took the copy of *Pravda*, opened it up and read out: 'Yury Tverdysh. Pass this on to my beloved . . .' Then leaning back more comfortably, he began reading with deliberately ironic expression, as though acting a part: 'Brothers, buddies, Russian soldiers! I once used to serve alongside you. I've sat with you in the blazing heat of armoured reconnaissance vehicles, I've breathed the black smoke from a Vasnetsov machine gun, I've shivered in Nangarhar, and I've fired round after round at the partisans . . . But now I've quit. I've had my fill of shooting! Tell my fiancée she'll not see me again. Tell my mother she'll never see me again either. And tell the same to my country. But tell them also this – that here, far away from them, I have remained a human being. I am not executing women and children, I am not burning up villages and settlements with napalm, I'm not poisoning people with chemicals, I'm not leaving booby-trapped toys in the road for children to pick up. I've remained a human being! I ask you, boys what is better? To come back to one's mother and tell her: "I am a murderer"? To return to one's wife and embrace her with hands that are stained with the blood of children? Or return perhaps in a zinc-lined coffin? Or else – even though far away from them – is it not better to remain a human being? What is better, buddies, I ask you? When you read this paper and then tear it up in case your political officer sees it, when you roll a home-made cigarette using my letter and first breathe in the smoke of that rough army-issue tobacco, try as well to take in the meaning of my question: "Is it better to kill, or not to kill? To live in one's homeland as a murderer, or else . . .?" And realise this: a government that turns its people into murderers cannot last for ever. You and I are only twenty years old! I am convinced that in five, ten, or maybe twenty years, the Kremlin's fascist rulers will fall and I shall return to my homeland. What if my girl abandons me, or my country forgets me? My mother will still greet me and I'll be able to tell her: "I didn't kill anyone, mother! I've remained a human being." Do you understand, buddies?' Stass laid the paper to one side and looked searchingly at Alexey. 'Well?'

'Well what?' Alexey said. But he had already realised: all this talk about whether it was better to preserve one's human dignity or return home a cripple and murderer – these were ideas that Yury Shalygin was always talking about. And all the addresses to his buddies and so on were typical of the expressions he used. Alexey could almost hear Yury's voice talking to him. So that meant he was alive! Yury was alive! But what was that strange surname? What was it? Tverdysh? . . .

'Did Shulygin write this?' Igor asked.

Alexey shrugged. 'You mentioned some other name, though . . .'

'That's not important!' Stass snapped. 'Do you recognise the style? They are all words that he uses – buddies, boys – aren't they? Well?'

Well, Alexey thought, if Yury is in England or even in Afghanistan with the Mojahedin, he'll not give a damn what these KGB officers think. Nevertheless, he answered cautiously. 'God knows. "Buddies", "boys" – half our men talk like that to one another. And even here at the works ...' He gestured through the window towards the workshops.

'But what about Nangarhar? The armoured reconnaissance vehicles and Vasnetsov guns?' Stass laughed. 'Your unit were in Nangarhar in winter, weren't they? And you drove those vehicles and fired Vasnetsovs, didn't you?'

Alexey said nothing.

'Is it true or not?' Stass suddenly slapped the table.

'Yes, of course it's true,' Alexey said hastily.

'So there we are! ...' Stass said with satisfaction. 'We're not here to play silly buggers. Not content with writing this muck and printing his counterfeit *Pravda* somewhere in Italy, this Shalygin actually brings the stuff into Afghanistan and drops it at our bases!'

'But you read out some other name ...'

'Tverdysh,' Igor said. 'Tverdysh is a small settlement in the Kurgan region. It's the place where Shalygin was born and where he lived until he was called up. And his mother still lives there....'

'Why bother telling him that! He knows it already!' Stass interrupted. 'The two of them were friends for a whole year!'

At this point Alexey remembered: of course, Tverdysh village, 22 Maiskaya Street – the address of Yury's mother. Two years ago he had memorised it, but since he was wounded he had forgotten everything. Yury! You're alive! Alive, but where the hell have you ended up – Britain, Italy, with the Mojahedin?! You're a fool, mate, these jokers can get you wherever you are – Moscow or Madagascar – it makes no difference!

Stass had meanwhile opened his attaché case yet again and this time hauled out a small tape recorder. He set it on the table and pressed the 'record' button.

'So,' he said harshly, 'How did you get to know Yury Shalygin?'

'How did I get to know him? In the usual way ...' Alexey glanced apprehensively at the quietly whirring recorder spools.

'Tell us in detail!' Stass ordered.

'What is there to tell? When he came to our battalion I'd already been in Afghanistan for a year. He was just a greenhorn, and they assigned him to our unit, that's all.'

'And what was the other soldiers' attitude towards him?' Igor sat down on the party secretary's seat and propped his elbows on the desk. 'Tell us everything, Alyosha. What was he like, this Shalygin? Any information might be useful to us.'

'He was ... well ... ordinary, really.' Alexey scratched the back of his neck thoughtfully. 'To be honest, the lads didn't really like him.'

'Why?' Igor leaned back in his chair.

'I don't know. Because ... maybe because he never shared the parcels he got from home.'

'So he was a greedy, selfish type?' Stass asked.

'I wouldn't put it quite like that ... Only ... well, he's from the country. And these country types from the villages aren't all that ready to share their things.'

'And how did you get to be friends?' Igor smiled.

'We didn't get to be friends! Our commander detailed me to put him through his paces and train him up.' Alexey was now beginning to get a hunted look and his glance kept shifting back and forth between Igor and Stass. 'There are mountains out there, you know,' he went on. And when these new men come their knees are weak! They can't even drag their own kitbags – they even pull the plates out of their armoured vests to make the going easier uphill. Don't you know about any of this? Anyway, I trained Shalygin up, and after that he tended to cling to me. He once even showed me a picture of his girl ...'

'I see, I see,' said Igor, perking up somewhat. 'What was her name?'

'I don't remember. I'm not sure he ever told me ...'

(Good grief, what was this nonsense he was talking?! Would they really buy this story about the girlfriend? These KGB people could check everything! And apart from that, everyone in the battalion knew that he and Yury had been as thick as thieves. They had always done duty together. And how often had Yury covered up for Alexey when he had hived off without leave?! And Yury had always shared the rare parcels he got from home with Alexey.

But there had been no one to send parcels to Alexey Odalevsky. His mother had died before he was a year old, and of course he didn't remember her. For some strange reason his father had kept no photo of her. Only his grandma Masha had had a little yellowing picture with tattered edges hanging on her wall. And from behind the glass a serious ten-year-old girl with thick dark pigtails had peered ...

Alexey's relations with his father, who died six years earlier, had always been strained. Even as a child he noticed that his father found him a burden, and then he realised why: his father had never loved his wife. He had married her only because she got pregnant. And Alexander Odalevsky, a communist party member, had had to get married to a seventeen-year-old factory girl whom he had almost raped after some drunken party. As long as Alexey could remember, he had never had a home. First there had been day-nurseries and a kindergarten with irritable supervisors. Then a boarding-school where the teachers had cuffed and slapped the children a hundred times a day. And there were rare visits, sometimes only once a year, from his father, who was forever on the move, changing jobs and women in rapid succession. But while fat, garrulous grandma Masha was still alive, Alexey had at least had somewhere to visit on Sundays. And when she died there was nowhere. So he was left to while away the weekends and holidays in the empty school, lying on his bed and trying to sleep through the long lonely days.

He was an indifferent pupil. His teachers all agreed that laziness was his ruination, and he hated spending more than half an hour on any homework. So when school was behind him, he was not in the least upset at being called up into the army.

At the training camp near Ashkhabad, like all new recruits, he had to undergo the usual tormenting period of 'quarantine', and the sergeants and others with some service behind them had all made fun of him. He had had to scrub out toilets with a toothbrush, crawl around in the mud, peel potatoes at night in the kitchens, and get punched about by drunken officers. But while many newcomers found this a period of humiliation and despair, for Alexey it was not particularly new: the laws of army life were not unlike those of his boarding-school.

Alexey never thought to question those unwritten rules. He had bowed down to them years ago while still a child. The people who came out on top were always the strong, cruel or evil ones ... whoever had the sharper teeth, the heavier fists, and could down most drink! Was it really so unfair? That was how he had lived and how others around him had lived; in the army he was in his native element. So Alexey Odalevsky had made a good soldier. And when they were sent off to Afghanistan, the whole battalion had sung songs as they boarded the planes. Why not indeed?! They were off on a trip abroad! 'Our Aeroflot TU-104 will shortly be leaving Ashkhabad on its flight to Kabul,' the little snub-nosed stewardess had announced. 'We shall be cruising at a height of twenty-five thousand feet. The temperature in Kabul is 26 degrees centigrade – and the spring tulips are already out in the mountains!' Her announcement was greeted with a roar of applause from the whole plane. And that was how they had flown out there. But now that the Mojahedin had acquired American 'Stinger' rockets, army personnel no longer flew by Aeroflot. Instead they went on Antonov troop carriers. But at that time they had travelled in comfort, with soft seats and stewardesses. It was true, though, that once they were transferred from Kabul to Nanganhar, they had little time to admire the tulips.

'Try and remember.' Igor got up from his chair and went over to the window. 'Try and remember, Alyosha. If Shalygin had a girlfriend, we need to find her. That's absolutely vital! Try and remember her name, and where she was from. Was she from Tverdysh as well?'

'I can't remember, dammit! After I was wounded I was ...'

'He's just trying to play stupid!' Stass suddenly said in a firm voice. 'Can't you see? It's a lot of eyewash, this tale of a girl and a photograph! And there's bugger all there to prove it!'

'But I've told you, that after I was wounded ...' Alexey spread his hands helplessly and began raising his voice just as he once did in schoolboy squabbles. 'I spent three months in hospital! I've got a medical note!'

'Cool it!' Stass banged his fist down on the desk. 'Cool down! No need for that. Just remember this, Odalevsky: for the time being,' – and Stass emphasised this last phrase – 'for the time being nobody's accusing you of anything. What we want is information about a man who's betrayed his country. And reliable information! Do you understand?'

'Did he ever tell you he wanted to get away?' Igor asked, moving unhurriedly to the spare chair by the wall.

'No. Never!' Alexey tried hard to sound indignant. 'If he had, I'd have ... I'd have dissuaded him, dammit!'

Igor perked up at this.

'You'd have dissuaded him? Why?'

'Well, because ... because ...'

(I'm sorry, Yury, old pal. I wasn't able to dissuade you. What a pity! I've never had a friend like you, and I'll never have another like you. But right now I've got to get myself off the hook – you're all right. But I have to save my own skin. And I'll do what I did at school – stir the mud up good and proper, kick over the traces. I'll pretend I'm an idiot who got wounded and simply can't remember ...)

'Because that is an act of treason!' Alexey blurted out in a single breath, and looked Igor straight in the eye.

The other man seemed disappointed by Alexey's answer.

'What a truly sincere answer to give! Good for you!' he drawled mockingly. 'All the same, tell us a bit more about him. The two of you served together for a year after all ... What sort of a chap was he? Did he like reading, for instance? As one ancient philosopher once said, "Tell me what books you read and I'll tell you who you are".'

'Books?' Alexey laughed openly. (Stass, you utter fool! Just you try spending even a month out there, manning some outpost or a roadblock in the mountains. Out there in winter you almost seize up with cold and terror, and in the summer heat you've only a helmet and armoured vest to protect you. You crawl along like a worm, expecting to catch a sniper's bullet any moment, or else have one of the Mojahedin spring you from the rear. Just you try crossing a minefield, or try a stint of mine-clearing.... You wouldn't go asking about books! You'd have only one thought on your mind – how to get hold of some vodka or a joint of hashish, just in order to forget everything and switch off ...) 'Shalygin didn't read any books! Nobody out there reads any books! There's no time for reading!' Alexey answered. He waited for some reaction. Stass said nothing. Which of the two was the senior man, Alexey wondered? Who was the boss? Which of them should he play to?

'I just wondered, that's all,' Igor eventually said with a smile. 'Obviously when you're fighting a war you've no time for books ... So far as we know, Shalygin disappeared during the same battle where you were wounded. And Sergeant Zhebotko saw the two of you together during that battle.'

Alexey felt his left eyelid give a treacherous twitch and his hands began trembling. It was pointless to play the fool with them: they knew everything. Zhebotko had seen them ... But what precisely had he seen?

'What exactly happened during that battle? Can you tell us in a bit more detail?' Igor asked gently. He sat back more comfortably and crossed one leg over the other.

'What is there to tell? You surely don't call that a battle? We landed in an ambush. I almost got zapped by the first grenade they threw at us. Anyway, I was injured by it and lost consciousness. The last thing I remember was our senior lieutenant shouting "Get back in the car! It's an ambush!" Then some bloody thing hit me!'

'And where was Shalygin all this time?'

'He was next to me – in the car, that is. But where he disappeared to after that – on my word of honour, I really don't know.'

'Well, Zhebotko tells us that after the order to get back, Shalygin ran over towards the partisans and that you got into the car, then suddenly tore off after your friend. And only then, at that point, were you hit. So don't play the fool, Odalevsky! You decided to go along with him and run for it, but you were unlucky! Or else perhaps you were lucky – depending how you look at it! You were injured, and your bosom pal saw it happen and he didn't even stop. He had other ideas on his mind: he was bent on surrendering to the Mojahedin! Is that how it was?' Igor spoke quietly, and his bright eyes looked straight at Alexey.

Alexey blanched. He realised the moment had come to shout out, otherwise no amount of protesting later on would help. Especially since his conscience was quite clear on that account! He had never had any wish to desert! It was simply that as he got into the reconnaissance car, he suddenly realised he was losing his friend Yury for ever. He didn't even know what to do – yell to him, fire at him, or try and drag him back by force! Only once before had he felt such an agonising sense of loss – when his grandmother's coffin was lowered into the earth . . .

'No, that is *not* how it was!' Alexey shouted. 'I wouldn't be so daft as to try and surrender! I know what those bandits do to our men! You're better off with a bullet through your head! And as for the garbage that bastard Zhebotko has told you ... I can tell you that out there everyone had the measure of *him*! He always shat himself with fear and he hated anyone else who didn't – Shalygin and me included! After one engagement we actually put his trousers on show to the whole unit! If you go listening to people like Zhebotko, you'll never find out the truth! Anyway he wasn't one of our platoon!'

'Cool it! What's all this cock-and-bull you're telling us?' Igor's lips twisted in a mocking grin. 'You mean to say that you weren't about to desert along with Shalygin?'

'Not only was I not about to, I was absolutely against the idea!'

'Aha, so you *did* know that he was going to run?' Stass chimed in again.

'Don't try and catch me out! I never wanted to desert, and I know nothing about Shalygin deserting. I was sure he'd been killed.' Alexey nodded towards the window. 'You can ask the other lads in the works here! I told them about having lost a pal out there. And I was against ... well, I am against anyone who's a traitor to his country!'

There was a cautious knock at the door. Stass switched off the tape recorder. 'Come in,' he called. Gushchin came in with a radiant smile and carrying a large tray.

'Here's some tea for you, and some bread and butter. And for those that are specially hungry here's a nice hot goulash too. Zina our cook is an expert at goulash and buckwheat porridge.'

'Thanks, Ivan Mikhailovich. Many thanks. It smells first-rate!' Igor breathed in deeply as he caught the aroma of braised meat. 'Put it on the table there ... And then go and sort out that drunken work force you've got down there ... That is, if you haven't got any urgent party meetings, of course.'

Gushchin gestured his agreement.

'Of course, of course! I'm on my way to do just that! ... And if there's anything you need, just give a shout. And by all means take as long as you like for your talk!' And with that he made a hasty sideways exit, closing the door behind him carefully.

The fair-haired man went over to the desk where the tray stood, and appraised the food critically. Gushchin's efforts had produced ten times more meat than in a normal canteen portion.

'What do you think?' asked Igor. 'Are we going to survive after this little lot? Are you going to have some, Stass? Alexey, you can bring your chair up as well. Come and join the factory feast!' Igor settled back into Gushchin's chair and drew a plate of goulash towards him.

'Hmmmmm! Not bad at all!' Igor looked round at the others ironically. 'It actually is real meat! But the buckwheat could be better. Now my grandmother's the one who really knows how to make buckwheat – really feathery, with every grain separate! What about your grandmother, Alexey? Did she make it nice and crumbly too?'

'I don't remember,' Alexey answered glumly.

The bastard had asked about his grandmother! But he was only trying to show that he knew all about Alexey. On the other hand, why should Alexey stand on ceremony with them? Since they offered, he ought to accept and have done with it. That way it would seem more natural ...

'You know, Alexey, as the old Russian saying has it: rake over the past and you'll lose an eye. So let's act accordingly. Let's forget about the past,' Igor said as he chewed avidly at the hunks of meat. 'By now it's hard to prove whether or not you actually tried to run for it with Shalygin, or whether Zhebotko's just telling tales ... Although, if we need to, we can prove *everything*! Isn't that right, Stass?'

And anyway,' Stass smirked, 'It wasn't just Zhebotko that saw what happened in the skirmish. There was Durov, Kashchenko and Semakin too. And they all confirmed that Odalevsky and Shalygin were running away from the car.'

'What the hell could those men have seen?' Alexey boiled up. 'Durov was out cold, and lying there injured for a start! His car was the first to hit a mine! Why are you trying to pin this on me? And Semakin and Zhebotko weren't even in our platoon!'

'Really? It certainly is strange ...' Igor looked at Alexey thoughtfully. 'Four men quite separately all confirm the same thing. Yet it turns out that one of them was out for the count, and another was a scoundrel and an informer ... What do you make of it all, Stass?'

'What the hell are you driving at?' Alexey smashed his plate down on the desk. There was a tearful note in his voice. 'What is it you want? I've told you the truth! Yes, I did see Shalygin set off and run towards the partisans. And he was without his rifle! So I tore after him. Because for all I knew, he might have flipped his lid, dammit! Or else was trying to be a hero – like Matrosov who went and threw himself in front of one of their machine-guns. But at that moment I was injured myself. That's how it was!'

'Stop shouting, and cut out the hysteria!' Stass snapped angrily. 'Think yourself lucky that we're still talking to you in a half-normal manner! And that you've not been run in already! Do you get me?'

'Gently, Stass,' said Igor, 'Calm down. Alexey simply doesn't realise how serious things are, that's all. But, Alexey, Stass is right of course. You can see we're not accusing you of anything – heavens, we're even sharing our lunch with you! But if this affair were to be handled by someone else, it might be handled very differently. That's all.' Igor pushed his empty plate away, took a handkerchief from his pocket and sedulously wiped his lips and chin. 'I'm not trying to make out that we're angels or anything. You wouldn't believe that anyway. It's simply that at present there's no need for us to lock you up. We have a different job on our hands. Stass and I have worked out a plan.' He folded his handkerchief and returned it to his pocket. 'I'll not go into details – they belong to what we call the "secrets of our profession". But this plan of ours doesn't involve any quarrel with you. On the contrary, we need your co-operation.'

'But don't try any funny business, or we can soon cut you down to size!' Stass slurped his tea noisily from the thick glass tumbler.

'Cut it out, Stass! Alexey mustn't think we're like investigators at the movies, and that one of us is playing the nice guy, and the other one's a villain. I can assure you that, if need be, I can be far nastier than Stass has been just now.' Alexey could have guessed that without Igor's warning. 'But let's return to the matter in hand.'

Igor stood up and paced around Gushchin's office. He looked thoughtfuly at the large portrait of Gorbachev, then at the bookcase. Its top shelf was lined by a set of Lenin's complete works, while the other one below had a new set of blue volumes embossed in gilt: *M.S. Gorbachev. Perestroika – The Vital Concern of Our People. Speeches and Addresses 1985–1987'*.

'Alexey, we need you to write a letter to Shalygin,' Igor said, turning to look at him. 'One letter to start with, then another a bit later. We'll tell you how many. But the main thing is that these letters have to come from you as a friend, you understand?' Igor planted his chair in front of Alexey and sat down on it. His voice now had a hard ring, and he clipped each word. 'We could, of course, write these letters without your help. And we could even copy your hand-writing. But there's a fine point here: really these ought to be your own letters, using expressions of the sort that only you would use, and which only a friend of yours would recognise. A friend like Shalygin, say. Furthermore, I can tell you that it's very convenient indeed for us that Shalygin had a friend like you . . .'

Alexey looked at Igor, dumbfounded. What was this – another of their traps? In order to prove he had been Yury's accomplice?! What sort of plan had they cooked up?

'But do you know his address?'

'Of course we do.'

'But you say he's in Afghanistan, with the Mojahedin?'

'But his postal address is in London. Either messages are sent to him, or else he calls there to collect them.'

'But a letter from me? He'll realise immediately that something is up. Where could I have got his address from?'

'A very sensible question, Alyosha, you're on the right track!' Igor's voice now sounded soft and gentle. 'You'll really have to ponder every word. Shalygin has to believe you. But the address is easy to explain: you got it from his mother. She's already sent him several letters and has even got a reply from him.'

'And what does he write?' Alexey could not resist enquiring.

'Oh, various things . . .' Igor smiled evasively. 'And I think you'll get a reply from him too.'

It was quiet in the room. Stass gazed glumly into his empty glass. Igor rose from his chair and again walked leisurely about the room. Alexey waited, looking expectantly at each of them in turn.

'It isn't a question, Alexey, of whether you agree to do this or not. We are quite convinced you will. But it's important to us that you don't drop the slightest hint in any of these letters which could give the operation away and frighten Shalygin off. And if that were to happen I may as well tell you straight: every one of your army pals would have no trouble at all in recalling exactly what it was they saw you do! . . .' Igor moved over towards Alexey and placed a hand on his shoulder. 'I'm not trying to scare you, Odalevsky. In my opinion there's always a pleasant way of doing things, so that everyone stays happy. I wouldn't mind betting, for instance, that by now you're pretty fed up of living in a worker's hostel. You'd be more than ready to find a flat of your own, where you could take your girlfriend and the like. After all, you've spent almost all your life in boarding-schools, barracks and hostels. But that's surely no life for a grown man?' Igor looked at Stass. 'I really think we ought to give him a helping hand, Stass, don't you?' He turned to Alexey again. 'We couldn't promise you more than one room. But we could put you at the head of the queue for a bed-sitter – in your capacity as a wounded veteran who only performed his internationalist duty. Nothing could be simpler. And just in return for writing a couple of letters. It's surely worth it! And don't worry – we're not going to be sending him a bomb or a dose of arsenic with your letters!'

Igor was smiling now. But it was hard to tell whether there was a note of irony in his voice, or whether it was merely one of practical calculation.

'So what do you need my letters for?' Alexey sensed that they had him cornered – they had him trapped even more securely than in that ambush. At that moment he would have been happy to empty his Kalashnikov into Stass's sneering face and the deceitful, foxy features of Igor. What a relief it would have been to slam the office door behind him and leave those two KGB agents lying on the mat! But it was impossible, and his hands almost ached in frustration. 'You coward!' he thought to himself bitterly, as though he actually had a weapon on him.

'Odalevsky!' Igor was now suddenly serious again, as though he had read Alexey's thoughts. 'I want to say something important. Listen. You'll have nothing, absolutely nothing, to reproach yourself for!' One had to hand it to this KGB man: he was a good psychologist. 'I'm quite sure that anyone in your position – anyone, and especially Shalygin – would do what we require of you. And what we require is in fact a mere trifle! Just a few letters! Hi there, Yury! A few days ago I met one of our buddies recently demobbed from Afghanistan and he had a copy of *Pravda* with him. We started reading it, and straight away remembered you! So I rushed to the enquiry bureau to find out your mother's address, as I knew the surname and remembered the name of the village – Tverdysh. They gave me her address – 22 Maiskaya Street – and I found out from her where you are now. How are you doing, old mate? It'd be nice to meet again, but fate seems to have planned otherwise, dammit! ...' And so on and so forth, in that vein. And you *would* like to see him again, wouldn't you?'

'What? D'you think he's an idiot? Do you think he'd come back here just to see me?'

'Why here?' the blond man grinned. 'You could meet up in Afghanistan. We've not only got our army there. We're pumping oil out of the ground there, we're mining copper in Hainak, and uranium in Havaya Ravash. With our help you could quite easily sign on to work at Hainak. And Shalygin in turn has to get rid of his leaflets, so he'd obviously try to recruit you. You understand? But this is all looking ahead, of course! Meanwhile though ...'

So that was their plan! They wanted to use him as a decoy and lure Yury into a trap. And to do that they were even ready to send him to Afghanistan ... Bastards! Somehow he had to get away from them, disappear, go underground. Although even if he gave them the slip ... they'd manage to find Yury even in London. And here, where every other person was an informer, in a matter of seconds they could unearth anyone and twist his balls off. The swine! ...

'So just you go home, Alexey. And think about writing that letter. And in three days' time you can come and see us in Moscow and bring us a rough draft. They'll let you off work. It'll all be official. But you just try and write him a nice letter. And the thing is simply to write the truth – write about yourself, tell him about the works here, about life in the hostel and so on. But don't get carried away. He's not a fool – he realises that letters going abroad are censored. On the other hand, don't be too restrained either. We'll give you a hand to edit the thing. Here's our address and phone number ...' Igor tore off a sheet from Gushchin's desk diary and quickly jotted down the details.

Alexey got up quickly, took the paper and strode towards the door.

'Alexey!' Igor called after him and stopped him in his

tracks. 'Wait a moment. How's that great aunt of yours in America, by the way? Any sign of life from her?'

'Great aunt? What great aunt?' This time Alexey's surprise was genuine.

'The one from Florida – Tatyana Stepanovna Odalevskaya. I don't suppose she's sent you any more invitations to go and visit her?'

'Oh, her! No, no, I've not heard anything for more than three months. But you've got nothing on me on that count! I took all her letters and handed them straight to the Party committee. They know all about it! You can ask Gushchin yourself. The old girl's a bit twisted, if you ask me. A relative indeed! Suddenly appearing out of nowhere! Anyway, she seems to have given up writing.'

'But why are you so hostile towards her? It does look as if she's some sort of great aunt twice removed. Isn't that what she writes?'

(But you're not going to catch me out there, Alexey thought. There are absolutely no flies on me on that score!)

'Well, that still has to be proven!' he said, 'Odalevskys are two a penny. There are twelve of them in the Moscow phone directory. She writes that my grandfather Pyotr Odalevsky was a prince. But that's absolute rot. I've seen his papers. Pyotr Odalevsky was a Party member, a Red Army commissar who fought against Kolchak. That was why he was posthumously rehabilitated.* And that, incidentally, is something you can also check quite easily. But I've never heard of there being any communist princes. So that old girl will have to go and find herself another grandnephew. Half of Moscow might be ready to apply in return for a pair of American jeans. But you'll not catch me doing that!'

'What happens, though, if it suddenly turns out that she really is your great aunt?' Stass said. 'Would you go and see her then?'

*i.e. in the de-Stalinisation process after 1953 – *Tr.*

'Go where?'

'To America – where else?'

'What are you on about?' Alexey smirked. 'Who's going to let me go there?'

'Well, what if we were to let you go? After we've finished our business, of course . . . the letters and so on . . .'

(My God, how they buy people! Alexey marvelled to himself. But Yury had certainly done the dirty on them with his private edition of *Pravda*! They didn't like it when people besmirched the reputation of holy writ!)

'No, I wouldn't go,' said Alexey firmly.

'But why?' Igor pressed him. 'Since you were a child you've been virtually an orphan, and here at last a great aunt has turned up – twice removed, it's true, but at least she's a relative. And what's more, she's a princess too!'

Igor's eyes expressed genuine curiosity and puzzlement. But Alexey had to respond and his answer must sound serious, consistent, and genuine. Why, after all, could he not say what he thought? Why shouldn't he admit what it was that maddened him each time he received those nice oblong envelopes with their US stamps? Although they were KGB men, they could maybe appreciate certain feelings . . .

'Well, if she really is an aunt of mine, where was she all the time I was cooped up in boarding-schools and made to sleep on those piss-stained mattresses?' he said angrily. 'A fine aunt she was! Where was she when I had meningitis and was put in a children's hospital? "Princess" indeed! Where was she when I nearly snuffed it in a military hospital? The fact is I don't have an aunt who's a princess, and I never had one! So don't try and foist her onto me! I've got enough with this Shalygin business as it is!'

'Well, that's certainly true,' Stass smiled for the first time. 'OK, on your way then, Prince Odalevsky. If you don't want to go to America, more fool you. Anyway, write that letter and come and see us in a couple of days' time. All right?'

'And one more thing,' Igor recollected. 'If that wasn't a lie you told about Shalygin having some girl, try and remember her name. All right?'

'Right-ho. Bye!' Alexey opened the door and went out.

The blond KGB agent did not move, but looked at Stass. 'Well? What do you make of him?'

'A complete wimp!' Stass got up and straightened his leg which had gone stiff at the knee. 'He'll do everything he's told to. Have you any doubts?'

'I don't know,' Igor closed his eyes and stretched. 'I don't go for him. On the one hand he's just a shell-shocked little plebeian. But he has a wolfish look in his eyes. That's your mixture of princely blood with a fourth-grade metal worker! My grandad incidentally was also a metal-worker. And which of us is more a prince now – him or me?'

3

The cost of the trip included three meals a day. The standard set breakfast consisted of three slices of broiled sausage with sauerkraut, curd fritters with sour cream, and a glass of coffee. Elizabeth, who was used to her toast and marmalade, studied the buffet display cabinet attentively. There were half-litre bottles of yoghurt, processed cheeses wrapped in foil, hard-boiled eggs, salads of fresh cabbage and grated carrot, miniature pots of black caviar, and little almond tartlets. But it emerged that even a refill of coffee poured into the same glass cost an extra 40 kopecks. So, economical as she was, Elizabeth made do with the standard set breakfast. Pursing her lips grimly, she carried her tray over to the table where Tanya was already sitting with the blond woman from New Jersey. Tanya poked cautiously at the curd fritters with her fork, but was suspicious of the sausage and left it on the side of the plate. The New Jersey woman looked in surprise at the Russian bank-notes they had just been given in exchange for their dollars down at the hotel exchange bureau. The diminutive multi-coloured notes actually resembled toy money: each had a portrait of Lenin barely larger than a postage stamp. But for every American dollar they were given only sixty-eight kopecks in exchange.

'Monopoly money!' someone quipped.

'What? And people here work to earn this sort of money?' the New Jersey woman exclaimed.

'Well, at least there is food available here ...' Elizabeth

volunteered diplomatically as she took her seat at their table.

'And I can't see any bears roaming around on Red Square either,' said Tanya, imitating her tone.

Red Square was in fact almost next door to them. From the tenth floor windows of the Rossiya Hotel there was a fine view of the Kremlin, the Spasskaya Tower topped by its ruby-coloured star, St Basil's Cathedral with its cupolas, and the frozen Moskva River, with the Crimea Bridge in the distance. But all the tables by the windows were occupied already by some people that looked like Turks or Uzbeks; they all wore turbans and robes with dark jackets over them. There were about thirty of them, and they were being carefully looked after by three waitresses and several young Russian men all in identical grey suits. These men were busy distributing small badges with a portrait of Lenin to their guests and setting up little flags with a star and crescent on the tables.

'Who are they?' The New Jersey woman turned to their guide Oleg Petrov who was sitting at the next table devouring a plateful of cabbage and carrot; the gusto with which he ate suggested either that this was his favourite dish, or else that cabbage was in short supply in Russia. Or maybe both ...

'Those are some of our guests from Afghanistan,' Oleg explained, wiping his mouth with a serviette. 'They've come to attend a course on combine-harvesting and tractor maintenance.' Then he quickly changed the subject: 'Ladies and gentlemen! Your attention please! This evening we shall be going to the theatre – the celebrated Moscow Arts Theatre – to see Chekhov's *The Seagull*. But until then you are free to relax. You've been flying all night, so this is your one day for resting and getting acclimatised. However, if any of you are anxious to do something immediately, could you please raise a hand? We have the chance of going to the Tretyakov Gallery.'

'But according to the schedule, we have the Tretyakov Gallery the day after tomorrow,' somebody objected.

'Oh, but the Tretyakov is an enormous place,' said Oleg. 'We shall be going there for the day in any case. Today is just a short extra visit for those who would specially like to. So ... one, two, three ...' Oleg began counting the show of hands.

Tanya immediately glanced anxiously towards Judy Sanders, who was sitting three tables away. But Judy was bent over, concentrating on her plate of fritters.

'I'm sorry, Mr Stark, are you coming or not?' Oleg called to one of the men from Minnesota. 'You are? Good. So that makes eleven in all ...'

'And when do we get our passports back?' Mr Stark asked. (Everyone's passport had been collected in when they registered and were allocated rooms, and this had evidently perturbed some of the visitors.)

'Oh, don't worry about that.' Oleg gave a calm and condescending smile. 'You'll get your passports back tomorrow. They're needed just for a quick bureaucratic procedure. We have our own bureaucracy here as well, you know! ... And you, Mrs Wollens? Are you coming to the Tretyakov? I think you had your hand up too?'

'Oh, me?' Elizabeth looked round at Tanya, bewildered. Then she said hastily, 'Oh, no. I'm not feeling too good. It's my blood pressure, you know ... after the flight ... And I've also got a bad knee.'

'And you, Mrs Goehr?' His glance passed to Tanya, but was then immediately drawn to the rings on her right hand.

'I can't come now,' said Tanya somewhat brusquely. 'I need to rest too.' She was annoyed at Elizabeth's clumsy acting. How often had she warned her not to be different and not draw attention to herself. None of them must attract attention – especially not the guide's ...

'Of course, certainly. You stay and relax,' Oleg said without a pause. Then reluctantly tearing his eyes from her rings, he turned to the rest of the group. 'Right, ladies and gentlemen, I am now talking to those of you who do not wish to come with us to the Tretyakov. Please, if you do go walking outside the hotel, don't forget to leave your key with the landlady on the floor and collect a hotel registration card from her. It has your name and room number on it and is your pass to get into the hotel. Also it can be of use when you are outside. Some people think that every foreigner in Moscow is followed by the KGB, so there's no fear of getting lost! But I can assure you that there'll be nobody following you. But I should warn you that by no means all Muscovites speak English. So if you do lose your way, the best thing to do is to go straight to a militiaman and ask for help. Show him the hotel registration card and he'll help you get a taxi or else ring the hotel. And one more request: please be sensible – don't go too far away from the city centre. Remember that tourists in Moscow are subject to a fifteen-mile limit ... But I don't expect that many of you will be rushing out of town immediately to visit a collective farm! ... Are there any more questions at all? ...'

Some people immediately raised their hands. Tanya laughed. Elderly people in tourist groups always behaved like children, especially at the start.

The blond woman from New Jersey hastily left to go and change ready for the outing. That was good. Now Tanya and Elizabeth were alone at their table. Tanya glanced again in Judy's direction. Well done! She was still bent over her plateful of fritters and was sitting there quiet as a mouse – precisely what was needed. And besides, considering how much money she was getting for her part in the operation, anyone would have consented to swallow a few curd fritters and boiled sausages! So, everything was in order. They could commence their plan of action – especially since the guide had reassured them that today they would be left to themselves.

The group of Afghans had got up with a loud clattering of chairs, and led by the cohort of men in grey they were now making their way to the exit like a herd of sheep. As they walked past, the American visitors all fell silent. And as the flock of Afghans followed their beefy

Russian herdsmen, the slightly protruding eyes of these would-be combine-operators and tractor drivers seemed to betray a look of almost animal fear and repression.

'They look like frightened rabbits,' Elizabeth said, then suddenly bit her tongue as she caught Tanya's sharp glance.

'You stay here, and then go down and make sure when the people in our party leave,' said Tanya. 'And then, only when they've left, you come up to our room. Got it?' She picked up their room key from the table, stood up and headed for the door. Elizabeth sat there at the table with bated breath, anxiously watching Tanya leave the restaurant followed by Judy. A few other tourists who had finished breakfast were also leaving.

Tanya set off down the corridor without a backward glance. The key with its heavy metal weight stamped 'room 1032' weighed heavily in her hand. Their room was not on the main corridor of floor ten, but down a small side-corridor where there were special luxury rooms. On a table at the corner was a large decorative samovar, and opposite at a large desk sat the female floor attendant. Judy had meanwhile gone her own way; her room was on the floor above.

In an effort to look younger than her age, the floor attendant had on heavy make-up and a bouffant-style permanent wave. Tanya avoided catching her eye and turned off down her own side corridor. Even the carpet here, she observed, was different from the one in the main corridor. It was spotlessly clean and had a proper pile. 'The luxury corridor,' Tanya smiled to herself as she opened the door. In fact this was the one luxury she could not resist. As the owner of four first-class Florida hotels, and with an annual income of around $540,000 – quite apart from the fact that she was a princess – Tanya could not abide staying in cheap accommodation. And certainly not in Moscow – *her* Moscow! All the more since she had heard enough already about the splendours of standard Russian hotel service . . .

Once in the room, Tanya locked herself in and quickly looked about her. Her own large case and Elizabeth's more modest one stood in a niche by the entrance. Nobody appeared to have tampered with them. Her coat was also hanging in its place. The room itself was spacious. In the reception room was a large rug – slightly worn, but again, spotlessly clean. There were heavy velvet curtains at the windows, and on the wall were two picture reproductions of works by Repin and Aivazovsky. There was a fridge, a television with some sort of gigantic handles made of dark plastic, a table and armchairs, and a settee. There was also another small side-table with an electric samovar on it and some instruction sheet or other beneath the glass top. To the right was the bedroom door. Tanya took her case and dragged it over to the settee and opened it. Then, once again she looked around her, as though someone might still be watching. Who was to know, after all, with these Bolsheviks? What secrets lay hidden behind that mirror, for instance? Who needed a mirror in the drawing room anyway? Or was there a camera hidden behind it?

Tanya went over to the mirror and tugged at its thin wooden frame. Hanging just by one hook at the top, the mirror easily came away from the wall. Tanya felt behind it. The wall was solid enough. A slip of paper fell out from behind the mirror. She bent to pick it up: 'Instructions for evacuation in the event of fire'!

She did not trouble to read the rest. If there was a fire in the hotel, who on earth would think of looking for instructions behind the mirror?! She thrust the piece of paper back in its place and returned to her suitcase. Opening it up, she began taking out the clothing she had prepared. A dingy woollen skirt, a thick, coarsely knitted blue sweater, dark woollen gloves and a similar dark-brown knitted headscarf. And the main item was that dark-blue overcoat that had caused so many problems back in New York. The friend who advised her (a Russian Jew who had recently emigrated, and whom she discovered in the editorial office of an émigré newspaper) had spent three days looking out clothing for herself and Judy. They had spent many hours of searching and cursing, in the cheapest and shoddiest of American stores, but there was nothing to be found that looked remotely like what ordinary people wore in Russia. Only the Salvation Army store at West 49th Street had had what they were looking for – a loose-fitting dark coat with a worn fur collar for Tanya, and a similar rough jerkin for Judy. He had also tried persuading Tanya not to take her expensive rings with her. But one of them had been a gift from her late husband, and the other two were family heirlooms. And anyway, as she told him, 'I am a princess, and I said so on my visa application. But they've still given me a visa. So I shall go to Russia as a princess. And I shall wear my rings there and live in luxury! Like a princess!'

In the dark skirt and sweater, Tanya looked even more gaunt than usual. Surveying herself in the mirror, she felt satisfied. The main thing was to wear nothing at all striking. She had to blend completely with the ordinary folk on the street, and nothing must give away that she was a foreigner. And of course, nowhere under any circumstances must she take off her gloves and reveal those rings ... Heavens! She had completely forgotten how to tie a headscarf! Her Russian nanny always did that for her as a girl. Very well, she would put it round her shoulders for the time being. She glanced at her watch. Where was Elizabeth? She could not leave before Elizabeth came up to announce that the bus and their porcine guide had left for the Tretyakov. What if Judy had already left the hotel? As an insignificant, mousy NYU student, it was far easier for her to slip away unnoticed than for Tanya, who had just told the guide she needed a rest. It was to be hoped that Judy wouldn't do anything silly – like taking the first available taxi from in front of the hotel. Her Jewish émigré adviser warned them against taking taxis outside the hotel, and had told them instead to take a walk down the road for a few blocks and then find a taxi: 'The taxi drivers operating from Intourist hotels are usually working either for the KGB or else for some prostitution ring. And you don't want to get mixed up with either of them. Take a walk away from the hotel. Then just stand by the roadside and hold up a packet of Marlboros, and any car will stop for you . . .'

Tanya lit up a cigarette and paced from one end of the room to the other. Then she paused in front of the little table with the samovar. Under the glass top was a grey sheet of paper with a text in Russian:

DEAR HOTEL GUESTS!
THE FOLLOWING SERVICES ARE ALSO AVAILABLE AT THE PRICES INDICATED.

Then followed a numbered list of services and items to be had in the Rossiya Hotel. There were about thirty-five of them, including: hire of additional towel at 10 kopecks a day, bath towel at 15 kopecks, hire of iron – 5 kopecks per time, extra sheets at 20 kopecks each, extra pillows – also 20 kopecks, and so on and so forth. Even a shoe brush evidently cost an extra 5 kopecks. Tanya laughed. So these Bolsheviks were businessmen as well! If she tried introducing that sort of thing in her hotels in Florida, she would lose her entire clientèle, gathered over forty years, inside a single week!

But where was Elizabeth? Nervously Tanya switched on the TV. It gave a sharp dry electrical hiss. She immediately recalled having read somewhere that Soviet televisions often exploded when switched on, so she stepped to one side as a precaution. But the set did not explode, and a black-and-white picture soon appeared showing people in Caucasian national costume and black-whiskered men furiously dancing the lezghinka to the deafening sound of tambourines. Carefully Tanya approached the set again and turned the black plastic knob. The wild dancers disappeared, but nothing appeared to be on the other channels ... No, here was one. Of course, – Moscow had just two television channels, plus a third, educational one that came on just in the evenings. Their guide had told them that in the bus. Now a man appeared on the screen wearing a fur hat. Standing against some snowy rural landscape with an agricultural building in the background, he was intoning in a dull voice to the effect that 'the cattle from this collective farm are taken over 140 kilometers away to be slaughtered. Of course, on such a journey we tend to lose at least ten kilos on each bullock. And losses continue at the pre-abattoir stage, because it often takes several days to process them. And if cattle aren't fed, they lose weight. But our perestroika programme and team-contract system will help us to change the nature of our dealings with the abattoir, and to campaign for the introduction of new ...'

Tanya had little idea what this meat-producing automaton was going on about as he stood in the snowy wilderness of his collective farm. But she was suddenly gripped by the sharp nostalgia of that Russian country scene: grey sky, grey snow, the grey routine of a boring struggle to produce a piece of meat – and all that in a country that once used to export bread, butter, cheese and meat. She turned the knob back again, and there were the Georgians once again dancing their lezghinka ...

But where was Elizabeth? It was now at least half an hour since Tanya had left the restaurant, and Elizabeth was still not here! Tanya felt a shiver – partly from fear, and partly from the sight of that grey scene she had just seen on television. Surely things hadn't gone wrong already? But why? Why? She began nervously pacing the room again ...

When the First World War began, Tanya had been ten years old. They had owned a large private house in Moscow, at the so-called Patriarch's Pools. They also owned another house in Petersburg on the Fontanka, and there were family estates in the provinces of Kursk, Smolensk and Penza, not to mention two villas on the Black Sea, at Livadia. At Livadia the princely family of

Odalevsky had also been granted further massive landholdings by Emperor Alexander III, and these were rented out to a German wine dealer and vintner by Tanya's father. He himself meanwhile engaged in politics, busying himself with some liberal schemes in Stolypin's government and with endless debates over lunch at the English Club about ways and means of updating and modernising Russia's industry. And for that reason their houses in Moscow and Petersburg had always been full of guests and visitors – their father's friends, friends of her elder brother Petya, who was seventeen, her mother's lady friends, and of course the house servants and the governess for Tanya's two younger sisters Anya and Katya. And there were often special festivities for the children – they used to put on theatricals, play out charades, or else they would all go for a troika outing to Marina Roshcha.

But after the first few months of the War, guests began to appear at their house far less frequently. Just occasionally somebody called, but there was none of the earlier noise and jollity. At table the adults irritably discussed the failures at the Russian front, the rising prices, the government's stupidity, corruption and thievery among the cabinet, and of course Rasputin. Also they now had fewer servants, and those that remained were rude and careless in their duties. Mama used to get angry and flushed at the need to reprimand them, and then she would go to her bedroom to cool off. But one night Tanya was awakened by the sound of shouting downstairs in the drawing-room. She could make out the sound of her mother sobbing frenziedly. She had never known her mother raise her voice before, and now, still in her nightdress, she rushed downstairs.

In the drawing-room, dimly lit by two candles in candlesticks, her mother Darya was sitting on the settee, dishevelled and swaying in time to her own loud sobbing. Next to her sat her brother, Nikolai Andreyevich Trubin. He was a First Secretary in the War Ministry and was wearing a colonel's uniform. Tanya's father, tall and stocky, and dressed in a dark silk dressing-gown, was pacing the room distractedly.

Trembling with fright, Tanya rushed to her mother.

'Mama, why are you crying?'

'Tanya!' Darya took her daughter in her arms and hugged her violently. Her mother's embrace hurt Tanya; she was frightened and burst into tears.

'Dasha! What are you doing?' You're frightening the child! Take a grip of yourself!' Father came over to them. 'Nothing so very dreadful has happened yet. All that's happened is that Petya's run away to join the army. It doesn't mean that he's been killed!'

At these words, Dasha hugged Tanya even more firmly and moaned loudly.

'Dasha, darling, you're really scaring Tanya!' Uncle Nikolai leaned over and began carefully disengaging Tanya from her arms. 'The prince and I will use all our connections and we'll find Petya. I promise you, we'll have him back here at home within a few days!'

But Petya was not found within a few days. It took three months to discover his whereabouts. He was brought back home to Moscow very thin and mortally offended. His first words when he saw the family were: 'But I'm going back to the war all the same – as soon as I'm eighteen!'

Darya burst into tears and stretched her arms out to embrace him. But Petya started back and went off to his room. Mama turned to their father. Her face was flushed.

'So you see, he's not come back to us for long!' she said drily.

'We should really get ready straightaway and go abroad.'

A month later, at his wife's insistence, but somewhat reluctantly, Stepan Odalevsky left for Paris in order to prepare for his family's removal there.

In France Odalevsky managed to purchase a fine house twenty miles from Paris, engaged an estate manager and transferred the majority of his capital to a Swiss bank, and in general he arranged his affairs in the best way possible. Three and a half months later he was home again and in a lively, jocund frame of mind. At that time nobody imagined that none of his family would ever manage to benefit from these arrangements. Nobody, that is, except Tanya.

Spring came, then summer, followed by another winter. At home they even stopped mentioning the prospect of going abroad. Petya grew older and more manly. In the autumn he started at university, and his parents began to feel easier and joyfully followed his academic success. He became seriously absorbed in his medical studies and now recalled with amusement how he had once run away to join the army.

And then Lena appeared. Lena transformed the whole of his life. Petya fell in love with her. But not in the way eighteen-year-olds normally do – with exultation and rapture. It was a dark and jealous passion that consumed him completely. He turned thin, became tetchy and looked at the whole world with sullen eyes.

Lena was three years older than Petya. She smoked long thin *papirosy* and belonged to a secret revolutionary circle. She would often vanish only to reappear again unexpectedly; and she would then behave in a mocking, frivolous manner before disappearing once again.

This drove Petya to distraction. He imagined Lena with other lovers. He was gnawed by anguish, and from his red eyes it was obvious that sometimes he even wept. He lost interest in medicine, and when the February revolution of 1917 came he gave up his studies altogether; at that time in any event all students were dismissed for an indefinite period.

Stepan Odalevsky enthusiastically welcomed the February revolution, the abdication of the tsar and the establishment of a Provisional Government. As a liberal he was bound to welcome the democratic changes going on. But soon came October, and the new Bolshevik government became a fresh source of fear to the prince and his family.

The circle of arrests and executions gradually closed in around Stepan Odalevsky and his family. Several times men came bursting into their home and searched it. And after that their father dared not look anyone in the eye. Nothing was likely to save Prince Odalevsky from arrest – neither his liberal articles, nor his former revolutionary sympathies, nor his enforced and humiliating withdrawal into his home, where he now sat behind closed doors and with the blinds drawn.

In fact Odalevsky was saved only by his old friendly links with Timofey Razumikhin. From adult conversations she overheard, Tanya realised that as a young student at Moscow University her father had once saved Razumikhin from being sentenced to hard labour.

Exactly what had happened her father had never said. However, by this time Razumikhin was an all-powerful figure – something like the right-hand man of either Bucharin or Trotsky (Tanya couldn't remember exactly). And now it was Razumikhin who helped the prince's family not only to avoid arrest but also to file an application to emigrate.

Everything was shaping up successfully. They received their exit visas, their manager in Paris wrote that everything was ready for their arrival and in best order. According to their father, the money transferred in 1916 was quite sufficient for a long time to come; they could even afford to travel light as they left.

The sticking point, though, was Petya. Would he agree to leave the country? Their mother stated firmly that if he refused to go, then none of them should leave. But Petya said neither yes nor no. Every time they sat down to breakfast, lunch or supper, Darya contrived to point out that the lives of his father and sisters as well as her own, were in Petya's hands. But they all realised that the obstacle was not Petya himself, but his relations with Lena, who had not appeared in their house for more than a month.

Over the last six months, though, Petya seemed to be tiring of the affair. All too brief meetings with Lena followed by her frequent unannounced disappearances finally wore him down. He no longer seemed to swing so violently between rapture at her presence and jealous torment at her absence; and the long nights of sleeplessness over his unrequited love seemed a thing of the past. Finally, in fact, Petya had given up. One morning he emerged as usual from his room with his eyes all red, and gazing somewhere above their heads suddenly said in a loud voice bursting with resentment: 'Let's leave! As soon as possible! If everything is ready, I can be ready by tomorrow!'

After that the house was a hive of activity. And on the fateful 29th of January, 1919, they loaded their belongings in a cab and drove down to the station to catch the train for Paris.

The scene at the station was beyond description. It looked as if half Moscow was preparing to emigrate. Amid the bustle Tanya and her sisters clung close to their mother. Petya was gloomy and aloof and kept anxiously watching the teeming crowd. Amid the throng there were occasional glimpses of familiar and half-familiar faces – one-time professors of Moscow University, former counts and princes, and theatre personalities, the famous as well as the not so famous . . .

At last a train was shunted up to the platform and the crowd went wild. People were leaving behind their earlier settled lives, and none knew whether they would ever return again. But this consideration now became less important; the vital things now were their precious wooden trunks and cases stuffed with belongings, their ugly, bulky packages and bundles. Valuable burdens were carried on shoulders, dragged along or clutched like infant children. Even former aristocrats, professors and their wives were humping and dragging their baggage and were bowed under the weight of chests and trunks. People were carried along by a basic instinct for survival. Sometimes hunched and bent double, almost on all fours, they were unstoppable, and they paid no heed to the women who fell, or to the lost and crying children, or the old people who shuffled forward helplessly ...

Flushed and confused, Prince Odalevsky shouted at his wife for the first time in his life.

'Darya, hold this bundle! Are you blind or something? You've forgotten your handbag! Petya, check whether we've got everything! Anya and Tanya, you two can drag this case between you! Everyone on the train!'

Their hands chafing till they bled on the coarse rope that tied the heavy case, the girls managed with difficulty to get into the carriage. All the seats were filled with people and their luggage. They could see Petya up in front. He was angrily throwing someone's things off one of the seats. At a window nearby a small man sat with a stony look and a thrusting round belly. Suddenly he jumped up and shouted in a falsetto voice: 'Here, you, I'm a former war hero! You've no right to do that, you young puppy!'

'Well, I happen to be a prince, and I've fought in the army too!' Petya retorted.

'Ha, ha! Everybody's a prince these days! Or at least they used to be!' a bystander called mockingly.

Pale and angry, Petya continued clearing the seats for them. Their mother and eleven-year-old Katya, who was trembling, sat down. There were still about fifteen minutes before the train left.

Suddenly there was a loud call from the end of the corridor: 'Petya! Petya!'

Petya was bending over their luggage, but now stood bolt upright.

'Lena? ...' he murmured and rushed down to the end of the corridor.

Their mother turned pale and looked helplessly at her husband. Prince Odalevsky made a half-hearted movement to follow his son. 'Petya! We leave in a few minutes!'

But Petya was no longer listening.

'It's all right, darling,' their father said hesitantly. 'He just wants to say goodbye to her!'

For a few minutes they sat there in silence. Their mother gazed blankly out of the window, clutching Katya to her. Katya meanwhile was exhausted and already dozing off. Things settled down in the coach.

Everyone had taken their seats and were awaiting the departure.

'I can't! I can't just sit here and wait like this!' Darya was at her wits' end. 'Stepan, go and call him! The train will be off any moment! He'll miss it!'

Petya suddenly reappeared with a crazed look in his eyes. 'Mama! Papa! I can't come with you! I simply can't just now! I'll come later. We'll both come! I'll come with Lena!'

He was out of breath and could hardly get the words out.

'Oh, no-o-o-o-o!' Their mother moaned suddenly like a lamenting peasant woman. 'No! No!' She clutched Petya and hung on to him. 'Petya! I beg of you! Don't leave us, my son! Petya, darling!'

'Mama!' Petya too seemed close to weeping, but for another reason. 'Mama, dear, she's told me she loves me! She's never said that before! But now she's said it! She loves me! Mama, do you understand?!'

The train slowly began to move off.

'Goodbye, Mama! It's not forever though! It's *au revoir*!' Petya tore himself free and rushed to the door. 'I swear to you, I'll be coming soon!'

The prince seized his son by the sleeve.

'You're not going anywhere! You're coming with us!'

'You must be crazy!' Petya pushed his father off with some force and the Prince fell back onto someone's knees.

There was shouting. Petya's sisters burst into tears. The train was gathering speed. Petya dashed to the exit and jumped out.

Darya fell to the floor in a faint, and everyone crowded round her, trying to lift her up onto a seat. Nobody then realised that by appearing when she did Lena had saved Petya from the dreadful fate that lay in store for all the men on that train – princes, counts, professors, no matter who they were . . .

Suddenly there was a gentle knock at the door. Tanya started in surprise, suddenly brought back to the present.

'Who's there?' she called.

'Mrs Goehr? It's me, Oleg Petrov, your guide.'

Tanya was dumbfounded. She said nothing. 'We're done for!' she thought. 'They've come to get me!'

For a second she saw again the awful picture that had haunted her for half a century: the train . . . the shooting of the men . . . and her mother at the foot of the embankment, her mild-mannered mother uttering an inhuman shriek as two dirty unshaven soldiers with red bands in their buttonholes ripped off her dress . . .

'Mrs Goehr, your friend tells me that you're not feeling well. So I just thought I would call and check that everything is all right. Perhaps you need a doctor? We have excellent doctors here.'

'I . . .' Tanya tried to swallow a lump in her throat that prevented her speaking. 'No, thank you . . . It's not necessary. I don't need a doctor.'

'Are you feeling ill?' Oleg was getting perturbed on the other side of the door. 'I can send a doctor up immediately.'

'No!' Tanya fought back her fear and went to the door and now spoke quite cheerfully: 'I really don't need a doctor, thank you. I'm sorry, Oleg. I cannot let you in. I'm not dressed! You must forgive an old lady . . .'

'Oh, I understand,' he said somewhat dubiously. 'Don't forget that we are going to the theatre this evening. I hope you'll feel better by then.'

'Of course, certainly. Thank you for enquiring about me. Have a nice day.'

Exhausted by all this, Tanya took off her coat again and went into the bathroom to freshen up with cold water. But hardly had she splashed a first handful of water over her face when the telephone rang. Leaving the water still running, she rushed back into the bedroom and grabbed the receiver, thinking it was Elizabeth calling.

'Hallo?'

'Hallo, is that Frank?' said a husky woman's voice in English. 'How are you?'

She particularly stressed the 'you', and there was a heavy Russian burr on the letter 'r'.

'No, I am not Frank!' Tanya said angrily. 'And you should say "How *are* you?", and not "Khow arr *you*?"!'

'What? ... What?' the voice said, switching to Russian and clearly not understanding.

Tanya herself now switched to Russian and replied: 'To put it in a nutshell, there isn't any Frank around here!' She was about to hang up when the voice continued:

'So there we are! Speak perfect Russian, do we? Listen, then: what do you prefer, blondes or brunettes?'

Tanya's jaw dropped in astonishment. 'What? ... do I sound like a man?'

'What's the difference?' the voice went on, unembarrassed. 'Or are you only straight? I'll send you a nice young man. How old are you?'

'Eighty-three,' said Tanya. 'How old are *you*?'

After that there was no answer, only a series of pips ...

Tanya paused a moment by the phone, amazed, then went back to the bathroom. Shortly after that, Elizabeth appeared.

'They've left!' she announced, her eyes twinkling behind her spectacles. 'I watched them go. Why are you all flushed? Aren't you feeling well?'

'I'm feeling fine. It'll soon pass off.' Tanya placed a finger to her lips and pointed to the notepad she had ready to hand. Taking her pen, she wrote quickly: 'Has Judy left already? Did you see her go?'

'Yes,' Elizabeth wrote.

All the books about Soviet Russia maintain that the KGB bugs all foreigners in their hotel rooms. Tanya had specially consulted her Russian émigré friend on this point. He explained that the KGB are physically unable to listen in to all the conversations of every foreign visitor. Nevertheless all rooms in Moscow's Intourist hotels are equipped with hidden microphones, should the need arise to listen in. And this being the case, it was best to take precautions. Tanya felt almost like someone in the film series *Mission Impossible.* 'Go back down,' she wrote furiously on her pad. 'If you see anybody following me, you . . .'

Elizabeth seized the pen before Tanya could finish.

'I *know*! I *know* what to do!' she wrote, clearly offended. Then she ripped the sheet off the notepad, tore it in pieces and disposed of it down the toilet in the bathroom.

'I think I'm going for a walk,' Tanya said loudly for the benefit of the hidden microphone, and quickly put her coat on again. 'I have a slight headache. Do you want to come with me, my dear?'

Elizabeth emerged from the bathroom and looked at her in surprise. Then, realising Tanya was speaking for the KGB's benefit, she gave a loud theatrical answer:

'No, thank you. I think I'd better have a lie-down.'

Tanya seemed displeased and frowned, then made her way to the door.

'Wait!' Elizabeth suddenly said softly. She went to Tanya and held out her arms to embrace her. At any other time Tanya would have laughed or made some caustic remark. But now she hugged her friend gratefully and held her for a moment. Who could know how things were going to turn out? . . .

Elizabeth clutched Tanya feverishly and the whole of her body started quivering.

'Huh, she's started! She's crying,' Tanya thought contemptuously. 'Why on earth did I . . .'

'Elizabeth, stop it at once!' Tanya brusquely disengaged herself and walked out of the door without a backward glance.

4

The hostel where he lived was three stops away. But there was no sense in waiting for a bus – right now, at noon, in the middle of a shift, you could spend an hour or more waiting for the next one. Alexey thrust his bare hands deep into his jacket pockets, put his head down and set off walking. The cold wind lashed his face; it found its way through the thick padding of his quilted jacket and rasped his body with its icy needles. His feet quickly froze in his worn boots. At the food store there was a small queue to buy eggs. They had been on sale since the morning. When Alexey had hurried by earlier on his way to work, the queue had been enormous – about three hundred folk waiting. But now, though, it seemed all of Mytishchi had been supplied with eggs, and only about twenty people were still queueing. The customers' main concern was now how to get the eggs home intact. A woman was coming towards Alexey along the icy pavement like a circus tightrope-walker. In front of her she held a square cardboard tray with white hen's eggs nestling in the indentations. 'She's bound to fall any minute,' thought Alexey. But at that moment he almost fell himself as he skidded on a frozen mass of egg yolk that decorated the entrance to the store.

Cursing lustily, he rounded the food store and set off, half-running over the waste ground to take a short cut. He immediately regretted doing so. The hostel seemed not far away – there it was across the railway line, a four-storey brick building. But the icy wind cut through him as though he had no clothes on, and his knees were growing numb already.

'Faster, faster! ...' The words seemed to hammer in his head. 'I mustn't fall now! ...'

He ran along, bent almost double, forging a way with his left shoulder and shielding his head and ears with his quilted jacket. As he ran, memories of the past came flashing back. He had a sudden vision of Kolya Guryanov – the one who had had his legs blown off as the two of them took it in turns to help drag Yury Shalygin back from his first duty on a road block in the Chagar Ravine. They did not come under enemy fire that night, and had no cause to fire a shot themselves. Yury had simply gone and twisted his ankle because their wretched quartermaster had issued him with the wrong size of boots. Nobody of course dreamed of having gym shoes, which would have been the only suitable footwear for such slopes, but at least you should be able to expect boots of the right size! Then the faces of those two KGB agents floated before him – the ones he had recently seen in Gushchin's office. 'The bastards! They really put me through it! But I'm not going to give in all that easily to scum like them! I'll show them!' He swore aloud bitterly. His hands and feet were frozen almost rigid by the cold. Then, as if to spite him, just as he was about to emerge on the railway embankment, a train suddenly appeared and he had to wait till it passed ... Finally, however, Alexey reached the hostel, heaved open the heavy entrance door and was suddenly bathed in warmth. He stood there leaning against the wall in order to thaw out. The caretaker at the entrance sat reading his usual copy of the Moscow Young Communist paper. Egor Ivanych was a bald, grumpy old man and he looked at Alexey suspiciously over his glasses.

'What's up? Why aren't you at work? Are you canned already?'

'I was let off early, Ivanych ... What are you gawping at? If you don't believe me, ring the Party organiser,

Gushchin.' Alexey stamped noisily past him in his boots. Of course it wasn't a good idea to talk like that to Ivanych. The caretakers were often useful men to know if you wanted to bring a girl in for the night or borrow three roubles. And Ivanych was good for even larger sums, especially if you paid interest ... But just now Alexey couldn't care less. The main thing was to get to his room as quickly as possible.

Still panting, scarcely able to drag his numb and frozen feet, and cursing everything and everyone to high heaven, he finally made it up to the top floor. After his back injury he really was a physical wreck – fancy being out of breath after only three flights of stairs! He was certainly not in good form for a young man of barely twenty-two!

Alexey unlocked the door to room number 47, and without taking off his coat he made a rush for his bedside table. On the bottom shelf, amid a bundle of crumpled linen he kept a bottle of vodka hidden. Ever since Gorbachev had put half Russia on the wagon and forbidden liquor sales before 2.00 p.m. Alexey had bought in a supply and hidden it there for an emergency. And this was an emergency if ever there was one!

He wrenched the linen out onto the floor, found the bottle and greedily tore off the aluminium cap. For a second he was surprised how loose it was – the cap flew off almost without help. But there was no time to pause and think as he hastily pressed the bottle to his lips. Suddenly, after a few hasty gulps, he jerked the bottle away and with a cry hurled it against the wall.

'Bastards!'

Instead of vodka, there was only water in the bottle. One of his room-mates had drunk his vodka! Furiously he aimed a kick at the bedside cabinet. The nearest liquor store would not open for another hour and a half.

Alexey went over to his bed and turned back the mattress with a jerk. With his fingers he felt out a small packet sewn into the cover, then knelt down and began tearing open the seam with his teeth. In a couple of minutes he was holding a little cellophane packet with white powder in it. He swept everything from the cabinet onto the floor, laid out a sheet of newspaper, and carefully unwrapped the packet. He tipped a pinch of the powder onto the news-sheet, then with two fingers raised a crumb of the powder to his nose and breathed in deeply. He held his breath for a few seconds, then repeated the process. Sensing a slight rush of blood to his head, he inhaled one more pinch of the powder, just to be sure. Then, still in his boots and jacket, he lay down on the overturned mattress and awaiting the return of a sensation he had not experienced for a good long time.

'You can all go to hell!' he thought, as a calm came over him. 'It's true I promised myself never to take any more cocaine. But who was to know those bastards would turn up and ruin things? To hell with them though! What can they do to me? Lock me up? Shoot me? Ha-ha! Oh no, I'll put *them* inside – stinking rats! I'll show them who Alexey Odalevsky is! And Yury's made a wonderful job of his imitation *Pravda*! You only made one slip, though, old pal: you signed the article with the name of your village! You couldn't resist that, could you? And that's how they twigged who you were! But don't worry, Yury, Odalevsky isn't going to give you away. They've got the wrong man if they think I'll do that!'

Alexey closed his eyes happily and enjoyed the increasing narcotic effect. His head cleared, his legs ceased to ache, and the whole of his body became weightless. Once again he felt healthy and strong, just as he was before his injury.

It had been the best month of his life. In April the days were calm and warm. In the mountain valleys of Afghanistan, which had been dead and parched during winter, suddenly whole fields blossomed and were ablaze with poppies. In the villages within the Soviet military zone, there began a period of springtime Moslem feasts. On holidays such as this, the Mojahedin forgot about the war and were busy praying to Allah. It was therefore a good time both for them and for the Soviet army units. In the villages children ran around looking clean and washed, and there was a smell of roasting meat in the air. Alexey and Yury used every excuse to go off to the village of Tapbil – whether to help teach the local children Russian, or else to help the older men master the use of a gift which the Soviet command had presented to them to mark the feast. It was a new Belarus tractor, which the locals nevertheless managed to overturn on a mountain slope the very first time they used it for ploughing! But Alexey and Yury had their own reasons for escaping to that half-empty village where lean old men in long beards sat around on the streets, and women walked about dressed in black and with their faces hidden.

Yury kept his reasons to himself. But now it was clear to Alexey that he was then probably trying to establish contact with the Mojahedin. Perhaps he was already in touch with them? Perhaps during that ambush when Yury ran towards the enemy, they were already waiting for him and for that reason did not shoot? . . .

Alexey's reason for visiting Tapbil was Ulima. She would be there waiting for him, and he would rush to meet her as fast as his legs could carry him. The only things he could get at the store in their mess were 'Acidola' (which was a paste for polishing uniform buttons!), some bitter Yugoslavian sweets, and jars of condensed milk. The idea that Soviet soldiers got such things as chocolate and oranges as a reward for carrying out their 'internationalist exploits' was a sad delusion. There was neither vegetable nor fruit to be had, even if you had the money to pay. Even in the army hospitals such things as apples and gherkins were a rare treat. And very often, when the Motherland occasionally sent a planeload of such things as potatoes and cucumbers, they would unseal the crates to discover that the contents were already rotten. The soldier's basic fare in Afghanistan was so-called 'shrapnel' – a gruel made of peas and either oats or wheat: a healthy body meant a healthy mind! So Alexey would chuck three of four tins of milk and a packet of those sweets into his kitbag and hurry off to see Ulima: She seemed to like the awful Yugoslav confectionery! And of course Yury would go along with him – the two of them only parted when they got to the edge of the village, where Ulima's hut stood.

Yury would give an understanding smile and promised to cover for Alexey if the need arose. Meanwhile Alexey never paid any serious heed to his friend's oaths and muttering against the war, the people in command, and the distant 'bosses in the Kremlin'. Several times Yury had argued that he would flee to Pakistan and join the partisans rather than endure this feeling that he was a butcher sent here to slaughter innocent, defenceless children and old people. 'We are fascists – that's all we are! Pure and simple fascists!' he muttered almost absent-mindedly when no one was within earshot. Such moments were rather rare however. Every platoon lived under canvas, seven men to a tent. All around them was a ring of mine-fields; and inside the circle were their tents, a parking area for the artillery and other equipment; and in the middle was their HQ, the clubhouse, mess, and the officers' prefabricated quarters. The officers themselves openly drank and hardly disguised the fact. When drunk they often fired off their signal pistols in a mock salute. But since the common soldiers had nowhere to get their vodka, they turned to hashish. In order to obtain it they flocked to help the local Afghan 'collective farmers', taught them to plough the hard red Afghan soil using tractors, and even made school benches for them – anything to improve the chances of getting hashish by purchase or barter! Stuck with nothing to do inside this barricade of minefields and in the baking heat, confused and uncertain about their position, and waiting to be attacked or bombarded at night, the majority of soldiers and officers welcomed every new military operation as an opportunity to let rip. During raids and sorties into partisan territory, there were also chances for plundering and for avenging the death of recently killed comrades, as well as earning a routine battle decoration. So that when you were demobbed you could return home with a breast full of tinplate. And some of them – Sergey Sukhar, for instance – had managed to combine all of these activities. Like most of them he had stolen anything he could lay his hands on – clothing, watches, transistors and ballpoint pens. But in addition to these, the first things he grabbed from ruined houses and mosques were copies of the Koran. And if he couldn't find any, he would force women prisoners at gun point to bring him the 'holy books' they had hidden. He would simply point his Kalashnikov at the children and yell to their mother or grandmother to bring him a Koran. Alexey recently heard that through the sale of these Korans Sukhar had become a rich man in Dushanbe. In the Moslem republics of Soviet Central Asia the Koran had apparently not been printed for seventy years. Consequently on the black market there every such book would fetch three thousand roubles; they almost tore them out of your hands and went off praising Allah and thanking you into the bargain. And Sergey Sukhar had managed to swipe almost three hundred Korans while in Afghanistan!

But Alexey had no time for such business deals, and no time either for his friend Yury Shalygin's outpourings of conscience. Whatever he managed to filch within their unit he brought to Ulima. And she was always there to greet him in the same pose: seated on her bedmatting in the corner with her legs tucked under her. It quickly emerged that she lived alone. Her parents had been killed by a Soviet bomb at the start of the war, when she was nine. In the same raid she had also lost three younger brothers. Her mother's sister had taken her in, but she too soon perished, blown up by a mine. It was not a Soviet mine, though; it was an anti-tank mine laid by the partisans – and this particularly incensed Ulima. Not that it made any difference to her aunt . . .

Whenever he managed to obtain vodka or wine from one of the cooks or medical orderlies who exchanged it for hashish, Alexey would take it to Ulima. But she herself never drank, preferring hashish, which she obtained by bartering the clothing that Alexey used to bring her. Such items were considered luxury goods among the Afghans. They paid well for shirts, vests and socks; and boots fetched a specially good price.

Alexey half-guessed that the clothing he brought was passed on to the Mojahedin, but that did not unduly worry him. Ulima never asked him to bring weapons or ammunition in return for hashish – she was too intelligent to suggest it, and he was unconcerned by anything else. The only thing he did not understand was why she seemed unafraid of being with him, a Russian soldier ...

Once, however, when he called on Ulima he found she was out. He surveyed the empty house in bewilderment. Leaning against the cold clay wall, he took a sip of the vodka he had brought, then lay down on the bedmatting. He dozed off immediately and must have slept for some thirty minutes. He awoke at the sound of someone quietly sobbing. The room was dark and Alexey could make out nothing.

'Ulima!' he called, 'is that you?'

Silence.

He got up and went to the doorway. There he saw a dark hunched figure barely recognisable in the gloom.

'Ulima!' He bent down and carefully touched her rough hair. 'What's the matter?'

She began weeping loudly, rocking from side to side, and uttering angry guttural words in Afghani. Alexey sat down next to her and embraced her shoulders.

'Have you ... have you vodka?' she asked in Russian, and flinched at his touch.

'Yes, over there.' He nodded inside. 'Shall I light your lamp?'

'No. I can see.' Ulima got up and went inside.

Alexey heard her grasp the bottle and begin drinking from it. The burning taste gave her a fit of coughing. She swore in Afghani then took another swig. In a few seconds though, all was calm again and she lay down on her matting. A short while later he saw the flare of a match and heard her moan as she drew deeply on a cigarette.

He sat there in the entrance and could not think what to do. Should he sit with her and try to find out why she was so upset? Or should he wait till she calmed down of her own accord and called him to come?

Goodness knows what had happened! Perhaps one of her relatives had been killed, or maybe someone in the village had cursed her for getting involved with Russian soldiers. They were fanatics, these Afghans. Then it occurred to him: suppose she had been raped by one of their own men? The officers were such a randy bunch. Give them half a chance with a young Afghan girl . . . But if one of them has touched her, Alexey thought, I'll kill the bastard. I'll put a bullet through him! . . .

Suddenly, for the first time in that shortest and happiest month of his whole life, he realised to his surprise that he loved her. He loved her so much, that if anyone had really hurt her he would have stopped at nothing. He was quite prepared to gun down or knife the guilty man, and afterwards he would happily face whatever charge!

'Alyosha,' she suddenly said in a soft voice, using the tender short form of his name. 'Today I am happy. Today I am very happy!'

She said no more.

What was one to make of these women, Alexey wondered, puzzled yet relieved. When they were sad they blubbered, and yet they did the same even when they were happy!

'Then why are you crying?'

Ulima said nothing. Alexey went over to her, settled down on the matting, felt for her face and stroked her moist cheeks. The discovery of his love for her moved him with tenderness, and he felt that he should tell her of it.

'Alyosha, today is the birthday of my son!' Ulima said softly.

'Your son?'

He thought he might have misheard or that she had used the wrong word. She often confused Russian words and was, for instance, quite capable of saying 'a lot' when she meant 'a bit'.

'Did you say your *son*?' he asked cautiously.

'Yes, my son. He today two ... two year old.'

'Two year*s*,' Alexey corrected her without thinking. 'And where is he?'

'I don't know.'

It was dark in the room. Her cigarette with its faintly glowing tip seemed to float in the air on its own.

Alexey breathed deeply. His recent thoughts of loving her now seemed almost comical. She was a secretive person, it seemed – still a stranger to him. How often had he come to see her, yet she had never dropped a syllable about having a son! When had she managed to give birth? After all, she was only fifteen. She probably had only one idea in life – onto the bed, light up a cigarette and drop her skirt. He shifted as he recalled her hard dark nipples. He felt an urge to seize her again, fling her back, sink his teeth into her small childlike breasts and hear again her hoarse, almost animal moaning.

'Alyosha, I watch you long time ... you and your red-hair friend.' Ulima said with a gentle laugh. 'Your friend used to shout at me. He wanted some grass. He gave me a tin of meat. And I gave him dry leaves as a joke. Can you remember?'

She giggled again.

Alexey tried to recall when he had seen her first of all. But he could only think of when Ulima had flung off her jacket and put on his shirt. No, he couldn't recall having come here along with Yury. She was fibbing probably. Just fibbing.

'But I watching you even before. You were always together ... always with friend.' Then after a silence, she said, 'Alyosha, when are you go home?'

'So I'm boring you, am I? In that case I'll go right away!' he said roughly.

'No, home to Russia ...'

'To Russia?' he said in surprise. For the last month he had never spared a thought for the fact that he would soon be demobilised. Where was he going to go? Who would be waiting for him back there? He had no home in Russia. And none here either. He suddenly felt miserable. Her hut had become his home. Perhaps he could stay on and extend his service? But now it turned out she had a son! 'I don't know when I'm going back to Russia,' he said.

'But I know. It will be soon ...' Ulima leaned her body against him, but this time not as before – trembling with desire. This time she was weak and pathetic.

'Ulima, where is your son?'

'I don't know,' she said, still pressing against him. 'He was taken away half a year after.'

'Half a year after what?'

'After he born. First Allah call Kolya, his father. Then a Russian general came with soldiers and a tall woman. Woman – she political agitator, not *shuravi*, but Moslem, from Tashkent. She speak good Afghani. She see, my son have white hair – like Kolya. Woman take my son. She say, all the same, Afghan people kill son because he have white hair. I tell her, Kolya became Moslem before he die, he take Islam. She say that Kolya – he traitor to Russia. So Russian general took Ulima's son. She say he send son to school in Russia. In airplane. Other village too has many children taken on airplane. They not have white hair – but all the same they take to school in Russia ...'

Alexey felt for the bottle of vodka and took several swigs. So that was it! Some Kolya or other, from the Ukraine probably, had gone over to the Afghans, converted to Islam, and then been killed – 'called by Allah'. And after that the Soviet authorities had sent his son off to Russia... Alexey realised of course that many Afghan orphans had been sent back to the Soviet Union to boarding-schools. But to take a child away from his own mother!

'And this man Kolya?' he asked carefully. 'How old were you then?'

'Ulima twelve. He also come to change *tapbil.* Exchange watch for hashish. But I not want him. He beat me. Every time he come he beat. But I no crying. Then he stop beating. He love Ulima. And our people come and want to kill him and me. But he already speak Afghani. I teach him. I love Ulima, he say. I want marry Ulima, he say. I want go with you to *kiriz.* He become Islam, then Russian mine blow up and Allah call him. And my son taken in airplane to school. Now nobody can marry Ulima, only Kolya's brother. But Kolya has no brother. He say me: I have father, I have mother, but nobody else ...'

So that was how things were. Alexey got up and went over to the wall. He groped on the floor and found the kerosene lamp and spent some time trying to light it, his hands trembling nervously. So that was why she was not afraid to receive him. For her own people she was already a widow, the widow of a Russian convert to Islam – a widow. That was the sort of story you could never read in *Pravda* or the *Red Star* magazine! Nor could you even hear the like on the BBC! But perhaps she was now expecting Alexey to convert to Islam for her sake? What a joke! It *was* funny, wasn't it? First Kolya had gone crazy over her, and now he, Alexey, was in the process of doing the same!

At last he managed to light the lamp. It glowed with a smoky flame and a warm light spread through the room. Alexey returned to the corner where Ulima lay, and for a long time he stood there gazing down at her. To his surprise, he discovered he was not in the least jealous of Kolya, who had first of all raped and beaten her and then fallen in love with her, deserted and joined the Mojahedin and converted to Islam. How lovely her eyes were ... they had a velvety look, and her lips too ... And how slender and fragile she seemed. And the things she had gone through – more than some women in a long lifetime. All her people had been killed – father, mother, brothers,

Kolya. And her son had been taken away. 'Good God! What the hell are we doing in this country?' Alexey wondered. 'And why?'

Alexey knelt down and gently embraced her about the shoulders.

'When did all this happen? Do you remember when it was that they took your son away?'

'Yes. Autumn. November in Russian.'

'That means November of 1984. And what did you say they called him?'

'Akhram, like my grandfather. Why you asking?'

'And his surname? Did they write down his Russian surname?'

'They not ask. They know name of Kolya already. Kolya Batkov. Why you want to know?'

He held her firmly in his arms.

'Ulima, I'm going to find your son. I swear to you, I shall find him!'

'No, Alyosha. Soon you leave here. You leave for ever. I know.'

'Where shall I go? What are you thinking about? I'm not going to go anywhere. I still have six months before I'm demobbed!'

'No. You leave soon,' she repeated insistently and burst into tears again.

'What on earth are you going on about? Silly! Why keep on saying "You'll leave, you'll leave"?' Alexey pressed her head against his chest. 'I'll never leave you. I swear it – never!'

But Ulima was right. One hour later, as they lay there in one another's arms, Yury Shalygin came running in panting and announced that they must return to their unit immediately.

'Quick! There's a general alarm on! They've all gone crazy back there! The officers have got the men to fall in – and some of them are tanked up to the gills! Some others are zonked on hash, and some of them are like you – absent without leave! And the old man's breathing fire and brimstone: anyone not back within the hour will be up on a charge – court-martialled!'

'What the hell do you mean? For God's sake what is this?' Alexey asked as they hurried back. 'It's still Ramadan. None of them are fighting now!'

'Bugger Ramadan! A commission's just flown in from Moscow, and they're bawling *us* out for not fighting!'

Alexey could not imagine he would never see Ulima again. How could he have guessed that they would be herded like cattle into transporters and armoured cars, and that at any moment they would be on the move? In fact it was at the start of that fatal advance down the Lohar valley that Yury Shalygin ran and joined the Mojahedin, and that Alexey, unconscious and with a serious back injury, was taken to hospital . . .

5

Judy took the bus to the Yaroslavsky Station on Komsomolskaya Square. But hardly had she got out and surveyed its quaint old-fashioned architecture, reminiscent of a church, when she realised they had been wrong in one of their calculations. The massive carved semi-circular doors of the main station entrance, where she was supposed to wait for Princess Goehr, turned out to be shut, and streams of passengers and others were entering and leaving by the small side entrances quite some distance away. Back in New York, Judy and Tanya had studied the station building from photographs and guide-books, and Tanya had marked their meeting point with a cross, on the steps in front of the apparently crowded main entrance. But now there was no way for anyone to stand and wait in that deserted area without drawing attention to themselves. She would stick out like a sore thumb!

The taxi driver offered her only a five-rouble note as change for her ten roubles, and with an impudent 'Thank you!' he drove off, although Judy could see quite clearly that there were only three roubles twenty kopecks on the meter. But who could tell: were five roubles too much or too little to offer him? . . .

As she paced up and down on the empty frozen pavement in front of the station, Judy took in her surroundings: the huge station square, a clump of grey taxis identified by the chequered pattern on their doors, the crowds of people carrying bags who stormed the doors of buses, a small queue of people waiting at a street stall to purchase hot pies, the brick-red building of the Kazansky Station on the other side of the square, a bridge over to the right, and the spire of a sky-scraper building with lettering she had difficulty making out against the sun ... 'LENINGRADSKAYA HOTEL' ... So this was Moscow – the Moscow Judy had dreamed of visiting ever since high school, the Moscow that writers like Pushkin, Chekhov and Tolstoy had written so much about ... It was a bright frosty day, but breathing was difficult – not because of the cold, but because of the acrid smell of exhaust fumes from the taxis, cars and buses with their roaring engines, squealing brakes and trails of dark grey exhaust smoke. What a pity Princess Goehr had forbidden her to bring her camera! Should she buy one of those hot pies or not? There were Russians standing there eating them around the stall. They bit off large pieces and clouds of vapour rose from their mouths – either because of the keen frost or because the pies were so hot. But how was it that all of them had such sullen, blank, grey expressions? In the USA the papers kept writing every day about glasnost; almost every newspaper had a smiling picture of Gorbachev, and one might have thought the Russians were enjoying a constant feast of renewal, almost like a carnival. But where were the signs of it here? The elderly saleswoman had a raw, red face. Dressed in a sheepskin, felt boots, and gloves with the fingers cut away, she gave not a smile as she forked up the pies and handed them to her customers. With no napkins on offer and no welcoming smile, she wouldn't have done a very good trade in New York!

'Three hamburgers and three Cokes! ... A Big Mac and a Sprite! ... Two cheeseburgers with fries! ... Regular fries and a coffee! ...' Judy laughed as she thought of herself only two weeks before, working in McDonald's on West 97th Street. She had hardly time to punch out the various items, take the customers' crumpled dollar bills, hand out change and set the hamburgers, cheeseburgers and cardboard cups of coffee on the trays, together with the cartons of fries, the Coke and napkins, more napkins and ever more napkins. And still you had to keep smiling! ... 'Three hamburgers and three Cokes! ... Thank you. Have a nice day ... A quarterpounder with cheese ... Thank you. Have a nice day ...' Your legs got tired of standing on one spot, your hands were aching after two or three hours of morning rush-hour business, and your nose was bunged up with catarrh from the constant smell of coffee ... But those two elderly women – the tall thin one in the expensive cream-coloured leather coat and kid gloves, and the little rosy-cheeked one in spectacles – she had noticed them straight away. They had ordered just two Diet Pepsis, had sat down at the nearest table to the till and proceeded to stare hard at Judy. And they had continued gazing at her for a full hour! They never took their eyes off her. Then the older one said something to her small companion and they both got up and went away. But the following day, there they were again, early in the morning at eight o'clock! And the small one again ordered just two Diet Pepsis, while the tall one sat at the next table. And once again they sat there and watched Judy, inspecting her like a horse at a sale. They must both be lesbians, it's obvious, thought Judy. But why on earth do they both sit there and gaze at her for two days in a row?! She felt like going up to them and telling them to leave her alone – she was straight, dammit!

Just then a taxi drew up barely a yard from where Judy stood. The bent figure of the Princess emerged, but once out of the car she stood up to her full height.

'Why have you come without a hat?' she asked Judy in an almost hostile voice.

'I forgot ...'

'Not so loud!' Tanya interrupted and looked round anxiously. 'Stop that loud talk in English! And fancy standing here in such an obvious place. You stand out terribly! I asked you to ...'

She stopped short. An elderly man in a black coat and shabby fur hat with drooping earflaps had stopped next to them. He had no gloves on and in his chapped hands he carried two net bags stuffed with empty bottles. He seemed to Tanya to be eyeing them suspiciously. She smiled at him, in the way people the world over smile if their glances happen to meet. But there was no answering smile. On the contrary the man gave an unfriendly scowl.

'What is it?' he asked.

Tanya did not know what to answer and turned away.

'An old hag like you, and still at it!' he grated, and spat on the ground angrily. 'Ugh! *Koorvy*!'

With a shudder as though someone had lashed her with a whip, Tanya grabbed Judy by the elbow and quickly headed towards the side entrance of the station.

'What does *koorvy* mean?' Judy asked. She had never met the word in Tolstoy or Dostoevsky.

'Quiet!' Tanya snapped and continued to drag Judy after her. 'Koorvy is a vulgar word meaning "prostitutes".'

Judy followed at Tanya's side and kept glancing at her curiously. Something in Tanya Goehr had altered. The dark scarf tied about her head emphasised the angularity of her broad cheeks; her face without make-up now seemed grey; and her wrinkles were more pronounced. Dressed in a coarse navy overcoat, she looked just like all the other old Russian women around them. Only she held herself straighter; the Russian women were hunched forward under the weight of their heavy bags and carriers in both hands.

'But she is afraid too!' Judy thought jauntily as she felt the Princess's hand trembling as she gripped her elbow. Judy had no fears though. Oh, no! Up to now she had found it terribly difficult to restrain herself and to have to play the part of a demure little tourist who wouldn't say boo to a goose. And now she felt a surge of energy – she wanted to see more action and enjoy a few dangers and adventures, like in the film *Romancing the Stone.* And now it was beginning – they were about to leave Moscow and go beyond the twenty-mile limit. True, they were going only four or five miles beyond, but still . . .

In the booking hall at the rear of the station only five of the sixteen ticket kiosks were operating – just like at Grand Central. But the queues were different. People pressed up against one another and pushed those in front of them. And every few minutes a metallic female voice could be heard over the loudspeaker, announcing the departure of trains to Zagorsk, Fryazino, Mytishchi, Monino and elsewhere ... It was not very nice being elbowed forward with people breathing down your neck. And ugh! What an awful smell! But Tanya squeezed Judy's arm as if to say 'Stand just as you are and don't turn round.'

At last they made it to the front and it was their turn. Tanya handed a red ten-rouble note through the small round ticket window, and without a smile ordered 'Two to Mytishchi'.

The fat woman cashier had on a navy sateen smock over her warm overcoat.

'What sort?' she snapped without looking up.

'What was that?' Tanya asked, bewildered.

'If you can't hear, grandma, you should stay at home!' the woman snapped angrily. 'Single or return?'

'Oh, return of course! Certainly, return tickets!'

'Huh! Woken up at last, have we?' The cashier slapped the two tickets down. 'How am I to know what sort you want?'

'The next train to Zagorsk leaves from platform number six in two minutes' time,' the loudspeaker announced. 'Calling at the following stations: Yauza, Losinka, Mytishchi, and all stations thereafter. I repeat ...'

'That's ours!' With her gloved hand Tanya quickly seized the tickets, and had turned away and set off with Judy in tow. But the young woman next in line stopped them: 'What about your change?'

Tanya looked inquiringly at the cashier, and Judy peeked inquisitively from behind her shoulder. She was just in time to see the cashier's plump short-fingered hand sweep up the seven roubles and kopecks Tanya had forgotten. Without a word, the woman produced the money again from her drawer and threw it out through the window. There were no apologies though, and all she did was to shout loudly, 'Next!'

Tanya took her money and made for the exit onto the platform. There were hordes of people, but Tanya grimly barged her way through, all the while clutching Judy's arm with one hand. Judy had never imagined an 83-year-old could have such a strong grip.

'Please let go! You're hurting me!' she blurted finally.

Tanya did not answer but kept on going. Finally they reached platform six. It was half-empty. Only now did Tanya pause. She leaned over close to Judy and said quietly in Russian:

'Now, I'm asking you: don't say a word from now on! Not a word to anyone! Don't look at anyone either. And don't smile. Otherwise everything could be ruined.'

'All right, all right ...' said Judy.

'Shut up!' Tanya whispered furiously straight in her face. One more word of English and I shall pack you straight back to New York!' she continued in Russian.

'*Khorosho, khorosho* ... Very well,' Judy said resignedly, reverting to Russian. 'Only don't get so excited!'

The coach was cold and empty. On each side of it were rows of hard wooden two-seater benches, with narrow metal shelving overhead for luggage and parcels. Tanya moved ahead unhurriedly down the coach and tried surreptitiously to get a look at the few passengers already seated there. There were two portly women wearing identical knitted mohair hats, a young couple carrying skis, and an unshaven man in a tall cap with ear-flaps.

Seeing nothing suspicious, Tanya settled down on one of the benches at the far end of the coach and gestured to Judy to sit down next to her by the window. It was a pity there were so few people, since it made the two of them more conspicuous. On the other hand, it made it easier for them to observe the passengers. And if anything appeared suspicious they could easily slip through into the next coach. Tanya was also desperate for a cigarette – but heaven forbid! Who could tell whether smoking was allowed on trains or not?! It might in fact be a good idea to pretend to doze off like the unshaven man there: he had his feet up on the seat opposite and had leaned back and closed his eyes, using his cap as a pillow. If only Petya, who jumped off a train on 29th January 1919, had known what lengths she was going to today, sixty-eight years later, to try and find his grandson!

Suddenly, from above there came a loud hissing noise and the two of them gave a start. Then a hoarse male voice announced over the Tannoy: 'Attention, please! This train is the 10.05 to Zagorsk, stopping at the following stations: Yauza, Losinka, Mytishchi, and all other stations after Mytishchi ... Stand clear of the doors!'

The doors slid to automatically, then the coach gave a jerk and the train began gliding down the empty platform. On the track next to them meanwhile another train was pulling in.

'Thank God we're off!' Tanya thought with relief. For some reason she believed that once the train set off all danger would be left behind – nobody would stop them, send them back to Moscow or arrest them! Only one thing remained to be done: find Alexey, fling her arms about him, and ...

Judy felt Tanya's enquiring gaze resting on her again, sizing her up, so it seemed, as she had once before, back in New York ...

Judy finished work at McDonald's and eventually emerged at 3.15 p.m. At four o'clock she was due to start her shift at the Answering Service in a stuffy little cabin on 37th Street, in the block between 7th and 8th Avenue. There at least she could sit down as she worked, instead of standing. Thank God, though, tomorrow was Saturday – she didn't have to work and could sleep in and recover from the week's exertions. Her boyfriend Craig kept telling her that only donkeys would stand for such punishment – 7.00 a.m. to 3.00 p.m. at McDonald's, and after that another six hours at the Answering Service. But how else could she pay her way through university? Her father had died two years before, and her mother had immediately gone and married some swine called Tom – on top of which she had started drinking like the wife of President Ford. Unfortunately, though, her mother was not married to President Ford but to a bastard who was eight years younger, and who not only joined her in her drinking bouts but had also started interfering with Sharon, Judy's twelve year old sister . . .

A thick snow was falling. No, it wasn't even snow, but a ghastly cold porridge of sleet that gummed up her eyes and turned Broadway into something halfway between a gigantic gutter brimming with mud and melt-water and a landscape painted by some woebegone impressionist. Within a few seconds her sneakers were sodden from the snowy swill and her face was streaming. Quick! Down into the subway where at least it was dry! . . .

But suddenly, through the shroud of sleet Judy thought she heard someone calling her name.

'Miss Sanders!'

She glanced round bewildered.

'Miss Sanders!' There it was again, from somewhere behind her! It seemed to come from the open door of the long black limousine that was slowly rolling along right next to the sidewalk.

No, it couldn't be her they were calling. Nobody she knew rode about in a limousine, a Rolls Royce, or even a Mercedes! Craig of course had a 1973 Ford, but that wasn't quite the same thing! Judy looked about her. There must be someone else around called Sanders. How strange!

'Miss Sanders! Judy Sanders!' It was a woman's voice calling insistently from the approaching car. Only then did Judy see through the freezing curtain of sleet who it was waving from the open door: it was the little old lesbian who only that morning had spent a whole hour gaping at her in McDonald's. And next to her on the back seat sat the other woman – the tall one in the light coat. Ghastly old harridans!

Containing her anger Judy stepped over towards them. 'What is it? What do you want?'

'Please take a seat. We want to talk to you.' The little old lady's cheeks puckered in a smile. She pointed to the fold-down seat in the rear of the car.

Judy turned on her heel and walked away. But the limousine moved along next to her, and the old woman continued shouting for all the street to hear:

'Miss Sanders! Wait a moment! Why are you walking away?'

'Get away! I'm not a lesbian!' Judy snapped, still striding along. Then she stopped: 'D'you want me to call the cops?' she called.

The old woman's jaw dropped in astonishment. She turned to her companion and stuttered: 'She ... she ... Oh my God, she thinks we're lesbians!'

Judy didn't wait to hear the other woman answer, but turned and set off again, stamping through the puddles in her fury. But the limousine still followed and eventually overtook her. And as Judy strode along, the little old woman leaned intrepidly from the open door and began beseeching her:

'Listen, Judy! I am aged seventy! I have four grandchildren almost the same age as you! We're not lesbians! Where did you get that idea? We simply need to talk to you – just five minutes! Please, I beg of you! ...'

She talked so loudly that other passers-by were turning round to stare at them.

Judy stopped, and the limousine also drew to a standstill.

'Okay', she said, 'Say what you have to say!'

'But we can't talk like this! Have a seat in the car. If you want, we can run you down to the Answering Service on 37th Street.'

Judy hesitated. It wasn't just that her feet were soaked,

or that they knew where she was heading ... But God knows, maybe these women were from Hollywood?! Or from the TV? After all, anything could happen in New York! ...

Judy looked around. After all, what could two old women do to her sitting in a limousine in the middle of Manhattan at three in the afternoon? Two old women who drank only Diet Pepsi! ...

'Okay.' She jumped into the car and perched on the folding seat opposite the old ladies. 'Only five minutes, mind! ...'

The little old lady reached forward to close the door, but Judy quickly wedged it open with one of her sneakers.

'Oh, no! We'll have the door open, if you don't mind!'

'But it's so windy! And there's all this snow!' the woman complained. 'We can't drive like this ...'

'Never mind. We'll stay here. What is it you want?'

'My name is Elizabeth Wollens,' she began, 'and this is my friend Tanya Goehr. We're from Florida, but we've been in New York for three weeks now.'

Judy glanced at Tanya Goehr. She had a Russian name – Tanya – the same as Tatyana in Tchaikovsky's *Eugene Onegin*. She had unbuttoned her suede coat and Judy noticed that she had around her neck three strands of white gold with a diamond of goodness knows how many carats. And she exuded the aroma of some fine perfume. Was this something out of *Dynasty*?!

'Please, perhaps after all you would let me close the door? I suffer terribly from rheumatism,' Elizabeth Wollens pleaded, holding her knee.

Judy removed her foot.

'Thank you,' said Elizabeth and closed the door. Then, turning to her friend: 'I told you Miss Sanders would be a kindly girl! We've simply gone and scared her – coming up to her on the street like this!'

'Okay, so you've come from Florida? What is it you want to tell me?' Judy asked impatiently. She noticed the chauffeur behind the glass partition was wearing a braided Limousine Service uniform. He showed no sign of starting off and sat there waiting for instructions.

'Tell me, Miss Sanders, how old are you?' asked Tanya Goehr, screwing her eyes up slightly. Her voice was dry and low-pitched, obviously from much smoking, and she had a faint Slavonic accent.

'She'll be twenty-one in seventeen days' time,' Elizabeth Wollens answered before Judy could speak.

Tanya Goehr gave an irritated frown.

'Elizabeth, I am sure Miss Sanders can answer for herself!' Then she suddenly switched to Russian and asked, '*Skazhìte*, tell me, are you going to continue your college studies? Answer me in Russian if you possibly can.'

But Judy continued in English.

'But why do I actually have to ...?'

'I would ask you, please speak Russian to me!' Tanya Goehr interrupted. '*Pozháluysta, govoríte po-rússki*!', she said, pronouncing her words firmly and deliberately. 'Or don't you understand me? At N.Y.U.* they told us you were one of their best Russian students. I did want to hear you speak Russian.'

'Look here,' Judy finally exploded, still in English, 'Until you tell me exactly who you are and what you want, I'm not going to talk to you in either Russian or English!'

'Aha, you see, a girl of spirit!' Elizabeth said to her companion and immediately patted Judy on the knee. 'Judy, my dear, please do what the Princess asks. You've no idea what a surprise we have in store!'

(So this tall woman Tanya Goehr was a Russian princess! Perhaps that was how she got her diamonds? Were there really still Russian princesses around? Well, maybe, if she was eighty or ninety years old ... But what was that she was saying ...?)

'Unfortunately, Miss Sanders, until I've checked on

*University of New York – *Tr.*

your Russian, we cannot discuss this piece of business of ours.' The Princess seemed to wear a slightly mocking frown. 'I wanted to offer you some work, but I have to check on you first. I hope you don't object?!'

'Heavens,' Elizabeth interrupted again, 'The girl must need money badly! How much can anyone earn at McDonald's? And on night duty at the Answering Service?! Six dollars an hour. D'you call that money? The poor girl must be desperate ...'

(Damn it, perhaps they knew all about her mother, Tom and Sharon too? But that wasn't so important. Most likely Princess Goehr was looking for a private secretary with a good knowledge of Russian. Of course, that wasn't why she'd studied Russian at high school, at N.Y.U., and at the Norwich University Russian summer school – simply to be an old woman's secretary! But on the other hand ... how much did a secretary earn with a foreign language? Steady now, Judy, this could be your chance: thirteen hundred a month, not a cent less! Perhaps even fifteen hundred!)

Judy put on her friendliest smile and said in Russian: '*Chto vy kholíte?* ... What do you want me to say? You want to know whether I hope to graduate? Of course I do! *Konyechno*!'

From the twinkle in the Princess's eye Judy realised her Russian must still be in good form, despite her six months at McDonald's. So all that time spent in the language centre and at Norwich had not been wasted.

'When did you start learning Russian?' the Princess asked. 'And why?'

'I began in high school ...' Judy glanced at her watch. If they didn't take her to 37th Street by car she would be late for work. And she still didn't know whether she was going to get this secretarial job!

'Perhaps we should be on our way?' Elizabeth said. 'Otherwise the girl's not going to be in time for work ...'

Princess Goehr extended a suede gloved hand toward the glass panel. The chauffeur turned round, and she said quickly in English, '37th Street, please, between 7th and 8th Avenue.'

The limousine moved off.

'Yes? I'm listening,' Princess Goehr resumed in Russian. 'So you began learning Russian at high school? Why was that?'

'I don't really know,' Judy shrugged. 'Several of us began taking Russian when a Russian teacher came to the school. He was a Russian émigré, a journalist from Leningrad. Then at least half of them gave it up. But I didn't. I'd just started reading Gogol. You'll have read Gogol of course?'

Elizabeth, who obviously didn't understand Russian, looked anxiously from Judy to the Princess. (Who was Elizabeth? Was she Princess Goehr's friend? Her companion? One thing was clear however: Elizabeth was 'rooting' for Judy and anxious for her to pass this test with flying colours ...)

Judy's question about Gogol was left hanging in the air. Princess Goehr said nothing and gazed at Judy – just the way people size up a horse at the races, Judy thought bitterly as she looked out of the tinted window ... Yes, they were heading along Broadway.

'How's she doing, Tanya?' Elizabeth could contain herself no longer. 'Why are you saying nothing?'

'Not at all badly ... She does have an accent, of course, but that isn't so important ...' Princess Goehr continued to look searchingly at Judy, as though still double-checking on something. 'I think, though, that she really resembles the sort of girl I'm looking for ...'

'I'm delighted to hear it!' Elizabeth exclaimed and leaned forward towards Judy. 'I must give you a hug, my dear!'

Judy felt embarrassed but made no response.

'Elizabeth! Sit back in your seat, for goodness' sake!' Princess Goehr said sharply. 'Or she'll think we really are lesbians!'

Elizabeth shrank back in alarm, blushed and resumed

her seat. But why hadn't Judy been asked yet whether she could type in Russian? Or had they found that out from her university already?

Princess Goehr looked round and from behind the seat pulled out a thick copy of the *Village Voice*. She opened it at the advertisement page and handed it to Judy. In the 'Vacancies' column there was a little notice which someone had ringed with a felt-tip pen.

'Did you read this?' asked the Princess.

(How could she have read it when she had stopped buying the *Village Voice* three months ago? After all, it cost all of one dollar!)

'Read it,' the Princess said.

'Elderly lady seeks student-companion with good knowledge of Russian for two-week tourist visit to the USSR. All expenses paid, plus generous remuneration. Phone: (212) 687-91-06, extension 378.'

Judy sighed in disappointment. So it wasn't a secretarial post, but just a short-term job. Of course, a trip to Russia with all expenses paid would be no bad thing. On the other hand, it might mean she lost both her other jobs, at McDonald's and the Answering Service.

'How much are you offering?' she asked casually, having lost all interest already.

'Fifty thousand,' said the Princess.

Judy couldn't believe her ears.

'*How* much did you say?!'

'I said fifty thousand, Princess Goehr repeated.

Judy could still not believe it. Fifty grand for just two weeks?!

'*Dollars*? ...' she gasped.

'Well, certainly not fifty thousand roubles,' Princess Goehr laughed. 'I don't have roubles anyway. No, fifty thousand American dollars is what I'm offering. And ten thousand as an advance before the trip. That should be enough to pay your way through university.'

(One of them must be crazy – either the old woman or else Judy! Fifty grand! And ten in advance!)

'What do I have to do?'

'What the two of us have to do is find a certain person in Russia and bring them out to the West.'

Judy looked away again in disappointment. Of course, they were crazy. Smuggle someone out of the Soviet Union? What should she do ...? Tell them to stop the car right now, or let them take her to her destination? By now they were at 57th Street and the Lincoln Center. Outside it was still sleeting and her sneakers were saturated. But the chauffeur at least seemed normal enough – he had stopped at a red light! Okay, let them take her on to where she was going ...

'And how exactly are you going to get this person out of Russia?' Judy laughed. 'In a suitcase?' And then, to cover up this obvious mockery, she asked quickly, 'Is it a man or a woman?'

Princess Goehr realised of course that Judy was laughing at her, but did not react. During the pause in conversation she silently peeled off her suede gloves, opened her handbag and took out an expensive cigarette-case also made of cream leather, shook out one cigarette and flicked her lighter – 'Gitanes' – Judy recognised them by their heavy odour. But all the time she was looking not at the old lady's face but at her hands. What fantastic rings! Judy had never seen the like before – not even on the fingers of that pianist ... What was his name? ... Liberace!

Princess Goehr drew deeply on her cigarette, exhaled and looked at Judy through the smoke.

'The person you and I are going to find in Russia is my grand-nephew. You see, I'm not interested in having a nephew over there – I want him here. But you can't just bring people out of Russia in suitcases. In fact it's not been at all easy to get out of there for the last seventy years. That's why I need *you*,' the Princess said.

'What for?'

'You'll get married to him – a fictitious marriage of course. You'll bring him back here, and afterwards I'll look after all the divorce expenses.'

Judy looked at her intently. No, this old Russian lady was not crazy. She was simply rich and shameless – trying to buy Judy's services as if she were some whore on the street! ...

'Just think, poppet!' Elizabeth leaned forward again. 'We'll be able to walk through the streets of Moscow! We'll go riding in a Russian troika, and go to the Bolshoi too!'

'Stop the car!' Judy turned to the chauffeur and grabbed the door handle. But the chauffeur kept going at full speed, following the traffic stream.

'I said stop the car!' Judy addressed the Princess agitatedly.

'Very well, very well, right away ...' Princess Goehr looked at her calmly. 'But before you get out, just count up to ten and think about it. I'm offering you a deal. You're a talented girl. I know that, I've read your dissertation on Chekhov. I don't know whether you thought of the idea yourself or got it from somewhere. But I have always thought as you do, that Chekhov was less of a humanist and more a destroyer of the human personality. But be that as it may, you're a girl with talent and you ought to be studying, not working at McDonald's. You need money in order to get through university – and I need my grand-nephew!'

'But I'm not a prostitute for hire! Stop the car!'

'Nobody's ever suggested you had to sleep with him. I'm talking about a simple honest business deal ...'

Judy looked at her again curiously. A few moments ago the old lady had appeared like Cinderella's fairy godmother. She had filled her with hope and offered her a ticket to the ball. But now, alas, her fairy godmother had turned out to be in reality nothing more than a procuress, and Judy was filled with hatred.

'Honest business deal indeed?! Would you have made me a proposition like that if I'd been your daughter?' Judy asked with cold sarcasm.

Princess Goehr looked her straight in the eye and calmly turned to the chauffeur.

'Would you stop, please.'

The chauffeur veered in towards the sidewalk and stopped at the intersection of 44th Street and Broadway.

'Tanya, wait! Judy, my dear, you don't understand! ... Tanya doesn't even have a daughter!' Elizabeth wailed, confused and upset. 'She doesn't have anyone! Tanya, explain to her! ...'

But Judy was already getting out.

'Bye!' she said, slamming the door as she stepped out into a pool of sleet.

Slowly the limousine moved off again, and with its right-hand rear winker flashing it disappeared in a stream of traffic and a thick shroud of falling snow.

Judy set off along Broadway, walking quickly although she could hardly see where she was going. 'Got anything to smoke?' asked a black youth wearing a dark anorak with its hood raised. Judy strode past angrily. She stepped into the road then pulled back with a start as a taxicab honked loudly and roared past an inch in front of her face. The driver turned, shouting something and wagging his finger at her.

'Damn you!' Judy shrieked after him – so loudly that an old lady turned round to look and shook her head in dismay.

But Judy saw none of this. She was haring away along Broadway, splashing through the snowy swill in her saturated sneakers. Thanks to the lashing sleet she was unable to feel the tears running down her face. 'Damn you! Damn your fifty grand! To hell with your Chekhov and your Gogol! To hell with everything!'

One of the doors at the end of the carriage opened with a crash and in came a man wearing the black railway-man's uniform. He quickly made his way down to the other end of the coach. After him there came three noisy youths wearing jerkins hung with a variety of metal badges. They had bare shaven necks, like slaughtered chickens. Meanwhile a woman, also in railway uniform, was hovering over Tanya and Judy with her clipper held ready.

'Tickets!'

'There you are ...' Tanya handed her their tickets and the woman punched and returned them. Then she quickly moved to block the way of the man who had been sleeping and who had now jumped up and was making his way to the exit.

'Stop! Where are you going?!'

'I'm getting off ...'

'Where's your ticket?'

'I tell you, I'm getting off!' He tried to dodge past her, but she grabbed him by the sleeve and hurled him back with quite unexpected force so that he almost measured his length in the aisle.

'First you buy your ticket, and then you get off! This way! Come on!' She began heaving him forward roughly towards the group of youths and the other ticket inspector.

'Hey! Who do you think you're shoving? What's all this pushing?!' the man snarled. Nevertheless, he moved in the direction required.

Then she punched the other passengers' tickets and together with her colleague ushered the unticketed youths and the man towards the exit. After which the doors closed to on them.

Tanya and Judy exchanged glances. Tanya unbuttoned her coat, which was pinching her around the chest, and leaned back in her seat. Outside the window there was a rapid panorama of brickbuilt factories, snow-covered yards separating various extended workshops, several five-storey residential blocks, groups of lorries and Soviet versions of the Fiat queueing up at the level crossings, and every now and then there were faded red banners with slogans on them such as 'PEACE TO THE WORLD!' and so forth.

'This is Yauza! This is Yauza! ... Next stop Losinka,' came the announcement over the loudspeaker.

For about half a minute the train stood in silence at an ice-bound platform. Then there was another jerk and off they went again, gathering speed. Outside, the ugly grey and brown buildings of Moscow's suburbs gave way to empty fields covered in sparkling snow and divided by strips of forlorn and wintry woodland.

To Tanya it seemed as if she was travelling back in time to that awful train journey of January 1919. No, no! Heavens, couldn't she be spared these memories? Then, too, there had been snowy woodland sunshine ... then suddenly there was the squeal of brakes, a sharp halt, bursts of machine-gun fire, the tinkle of broken windows, shouts, people crashing down from the bunks and shelving, then an ugly unshaven gang of men with red bands on their sleeves who came bursting into the carriage. They immediately seized her father along with all the other male passengers. They hurled them out of the coaches and down the embankment, removed the coats and boots from each of them and then gunned them down on the spot as the women watched from the train windows, screaming hysterically.

With a fearful cry, their mother bundled Anya, Katya and Tanya under the benches of the compartment, shoving in various cases and bundles to cover them. And at the last minute she also stuffed something down the top of Tanya's lefthand felt boot – a little bag containing her valuables, rings and earrings, necklaces and grandmother's pendant. But now the Bolshevik soldiers were in a frenzy after the slaughtering and were coming through the coaches once again. This time they drove everyone at bayonet point towards the exits. All the luggage was dragged out from under the seats. And all the girls and women were hurled off the train and dragged underneath the carriages where the soldiery ripped off their clothing and raped them there and then, on the ice-bound frozen sleepers ... mother, Anya, Katya and ... Lord, to her dying day she would remember their mother screaming 'Kill us instead! Why don't you kill us, I beg you! ...'

Then there was the bayonet at her own throat and the stubble and two metal front teeth of the man who raped her, the icy sleepers under her bare shoulders, and a searing pain in her abdomen ... and then ... and then ... and then there was silence, an icy stillness, snow on her eyelashes and on her bare and bloodied stomach ... and something hard pressing inside her left boot ... How had she survived? Why hadn't they shot her too? Had they forgotten? Did they think she was dead already? Were they in a hurry to drive the train off with their plunder? Along the deserted railtrack where the twenty-five coaches had stood lay a host of naked, bloody corpses, smashed and empty suitcases, and torn cambric underwear. Some distance away stood a hand-operated rail trolley and an old railway linesman was going from corpse to corpse taking here some woollen socks, there a set of underpants ... He removed their own father's drawers, and from Katya's dead body – her little felt boots and bloody woollen stockings ...

'Losinka! This is Losinka! Next stop Mytishchi!' the loudspeaker rasped.

Quickly Tanya buttoned up her coat, not so much in readiness to get off, as to try to dismiss these haunting memories ...

The old linesman had to tear Tanya away from her mother's frozen corpse by force. Then he loaded her onto his trolley and covered her with some sacking. He left her boots on her feet. In that at least he spared her ... And five months later, partly with the help of that little bag of valuables stuffed down her boot, she found herself in Paris ... For his work in registering her as official heir to her father's fortune, the lawyer managed to wrest almost half the inheritance for himself. And by the time that Tanya met her future husband, Sergey von Goehr, all that was left of her fortune were two rings, her mother's two rings ... In the US she and Sergei had started again from nothing. He had driven a taxi in Chicago and she washed dishes in restaurants. On their sixth wedding anniversary he had given her his own mother's wedding ring. Two years ago, he had died and she was left alone in the world, but as the owner of four hotels in Florida, with an annual income of over half a million dollars and real estate assessed at sixty-seven million. A year ago, in a book of memoirs about the Soviet labour camps, she had suddenly lighted on the name of her brother Pyotr – or Petya Odalevsky. She rushed to look up the author of the book. It turned out he lived in Israel, and she had flown out to Natanya to see the old man. Mark Zusman had spent 1935 to 1957 in Stalin's camps and had survived only by a miracle. In the camps he had organised various artistic ensembles among the prisoners. He had spent half a year in the same camp as Petya, near Vorkuta in the far north, near the Arctic Circle. It emerged that Petya had concealed his aristocratic origins and became a Bolshevik and an ardent supporter of Lenin – just like Lena, his lady friend. During the Civil War he had been commissar of a partisan detachment and had fought against Kolchak in Siberia. By a monstrous irony of fate, Tanya's future husband Sergey had at that time been fighting in Kolchak's army: the two of them might well have exchanged fire in some battle or other! But how different their fates had been! In the 1930s, on the money saved from his taxi driving, Captain Sergey von Goehr bought himself a gas station down in Miami, while Petya Odalevsky was wearing a prisoner's quilted jacket and labouring on a railway at Vorkuta. Petya evidently recalled his wife only rarely, and with bitterness: she had either renounced him or else left him even before his arrest. And old Zusman could no longer remember whether her name was Elena or something else. But he clearly recalled Petya talking always about his sons. Apparently Petya died there in one of the barracks huts of that camp – he simply failed to wake up one morning. 'But he had two sons. There were two sons!' Zusman had insisted.

The next stage of an apparently simple operation had

taken six months and cost Tanya ten thousand dollars. A Soviet relative of some recent émigrés discovered through the normal enquiry bureau in Moscow that Konstantin Petrovich Odalevsky was born in 1921 and had fallen in the war in 1941; Petya's other son, Nikolay, was born in 1929 and died in 1980. And his son Alexey Nikolayevich Odalevsky was born in 1964 and lived in the Moscow region, at Mytishchi, 9 Okruzhnaya Street, Apartment 7. And the day she discovered this, Tanya's life took on a new meaning. This boy Alexey was her grand nephew, virtually her grandson in fact! He was the only relative she had in this world, and despite all the horrors that the October Revolution had unleashed on them, he was the last descendant of the princely family of Odalevsky. And Tanya now felt obliged to get him out of Communist Russia – for the sake of her mother's, father's and sisters' memory. The fact that so far he had not answered any of her letters did not worry her. It was quite understandable. Both Zusman and another Russian émigré who had advised her in New York had assured her that many people in Soviet Russia were afraid of corresponding with relatives abroad. Back in 1937 or 1946 just one such exchange of letters would have been sufficient to land you in a labour camp. Zusman advised her to send Alexey another letter, requesting confirmation of delivery. And that confirmation had come back with an oblique signature on it: 'A. Odalevsky'. After that Tanya had rushed around various Russian departments in American universities, trying to find a fictitious bride for Alexey, someone who would go to Russia, marry him and get him out. Of course she could have found someone willing to agree to such an adventure for as little as ten thousand dollars. There had been about fifteen candidates, but one by one Tanya had eliminated them all. Not because of their Russian – some had spoken it quite tolerably. But Tanya knew what she was looking for: she was looking for another Lena – someone similar to the Lena that her brother had fallen for back in 1918. What else could she offer this young man whom she still did not know and who didn't even answer her letters? Perhaps he was a Young Communist, after all, and had been thoroughly brainwashed by the Bolsheviks? What could she put up to challenge his Communist ideas? Offer him four hotels in Florida?! What a joke! But if he was the grandson of Petya, then possibly a girl who resembled the one that had turned his head back in 1918 ...? Of course, it all sounded slightly mad, but it was better than nothing – better than just four hotels in Florida! And that was why, when she set eyes on Judy serving at McDonald's, she had said to herself: 'That's the one! That is the one ... at any price!'

'This is Mytishchi! This is Mytishchi! ... Next station Stroitel!'

Tugging Judy by the sleeve, Tanya rushed for the carriage exit. Mytishchi turned out to be a large station with a dozen different railway lines and a long bridge spanning them. Tanya and Judy followed several other passengers and made their way up the slippery steps of the viaduct bridge, towards the exit. From the bridge they had a view of Mytishchi. It was a large industrial settlement – almost a city in its own right. From several factory chimneys a thick yellow smoke came pouring, and instead of dispersing in the frosty air it hung over the area in dense billowing clouds that gleamed in the sunlight. And through this haze the whole townscape appeared slightly blurred, with pinkish sun-glints on the white walls of the houses and snowdrifts on the streets.

Crossing the footbridge, they descended onto a broad snowy square surrounded by four- and five-storey brick buildings, and with a snow-bound garden in the centre. The groundfloor frontages were occupied by shops, variously advertised as 'Bakery', 'Wines and Spirits', 'Delicatessen', 'General Store' and so on. Judy read off all the names like a dutiful student. A crowd of about twenty were gathered outside the locked doors of the liquor store. To the left was a small square marked 'Taxi rank'. There were no cars there. Instead there stood a green lorry and a little girl of about eight was looking out of the cabin window.

After about ten minutes of fruitless waiting for a taxi, Tanya decided to ask the whereabouts of Okruzhnaya Street. But the place was deserted, and she did not feel like crossing over and asking that crowd of alcoholics standing outside the liquor store. Instead she went and asked the little girl in the lorry. The girl smiled and Tanya handed her a chit of paper with an address.

'Do you know if Okruzhnaya Street is far from here?'

'I don't know,' she said. 'We don't live here anyway. We live in Podlipki. But my dad will know. He knows everything!' She smiled again and pointed to the glass and concrete station extension with a sign above the door reading 'Station Restaurant'. 'You just go in there. Don't be afraid,' she said. 'My dad's in there having his morning beer. But he's only having a beer, so he'll be able to tell you all you want to know . . .'

'Thank you!' Tanya surveyed the empty square again, took Judy by the arm and the two made their way to the restaurant entrance.

On entering they were met by a waft of sour bread and fried onion. The tables in the large eating area were covered with grubby white tablecloths. At several of them, noisy groups of men were seated, drinking beer out of bulbous cut-glass tankards. The waitress was tall and a trifle overfed. She wore a perky little apron and white lace headpiece over her fluffed-up fair curls. Her gold front teeth flashed as she laughed and bent down to speak to one of the young men. Tanya went up to her.

'Excuse me, could I talk to you for a moment?' she asked cautiously. The waitress stood up and surveyed her in surprise.

'Can you tell me where Okruzhnaya Street is?' Tanya asked. 'We've already waited ages for a taxi . . .'

'What number on Okruzhnaya?' the waitress smiled.

'Number nine . . .' Tanya answered reluctantly.

'Oh, that's hostel number seven,' the waitress said.

'You don't need a taxi for that short distance. It's quite near here.'

From close quarters her face looked quite attractive, but her smile was spoilt by her gold teeth. Her heavily made-up brown eyes had fine lines spreading from the corners – not from age (she was only about thirty) but probably because she enjoyed a good laugh.

'Who are you looking for there?' The waitress took a lighter and packet of 'TU-134's from her apron pocket. Pinching the cigarette slightly between her fingers she lit up deftly.

'Oh, just someone we know ...' Tanya said evasively. 'How do we get there?'

'The only thing,' the waitress went on, 'is that all the workmen tend to hang around here. Especially when there's a new consignment of beer in. Those guys over in the corner ... they're from number seven. Have you come from Moscow?'

'Yes, from Moscow,' said Tanya, straining for a glimpse of the men at the table over in the dim corner.

'I could see you weren't from here,' the waitress said. Then: 'Volodya, come over here a moment!' she called. 'These people are looking for one of your lot. You might know where he is ...?'

A broad-shouldered young fellow of about twenty-five got up from the corner table and sloped over towards them.

'Now, who is it you're wanting, ma?' he asked gently.

Taken aback, Tanya did not answer.

The young man looked uncertainly from Tanya to the waitress. 'Who are you looking for?' he asked more deliberately.

'I'm looking for ... er ... Alexey Odalevsky ...' Tanya answered, realising that now she couldn't avoid naming him.'

'Ha, Alyosha!' Volodya gave a laugh, and then, to the waitress: 'Why come and ask me? You could have told them yourself. He was here not long ago,' he told Tanya.

'You've just missed one another! He heaved off about an hour ago. Did he say where he was going?' he asked the waitress.

'He seemed rather out of sorts today,' she smiled. 'I think you'll find him back at the hostel. He had quite a lot on board. Can you show them, Volodya? They don't know the way. I'll look after your beer.'

'For you, Maryuta, darling, I'd do anything,' he said.

'It's all right. You don't have to come with us,' Tanya said warily. 'We'll find it ourselves if you tell us.'

'Quite all right, ma, I can take you there in a jiffy. Begging your pardon, though, that granddaughter of yours is going to catch her death of cold without a hat. Heavens above!' He strode back to his place, took his jerkin off the back of a chair and made for the exit.

Tanya followed and turned to the waitress as she passed. 'Thanks, many thanks!'

'So how do you come to know Alyosha? Is he a relative of yours?' Volodya asked with leisurely deliberation as they went.

'Oh, no, we're just ... just friends of his,' said Tanya, trying to sound natural.

They walked along a pathway that had been trodden through the snow alongside the railtrack, and as they went Volodya cast an occasional interested glance in Judy's direction. Then turning to her again, he asked directly:

'Beg pardon, but what's your name?'

Tanya quickly intervened. 'My name is Tanya ... Tatyana Stepanovna,' she said, afraid lest Judy answer and cause unnecessary questions because of her accent. 'And her name's Zhenya,' she said. 'Only she can't talk. She's a deaf mute.'

'Deaf and dumb?' Volodya said, a note of disappointment and of genuine pity in his voice. 'Completely dumb, is she? But perhaps she can hear? Can she hear? ... Can you hear me?' he asked Judy loudly.

Judy smiled and nodded her head.

'What lovely teeth she has! She's a real beauty, she is!

What a shame. Has she always been like that, or did something happen to cause it?' he asked.

'Since birth.' Tanya wished their sociable companion would go a little faster. But he was not to be hurried. Stoked with beer and his interest aroused by a nice girl, Volodya wanted to talk and see as much of her as he could. Eventually, however, they rounded a fence, and halted at the entrance to a four-storey brick building.

'Well, here we are ...' said Volodya disappointedly. But as his gaze lighted on Judy again, he suddenly volunteered cheerily, 'I know, just to make sure you find the way, let me take you up to his room. Just in case ...'

Tanya tried to stop him but it was too late. He had already swung open the door and ushered Judy in ahead of him.

By the entrance in the narrow corridor was a wooden desk, where a fat and balding old man sat with his spectacles on, reading a copy of the Moscow Komsomol* paper.

'Ivanych, these folk are going to number 47, to Alyosha. Is he in?'

'Yes, he came in not long ago.' The doorman folded his paper neatly and pulled towards him a fat exercise book lying open on the table before him. 'I'll need to see your documents,' he said politely addressing Tanya.

'Why?' she said in surprise.

'How do you mean "why?"' The old man peered at her over his glasses. ''Cos the rules of the house require it.'

Bewildered, Tanya clasped her handbag and wondered what to do. To show him her American passport was out of the question. Yet to turn round and leave would be even more stupid! Fancy getting so close to Alexey and then not managing to see him!

'Oh God, we've not brought our papers! I've left them at home!' Tanya looked pleadingly at the doorman.

*Komsomol – The Young Communist League. *Tr.*

'Couldn't you let us in, please. It's very important ... I didn't realise I'd need them!'

'Nobody's supposed to enter this hostel without showing their documents,' he rapped.

'Aw, come on, don't bugger them around, Ivanych!' Volodya said. 'Let the ladies in. They've come especially from Moscow. And this girl here is deaf and dumb. And look how thinly dressed she is! Let them in, Ivanych. If you want, I'll leave my passport here instead.'

'What good's *your* passport?' The old man studied Judy carefully. 'I'm supposed to see *their* papers!'

Tanya looked feverishly from one to the other. 'What on earth are we to do?' she wondered.

'Volodya, can I talk to you a moment?' she asked and led him to one side. 'Perhaps I should offer him some money?' she whispered hastily. 'But how can I do that? I can't ...'

'That's an idea. Leave it to me. Let me handle it ...'

Tanya took a ten-rouble note from her purse and slipped it surreptitiously to Volodya.

'What on earth are you doing?' he objected. 'Three roubles is enough for an old turd like him!'

'Give it him, please!' Tanya whispered, almost pushing Volodya back towards the doorman. The rest of it took no more than a minute. Volodya bent down, slipped the note into the old man's pocket and said something to him in a low voice.

'Only we do have a rule that guests can only stay in here till ten at night. After that there could be a Komsomol patrol, so after that I can't possibly ...'

'No, no. It's all right. We won't be here long,' Tanya promised hastily.

'That's what they all say. And next thing we have to fetch the militia in to them!'

They climbed the narrow stairs to the third floor. At the top they turned left and went almost to the end of a long bare corridor.

'Forty-three ... forty-five ... forty-seven!' Volodya

counted the numbers aloud as they went past. 'Here we are. This is where he hangs out.'

'Volodya!' Tanya grasped his arm just as he raised a hand to knock, 'I am most grateful to you,' she said. 'But now, please, leave us on our own with him.'

Volodya looked in surprise at the old lady. What was the matter? She had grasped his arm like someone crazy and was talking in a whisper ...

'What's the matter, ma? I was only trying to help!'

Tanya realised she had offended him.

'Don't be angry, Volodya! If only I could thank you properly ... Look, here ...' She quickly produced her purse from her handbag. 'Good grief, ma, are you crazy? I only did it to help you, that's all!' He looked again at Judy. 'But it turns out.... Anyway, goodbye, fair lady! But you, madam, at your age, you should know better than that!' he said, clearly offended at Tanya. And throwing his head back proudly he went off down the corridor.

Tanya waited till he was out of sight, then knocked at the door. There was no answer. She knocked again ... and again ... but all was silent. Then Judy cautiously pushed open the door, looked around it, and went inside.

The room was in semi-darkness. The blinds on the windows were fully drawn. A small square table stood in the middle. It still had the remains of some meal on it, either breakfast or yesterday's supper. A chair lay over-turned on the floor next to it. Along the walls were three identical beds, and above them were pinned some faded magazine photos of women. Two of the beds were empty and covered over in a rough and ready manner with coarse green woollen blankets. On the third bed by the window lay a man, face down and still wearing his boots and jacket. Above him on the wall, next to a coloured magazine illustration of a seaside resort, there was a black and white army photo. It showed a group of seven Soviet soldiers deliberately posing for the camera and elegantly arrayed on the back of an armoured troop carrier; each of them held a sub-machine gun.

Tanya went over to the recumbent figure.

'Alyosha!' she called softly. 'Alyosha, are you asleep?'

The man did not stir.

Tanya turned to Judy helplessly. Judy was filled with curiosity. She too went over to the bed and gently shook the sleeping man by his shoulder.

'Alyosha,' she said, 'Alyosha, wake up!'

The inert body suddenly twitched and gave out a deep moan.

'Ulima! Ulima!'

'What's he saying?' she asked.

'I can't understand him,' Tanya shrugged and was confused.

'Alyosha! Alyosha!' Judy tapped him again on the shoulder.

Again he moaned loudly and slumped over heavily onto his back. Judy started back in horror. The man's face was covered in blood. His long dark hair was plastered across his forehead and over a deep cut in his brow. He was struggling for breath through parched lips.

Tanya too looked at the bloody features and was horrified. Who was it? Was this Alyosha? Was this dirty beast with the heavy stench of alcohol on his breath really Pyotr's grandson, the last heir of their princely line? She turned away, revolted, and made for the door. 'I've got to get away,' she thought. 'We must leave before he wakes up!' Tanya grabbed Judy by the arm and yanked her towards the door. But apparently Judy had no intention of obeying. She snatched her arm away and quickly looked round the room. Taking a freshly laundered towel from the edge of the other bed, she sat down by Alexey and began carefully wiping the blood from his face. He moaned with pain and tried to push her hand away.

'Alyosha! Alyosha!' Judy kept saying patiently. 'I am just going to wipe it . . . It's not going to hurt.'

'Ulima . . . Ulima. . . . How good of you to come!' he gasped pathetically.

The dry towel did not wipe the clotted blood away very effectively. Judy got up and looked around the room again. There was no wash basin or toilet. Seeing an empty vodka bottle on the table, Judy took it and held it to the light. There were a few drops left in the bottom. She poured them onto a corner of the towel, and, as she turned to Alexey again, she saw he had opened his eyes and was watching her carefully.

'Who . . . who are you? . . .' he asked. He had difficulty moving his parched tongue. Judy turned and looked quizzically at Princess Goehr.

'Are you . . . Alexey Odalevsky?' Tanya asked, overcoming her distaste.

Alexey struggled to sit up. It took him some time, but he managed it. He shook his tousled head once again and looked questioningly at the two women.

'Alyosha,' Judy began cautiously.

He recoiled at the sound of his name as though someone had struck him a blow. The two women looked at him in surprise. His eyes were wide with fear.

'Who are you?' he asked as though still half asleep, his voice quavering.

'I am Judy,' she said in the same gentle voice, but for safety's sake took a step to the side. It was best to stand back a little: there was no knowing what this drunkard might get up to.

'Judy?' Alexey echoed, and looked plaintively at Tanya. 'Who *is* she? he asked.

'She's told you – her name's Judy,' Tanya said sharply. Her only feeling for him was one of revulsion. 'And you, begging your pardon, who are you? Are you Alexey?'

'Yes. . . . I'm Alexey.' He looked at Judy as though hypnotised. 'But why do you talk like her?'

'Like who?' Judy asked.

'Like *her*. Like Ulima.'

'And who is Ulima?'

'Ulima?' Alexey still seemed unsure whether he was awake or asleep. 'Well, Ulima is . . .'

'I am *not* called Ulima,' said Judy, smiling. 'My name is Judy. And this, Alyosha, is your great-aunt.'

'Alexey, I wrote to you ... I wrote to you from America ...'

'From America?' Alexey stared at Tanya, now totally confused.

'I realise all this is very unexpected, Alexey ... But try and concentrate. We've not got much time. We have to return to Moscow.' Tanya was clearly tired and she sank onto a chair.

A wicked thought flashed through her head: 'So this is the meeting you've been waiting for! It serves you right, you old fool! That'll teach you to go digging up the past!'

'Perhaps you should take a shower?' Judy said. 'What happened to you? Have you been beaten up?'

'A shower?' Alexey asked, still confused. 'I can't have a shower. You can only get hot water here after five o'clock.'

'Why?' Tanya asked. His almost childish bewilderment made her slightly more favourably disposed. 'Anyway, never mind about that. But at least wash your face, you've got blood on it ... Have you been in a fight?'

'What? Yes ... no, that is. Not an actual fight, just ... My neighbour and I had an argument.' Alexey was gradually coming to himself. 'I'll have a wash in a moment. So you say you're from America. And you're my great-aunt? That's a good one!' He suddenly burst out into a gale of merry laughter. As he did so his face altered and became suddenly young and boyish.

'What is it, Alexey?' Tanya was infected by his reaction and gave a smile. 'Why are you laughing?'

'That's funny! That really is funny!' he said, standing up unsteadily. 'And her name's Judy? Ha-ha-ha!'

He stood for a while on unsteady legs and looked mockingly again at the two of them. The two women looked away in embarrassment. His flies were unbuttoned, and his dark glossy pants showed underneath. Alexey fastened his leather belt, which had a star on its buckle, and made his way unsteadily towards the door. Then he stopped.

'I'll just . . . I'll just rinse my face!' he said, and laughed again. There was something familiar about his features when he laughed.

'Alyosha, take your jacket off. You'll have a job trying to wash with your jacket on!' Tanya smiled.

'My jacket?' he said. 'Oh, never mind!' and went out.

Reaching the toilets, Alexey went straight to the wash-stand. Turning on a tap, he placed his palm beneath it and took several gulps of water. Then he bent down and put his head under the running tap. The cold water seared the back of his throat, but he held his head there, washing off the blood, and at the same time he kept filling his mouth with water, as though he had never drunk before.

So now they had even sent his great-aunt to see him! My God, these chaps were full of ideas! One had to hand it to them! Finally Alexey stood up and with the tap still running, leaned against the wash basin and looked at himself in the mirror. A fine one he was, and no mistake! God alone knows why he had to go and have a dust-up with this neighbour today. The little rat was nothing but an informer, though, and Alexey had had enough of him. Everywhere he went he kept seeing that man's dirty mug! He'd been recruited by the KGB of course, to spy on him. And the wretch had even gone and told them about Ulima! And now they had invited Alexey's 'auntie' over to visit him! They'd be the death of him yet! As if it wasn't enough for him to go and smash his arm, in order not to have to write that letter to Yury! He'd only had the plaster off yesterday, and now here they were plaguing him again! And this time they'd sent him a great-aunt complete with a junior sidekick! And the way that young KGB tart spoke – the way she pronounced his name, just like Ulima – it almost made him sick to hear it – 'Ally-osha!'

Alexey wiped his face dry with the sleeve of his jacket, smoothed his hair, turned the tap off and went out.

6

Elizabeth sat in an armchair in their hotel room. With one hand she continued massaging her leg with Ben-Gay, while using the other to support the telephone receiver which she cradled on her shoulder.

'And what's your name?' she asked flirtatiously, evidently chatting up some stranger who had dialled their room number. His English had a heavy Russian accent, but the voice had a pleasing baritone timbre. 'Peter? Oh, that's great. I like it ... What's that? What's my name? I'm Elizabeth ... No, not Elizabeth Taylor. A little bit older! ... Not too much though ... Oh, so you like older women? But I'm not actually old, you know! How old are you? ... What? Just nineteen?! ... Oh, I'm terribly sorry! ...'

She hung up with a sigh and continued rubbing her knee with both hands ... All the same, these Russians certainly had a nerve – ringing your room number like that and making heaven knows what sort of proposals! ... But her rheumatism had still not gone away and the room was full of the pungent smell of Ben-Gay! If only she could open the window – but the windows in here were apparently not of the opening sort.

Elizabeth looked at her watch. It was ten to three. In ten minutes they were due to be served a meal, and if Tanya was not back in another twenty minutes after that, Elizabeth was going down to the restaurant to say that her friend had just gone out for a breath of fresh air to try and get rid of her migraine ... What a pity, though, that

Tanya had not taken her along! She would so much like to have seen the Princess's first meeting with her grand-nephew. It was probably just like in the movies! The boy would be deeply moved and throw himself into the arms of his stately aunt, and she would be unable to restrain tears of joy and would be weeping loudly: 'Well, my boy, at long last the two of us have met! And you're so like your grandfather, Prince Odalevsky. One can always recognise the old family likeness!' . . .

Elizabeth then recalled that she had never once seen Tanya weep. But surely on this occasion she'd be unable to restrain a tear? Elizabeth had met her two years before in the Sarasota hospital where doctors had referred her with a blood circulation problem. While she was there, a woman had come hastily into the hospital vestibule carrying a large handbag. She strode towards the elevator and suddenly halted right in front of Elizabeth. Then, with a sudden cry of 'Oh, I've forgotten to bring his socks!' she made a sharp about-turn and then . . . crashed to the floor in a faint. Of course, hospital orderlies and nursing staff came running to assist – and they took her away on a stretcher. Elizabeth brought the bag that the woman left lying on the floor to the registration desk. It turned out the woman's name was Tanya Goehr. Her husband had died in the hospital that morning, and the bag contained various items of his clothing. Elizabeth had herself once been a volunteer with the Red Cross and in an old people's home. Her own husband died twenty years before, her two grown-up sons were married and lived one in Canada, in Vancouver, and the other in Los Angeles. She would visit them once a year and bring gifts to her grandchildren in summer, during the Florida heatwave. But during the still warm winter months what was there left for her to do in Florida but volunteer work? The next day she rang the hospital to find out how the woman who fainted was. They told her Mrs Goehr was still unconscious. They asked also whether Elizabeth was by any chance a relative of hers, because Mrs Goehr's medical record mentioned no next of kin who could be rung in case of an accident. And Mrs Goehr's husband had died the previous morning. And to think that this was Florida, Elizabeth pondered. There they all were, a set of lonely old people. They came to live out their days in the warmth, but when the last days and hours came, they had nobody even to hold out a hand ... Needless to say, forty minutes later a sympathetic volunteer worker called Elizabeth Wollens turned up at the hospital. And she spent the next eight days by Tanya Goehr's bedside, because although the patient came to on the fourth day, she was not completely conscious. She did not know where she was and she spoke not a word, as though she had clean forgotten the English language. But Elizabeth did not give up. She sat by the sick woman's bed, held her by the hand and talked to her endlessly. She told Tanya about her sons and grandchildren and heaven knows what else, and even sang her a few simple Scottish folksongs. Tanya's memory returned on the ninth day and she asked to be taken to the cemetery where her husband had already been buried on the instructions of their lawyer. Yet even on that day Tanya had never shed a tear. She stood by her husband's grave, gaunt and silent like the Russian princess she was. And Elizabeth realised this woman was going to need her to be around for a good long time yet ... And that was how it turned out; the two women in fact became inseparable friends and companions. And how that starchy, austere Russian princess had come alive when she discovered that somewhere in Russia she had a grand-nephew! She seemed to light up and became furiously active, and she spent so much money and time on scouring the universities of Washington, Boston and New York in search of a suitable bride for this Alexey ... She had a Russian, almost bear-like persistence – just like that new leader of theirs ... What was his name? ... Gorbachev!

Suddenly the door of their room swung open and in came Tanya.

'Thank the Lord!' Elizabeth heaved a sigh of relief. 'I was getting really worried! ...'

But Tanya neither spoke nor looked at Elizabeth, but instead stalked straight through into the bedroom. Elizabeth heard her flop onto the bed without even a pause to take off her coat. Quickly she ran through to her, forgetting all about her rheumatism.

'What's happened?'

Tanya lay there on the bed still wearing her boots and that awful Russian-style overcoat. Only her headscarf lay loosely by her pillow. Her features were drawn, and she was gazing woefully up at the ceiling.

'What's happened? Did you find him?'

'Nothing happened,' Tanya said shortly. "Leave me be." And she closed her eyes.

Elizabeth pursed her lips and went out, obviously offended. These Russians really were awful – even Russian princesses! Elizabeth replaced the plastic lid on the Ben-Gay and looked out of the window. On the sill outside sat a lonely pigeon with its feathers puffed out. Beyond it, down below, was Red Square with the cupolas of an old Russian cathedral. Was it worth coming all this way to Russia in order to be treated like dirt? And all for nothing – just because Elizabeth had shown some concern!

'Yes, I found him all right! I found him!' Tanya's cry came from behind her back. Elizabeth spun round and saw Tanya standing there in the bedroom almost literally ripping off that awful old coat, skirt and sweater and flinging them on the floor. 'To hell with all this conspiracy! Yes, I saw him all right! Only he ran away from me! Do you understand? He ran away! Here I come flying over land and sea like an idiot to come and meet him, and he runs away! He didn't even want to talk to us!'

Elizabeth immediately forgot her hurt feelings and ran to Tanya's side.

'Tanya! Tanya! What is all this? Why are you shouting? You yourself said that all the rooms are bugged,' she said in a frantic whisper. 'Calm down and tell me what happened. How do you mean, he ran away? Where's he gone to?'

'If only I knew!' Tanya sat down on the bed in just her underwear; her thin bony shoulders were angular beneath the shoulder straps. 'He went to the bathroom to wash his face and then disappeared. We sat and waited for him, but he simply never reappeared. I went to the men's room – I thought perhaps he might be ill. Be he wasn't there. We sat there and waited in his room for a whole hour. After that we went looking for him outside in all those awful bars and restaurants! But it was hopeless. He'd gone! But why? Why? I'd simply like to know *why*!' By now Tanya was no longer shouting. Softly but bitterly she simply kept repeating the same question over and over.

Elizabeth stroked her shoulder and tried to console her.

'Tanya! You mustn't take on like that! There's probably some very good reason why. You can go and see him again, and he'll probably explain everything. The main thing is that you've found him. He really exists ...'

'It would be better if he didn't! ...'

'Don't talk like that, Tanya! Next time I'll come with you, and everything will be all right. You'll see.'

'You should have seen him!' Tanya said softly after a pause, and gazed fixedly at one spot. 'He was lying there asleep – still wearing his jacket and with his face all covered in blood. And he reeked of vodka so much, I was scared to go near. He looked such a filthy lout ... And he kept on talking about some girl called Ulima and laughing all the time like an idiot! And then he dashed out of the room and disappeared! But why? If only he'd said why! ...'

'Tanya, dear, it's all right ...' Elizabeth sat down next to her and whispered various words of comfort. 'We'll go and see him there again, and everything will be cleared up. And what about Judy?'

'Oh, Elizabeth, I'm so tired! Why on earth did I start all this business?'

'Don't get upset. Try and take a grip on yourself. You know perfectly well why you've done it. And when you've calmed down, the two of us will go and see him again ...'

'No!' Tanya closed her eyes and shook her head in emphatic denial. 'I've no further desire of that sort! ...'

There was a knock at the door. Elizabeth rose to go, but Tanya restrained her.

'I'll go,' she said.

She got up, took her dressing-gown from a hanger and putting it on went through to the reception room.

'Who's there?' she asked.

'It's me,' Judy's voice said from outside the door.

Tanya opened up and let her in. Judy had already changed after their trip and was now wearing jeans and a light woollen sweater. She was holding a sheet of paper which she handed to Tanya.

Tanya read: '*I think we should go back and see him again. This evening, instead of the theatre.*' She handed the note back to Judy.

'We've discussed that already,' she said sharply.

'I think you're getting too worked up,' said Judy, lowering her voice. 'Perhaps there's something he hasn't understood.'

'Judy!' Tanya said, emphasising every syllable, 'You've seen him yourself. That man is not my nephew! And there's an end of it. I set this whole thing in motion, and now I'm calling it to a halt. But don't you worry. You shall get all that I promised you. Is that clear?'

The two of them eyed one another again, straight and hard, just as at their first meeting when the three of them had sat there in the limousine.

'You know, I think Judy is right,' Elizabeth said gingerly.

'That's an end to it!' Tanya snapped again. 'I've told you already ... the whole thing is finished. So just get on and enjoy your stay in Moscow. Go to the theatre and the museums. And forget about all the rest. That's the end of the matter.'

She turned sharply, went through into the bedroom and closed the door behind her.

From the street side facing Red Square came the jangle of Kremlin bells, and then the single heavy chime: one . . . two . . . three . . .

For a few seconds Judy gazed after Tanya as she disappeared. Then she herself went to the door and walked out.

7

Over a late lunch in the restaurant, Tanya Goehr tried not to look in Judy's direction. After the brusque manner in which she had spoken to her, Tanya felt uncomfortable and realised she ought to go and try to smooth things over. After all, none of this was Judy's fault. It was she, Tanya, who had exploited Judy's position – her lack of money, her need to get her young sister away from an alcoholic mother and dissolute stepfather. And of course she would give Judy her fifty thousand ... well, maybe not fifty: after all, that was a bit much for making one short trip out to Mytishchi! But she would help Judy to set her sister up in a good private boarding-school, and she would pay for the first year – that would not set Tanya back at all. But for the time being Tanya just wanted to be left in peace. But Elizabeth was sitting there in silence and demonstrating her disapproval of Tanya as she forced down spoonfuls of Russian borshch, and Judy ... But Tanya couldn't go up to her now in public and start apologising! And then there was their rubicund guide Oleg who of course had to put in an appearance at their table:

'Well, Mrs Goehr, how are you feeling? Are you coming to the theatre this evening?'

'Thank you. I'll certainly come.'

'Good. I'm glad to hear it. We're meeting at seven o'clock down below in the vestibule.'

'Thank you.'

Without finishing the main course, which was a rather good beef stroganoff, Tanya got up and went to her room.

At about six o'clock she awoke and found everything terribly silent. She walked out of the bedroom, looked round their reception room and glanced into the bathroom. But there was no sign of Elizabeth, and to judge by her still unruffled bed she had not been up in their room since the meal. So she was still putting on an air of disapproval and offence, was she? Probably she was sitting down below, chatting with someone in the hall. But it was time to start getting ready for the theatre, time for a shower. Fancy there being no bath towels provided! Only these linen ones – no better than a tea cloth! She would have to ring the floor attendant and order a pair of bath-size terry-towels. Imagine it! The very idea – having to *hire* a bath towel!

Tanya had reached out for the telephone when the door opened and in came Elizabeth.

'Where have you been?' Tanya asked in a calm and casual voice. 'We ought to be getting ready for the theatre.'

Elizabeth said nothing and walked through into the bedroom.

Tanya lifted the receiver and dialled the floor attendant.

'This is room 1032,' she said in Russian. 'I want to order two bath towels.'

'Thirty kopecks per day. I'll bring them right away.'

'Thank you.'

And indeed, not ten seconds had passed before the attendant was knocking at their door. Tanya was waiting for her, handed her a rouble note, and took the two white bath towels from her.

'I'll bring your change and the receipt,' the woman said, trying to peer round the door which Tanya deliberately opened only slightly.

'It's all right, keep the change ...' Tanya closed the door again. She sniffed at the towels as she carried them through into the bedroom. They smelt of either bleach or some disinfectant wash-powder. Well, at least they were disinfected, Tanya thought ...

Back in the bedroom Elizabeth was getting changed. Her appearance suggested a sense of total indifference to everything.

Tanya threw a towel down upon her bed.

'There. Now you can have a shower ...'

Elizabeth said nothing.

'All right then, you're right! I agree. You're right! I admit it!' Tanya finally exploded, and chucked the second towel down as well. 'I behaved like a pig! I'll go right away and apologise to her.'

She thew off her dressing-gown and began climbing into a skirt.

'You needn't bother,' Elizabeth said. 'She's left already.'

'Where's she gone?'

Elizabeth did not answer. 'But it's another hour before we leave for the theatre!' Elizabeth still said nothing. 'Why don't you answer?' Tanya insisted. 'Where has Judy gone to? ...'

At that point Tanya suddenly realised. She seized Elizabeth by the shoulders and shook her slightly.

'No! You don't mean to say that she's gone ...? She's not gone to see *him*?!'

'Don't hold me like that,' Elizabeth said calmly, staring back at her. 'You know, Judy is right. You *have* to make another attempt to see him. Otherwise you'll regret it for the rest of your life. And Judy is a fine girl – she's both brave and good-hearted. And she's far better disposed towards you than you are to the two of us ...'

'When did she leave?'

'An hour ago.'

'Oh, my God!' was all Tanya could gasp, and she sank down feebly onto the bed.

8

'What bastards they are! They'd even drag you back from the grave if they saw fit!' Alexey was sitting on the bed wrapped in a blanket. He looked angrily at Judy. 'Who told you I was here?'

'Your room-mate in the hostel.' Judy still held her shoulders hunched from the chill air outside and looked around for a chair to sit on.

The little cramped room was not very cosy, but it was clean. Even Alexey's underwear, carelessly discarded on the floor by the bed, did not disturb the general impression of order. On every available surface in the room there were lacy paper doilies, and a bouquet of artificial flowers stood in a vase on the table. Over the bed where Alexey sat was a photograph of the waitress from the station restaurant. She had taken a long time to open up, and surveyed Judy suspiciously with the chain still in place, quizzing her as to why she needed to see Alexey. Finally, though, she had let her in and then quickly disappeared.

'So that means Vasya really is working for you?' Alexey said. 'The bastard! Well, why have you come?'

'I need to talk to you,' Judy answered.

'Talk then!' Alexey fixed her with a harsh, sullen glare.

'Can I take my jacket off?' Judy's hands were so frozen, she had a job unzipping her coat. 'The frost out here is so keen I thought I'd never make it. Is it always as cold as this where you live?'

'And what about where *you* live? Isn't it quite so cold there?' Alexey laughed mockingly.

'What, in New York? It's sometimes cold, but never frosty like this ...'

'So you live in New York, do you?!' Alexey seemed about to roll off the bed with laughter. 'Ha-ha-ha! At your place in New York! She lives in New York!'

Judy looked at him in amazement.

'I don't understand. Why are you laughing, Alyosha?'

'Look here!' His face suddenly twisted with fury. 'Just don't call me Alyosha! All right? Otherwise I'll not answer for the consequences! ...'

'Why?'

'Because I'll let you have it. Understand? I'll clobber you over the head! Call me Alyosha once more, and I shan't bother whether you're a girl or not ... Anyway, what sort of girl *are* you? What's your rank in the service?'

'What?' Judy was totally confused. 'How do you mean "what rank"?'

'Never mind. Forget it. I know you're not supposed to say. Only don't try it on any more with New York and my American auntie. It's quite obvious you're from one of the Baltic republics! So out with it! Why've they sent you here?'

'Nobody's sent me. I decided to come myself. Tanya was against it, but I've come all the same. Why did you run away this morning? Did we give you a fright?'

'A fright? Whatever next! Some fright! I got stomach cramp, that was all, and I went off to get something for it. So you thought I was afraid?' He wrapped himself more snugly in his blanket.

'No, we simply couldn't understand ...'

'Well, what have you come for now? Is this some new trick?'

'What trick? I don't understand, Alyosha,' Judy suddenly stopped short. 'I'm sorry ... Can I call you Alexey?'

'Okay, go on.'

'There's a lot that I don't understand. Please talk more slowly, I don't know Russian all that well.'

The owner of the apartment reappeared. She looked hard at Judy and Alexey, then demonstratively sat down at the table. She had put on a floral dress and done her hair.

'I'm sorry,' said Judy, 'I've left wet marks on your floor. It's the snow outside ...' She smiled guiltily.

'Never mind ... We can wipe it up ...' the woman said brusquely.

'Don't get angry, Maryuta. "Madam" won't be here for long. She'll just ask me a few questions, and then she'll be off again – to New York, if I understand correctly?' Alexey gave a laugh.

'You could at least introduce us," said Maryuta, looking hard at Judy. Without waiting for an answer, she asked bluntly, 'What's your name?'

'Judy ... I mean Zhenya!'

'Did you hear that? They recruit them from primary school these days! ...' Alexey laughed.

'But why did Volodya say this morning that you were deaf and dumb?' Maryuta asked sternly.

'Her ... *dumb*?!' Alexey asked in amazement. 'That's a new one on me!'

'Alexey, I need to talk to you! I need to talk with just *you* for a moment,' said Judy in despair.

'Right. Maryuta, could you excuse us,' said Alexey. 'Sit in the kitchen for five minutes, and I'll soon be finished with this hell-hag.'

The reference to Judy as a 'hell-hag' evidently allayed Maryuta's jealousy. She looked at Judy again, then at Alexey, then went out without another word.

'Well?' he barked as the door closed. Judy was aware of using her last ounce of restraint. although she hadn't heard the expression 'hell-hag' – *kikimora* in Russian – she could tell by his tone that it was far from being a compliment. She felt a sudden flush of anger. Fool! Idiot that she was, she had never been in such a stupid situation as now! She had thought it would be quite simple, and the right thing to do, to come and talk with Alexey! But now she had run up against this inexplicable brick wall of anger and mockery. What on earth was he thinking of? He was still sitting there brazenly on the bed, half-dressed. He could have quite easily gone and smartened himself up. Instead of which he was simply sneering at her . . .

'Alexey, I don't understand why you find all this so funny,' she said, still trying to restrain herself. 'As far as I know, I've not said anything very amusing.'

'Huh! As far as you know! Why don't you cut out the funny talk and just get down to business?'

For a few seconds she studied him carefully, restraining an urge to slap him in the face then get up and go. Then she looked down at the floor and said quietly:

'We have come in order to try and get you out to America.'

'I'm not with you! Can you say that a bit louder?!'

'I can't. Nobody must know about this. Not even . . .' Judy looked apprehensively towards the door. 'Not even your friend here.'

'Listen! What exactly are you burbling about? *Who* mustn't know *what*?'

Judy got up and moved her chair closer to the bed.

'The idea is that you get married to me and that I take you out to America. In a year's time the two of us can get divorced. Tanya, your great-aunt, will pay for everything.'

Alexey looked at her and said nothing. Judy continued.

'She has lots of money. And she wants you to leave here and go and live with her in America. You've no other relatives over here, so all her money will be yours one day. On condition, that is, that you leave here.'

There was a silence. Now it was Judy's turn to look mockingly.

'Well, have you swallowed your tongue? You *do* look amazed! Didn't you expect any of this?'

'Maryuta!' he called out suddenly. 'Get me a drink of something!'

The girl came in again and stopped. 'I don't have anything! . . .' Then, after a moment's thought, she went off down the corridor. 'I'll just run and call Klavka in the next entrance. She might have a half-bottle.'

'Never mind, Maryuta! I didn't really mean it. My throat just went dry for a moment.'

But Maryuta was already draping a beaver-lamb jacket around her shoulders. 'I'll be right back! I feel like something to warm me up too.' And out she went.

Judy looked hard again at Alexey. He was lost in thought and gazed at the window, apparently oblivious of her presence. All his earlier self-assurance had disappeared, and he now looked like a sick old man. There were deep shadows under his eyes, the corners of his mouth drooped, and his cheeks were furrowed by sharp creases which emphasised his leanness even more.

No longer afraid of being overheard, Judy began again more loudly, 'Alexey! We don't have much time. We've come to Moscow for only two weeks! You've got to make up your mind quickly!'

'What do you want me to do?' He stared hard at her. 'Why are you doing all this? You're a lovely young girl! Why do you do this? Couldn't you find any other work to do?'

'How do you mean, "Why am I doing this?" I have ... Well, that'd take a lot of explaining. I simply need the money.'

'Money ...' he echoed. 'She needs money! So they've managed to buy your services. But they're not going to buy me! No fear, not for all the tea in China! They can leave me to rot in prison if they want! Or face a firing squad! But I'm finished. There's no life for me here anyway. Do you understand? So go and tell that to the people that sent you! I've finished with them! And not because Yury is such a dear friend of mine either, but simply because I don't want to dirty my hands on your lot! I don't want to filthy myself. D'you understand?' Alexey jumped from the bed, pulled the blanket around him, and went out into the kitchen.

Judy shuddered as the door banged. What was the

matter with him? What had she said? Was it the mention of money? But that was perfectly normal. There was nothing there for him to object to. How she chose to earn her money was her affair. Nobody was forcing him to be her real husband. But what was that about someone called Yury? And why should they leave him to rot in prison? ...

The outer door opened again and in came Maryuta. She was carrying a bottle of vodka, and by now her expression was slightly less glum. She actually smiled at Judy and proudly flourished the bottle labelled '*Vodka gvardeiskaya*'.

'It was a job getting her to part with this! Where's Alyosha?'

'He went into the kitchen.'

Judy got up from her chair and stood there uncertain what to do. Should she leave now or try to talk to him again? But probably Tanya was right: there was no point in getting involved with this lunatic. It was a lost cause.

'What? You're about to leave? Oh no, we can't allow that! I had such a job getting this bottle, and now you want to leave! Come on, have just one glass. That'll warm you up, and then you can go if you want. Alyosha! Hey, Alyosha, come here! Sit down, miss. Sit down, and I'll make us a snack. It isn't every day we get visitors. And especially *such* visitors! ...' Maryuta almost forced Judy to sit down again.

Alexey emerged from the kitchen, and shot them a sullen look. 'What on earth are you up to, Maryuta? Let her go back where she came from! Why are you stopping her?'

'Hey, mind your own business. Anyone would think you owned the place! It's my house and I'll do what I like. You can't let someone go away again without feeding them! And you'd best put some trousers on! Walking round, draped about like a statue! Sit down, stay where you are, miss. What did you say your name was?'

'Judy.'

'Well, just stay where you are, Judy. I want to ask you something while Alyosha gets dressed. Where did you buy a cardigan like that? I know, of course, you can get everything in Moscow. But how often do I get into town?' She gestured helplessly. 'You see this dress? A visitor from Moscow sold it to me. She took it off her own back and sold it me, she did. And she went back home wearing just her coat! It was killingly funny, but it's true! I paid her a hundred roubles for it ...'

Alexey came out of the kitchen barefoot. As he walked, he tightened up his leather trouser belt which had a five-point star on its metal buckle. Without looking at either of them, he went over to the bed, picked his socks off the floor and walked out again.

'He's taken offence, you see? Oh well, so what? He's that sort of character,' said Maryuta. 'But he's the loser by it! The idiot! Anyway, you sit here and I'll go and smooth his feathers. Otherwise he's going to spoil the whole evening for everyone.'

Judy was left alone. Her body ached with exhaustion, her head was heavy and she had a slight tickle in her throat. I'm falling ill, she thought. It was a crazy idea to come trailing out here in such cold weather. But I just felt sorry for Tanya!

Alexey appeared from the kitchen again, carrying a plate with some bread ready cut and three large glasses.

'Move your chair up to the table,' he said to Judy offhandedly.

Judy looked at him carefully. His face had lost its furrows, his eyes were bright, and a mocking smile curled his lips. Was it the prospect of a drink that cheered him up? Judy, however, was still bent on quizzing him:

'Alexey, I'd still like to know *why*! Why do you refuse this offer? Is it because of this woman? Are you in love with her?'

'What? Are you crazy?! Me in love with Maryuta?! Whatever next? Listen, let's drop this subject, okay? You've done your job. You've told me and I've listened.

And the answer is no. You're not going to use me as a stool-pigeon – not bloody likely! I'm not falling for a cheap trick like sending girls to me and luring me with promises of America! And that's final. Bugger off. Now let's have a drink! ...'

Maryuta came tripping out of the kitchen carrying two plates of assorted snacks.

'It's not all that much, I'm afraid. I didn't expect guests.' She surveyed the table quickly. 'But there we are – there's what the Good Lord provided, as they say. Let's have one glass now at least, and then if you're still hungry I can fry up some cutlets, and we'll have another drink! ...'

It was Judy's first taste of undiluted vodka, and awful stuff it was! She put her empty glass on the table, spluttering and with tears in her eyes. The fiery liquid scorched her throat like sandpaper, her head swam almost immediately and her legs turned to jelly.

'Judy, try some of this salad. Come on, don't stint yourself. Take more. And some herring! Heaven's, you've got tears in your eyes! You're not used to it, I can see that. *Gvardeiskaya* isn't exactly the best brand, of course! God knows what they brew it from!'

Judy mechanically ate everything she was offered. Maryuta had obviously warmed to her, but Judy meanwhile kept glancing warily in Alexey's direction. He evidently was not listening to his lady-friend's chatter. He picked at his food thoughtfully with a fork and kept eyeing Judy curiously.

They had a second glass. Judy tried to refuse, but Maryuta insisted, and Alexey said nothing, but smiled ironically. After the second full glass Judy began to feel a certain lightheadedness, and her visit out here no longer struck her as such a disaster. But she was still baffled by the inexplicable malice and mockery that blazed in Alexey's eyes whenever he looked at her. Very well, so he didn't want to go to America. To hell with him then! No doubt he had his reasons ... She tried to avoid catching his eye and looked just at Maryuta, who by now was all aglow and chattering away vivaciously. Of course Judy ought to have been on her way back to Moscow long ago. But it was so nice and warm here, and outside it was so frosty and windy . . .

Suddenly Maryuta started singing a long slow Russian folk song. She sang loudly as though on stage, and Alexey joined in, his heavy head propped on his hand. Each of them sang a separate part of their own. Judy would have liked to join in but, not knowing the words, simply enjoyed humming quietly.

Then they clinked glasses again. Judy lost count of how many glasses she had had. She liked Maryuta's devil-may-care way of drinking – with elbow held high and exhaling powerfully before each swig. Judy tried as well, but she ended up breathing out a mouthful of vodka straight into Alexey's face. He laughed good-naturedly. But she was very keen to get it right: she poured herself another glass, breathed out heavily and emptied the contents of the glass into her mouth. Maryuta applauded enthusiastically, then seized her by the hand and led her out to the kitchen. There they exchanged cardigans and then re-emerged to join Alexey with their arms around one another.

'Where on earth did they find a girl like you?' Alexey asked, suddenly very thoughtful. 'You really aren't like any Soviet girl. Or are you just pretending?'

Judy laughed, not realising exactly what he was talking about.

Maryuta shot them a sidelong glance and turned away to the record-player. Suddenly a powerful female voice sang. 'I so wish that summer had no ending . . .'

'Who's that singing?' Judy asked curiously.

'Alla Pugacheva. Don't you recognise her?' Maryuta held her hand out to Alexey, inviting him to dance. He got up reluctantly and, putting his arm round her, paced about heavily more or less on the spot. Maryuta leaned against him.

Suddenly there was a ring at the door. Judy looked at

the couple dancing and moved towards the door.

'Wait, let me go,' Maryuta disengaged herself from Alexey's embrace. 'The two of you can have a dance and I'll go and see who's there.'

Judy got up readily and joined Alexey. Looking him merrily in the eye, she placed both hands on his shoulders. He in turn placed his hands about her waist and took a few unsteady steps in time to the music. Then the record came to an end, and in the silence they heard voices talking quietly in the entrance.

Two men came into the room. One of them was tall with smooth fair hair brushed back. He gave a sardonic smile and nodded to Alexey.

'Good evening, pal. Enjoying yourself?'

The other man wore a wry, sombre expression. He said nothing and remained in the doorway. Maryuta peeked curiously from behind his shoulder.

'Oh, so you've rolled up?' said Alexey. 'Don't you trust your own people? Well, I've already told her everything. You can check and ask her. I'm not going to repeat it all.' He sat down demonstratively on one of the chairs.

'What's this?' The blond man looked at Judy inquisitively. 'Who are you?'

'Me? ...' asked Judy. There was something unpleasant about the blond man's self-assurance. 'Who are *you*?'

'I am a representative of the Committee for State Security – the KGB. My name is Igor. And this is my colleague Stanislav. What about you? What is your name?'

'My name's Sanders.' Judy felt a spasm of nausea in her throat.

'Sanders? And where do you live?'

'Me? ...' Judy's gaze shifted from Alexey to Maryuta. But there was no help from either quarter. 'I ... er ... I need to go to the bathroom. Maryuta, show me the way, can you?'

'Wait! First you'll answer my question and tell me where you're from! Where's your passport?' The fair-haired man spoke harshly and the smile had vanished from his face.

'I don't have my passport.'

'Comrade Vovchuk!' he called imperiously to Maryuta, but without turning towards her. 'Where is this person's handbag?'

'Here.' Maryuta came bounding up holding Judy's bag.

'Stass!' the man called, motioning towards the bag. The second man opened it unhurriedly and shook the contents out onto the table. Out fell Judy's make-up kit, purse and notebook. He opened the purse. In it were a hundred American dollars, fifty roubles, some change and the local train ticket. With his interest now aroused, the man picked up the notebook and leafed through it.

'So you're a foreigner? This is all written in English. Where are you from?'

'Let me have a look.' The blond man held out his hand for the book. Out of it fell a grey registration card for the Hotel Rossiya. The fair-haired man picked up the card. It had '*Judy Sanders, Room No. 1103*' entered in ink. 'So ... that's interesting, most interesting! Sanders, you said the name was? And how did you get to Mytishchi? As far as I know, this place isn't on any tourist schedule?'

He eyed Judy with interest from head to foot, then turned to look at Alexey.

'So these are the sort of contacts you keep, Odalevsky! Foreign girls as your friends? Well, well! And there you were pretending ... And what's more, as far as I gather, she speaks Russian? Curious, very curious ... I still haven't had an answer, Miss Sanders. Where are you from?'

'From New York,' she answered, realising that there was no point in fibbing.

'Wow! An American! Remarkable! Welcome to our midst! And what are you doing here? I mean here in Mytishchi, which is supposed to be off-limits?'

'I'm just visiting,' said Judy. The feeling of intoxication

had gone, but the fair man's words echoed dully in her head. What a mean role he'd chosen for himself! He kept smiling the whole time, yet his eyes were white and cold – just like the villain in a bad movie.

'Hmmm, I see ...' he drawled. 'Visiting, are you? But oh, Alexey, my dear Alexey, I did warn you, didn't I? ... I even asked you to try and keep things plain and simple. But what did you go and do? It's quite clear now why you tried hiding from us, and why you even deliberately injured your hand! You were trying to get back at us. And you decided to use this foreign girl to try and warn your friend that we were after him ...'

'Look, just cut out this play-acting!' Alexey said, though none too confidently. 'I guessed straight away what sort of girl she is. But what I don't understand is why you've invented this story about getting married?!'

'How do you mean "getting married"?' The fair-haired man stared in surprise. 'What are you talking about?'

'Okay, that's enough! You've got the wrong man for this altogether! I've seen through the whole scheme: "Auntie has come from America and wants to take you away, and she has lots of money!" That's a story for the nursery school!' By now Alexey had worked himself up into a towering rage. 'You want to play serious, and then you try something daft like this! ...' He spat contemptuously.

The blond man looked thoughtfully at Judy.

'So you're staying at the Rossiya?'

'Yes,' Judy answered, looking in surprise at Alexey.

'Stass, check when she arrived, and who with, and the general details ... you know what to do.' He handed Stass the hotel registration card. 'It looks as if she might be a more serious customer than she pretends!'

Stass turned to Maryuta:

'Where's your phone?'

'I don't have one. I rang from the neighbour's!' she answered readily, then bit her tongue. Alexey stared at her.

'You bitch!' he grated. 'I wonder how much they're paying for *your* services?'

'Take it easy, Odalevsky. Comrade Vovchuk was only doing her duty. Whereas you . . .'

'Why are you trying to put me to shame?!' Maryuta suddenly shrilled, interrupting the blond man and looking at Alexey. 'You think you're so virtuous! But there's only one thing you lot want Maryuta for! As soon as you feel like having it off, it's straight to her! Meanwhile my children have to live out of town with their grandmother! Do I have to leave them as orphans, just because King Stud comes panting? And now he even comes and hides out at my place, and brings foreign girls here too! . . .'

Stass stepped over and gripped her firmly by the shoulders and gave her a good shake.

'What's all the shouting for?! Cool it! Come on, show me where the phone is!'

Maryuta whimpered and looked up fearfully.

'It's next door, in the next entrance.'

Stass released her and the two of them left the apartment. Meanwhile the fair man sat down at the table, still wearing his overcoat. Lazily he took a glass and poured himself a vodka. He drank unhurriedly, in slow gulps, as though it were water, then set the glass down again. Using his fingers he fished a pickled gherkin from the jar, crunched it with relish between his teeth and leaned back. For some time he rocked back and forth on his chair, looking at Judy with obvious interest and then at Alexey, as though somehow comparing the two of them.

Judy would have liked to sit down but she remained standing. Her legs felt numb and lifeless and she leaned feebly against the wall. Only now did it dawn on her why Alexey had run away that morning. He thought they had been sent by the KGB. What an idiot! Thanks to him, she was now involved in this stupid affair!

'So you came here in order to suggest that Odalevsky should go back to the West with you?' the fair-haired agent said at last. 'Only I must advise you: if you ever want to see New York again, you'd better tell the truth! Or was it Odalevsky who summoned you here?'

'Look here!' Alexey suddenly cut in, 'Stop trying to blackmail this girl without any proof! She never said anything of the sort! It was me who ...'

'Shut up!' the other man snapped. 'Things are going to be a lot different for you from now on! And I think one or two of our folk are going to take a serious interest in this so-called "bride" of yours. And the old woman too. We knew someone was here to see you during the day today. And we might not have guessed who it was ...' – he spread his hands helplessly and grinned – 'but you've helped us find out. Well, at least you've done us that service! But now you're going to let us have what we want in writing! Okay?'

He paused and looked at Judy again. There was a brief silence, and then he rose easily from the chair and went over to her. She looked him in the eye, waiting.

'I must admit,' he began with a gently thoughtful air, 'I can still hardly believe it. Do you really mean to tell me you came here with the idea of marrying *him*? Be quite honest. It's all right. There's no need to be afraid. What are they paying you for doing this? Are you doing it for money?'

'Keep quiet!' Alexey ordered her. 'Don't answer! He doesn't have the right to interro ...'

Alexey had no time to finish. With one short professionally aimed blow in the face, the blond man had knocked him out. Alexey reeled on his chair and grabbed for the table. The tablecloth came sliding off together with the plates. Alexey fell to the floor with a crash and the crockery came tinkling down on top of him. As he struggled to rise the blond man looked down at him harshly.

'And here's one last piece of advice,' he said. 'Shut up now and just do what you're told. You've landed in it good and proper, in a way you never dreamed of.

Nobody'll ever prove it wasn't you who summoned this great-aunt of yours to come out here, and to bring this "bonny bride"! You wanted to use them to warn Shalygin off. And you know what article that comes under, don't you? Anti-Soviet activities and espionage! Both you and them!'

Alexey sat up on the floor, pulled a corner of the tablecloth towards him and wiped his bloodied lip with it. The fair-haired man left him there. He kicked a sliver of plate aside and walked over to Judy who was standing stock-still, propped against the wall.

'I'm sorry that that little show of force was necessary. But scum like him don't understand anything else. Do you smoke?' He pulled a packet of cigarettes from his pocket. 'They're not American of course, but they're not too bad. You might be interested to try one ...'

Judy's hand trembled as she took one of his cigarettes. He held out a burning match, which slightly scorched her eyelashes. As she inhaled she got an acid taste from the strong, unrefined tobacco. The entrance door banged and in came Stass and Maryuta.

'Well?' the blond man turned to Stass.

'Judy Sanders, American citizen, arrived today by Pan Am jet from New York. The whole group have gone to *The Cherry Orchard* at the Moscow Arts Theatre. They're not back yet. The show ends at 10.30, in twenty minutes' time,' Stass reported drily.

'Who's their interpreter?'

'Oleg Petrov. He's gone with them to the theatre. She's already been reported, incidentally, for having absented herself from the group.' Stass motioned towards Judy and looked at his watch: 'In an hour from now the criminal police would have been looking for you in any case. This isn't New York, you know! We take good care of our visitors!'

'Have you left instructions for Petrov to wait for us?' the blond man asked.

'Of course. And I have told them *where* to wait...'

'Well done! Okay then, you two love-birds can get ready and come along with us.' The blond man turned ironically to Alexey and Judy. 'Off we go to Moscow, as they say – just like that line in *The Cherry Orchard*!'

As they emerged on the street, Judy breathed in a deep, sharp, painful breath of frosty air. The street lamp on its tall post cast only a feeble light. In the blurred yellow halo around it, fine needle-like snowflakes were falling lazily. The engine of the black Volga saloon parked by the entrance gave a hollow rattle that echoed in the stillness.

'Get in!' The fair-haired man opened the front door for Judy. 'And you, Alexey, will sit behind with me.'

Stass took his place at the wheel, revved the engine and let in the clutch.

To her surprise, Judy realised now that she was no longer afraid. Tanya had briefed her, and the first thing she had to do, she knew, was to get in touch with the American embassy. Alexey had been quite right when he had tried to prompt her. They had no right to interrogate her – at least, not without an American embassy official present ... Where would they be taken? she wondered. Straight to the KGB, or to the hotel first? ...

They emerged on a narrow deserted road. She could see nothing outside the window – either there was some factory fence there, or else a long dark stretch of forest. The headlamps picked out only a narrow strip of rough, icy roadway.

It was stuffy inside the car and there was a smell of petrol. Judy unbuttoned her jacket and took several deep breaths. She felt as if she was about to be sick and she put a hand up in front of her mouth.

'What's the matter?' Stass shot her a sideways glance.

'Stop!' Judy mumbled, trying not to open her mouth. But Stass drove on. Suddenly, though, Judy could not restrain the nausea any more and shot a cascade of vomit all over the front windscreen.

'Stass, stop!' the blond man shouted from behind.

With difficulty Judy struggled out of the car. She bent

double over a snowdrift and writhed as the spasms continued. It seemed as though it would never end. She had nothing more to vomit up, but the waves of sickness kept on coming. Dimly she recalled Maryuta's words: "*Gvardeiskaya* isn't exactly the best brand of course . . ."

The blond man was standing next to her.

'Eat some snow. That'll help,' he said.

With an effort Judy eventually managed to stand up. She tried to breathe in.

A dumper truck laden with sand was slowly trundling along the road. Behind it came another, and then another. The night air was suddenly filled with the roar of their engines, which drowned out every other sound.

Then, all of a sudden, the blond man gave a gasp and fell forward into the snow. Judy wheeled round and saw Alexey. His expression was calm and concentrated. He had a heavy spanner in his hand. As she watched, he bent over and slipped it into the top of his boot.

'What's happened?' asked Judy in surprise, then fell silent. Next to the blond man's head where he lay, a bloodstain was quickly spreading across the snow. Judy panicked and instinctively turned to look for Stass in the car.

Stass was still sitting in the driver's seat. His head was thrown back against the headrest at an awkward angle. She could see his dark profile: his tongue was lolling out of his open mouth, and his right eye stared from its orbit and glinted horribly in the darkness. Next to him, draped over the back of the seat, was a broad leather belt with a metallic buckle. On the yellow brass a five-pointed star stood out in bold relief.

9

Judy squatted by the roadside on a flattened snowdrift with her hands clasped about her knees, her legs and shoulders shuddering. A single thought banged in her head like a heavy hammer: 'He's killed them! He's killed them! ...'

The engine of the black saloon was still ticking over steadily.

Alexey walked round the car, opened the driver's door and began dragging out Stass's corpse. He searched him quickly, removed his pistol from its shoulder holster, and transferred it to his own pocket. Then he dragged the body to one side, away from the road and into the darkness. Judy heard what sounded like the crunch of planking and the sound of Alexey puffing and panting and quietly cursing through his teeth. Finally he reappeared, then grabbed the body of the blond man and dragged it off in the same direction.

Judy gazed blankly into the darkness and gave only an occasional whimper.

Very shortly Alexey returned, with the second man's pistol also stowed in his pocket. Then, seeing the vomit on the front seat and windscreen, he swore and ran off again. In the distance a pair of headlamps appeared, but Judy had not the strength to get up and try to flag the vehicle down. A small truck swept past, splattering her with dirty wads of wet snow.

Alexey appeared again with the blond man's jacket. With it he quickly but carefully wiped down the seat and screen.

Stass's document case still lay on the floor. Alexey opened it up, removed the tape cassette and stuck it down the top of his boot. Then he flung both the portfolio and the jacket away from the road into the darkness and turned to Judy.

'Get in the car!'

She stared back in fear. His face through the darkness was white as a sheet. His eyes stared and his lips were tightly pressed together. He thrust his face close to hers, like a horrible mask. Judy squealed and crawled away on all fours, trying to rise. But her legs spreadeagled on the frozen snow. Disregarding the ache in her hands, she tried vainly to scramble to her feet.

'Where are you running to? Idiot!' Alexey bent over her and violently jerked her to her feet. She began to struggle.

'Let me go! Murderer! *Ubeetsa*! Monster! Let me free! *Tvar*! Animal!' she yelled in a mixture of Russian and English.

She managed briefly to tear herself free and quickly ran along the road towards the bright headlamps of an oncoming car. She began waving when it was still far off. But the Lada just swerved to avoid her and raced away, disappearing in the darkness.

Then Alexey's powerful hands grasped her from behind. He seized her roughly by the jacket and shook her like a rag doll.

'Get back to the car!' he yelled.

Judy must have lost her reason. She twisted and turned in his grasp, screaming and trying to knee him in the groin. Furiously Alexey stepped back and dealt her a swipe across the face. She cried out, then slumped into his arms. He lifted her up and carried her to the car. He did not try to sit her down but simply flung her onto the back seat and slammed the door. She came to at the sound. In front of her the man's leather belt and metal buckle still hung over the seat. Judy gagged in terror.

Alexey had walked round to the other side and sat in the driver's seat.

'Listen,' he said, panting slightly. He took the belt from the seat and began threading it back through the loops on his trousers. 'Can you think normally?'

Judy said nothing.

'You've got to understand that we had no choice . . .' he said nervily as he struggled with the belt.

Judy whimpered in the darkness. He turned round and silently studied her pale face in the darkness. Only now did he realise that the murder of the KGB men had not solved all their problems. Not even hers. Abandoning his half-threaded belt, he gripped the steering wheel.

'We're going to Moscow!' he barked. 'And you and my aunt must get out of the Soviet Union immediately. By the first plane you can get – to Paris, London, or God knows where! The main thing is for you to be out of the country by tomorrow morning!'

Judy looked blindly at the windscreen. The roadway was an old one, narrow and with a pitted surface. They were tearing along at high speed, however, and at every bump and lurch she banged her head painfully against the roof. Clutching at the seat in front of her, she looked with hatred at Alexey's harsh profile. It was all his fault! If only he had believed them at the start, everything would have been all right! She wouldn't have had to come out and see him again! She wouldn't have run into the KGB agents, and, there wouldn't have been any murders!

The image of Stass's disfigured profile swam before her gaze again . . . Murderer! He had strangled one man and killed the other with a blow! What if they did work for the KGB? They were still human beings! They probably had mothers, wives and children. What a monster! He might just as readily try and bump me off from the rear when I'm not looking, she thought. A fine husband she had found to bring out to America!

Judy felt hot as a new wave of terror swept over her, and she suddenly and quite involuntarily gave a loud hiccup.

'What is it?' Alexey said without looking round.

'Nothing ...' she murmured fearfully.

'Aha-ha-aa.' He let out an indefinable yawning noise, then fell silent again. In the gloom outside she could now see the whitish mass of high-rise apartment blocks with an occasional lighted window. The car turned off the roadway and headed down a narrow drive towards the nearest block of apartments and stopped by a lighted telephone booth.

'Now, ring up the old lady,' Alexey ordered sharply. 'Don't tell her anything. Just hint to her not to go to bed. She should be dressed ready and waiting for you. That's all. Okay?'

'Yes,' she answered obediently, still paralysed at the thought that he might kill her as he had killed the others. It was obvious: she was the only witness of his crime! While she was in the phone box he might come and clout her over the head with that spanner! Or he might strangle her with his belt! ... She sat huddled in terror in one corner of the back seat.

'Come on, get out!' Alexey turned to her and stopped in surprise. 'What's the matter with you?'

'Don't touch me! I beg you! I'll not tell anyone! Don't kill me!' she whispered.

He looked at her for what seemed an age.

'Silly girl!' he said in a distressed tone. 'You silly American girl! It was because of you that I killed them!'

That was all he said. Now it was her turn to stare in amazement. The way he had said that left her with no alternative but to believe him.

'Because of me?! Why?'

What could the KGB in fact do to her? She was an American after all! She hadn't committed any crime. All right, she'd gone to Mytishchi without permission ... So what? Did so few American tourists secretly or even openly meet up with Russian dissidents or Jewish activists in this country?! ...

'Why? You wonder why?' Alexey mocked her with evident annoyance. 'They were already trying to pin a treason charge on me in order to make me work for them. My pal managed to flee to the West, but they want to catch him and use me to help them! And now of all things, an American girl turns up! You heard what he said: he claimed I summoned you out here, in order to warn Yury. They'd have framed you and my aunt on a charge of espionage, and you'd never have wriggled out of it. I've been running from them for a month now! Ugh ... but you'll never understand!' He was annoyed at having to explain all this – and she still wouldn't understand a word!

Judy stared at him full of hate. So that was how things were. He was a criminal on the run, trying to escape the authorities!

'Go and ring her. Have you got a coin?' Alexey asked.

'I'll call collect ...' she scrambled out of the car. All she wanted was to hear Tanya's voice as soon as possible and tell her she would soon be back – and to get shot of this 'prince' as soon as possible! But Alexey was right: she had understood precious little of what he had been trying to explain to her.

'What does "collect" mean?' Alexey grabbed her by the coat.

'Well ... through the operator. And they'll put it down on our hotel account.'

'No, you can't do that here! You can't phone without money!' He rummaged in his pockets and produced a two-kopeck piece. 'There you are. ...'

With a glare at Alexey, Judy dashed to the phone booth and began searching her bag for her notebook. Only then did she remember that the blond KGB man had kept her notebook. He had taken it at Maryuta's and hadn't returned it. 'Shit!' Judy hammered the telephone with her fist in a burst of helpless fury. She leaned out and called to Alexey:

'How do you ring up "Information"?'

'What information?'

'To find the number of the hotel. My notebook's still

with ... with that guy from the KGB.'

'It's called *správochnoye* in Russian.' Alexey came and dialled 09 himself and obtained the number of the Rossiya Hotel.

'Do you know the number of her room?' he asked, as he dialled the hotel. 'This will get you the hotel switchboard. When they answer, speak English ...' He handed her the receiver. It took only one ring to raise Tanya in her room. The Princess's voice sounded strained.

'Hallo?'

'Hi, it's me ...' Judy began and stopped immediately. She was interrupted by Tanya speaking in an imperious, hasty manner: 'I'm afraid you've got the wrong number!' Tanya said. 'There is no such person here, and don't you try ringing here again!' Then there were rapid pips as the phone was hung up at the other end.

Judy looked in amazement at Alexey who was standing next to her.

'What was that?' he asked suspiciously.

'She hung up on me!'

'Bugger it, that means they've already got to her!' Alexey rushed out of the phone booth back to the car. Judy followed.

'Who are "they"?' she asked.

'The KGB. That's who!'

'How can you tell?'

'I just can, that's all!' Alexey flopped into the driver's seat. 'What did she say?'

'She said I wasn't to try ringing there any more.' Judy took her place next to him.

'My! That great-aunt of mine is some lady! Well done for her! She was warning you not to turn up there, do you understand? Somebody from the KGB was probably with her! That means there's only one route for you to take – direct to the airport, onto a plane, and ...' He pressed the starter.

'Wait! I don't have a passport or a ticket! Everything's in the hotel!'

They sat in silence for a few long seconds.

'Give me another coin!' Judy suddenly came to life. How could she forget? She had to ring the embassy. 'I'm going to ring the American embassy!'

'Do you know their number?' A flash of hope lit up his face.

'No, but we can find out from Information – from the *správochnoye*.'

Judy quickly jumped out of the car and dived back into the phone box. Just as Alexey had done a moment ago, she dialled 09.

'*Správochnoye*,' a woman's voice answered.

'I'd like the number of the American embassy, please.'

'What do you want that for?'

'How d'you mean?' Judy objected. 'What business is it of yours?'

'We don't give the numbers of foreign embassies,' said the voice and the line went dead.

Judy stood there dumbfounded. Then Alexey appeared again.

'They wouldn't give it to you, of course,' he said.

'But why?!'

'Use your brain,' he said with the same irritation as before, and went back to the car. The girl was becoming a millstone round his neck.

'Then ... then *take* me there!' she said getting into the back seat again. 'You know where our embassy is, don't you? It must be somewhere downtown ...'

'I know all right, but that won't work. There's a round-the-clock guard on the entrance. Without an American passport, not only will they not let you in, they'll collar you if you even try! ...'

'Then ... Oh God, what am I going to do? How am I going to get out of this?' Judy thrashed about on the seat in a fit of hysteria.

Alexey stamped hard on the accelerator and off they went.

We've got to get off the Yaroslavl Highway and find our

way quick onto the Circular, he thought, trying not to listen to her loud sobbing. Then along Shchelkovo Avenue out of Moscow, or else along the Ostashkovsky – that would be nearer. Then we must change cars quickly. We might have to heist a Zhiguli saloon perhaps – the owner wouldn't find out and report it till the morning, and by that time we could be a long way away! And they'll not find the KGB men's bodies all that quickly, especially if we dump the Volga on another highway. But they won't take long to start hunting for *us*! They'll alert all stations along the highways around Moscow and then.... Listen to that fool of a girl howling! It's enough to deafen you! What am I to do with her? If I disappear somewhere in the backwoods, and even if I keep absolutely mum about it all, in a couple of years – at most three – they'll find me and I'll get a death sentence for doing in these KGB agents. But what about her? Where can I put her? The KGB are waiting at her hotel! Goddammit! Only a turd like me would have decided she was in the KGB! On the other hand, though, it's dangerous for me to go around with her. She could get nabbed over the simplest thing – she talks with an accent and has bugger-all idea about things here. Fuck it, I'm really trapped!

Judy had quietened down meanwhile.

'Where are we going?' she asked.

'I don't know,' Alexey said after a pause. 'As far from Moscow as we can get.'

She felt like asking why. But recalling his phrase about 'using your brain', she said nothing. Wasn't it now all the same where they were hurtling to along this road in the dark and snow? She was sitting next to a murderer, and back in Moscow the KGB were waiting for her. To them she was a criminal – for wanting to try and smuggle out a man who was wanted for treason! He admitted it himself! And when she and her 'bridegroom' were arrested, they'd both be had up for double murder! How could she prove that Alexey had put paid to two strapping men from the KGB entirely on his own, and that her being sick wasn't just a piece of play-acting! Alexey was right: she couldn't go back to Moscow! Once the KGB started torturing her, she knew she would admit to anything, whether it was true or not ...

'Have you ever been tortured?' asked Judy, in an attempt to quell the trembling fit that had overcome her.

'Where? In Afghanistan?' he answered, somehow rather unwillingly.

'Why Afghanistan? Have you been there?'

'Yes, I have.'

'What were you doing there?'

Alexey looked at her in amazement for a second, then turned to watch the road again. Here was the turn-off from the Circular onto Ostashkovsky Highway. Now they'd be heading northwards, away from Moscow. And on the way they'd have to change cars somewhere ...

'Hmmm, yes!' he shook his head. 'I've read somewhere in the papers that there are sixty million illiterates in America. But I never believed it. I thought it was just our propaganda. Did you really not know that we've been fighting a war in Afghanistan for the last eight years?'

'Oh, you were out there in the war?' Judy looked at him curiously.

'No! I was there as a tourist! A tourist with a sub-machine gun!' and he gave an evil smirk.

'Now I understand ...' she said thoughtfully. 'That explains a lot.'

'What does it explain?'

'Well, for instance, the fact that you were quite calmly able to kill two innocent people!'

'Innocent!!' Alexey boiled up again. 'What do you know about shit like them? The innocent folk are those that went and got killed in Afghanistan, not their sort! You're a fool if you think otherwise! But just tell me this, how do you come to know Russian? And where did my great-aunt find you? You really are two crazy women ... rolling up like that and wanting to take me off to America! Who asked you to do a thing like that?'

Judy choked on another wave of anger. After all this he dared to talk to her like that!

'Who asked me! Your forbears and your ancestors asked me – that's who!' she said quietly, but with obvious hatred. 'Your grandfathers and mothers and aunts and all the others who were shot. Do you know anything at all about your family tree?'

'I couldn't give a damn about these bloody princes and princesses! I'd just like to be allowed to live in peace after that hell-hole I went through in Afghanistan. But apparently I'm not meant to do that!' He clouted the steering wheel angrily.

Judy looked miserably out of the window. By the roadside a post flashed past with a sign announcing the village of Chelobityevo. Then came the windows of several closed shops, snow-bound streets with an occasional passer-by and brightly lit windows in the houses. Walking along a footpath towards them there came a rather jolly group of about ten people. Their faces were flushed and merry. It looked as if they had enjoyed a good evening's eating and drinking. The men wore their coats unbuttoned and the collars of their shirts were open. Several of them were carrying hats and scarves. The women walked hand in hand, singing and dancing as they went. The men flanked them, clapping in rhythm.

Because of them Alexey was unable to halt by a group of private cars parked for the night in the shadow of a large apartment block. With a disappointed sigh he accelerated away again. Never mind, there would be more villages coming up ...

Judy turned in her seat and for a long time watched the little group of dancers. But then the revellers were lost to sight, the village came to an end, and with it the last sign of life. The houses were followed by a strip of dark woodland. Suddenly Judy realised that she actually was leaving Moscow, and she was afraid! Where were they heading? Back there in the city there were people, and there was life. But in front of them was only impenetrable darkness, forest, and fear! What had happened to her? Had she really taken leave of her senses? Why was she letting him take her away from Moscow? No, they had to go back! Even if she had to spend the night standing beneath the windows of the American embassy! And if she didn't manage to get into the embassy, then maybe she could find some American journalist? ...

'Turn back!' she ordered sharply.

'I don't get you ...' He didn't even bother turning to look at her.

'I said turn back! Back to Moscow!'

'Oh, wouldn't you rather we turned off and headed straight for New York?!'

'Didn't you hear what I said?! I want to go back to Moscow!'

'Sit down and belt up. I'm not turning round and going to Moscow,' he snapped angrily.

And then Judy had a fit of madness. She grabbed his arm and jerked it with all her strength. For a moment Alexey let go the wheel, trying to fight her off, then grabbed it again. But it was too late ...

It all happened in a split second. The car skidded sharply, spun round several times, left the road and mounted the verge. Then, like a child's toy car, it hurtled down a bank and crashed into a large stack of metal pipes that had been dumped there. There was an ear-splitting crash. The last thing Judy saw was a fireworks display of sparks from the front headlamps as they shattered. After that her head crashed through the front screen, and she knew no more.

10

When Tanya put the receiver down again, she heard how very quiet it was in the room. In his eagerness to try and overhear who she was talking to, Oleg Petrov, the Intourist guide, had come up almost indecently close. That was why Tanya had immediately cut in and never gave Judy a chance to say a word.

'I'm sorry. Where were we?' she smiled, then walked past him to the settee and sat down next to Elizabeth.

'Who was ringing just now?' Petrov asked sharply, forgetting his earlier courtesy.

Tanya looked at him reproachfully and smiled.

'I don't know. They got the wrong number. Why? Are you waiting for a call?'

'Mrs Goehr!' Oleg began rudely, but then corrected himself, smiled and shook his head, 'It would be very easy for me to check ...'

'So why are you asking? Go ahead. Check!' Tanya jerked her head provocatively then turned and placed a hand on Elizabeth's shoulder. 'My dear, I can see you're very tired. You should turn in. I'm sure Oleg won't mind ...'

'I don't want to sleep!' Elizabeth pursed her lips obstinately. 'I'm going to sit right here! ...'

'Elizabeth, I beg you!'

'No! I want to listen to Oleg as well. Please carry on. You stopped where you were telling us what a poor life the peasants had under the tsars. And then, when the Communists came to power, everything changed. Is that right?'

'Yes, indeed. Exactly,' Oleg confirmed, not taking his eyes off Tanya for a moment.

'And then? ...' the Princess said mockingly.

'And then there was collectivisation,' he mused, and looked at his watch. 'But you know how it is, it's always difficult being first in the field. Prior to that, history had never known anything like the collective management of agriculture....'

Tanya stubbed out her cigarette in the ashtray and gave an obvious yawn, covering her mouth with a hand. Elizabeth fidgeted and gave a meaningful cough.

'Forgive me, Oleg,' Tanya smiled. 'But you know, we're so very tired! And the ... What time is it? Goodness, after midnight! But as I understand it, you're expecting something to happen ... Is that right? I wonder what it is though? Perhaps we can help you? Meanwhile, though, you keep churning out all this historical make-believe. You see, I lived here in what you refer to as the tsarist period. And I can tell you, you're talking a load of trash! There were peasants of many different sorts – some were very rich, and some were poor. Some people liked to work hard, and they lived not at all badly. And it was precisely those people that you destroyed in the collectivisation – almost nine million of them! ...' Tanya got up and walked towards Oleg. 'To be quite blunt, though: what is it exactly that you want here? You've been sitting here for more than two hours, and I'm still lost for an explanation. After all, we did say goodnight to one another after the theatre. So what's persuaded you to come up here to our room and ...'

There was a knock at the door, and without waiting for an answer, in came two strangers. One was a man of about fifty, with a round face and smoothly combed hair. The other was a young woman. She was slightly too plump for the close-fitting suit she wore, and she had both hands stuck in her pockets as she entered.

Elizabeth stood up as they appeared and both she and Tanya looked at the newcomers expectantly.

'Ah, Nina! Have they arrived?' Oleg stepped forward to meet the woman.

'No,' she said quietly, looking past him to the two American ladies. 'Which is rather strange. We've tried twice to ring them at their office. The duty officer said they hadn't turned up there either. Tell me, Mrs Goehr, who was that who rang just now?'

'I'm sorry,' Tanya said in English, 'I don't think we've been introduced. You simply came bursting in here without asking! That's rather strange behaviour, don't you think? ...'

'My name is Katunova,' the woman replied in slow and heavily accented English. 'I work in the tourist security section of this hotel. It is essential that I ask you several questions about the American tourist Judy Sanders. Was it she who rang just now?'

'Please, Miss Katunova – or should I say Comrade Katunova – do come in and sit down.' Tanya pointed to a chair and placed herself on the settee, all too aware of how furiously her heart was beating. 'I'm afraid I can't tell you who it was that rang.'

'But why did you not allow the person to speak? You immediately cut her short and told her not to ring again.'

'That was ...' Tanya hesitated for an instant, '... because we are constantly getting rung up here by prostitutes and other people trying to buy jeans! It was probably another one of them....'

It was unclear whether the woman believed Tanya's fib or not.

'Mrs Goehr,' she said, 'Did you know Judy Sanders before your trip to Russia?'

'No, I assume you're referring to that young girl who flew with us from New York? We got to know one another in the plane. Why? Has something happened to her?'

'Yes, it has. Did she say anything about any friends she had here in Russia?'

'Oh, she and I aren't all that close. But what's happened? I didn't actually notice whether she was with us at the theatre, did you?' Tanya turned to ask Elizabeth.

'So, you're maintaining that you aren't acquainted with her? In that case why did she come to your room today before the theatre?' Katunova asked sharply, her dark eyes fixed on Tanya.

'Why did she come here?' Tanya was confused for a moment, then smiled and shook her head mockingly. 'You know, I'm sorry, I keep forgetting that I'm in Russia now! In this country, of course, nobody can take a step without someone else taking notice!'

'Mrs Goehr, just think what you're saying! Nobody so far has ever got away with defaming this country of ours! Answer me. Why did Judy Sanders come to see you?'

Tanya looked in silence at Katunova's face with its clumsy make-up. Then she got up and walked over to Oleg Petrov who was standing by the doorway.

'If this is some sort of interrogation, then I refuse to answer any questions without an official from the American embassy being here!' she said slowly and deliberately. Then she lit another cigarette.

'Mrs Goehr! Good heavens, this isn't an interrogation!' Oleg glanced in alarm at Katunova. 'Why should we involve the embassy? There are just a few routine questions. Don't get excited. You're simply being asked to explain why it is that Miss Sanders came to see you today.'

'If that's the case, then this woman here had better alter her tone! Why does she address me as if I were some sort of criminal? I'd like to know exactly what I'm supposed to have done. And what has that poor young mite gone and done? If you don't tell me, I'm not answering any of your questions!' Tanya rounded on Katunova challengingly.

Katunova looked her straight in the eye. 'Miss Judy Sanders,' she replied, 'has been found at Mytishchi by some of our KGB staff.'

'So what?' Elizabeth, who had so far kept silent, suddenly exploded.

Everyone turned to look at her. Tanya clapped a hand

to her mouth in fright. Only now apparently did Katunova notice Elizabeth's diminutive and dapper figure. Her brows shot up in surprise for one second, but turning back to Tanya again she caught her look of alarm.

'Mrs Goehr, I've no wish to intimidate you, but your past history ...' Katunova suddenly made a furtive overture in Russian. 'Or should I say, the history of your parents, gives us almost unlimited possibilities. So I would therefore advise you to speak the truth and to tell us: why did Judy Sanders come here and see you before she set off to go to Mytishchi?'

'You know,' Tanya resumed, 'I do prefer to speak English! English has been a native language of mine for a good long time now!' She walked over to Elizabeth, 'And I've no idea what these "unlimited possibilities" are that you're talking about. My parents tried to emigrate from Russia more than sixty years ago. Quite legally, as we had permission. And I was still a minor. What legal system in the world can judge me because of my parents' past?'

'Mrs Goehr, you are now in the Soviet Union! And here in this country we have our own legal system!' Katunova pronounced these words in English with a certain obvious pleasure.

'But I am an American citizen!' Tanya replied triumphantly.

'And a Soviet citizen! You left the USSR in 1919. Nobody ever took away your Soviet citizenship. And you, incidentally, have never applied to give it up. So that while you are in this country you are regarded as a Soviet citizen!'

By now Tanya was looking at her in horror. The face of the soldier who first began ripping off her dress all those years ago had never loomed before her with such frightening reality as now. And as she now looked at the fatty crows'-feet around Katunova's eyes, she recalled that face down to the last detail. But instead of a red wart on the upper lip, which trembled as the soldier slowly untied the dirty rope holding up his breeches, Katunova had only a small dark birthmark. But as for the rest – they were the same eyes, the same thin pale lips, and, most of all, there was that same intoxication with her own power, the same boorishness, authority and impudence.

Tanya felt again how she had felt as a fifteen-year old girl with a bayonet held to her throat ...

'Mrs Goehr!' Katunova resumed, 'A few minutes ago you were rung up by a woman. Was that Judy Sanders? What sort of mission was it that you sent her on to Mytishchi? Answer me!'

Tanya swayed slightly, and seeing Elizabeth's outstretched arms, collapsed feebly onto the settee next to her. She realised full well that these were normal KGB methods to intimidate people – make them aware of their own weakness, then extract everything by torture. But she could do nothing to control the wave of terror that now flooded over her. She felt faint and the room swam before her eyes ...

'Stop it! Stop this at once!' screamed Elizabeth suddenly. She was quite beside herself with fury and began bustling over her friend, who now lay prostrate on the settee with her head thrown back. She opened several buttons on Tanya's jacket and began massaging her temples.

'What's the matter with her?' Katunova demanded in Russian, obviously displeased. 'Oleg, call a doctor!'

'Get out of here!' Elizabeth yelled, rising from her seat and flushed with excitement. 'Get out of here right now! All of you! And you ... If you don't leave my room this instant, then I'll ...' She made straight for Katunova and stood staring up at her menacingly. She firmly clenched her small rounded hands and held her fists out in an almost childish gesture of defiance.

Katunova looked in surprise at the old lady confronting her and frozen in that strange stance. Oleg Petrov and the other man both advanced towards the two of them, evidently afraid that Elizabeth would let fly at Katunova any second. But Elizabeth paid them no attention.

'Go away!' she said to Katunova almost in a whisper. 'And don't even think of coming back unless you've got an embassy official with you!'

Katunova stared at Elizabeth and at Tanya, who still lay on the settee. Then, turning away, she motioned to the men and they all left the room. Oleg paused at the door and seemed about to say something, but thought better of it and went out, shutting the door behind him.

Elizabeth rushed to Tanya's side.

'How are you?'

'All right ... Better ... Better now ...' Tanya sat up and took a few deep breaths. 'My head started spinning. But it's gone off now. Thank you, my dear!'

'What for?'

'Well done! I got completely confused. God, what awful people!' Tanya pressed a palm to her burning cheeks. 'What are we to do now?'

'We're not going to do anything,' said Elizabeth firmly. 'Nothing at all. We're going to get some sleep. And tomorrow we'll get in touch with the embassy. They'll not abandon us. Just let anyone try anything on, and I'll go and see Reagan! I'll have the whole of Congress up in arms! I'll give them "Soviet citizen"! ...'

Tanya tried not to look as Elizabeth bustled furiously about the room. Reagan, Congress – they were all big names, of course, but ones that meant precious little to a Russian. Elizabeth of course had nothing to fear. She wasn't haunted by that awful scene of violation and the murder of her parents and sisters! Nor was she aware that the might of the whole Soviet state stood behind Katunova's brazen threats ... And poor Judy! Where was she? What had happened to her? Why had she been detained? Surely that monstrous nephew of hers couldn't have betrayed her? So long as the KGB didn't beat her up! Of course, they wouldn't use violence nowadays – this was no longer 1919. Although if need be Tanya would take all the blame upon herself. Good Lord, why had she hung up when Judy had rung her? But then how was she to know that she had been arrested? She had wanted to warn the girl not to come to their hotel room. The guide was sitting there, after all, and not by accident. But how terrible all this was! ...

Tanya closed her eyes and let her head fall back. Elizabeth said nothing, but remained close by her. Through the window drifted the melodic chime of the Kremlin bells ... They always played a sweet ringing melody before the single bell toll announced the hour.

PART TWO

11

The room was narrow and cramped. It had a low ceiling of heavy unpainted beams. There was only one tiny window, and the walls were made of the same dull wooden planks, grey with age. The room was either a carpenter's shop or a junk store. Apart from a bed and a lopsided cabinet it also had a large open cupboard crammed into it. The cupboard had neither drawers nor doors. It was obviously handmade and smelt strongly of freshly cut timber. Inside it were various joiner's tools – planes, chisels, vices, jars of lacquer and carpenter's glue. The jars all had labels of the same colour and written in Russian.

Judy had lain with her eyes open for some time already. Dim strips of light came from the window, which was covered with a thick curtain. She had no idea where she was. How long had she lain there on that hard, knobbly bed? One day? Or was it two or more? She had a vague recollection of someone lifting and carrying her a long way, someone breathing unpleasantly in her ear and changing her clothes ... But all of it had happened through a fog. Her main sensation was that of having a blinding headache. And then there had been people all around her. They had talked and shouted in alarm about something or other. Had she also actually shouted and sobbed, and pushed people's hands away? And she had been fed with a spoon. But one particular person had irritated her and she was horrified by his presence. But now there was nobody there ...

Throwing back the blanket, Judy sat up on the bed. She was wearing somebody else's flannelette dressing gown and had socks on her feet. Her head still ached, but now it was bearable. Oh Lord! They had shaved her head bare! And the whole of her skull was stuck with strips of plaster! What was all this? ... Oh, yes! She had gone head first through the windscreen of a car! Evidently they'd tried to suture her injured skull. Thank the Lord, it was still intact! ... But now she was bald! How dreadful!

She lowered her feet to the cold wooden floor and sat there looking around the little room in search of a mirror. But there was none. Slowly she got to her feet and took a few steps towards the dark door in the corner. Silently she turned the handle, and then screwed up her eyes as they were met by streams of blinding sunlight.

In front of her was another small room that evidently served as both dining- and living-room combined. In the centre was a large square table covered with a clean, light-coloured cloth. Around it were several wooden chairs. Above the table hung an orange lampshade with a fringe. A crockery cupboard by the wall stood as high as the ceiling, and set out in it were cut-glass goblets, coloured salad bowls and a brightly decorated tea service. There were several small cupboards with embroidered covers, trinkets and artificial flowers on them; there was a large valve radio with a record player standing on broadly splayed legs, a bookcase with books in it, a settee and a rug attached to the wall with a pattern of flowers and swans. Above the settee in a simple wooden frame behind glass were four rows of black and white army photographs – three pictures to a row. Judy had already seen one of them above Alexey's bed in his room at the Mytishchi hostel. It showed seven Soviet soldiers holding sub-machine guns and posing on the back of an armoured troop carrier. She recognised one of them as Alexey, only in this photo he was much younger. The other pictures showed the same group of seven, photographed against a background of tall snowcapped mountains, at a roadside halt, at dinner, on the troop carrier again, and so forth.

Underneath the photographs on the settee someone was asleep with his head covered by a heavy quilt.

Still dizzy and slightly unsteady on her feet, Judy slowly made her way around the room. There was no mirror here either. She stopped and looked at the sleeping form, trying to tell from the outline whether it was a man or a woman. Still uncertain, she went and looked through the kitchen door. There was nobody there. In a corner by the window was a wash-stand and an iron bucket beneath it. Next to it were various barrels and a sack of potatoes. On the wall were shelves with saucepans, and beneath them a homemade kitchen table with a cast-iron frying pan covered by a lid. Opposite was a large Russian brick stove in which blazing logs crackled cheerily. By the outside door was a pile of fresh smelling fir and birch logs. Here, hanging by the door, Judy found what she was looking for – a small dull mirror.

She looked at herself carefully. Good grief, what a sight! Her whole skull was stuck about with ribbons of dirty plaster, and between them short bristles of new hair were growing in tussocks. It was worse than the worst punk hair-do! And her face: her cheek bones stuck out, and because she was so bald or so thin her eyes seemed enormous, like the pictures she had seen of prisoners at Auschwitz.

Judy turned away with a sigh. She went to the kitchen table and lifted the lid off the frying pan. In it lay a single cutlet. It was cold and had a fringe of white fat around it. Gingerly she picked it up and bit off a piece. Pulling back the chintz curtain, she looked out of the window and saw a snow-covered yard with ready-cut firewood carefully stacked in even rows along the fence. Snowy whiteness stretched right to the horizon and dazzled her eyes to the point of tears. And over in the far distance, on the edge of the skyline, a train was trundling, barely visible, like a dotted line, and an engine whistle shrilled....

'Well? Pulling round, are you?' a voice said behind her.

Alexey stood smiling in the kitchen doorway. He had on a T-shirt and black shorts that reached down to his knees. Tattooed on his left shoulder were some numerals. Unembarrassed, he kept scratching his chest and ribs which had two dangling strips of plaster and several recent scars.

Judy shuddered in surprise at his appearance. She dropped the cutlet on the floor and was about to stoop to pick it up, when a stabbing pain in her head made her cry out.

'Don't make any sharp movements, silly!' Alexey came closer and she could smell the heavy reek of alcohol on his breath. 'Feel like a snackeroo?'

'A what?' she asked, not understanding.

'Do you want something to eat? Are you hungry?'

'Yes.'

'Go through to the other room and I'll bring something.' He began searching among the shelves and pans and evidently knew his way around.

A few moments later he turned up with a hunk of bread and sausage. Judy was sitting at the table. She looked in surprise at the green rind on the sausage and would not eat it. She chewed feebly, though, at the stale bread.

'If you've an appetite, it means you're on the road to recovery,' said Alexey confidently. 'But why have you left the sausage? Don't you like it? Eat, it's a rarity around here!'

'It's gone off!'

'Where?' Alexey didn't believe her and turned the sausage over in his hand. 'It's perfectly okay. Don't you want it?' She shook her head, whereupon he stuffed the whole piece into his own mouth. His cheeks were crammed and his eyes narrowed.

Judy gave a wan smile.

'Where are we?'

Alexey muttered something with his mouth full.

'Where?' Judy repeated.

'At my pal's,' he said again when he had finished

chewing. 'At my old army friend's. We served together in Afghanistan. This is his house. He bought it with his earnings out there. You'll see how he did it. But you're obviously a good strong girl! Well done! At one point I didn't think you were going to pull through. You just lay there in a coma, out cold. I didn't know what to do. But look how Liza's managed to stick your head up! Better than any doctor, although's she's actually only a dairy-farm milkmaid. Liza is the wife of my pal Nikolay. Right?'

Judy nodded. She studied Alexey carefully. He was thin and bony, and his broad shoulders had not seen the sun for a good long time. His dark, slightly screwed up eyes looked open and honest, but his lips often curled in an unpleasant smile. No, there was absolutely nothing to recall the noble pedigree of his well-groomed great-aunt. Only his tall stature, and his hands with their long slender fingers perhaps betrayed more refined origins. But heavens, the state of his nails, and the colour of his skin! . . .

'Were you injured as well?'

'Only a bit. I crushed my ribs against the steering wheel. But it's healing up.' He began peeling off a plaster.

'Was it you who fed me from a spoon?'

'Of course! Who else could it have been, do you think? Can you remember anything?'

'And who bathed me? Was that you too?'

'Yes . . .' A slight blush came to his cheeks. He stood up awkwardly and went out to the kitchen but peered back into the room a few seconds later. 'But you needn't get any ideas . . . Liza helped me! And later you asked to bath yourself . . .'

'Thank you,' Judy said quietly. She too was now embarrassed.

He came back into the room and placed a steaming bowl of soup before her.

'Eat this. You need to build up your strength. It's no joke only drinking water for five days!'

'How many?!' she asked, horrified.

'What's today's date? The ninth? You can work it out for yourself – it was Wednesday when the two of us had our bump.' He disappeared to the kitchen and returned with another plate for himself. 'And today is Monday. What you need, of course, is some chicken broth – only there isn't a single hen in the whole village! This is a collective farm! So you'd better get this cabbage soup down you at least. Liza made it. It's wonderful!'

Judy gazed stolidly into her plate. Five days! Where was Tanya meanwhile? And Elizabeth? What had happened to them? Had they been arrested?

'Where is there a phone here?'

'What do you want a phone for?' Alexey looked up from his soup in surprise.

'I need to ring Tanya, your aunt.'

'What, again?! Not so fast! You've already rung once! Don't you remember?'

'No!' Judy snapped insistently. 'I must ring her! Where's there a phone?'

'There isn't any phone here.'

'Well, at the neighbours' then. Where can you ring here?'

'Nowhere. The neighbours don't have one either. We're out in the country here. This isn't America!'

'How do they manage?'

'Just like that. And what's more, my dear, *you*'ll have to manage like this as well from now on. You may as well get used to it.'

'No!' She felt like shouting, but hadn't the strength. Instead of a shout, all that came out was a faint squeak. 'I won't live here! Nobody's going to force me to!'

'Of course not. Nobody's going to force you!' Alexey smiled. 'You'll stay here of your own accord.' And he bent over his plate again as though nothing was amiss and began eating his soup.

'Where are my clothes?' By leaning against the table, Judy managed to get to her feet.

'So you've started, have you?! . . .' Alexey wiped his lips

with a hand and was obviously displeased. 'Aren't you fed up of constantly kicking and rebelling? I'll tell you one last time: just sit quiet and stay where you are! And thank the Lord that you're still alive. I carried you six kilometres in my arms until a lorry stopped and picked us up. And if you want to volunteer now for a spell in the jug, just carrying on making a song and dance! But I'm washing my hands of you! I've had to swallow enough shit in the army to last me a lifetime.'

'Nobody's asking you to. You can sit your time out on the North Pole for all I care! Where are my clothes?' It took all Judy's strength to remain on her feet and prevent herself from falling. Her head began to ache intolerably again, her legs trembled, and she felt she was about to faint at any moment.

'Listen to what I am saying.' He suddenly adopted a different, almost pleading tone. 'Don't go away anywhere. The two of us will go to Siberia. I'll get us some documents. You'll be able to find a job, and you'll see, you'll like it there. Don't go and ruin your life. You'd not last a couple of months in a Soviet jail. It'd finish you!'

'No,' said Judy quietly. 'I must go back to Moscow. I shall explain everything to them . . .'

'Either you're a idiot, or else you're pretending to be one!' Alexey fumed and even rose from his seat. 'You surely don't think that after killing two KGB officers you'll be allowed to go back to America?!'

'Where are my clothes?' Judy repeated insistently. 'I haven't killed anyone . . .'

Alexey stopped and looked at her in silence. An expression of surprise and pity passed briefly over his face.

'Why the hell did I bother dragging you all that way?' he said at last. 'I should have left you, and you'd simply have died there in the snow without ever coming round.' But suddenly his anger boiled up again. 'So you want to go? All right, go! Here's your stuff!'

He scornfully chucked over to her a neatly tied bundle lying by the settee, then went out into the kitchen, slamming the door behind him so hard that it set the crockery in the cupboard tinkling.

Judy dragged the bundle of clothes over to her small cupboard-cum-bedroom. There she sat down on the bed and felt the last strength drain from her. Having got her own way, she realised that in fact she was incapable of taking even a few steps, let alone getting to Moscow. But how could she possibly stay on in this country? What madness was this?! And if Alexey was right about no one believing she had not helped murder the KGB officers, would she then go to prison?

She curled up on the bed. No, she mustn't think about prison! It was all a lie! She hadn't killed anyone! She was an American citizen! Or at least let them send her to an American prison. There she might get some help from her mother ... At the very thought of her, Judy burst into tears. What a fool she had been to agree to this trip, to this crazy adventure!

A door slammed again in the next room. Someone came over to her room, stood outside for a moment and then went away again. For a time there was the sound of nervous pacing up and down, then everything was silent.

He's probably gone to sleep again, she thought with disgust. And her anger boosted her strength again. She sat up on the bed, pulled the bundle towards her and slowly began getting out her things. Everything, including her underwear and the worn cotton jacket she got from Maryuta in exchange for her own, had been laundered and neatly ironed.

When she was dressed and emerged again, she saw that Alexey was indeed lying on the settee. He had his trousers on now, and he was not asleep but lay there staring up at the ceiling. Judy walked past him and into the kitchen to the outside door. It was locked. She tugged at the handle and also tried giving it a feeble shove with her shoulder.

'Open the door,' she said.

Alexey neither answered nor stirred.

'Do you hear? Open the door!' She leaned weakly

against the wall beams.

Alexey still did not come.

Gasping with a mixture of anger and weakness, Judy went back into the living room. There Alexey lay, his bare arms comfortably propped behind his head. She went over and looked at him, full of hatred. At the sight of his self-satisfied smile she grasped him by the shirt and wrenched him upwards with the last of her stength.

'Get up, you pig! Open the door for me!'

Alexey sprang from the settee with a single movement, stood up in front of her and grabbed her painfully by the shoulders, breathing straight into her face: 'One more move out of you, you bitch, and I'll finish you off myself! Better me than the KGB! Have you got that?! Right now, go back to your room and be quiet!'

'Swine! Scum! ...' She spat out her small supply of Russian expletives. 'You're just afraid for your own skin!'

'Yes, I am. I'm afraid all right! Afraid for my life!' He was still squeezing her shoulders in his grip.

'I knew you were! I knew it!' she said triumphantly. She felt like laughing in his face, but no longer had the strength to do so. All she could do was speak very quietly, with long pauses between phrases. 'It's all up with you ... They'll put you in prison! ... Scum! You're just afraid for yourself!'

'Shut up, you American idiot! One more word out of you, and I'll not answer for what I do!'

'What? What will you do? ... Do what you did to them? Kill me with your belt round my neck? Well, come on then! Come on, big hero!'

Alexey thrust her away. He did not push hard, but Judy was so weak that she immediately collapsed on the floor. The awful pain in her head made her cry out.

'Have you hurt yourself?' He bent over her in fear. 'Where did you hit yourself?' he asked.

She looked in surprise at his pallid features. Just a second ago they were twisted in fury, but now they were contorted with fear. With Alexey supporting her, Judy carefully picked herself up and without a word made her way back to her room. She collapsed face down on the bed and pressed her lips together in order not to burst out crying. But she could control herself no more and burst into tears.

Alexey came into the room quietly. He stood there for a while, then sat down next to her on the bed.

'There, there, that's enough crying.' His voice had a guilty ring, but Judy wept even louder. 'I didn't mean to,' he said. 'Forgive me ... But please try and understand: I really want to do what's best. You're wrong if you think I'm worried about myself. I don't care about myself. I've not done that for too long now. After Afghanistan my life hasn't been worth a halfpenny! I don't even want to go on living: after that you feel such a swine. You feel like turning your Kalashnikov on yourself! Human beings are worms! They crawl about even though they know they're not worthy of it. But I've no regrets about finishing those two KGB men off. For scum like that we were made to wipe out whole villages in Afghanistan – women, children and old folk! We didn't choose to do it. And you wonder how people can do things like that? Well, if you'd been forced every day to export Communism to other nations on the front of a tank, you'd be capable even of doing the sort of things we did! ...'

Judy slowly turned over onto her back and looked at Alexey intently. She even thought she saw tears running down his unshaven cheeks – but it was dark in the room, and she could have been mistaken.

'Do you want something to drink?' He suddenly livened up.

'What is there?'

'I have a quarter litre,' he said. 'Vodka.' He looked at her more closely, and his eyes twinkled.

'No, thanks.'

'Maybe it's just as well. If you have anything to drink now, it'll put you on your back again! But maybe I'll have a small drop ...' He got up quickly and went out. He returned with a small 250-gram bottle and sat down again on the floor next to Judy. He tore off the cap with his teeth, then raised the bottle and said: 'Here's to you! Good health, as they say, and the rest we'll buy! ... Even though we haven't got a sou! ...' He quickly raised the bottle to his open mouth and threw back his head.

There was an unsavoury smell of vodka and the sound of swigging and gurgling. Judy turned her face away as Alexey drank. Then there was a short silence.

'Are we far from Moscow?' she asked quietly.

'Eighty kilometres. Why?'

'Alexey, please try and understand: I can't stay with you.' She turned to face him and tears started to her eyes again. 'I want to go home,' she whimpered.

'Glory be! But what are we to do? You're not going to get home just by heading back to Moscow! They'll not let you out! Believe me!' He nervously ruffled his already tousled hair. 'Two of those shits have been done in! And who's going to believe it when you say you never laid a finger on them?! And even if I give myself up and come with you and own up to it, they'll say that you bribed me to do it, and that I'm simply trying to shield you ...'

'What am I to do then?' Judy burst into tears. She realised Alexey was not making all this up. 'All right then, let me go to prison. But they'll be obliged to send me to an American prison, and not keep me in one of yours!'

'What do you have for brains? Wood shavings?' Alexey said. There was no longer any malice in his voice, but even a trace of affection. 'Or do you really not understand anything about life here? "Obliged" indeed! They are not *obliged* to do anything! And they make up their laws to suit themselves!'

'Then what can we do? What can we do?!' Judy kept wailing mindlessly, her hands pressed to her temples. Her head felt hot, her eyelids were getting heavier, and the blood seemed to race through the nape of her neck. She felt she was fainting again ...

'Calm down, calm down! There's always a way out!'

He covered her carefully with the blanket. 'The main thing is for you to rest and not fidget around. I'll think of something. There's never been a time yet when they've had Alyosha Odalevsky pinned against the wall! But you sleep. You have a sleep!'

She never heard his last words. Sleep, exhaustion and apathy carried her into oblivion.

12

'Ladies and gentlemen,' said Oleg formally, 'Allow me to introduce to you Colonel Anatoly Ivanovich Anisimov of State Security. Nina Alexandrovna Katunova you've already met. Please do sit down.'

Tanya quickly went over to an armchair and settled into it. Ralph Stone from the American Embassy smiled genially. He undid a button on his jacket and adjusted the waistcoat covering his small paunch. His chair creaked slightly as he sat down next to Tanya.

'Mrs Goehr, we have invited you here in order to put some questions to you,' Colonel Anisimov began in a heavy bass. He was slightly over fifty, and might possibly have been described as handsome. He had a large head, lightly-coloured eyes with dark lashes, a straight nose and sharply chiselled mouth. His broad chin was slightly skewed and his hair was greying at the temples . . .

Katunova sat to one side of his desk, holding herself erect, like a good pupil. She had on the same severe suit as before, but today she wore her wavy hair higher, and her face looked younger and fresher thanks to her more carefully applied make-up.

In an effort to calm her racing pulse, Tanya quietly took several deep breaths and looked about her. So here she was at KGB headquarters! How simple it all was, and how unremarkable! They were in a half-empty, well lit room with large windows giving one a clear view of the Dzerzhinsky monument. Around the walls were several simple wooden chairs, and a glass-fronted bookcase with some heavy volumes of Lenin's collected works. And of course, inevitably, Lenin's features were also present in the form of a small bust standing on the cupboard. It looked as if it were carved out of soap; probably it was plaster though ...

'Mrs Goehr, on what date did you arrive in this country?' Anisimov asked drily.

'On the 4th of March.'

'Can you give us some more details about your acquaintance with this other tourist Dzhudi Sanderrs?' the Colonel said, stumbling slightly over Judy's name as he passed a hand through his smooth dark hair.

'There's nothing to tell you. We got to know one another in the plane on the way to Moscow.'

'Why did you go to Mytishchi on the first morning after your arrival?'

'Because the grandson of my brother lives there. I wanted to see him.'

'Did you know that foreigners are not allowed beyond the bounds of Moscow without special permission?' Anisimov seemed highly interested in Tanya's hands and his glance several times wandered back to them – or more precisely, to the rings she wore on her right hand.

'I didn't realise it was beyond the bounds of Moscow. I was in too much of a hurry. It was our only day in Moscow when there weren't any other excursions planned. It's only fifteen minutes there on the subway ...' Tanya realised it was a feeble excuse, but she could offer no better one.

To give the Colonel his due, he was well-mannered, unhurried, and he used his lovely deep voice with theatrical flair.

'And why did you take Sanders out with you to Mytishchi?' he asked benignly, and again stared at Tanya's hands.

Tanya said nothing. What could she say that would not have harmed Judy?

The Colonel interpreted her silence in his own way and

gave a laugh. Once again Tanya was surprised to note how different the KGB was from her preconceptions. Here she was, confronted not by an ugly, cruel monster, but by a tired yet supremely competent official who was simply forced to do his duty ...

'There's no point is saying nothing, Mrs Goehr.' Something in his tone suggested he was even discreetly attempting to help her. 'You were seen together with Judy Sanders in the station restaurant, and from there you went to the workers' hostel to look for Odalevsky. But why did you take this Judy there with you?'

'Well, she's studying Russian at university, and she was just interested to see something of how ordinary Russians live. And when I told her I was going to visit my grand-nephew, she asked if she could come along. I don't see any crime in that!' Tanya fired back.

Colonel Anisimov disregarded her last remark.

'And so you found Odalevsky at the hostel. What did you talk to him about? We'd like to know in detail.'

(Why is he so interested in my hands, Tanya wondered? Is it because he never looks people in the eye? ... Or ... is it my rings?! Lord, what was he asking me about?! All right, Judy and I were seen together at the station restaurant – there's no getting away from that, apparently. But there were no witnesses to our conversation with Alexey, and it's unlikely that anyone was eavesdropping.)

'Well' Tanya answered, 'It was a private conversation about family matters. Apart from which, it didn't last very long. But if you like ... Well, to be honest, we didn't have time to get acquainted before Alexey disappeared ...'

'Disappeared?!' Anisimov queried, obviously intrigued, and he thereby confirmed to Tanya that no one had overheard their conversation in the hostel. (That means they can't know anything. So the important thing now is not to blab it out by accident!)

'Yes,' she confirmed, now quite confident. 'He said he needed to go to the bathroom. He went out and that was it. We sat and waited in his room for about an hour, and then we left. Has something happened to him?'

'So you're claiming that you took Sanders with you to Mytishchi without any special purpose in mind?' Anisimov asked.

'Yes, absolutely! That's right!'

'Hmmmm ...' the Colonel said, with evident disappointment. 'I do hope, Mrs Goehr, that you realise that making false statements can have very serious consequences for you! You see, we know everything ...'

'Well, if you know everything, then why waste time asking me? ...' Tanya stopped suddenly, scared at her own gratuitous flash of annoyance. 'Pardon me, but we've been sorting this out for a whole week now with Madame ... I mean, Comrade Katunova! So why waste any more time? Yours, mine or Mr Stone's? ...'

Ralph Stone stirred next to her.

'Mrs Goehr,' he said, 'you and I are guests here. You don't need to worry about my time. The important thing for all of us is to establish the truth. Am I right, Comrade Colonel?'

Tanya gasped slightly at such open betrayal. Ever since his first appearance at her hotel room, this over-amiable Ralph Stone and his stupid prattle had done nothing but irritate her. He was incapable of finding anything out; he talked of the whole business with a certain disdain; and he was much too casual as he sat there with one leg crossed over the other and fondling his own ankles. Even a kindly soul like Elizabeth disliked having him there, even in the middle distance. And now he had revealed himself in his true colours! Tanya realised in horror that she would now have to fight a lone battle. There was no point in expecting any help from this empty-headed embassy official ...

'Mrs Goehr,' Colonel Anisimov began again, apparently ignoring the American's twittering remark, 'Mrs Goehr, were you aware that on the same evening Sanders went out to Mytishchi again to see your Odalevsky?'

'No, I didn't realise that.'

'But why then did she come and see you in your room immediately before setting out for Mytishchi?' the colonel insisted.

How awful, Tanya thought. What sort of man was this? What went on behind the cold façade and sonorous voice? Did he have any feelings at all? Or did he even talk with his children and grand-children in this artificially eloquent manner?

'As I've told Miss Katunova already, Judy Sanders just dropped in to say hello. She came for a chat, and to say she wasn't going to the theatre,' Tanya muttered irritably, cursing herself that she could not collect her thoughts better. She felt she might explode at any second, yet that was precisely what she must avoid doing.

'And who was it who rang you at seventeen minutes past midnight after you'd returned from the theatre?' Anisimov inquired again.

'I do not know. In that hotel the phone keeps going all the time. And it's always some girls or young men wanting to get to know you. All the tourists in our group have been laughing about it ...'

Anisimov moved back slightly from his desk, opened a drawer and produced a small tape-recorder which he placed on top of his papers. He pressed the button. There was a quiet hissing, and then Tanya recognised her own voice:

'Hallo?'

'Hi! It's me....' Judy's voice gabbled loudly. Then Tanya again: 'You have got the wrong number! There is no such person here, and I would advise you not to try ringing here again!' Then followed a series of rapid pips.

Anisimov pressed the stop button and looked up at Tanya expectantly.

'And as Oleg Petrov confirms,' Katunova intervened suddenly, 'that is the voice of Judy Sanders. So why is it you refused to speak with her?'

'But I never realised that? That sounds to me more like the voice of the impudent young hussy who'd already rung five or six times prior to that!' Tanya insisted.

'That's a lie!' Katunova barked. 'You realised immediately who it was! And you therefore cut the conversation short and warned her not to try ringing again and not to come back to the hotel! Oleg Petrov was in your room at the time! And as I've told you more than once, Mrs Goehr, your unwillingness to help the investigation is aggravating your position, which is already very serious!'

Tanya now turned to the American embassy official.

'Mr Stone, I must protest at the unwarranted threats this woman is making. She's already caused me to have one turn! I'm asking you to protect me from this assault! And if you don't ... I'll be forced to protect myself as best I can. I don't want to bring this weird affair to the attention of people in Washington, but if you leave me with no alternative....'

'Please, don't get excited, Mrs Goehr! Don't get excited!' Stone gave a fastidious frown and recrossed one leg over another. 'I'm quite sure that Miss Katunova has no grounds for intimidating you. But, ladies and gentlemen, please don't let's fall out over this! People at my embassy are extremely worried by the disappearance of Judy Sanders, who is an American citizen. And so if you can be of assistance, Mrs Goehr, please do tell us all that you know!'

Tanya could read the irritation on his face. He clearly saw her merely as an obstinate, uncooperative old woman – and he made only a poor effort to conceal the fact. The effect of this was to stoke her fury even more.

'I've already told you – and not for the first time either!' She turned away from him. 'Throughout the whole of this week they've been driving me crazy with the same old questions over and over again. But I don't know anything! *I do not know*! I'd like to know myself where my grand-nephew is! And where's that poor girl disappeared to? And what's going on? Why should I know more about their disappearance than the local authorities do?!'

'There's no need to carry on like this!' Anisimov shook

his large grey-templed head and looked reproachful. 'You know, we're not a bunch of schoolchildren here. And even to a child it must be clear that you are mixed up somehow in their disappearance.'

'Excuse me, Comrade Colonel,' Ralph Stone intervened, still wearing his genial smile. 'But if you do have any real evidence of Mrs Goehr's involvement in some crime, it would greatly help me to know about it – as a representative of the American government ... You understand?'

Tanya could hardly believe her ears. Had this thick-headed American official decided to try and protect her after all?! Maybe he was cautious in doing so, and he still had that idiotic smile, but it did now appear as if he could talk like a man!

'We'll get round to the evidence, Mr Stone! We'll get round to that. One piece you've heard already. Moreover, Petrov is not the only one to confirm that the voice is that of Miss Judy Sanders. Mrs Stern, who shares a room with Miss Sanders, also recognised her voice immediately.' Anisimov rummaged among the papers on his desk searching for a particular sheet. When he had retrieved it, he carefully smoothed it with the flat of his hand. 'You see,' he went on, 'we are not just investigating the curious disappearance of an American citizen called Judy Sanders, but something much more serious!'

He opened a fat green document file, found the page he wanted and, holding it in front of him, began to read unhurriedly:

> '... On March 5th of this year at 3.15 a.m. on Ostashkovsky Highway, at a distance of 18 metres from the traffic lane, a police patrol car crew discovered an overturned black Volga saloon, registration number MGK 25-77, belonging to the USSR State Security Committee. The windscreen of the vehicle was smashed, the left-hand door was heavily dented; the bumper, radiator and engine were damaged by an

impact, and there were bloodstains on the bonnet. On arrival at the scene, an investigation team from the All-Union Criminal Investigation Department of the USSR Ministry of Internal Affairs and an operation group of the KGB established the following: the Volga saloon, registration mark MGK 25-77, had on that day been used by KGB captain Igor Karpov and KGB Lieutenant Stanislav Koval.

On March 4th at 9.45 p.m. in the town of Mytishchi, Moscow Region, at the apartment of Maria Vovchuk, a waitress at the Mytishchi 'Station' restaurant, Karpov and Koval had discovered one Alexey Odalevsky, suspected of treason against the state, and one Judy Sanders, who claimed to be an American tourist. At 10.20 Lieutenant Pashkov, duty officer at the National Hotel, received a telephone call from Koval and confirmed to him that American citizen Judy Sanders was residing in the Rossiya Hotel; her physical features established from her passport corresponded with those of the person detained. At 10.35 p.m. Karpov and Koval left the apartment of Maria Vovchuk and, taking Odalevsky and Sanders (both of whom were detained) with them, set off back to Moscow in Volga saloon number MGK 25-77. This is further confirmed by the fingerprints of all four persons on the cabin of the Volga that sustained the accident. In addition to the above, on the floor of the car, by the right-hand front seat, traces of vomit were discovered. Analysts have established the presence of alcohol in these traces. However, no sign of the four passengers was discovered at the scene of the accident ...'

(Good Lord! thought Tanya as she listened to this drily factual militia report. What is all this 'suspected of treason against the state'? What has Alexey done? And what about the bloodstains and vomit? ...)

Anisimov paused and looked up at Tanya's strained features. Then he looked down again at the paper.

'But that is only the modest beginning, so to speak. Here is how it continues. And I think Mrs Goehr will be forced to admit that she has not been totally honest in answering our questions.'

Anisimov ran his eyes over the text and resumed reading:

> '. . . In view of the exceptional character of the incident – the disappearance of two KGB officers, an American citizen and Alexey Odalevsky (employee of the "Red October" factory in Mytishchi, who is suspected of treason against the state) a special search and investigation team was set up by the USSR Ministry of Internal Affairs and State Security Committee. All militia and highway patrol teams in Moscow and the Moscow Region have been put on alert.
>
> At 7.25 a.m. a report came through from Mytishchi that sixteen kilometres down the Yaroslavl Highway, at a distance of fourteen metres from the traffic lane, the cadavers of KGB Captain Karpov and Lieutenant Koval were discovered by building workers on a construction site for a new vegetable storage depot. A team consisting of criminal investigator I.P. Shchapov and medical expert N.N. Kisina established that Koval was strangled with either a broad belt or scarf, and that Karpov was killed by a blow with some heavy object to the parietal bone of the skull. The two officers' personal weapons – two Mark TT pistols – had been stolen. On the roadway at the same spot, traces of Karpov's blood were found together with frozen particles of vomit, analogous in chemical content to those found in the car. Furthermore, in Captain Karpov's pocket, a diary was found belonging, as it says inside the cover, to Miss Judy Sanders, 481, 180th Street, New York City, New York 10033 . . .'

Anisimov fell into a meaningful silence. For a few moments all was quiet in the room.

'As you can see, the affair has taken on a criminal character,' said the Colonel, leaning back in his chair.

'But forgive me, I don't quite understand what this has to do with Mrs Goehr!' said Stone in perplexity, as he stared down at the tips of his pointed shoes. 'How can she be of help to you? And where in any case has Judy Sanders disappeared to?'

'You don't understand? All right, then I will explain,' replied the colonel, picking up the piece of paper again and reading the conclusion of the report:

> 'After analysing the above-mentioned facts, the investigation team came to the following conclusion: on March 4th at some time between 10.35 and 11.00 p.m., sixteen kilometres along the Yaroslavl Highway between Moscow and Mytishchi, one of the suspects under arrest, either Odalevsky or Sanders, simulating a sudden attack of vomiting, asked for the car to pull up. During the stop the two prisoners Odalevsky and Sanders strangled Koval, murdered Karpov, hid their corpses on the nearby building-site, stole their pistols and drove off in police Volga registration number MGK 25-77.
>
> At 00.17, after the murders and while in possession of the car, Sanders telephoned Tatyana Goehr, maiden name Odalevskaya, at the Hotel Rossiya. Warned by Mrs Goehr of the fact that it would be dangerous for them to appear at the hotel, Sanders and Odalevsky left Moscow along the Ostashkovsky Highway, where they were involved in an accident. They abandoned the car and disappeared. (Signed: Officer in charge of the combined investigation team, senior investigator of the KGB Operative Division, KGB Major Nezvansky.)'

Anisimov put the sheet of paper to one side. He pensively arched his wrists, locked his fingers together and cracked them loudly.

'Well, how about that, Mrs Goehr? Shall we talk?'

'What do you mean?' asked Tanya quietly. She had already realised that this colonel with the good looks of an actor had something else ready up his sleeve, something that would break her for good and all.

'You know perfectly well what I mean!' he said sharply and turned to look at Stone. 'It is all very simple, Mr Stone. On March 4th your citizen Mrs Goehr, maiden name Tatyana Stepanovna Odalevskaya, arrives in our country. The purpose of her journey, as she claims, was quite innocent – to see her former homeland and to make the acquaintance of her brother's grandson, Alexey Odalevsky. "By chance" a young girl called Judy Sanders turns up on the same holiday, also a citizen of yours. On the very first day, pleading indisposition, Mrs Goehr excuses herself from the museum visit and secretly heads off to Mytishchi to meet her brother's grandson. Indisposition had nothing to do with it. She simply knew very well that she was committing an illegal act. The claim that she, the former Muscovite Princess Odalevskaya, did not know the location of Mytishchi is just laughable. At the same time, again "by chance", she takes Judy Sanders along with her. And once they are in Mytishchi things begin that are not "by chance" at all! But it would be best if I read you one more document.'

Anisimov quickly found the right page and began to read, making a fairly good job of imitating the female intonation and colloquial speech of the Mytishchi waitress Maryuta Vovchuk.

'... On Saturday, March 4th at about eight o'clock in the evening someone knocks at the door of my flat. Now I was already relaxing after work, I'd got undressed, I mean, and Alexey was also there. I was surprised at the knock, because I wasn't expecting anyone. She struck me as odd right away, speaking with an accent, and although she was dressed quite simply, all the same there was something not quite right about her. She asks for Alexey. I let her in, and then rush into the toilet to get dressed. She starts chatting to Alexey in the room. When I come out to join them, I look and see that Alexey isn't himself, he's angry. Then he says to me: stay out of the room for a bit, Maria, he says, I need to talk to her. Well, if he must, he must. I went off into the kitchen. But from there I could hear everything. Especially as, a week before this happened, when Alexey was having the plaster taken off his arm in the hospital, two comrades from the KGB had come to see me and asked me to keep an eye on him to stop him doing any more injury to himself. Half of Mytishchi knows that he visits me at home, so what was there to hide! Well, so I was keeping an eye on him, as they had said. I can hear this girl, she introduces herself as Zhenya, saying something in a whisper. So softly that even Alexey shouts at her: speak louder. Well, then she says that she has arrived together with Alexey's grandma from New York so as to take him to America. Get married to me, she says, and I'll take you away with me. Your grandma's got a load of money, she says, and it'll all be yours. Well, I thought right away that there was something wrong here, so I rushed to ring the number that these KGB comrades left with me . . .'

Anisimov stopped to take a breath. Katunova and Petrov did the same, as if ordered to, clearing their throats loudly and changing position on their chairs. The colonel stood and began to pace unhurriedly up and down the room. His round-toed black shoes squeaked loudly, and each step revealed the red woollen socks beneath the wide trousers of his uniform. The Colonel was obviously pleased with his thespian achievements, with the way in which he had mimicked the voice of the Mytishchi waitress.

'Well, there you are,' he said at last. 'And when this bride and groom, if one may call them that, were arrested, they killed the KGB officers, made off with their car and then disappeared. Meanwhile, Mrs Goehr warned the murderers over the phone not to appear at the hotel, as she was herself already under observation by Comrade Petrov.'

The colonel sat down at the desk and looked attentively at Stone. 'And now you may ask your questions ...'

Stone was blinking helplessly, wondering what line he should take now.

'But, I swear to you, I was absolutely against her going to Mytishchi,' said Tanya, unable to contain herself.

'Aha, so you did know after all that she was intending to go there?' said Anisimov, coming to life. 'Well, no matter. Carry on.'

Katunova also showed signs of animation, sitting up in her chair.

'Yes, I did know!' said Tanya. 'Or rather, I found out about it when she had already gone! ...'

'Where did she go from?' asked the Colonel, his bright eyes fixed on Tanya, scouring her distraught-looking face and her pale lips, and moving down to her hands folded on her knees.

'She ... she came to my room and said that I mustn't despair because Alexey had run away from us. That we must visit him once again. But I refused, I didn't want to visit him again! It was she ... It was she herself who decided to visit him once more!'

'But *why* did she decide to go? He is your relative, after all?! And you and she only got to know each other on the plane – according to what you have told us!'

'She ... I don't know! I don't know anything! But I was against it!'

'Ah, but *I* know,' said the Colonel softly. 'Because you are not the first to come to us with this "original" idea of removing a relative to the West by means of a fictitious marriage. You didn't get to know Judy Sanders in the plane, as you claim, but you recruited her in your own country, the United States of America! Am I telling the truth, Mrs Odalevskaya-Goehr? Answer me!'

But Tanya said nothing, pressing the palms of her hands to her ears.

'How much did you promise her for this operation?' he went on. 'Well? Are you going to say nothing?' Anisimov leaned his whole body forward, planting his elbows on the table, without taking his bright eyes off Tanya for a second. 'I don't know why he ran away from you at the first meeting, this grand-nephew of yours – he isn't your grandson, of course, only your grand-nephew – but I can easily imagine why this girl went back to visit him again! Because without her fictitious marriage to Alexey Odalevsky, you wouldn't have paid her what you had promised!'

'That's a lie!' screamed Tanya.

'It's the truth!' said Anisimov triumphantly. 'And this is the crux of the whole business. This shows, if you like, the fundamental difference between your country and ours! You can do anything you like for money – hire a murderer, buy a child or find some poor girl and drag her into international intrigue!'

'I don't think we should make generalisations like that,' said Stone with a condescending smile. 'Certain things can be bought for money in your country, too . . .'

'But not murder! Not murder!' replied the Colonel, drumming his knuckles several times on the table. 'So, Mrs Odalevskaya-Goehr, do you admit that you brought this Judy Sanders along with you with the express intention of marrying her to your relative, Alexey Odalevsky? Or do you, a former princess, lack the courage to speak the truth?!'

Silence descended on the room. Tanya slowly lowered her arms.

'Yes, I brought Judy with me so as to marry her off to my grand-nephew. It's true.'

'Well, there you are, Princess,' said Anisimov, letting out a deep breath. 'You see how everything immediately feels easier for you.'

Tanya even believed for a moment that he felt sorry for her. But, intercepting the self-satisfied look that the Colonel darted at Katunova and Petrov, she realised she was wrong. And she lowered her eyes helplessly.

'Comrade Colonel!' drawled Stone with a smile. 'I still cannot see what Mrs Goehr is supposed to have done wrong! Is it a crime to marry off a grandchild? That's all any parent wishes to do – to see their son or daughter happy. And Mrs Goehr, as far as I know, has no other living relatives. Only this grand-nephew of hers. Her wish was natural, not criminal!'

Tanya looked at Stone in amazement. 'What a great guy!' she thought. 'Quite right! And I had lost all my drive! I was already prepared to go meekly to prison. And for what? I haven't committed any crime! I must pull myself together. And fight to the very end!'

'That's your opinion,' snapped Anisimov angrily. 'And there *is* a crime. Two representatives of the authorities have been murdered. Both of them have children . . .'

'But Mrs Goehr was not present at the murders!' Stone insisted doggedly. He had the look of someone spending his time enjoyably in congenial company. 'You are surely not intending to prove that she was instrumental in these murders?!'

'No, technically she was not there! But she was directing the operation. She brought the murderer, this Judy Sanders, into our country. And she gave her the order by telephone!' Anisimov was no longer able to control himself and was banging the palm of his hand on the table, as if pronouncing sentence on someone. 'And for this she will have to answer before our courts of law!'

'And answer I shall!' interjected Tanya with a sudden show of temper. 'Answer I shall! Yes, I wanted to get my grand-nephew married to a nice girl! I am a lonely old woman. I wanted my only grandchild to share my final days with me. There's no crime in that! No court in the world will be able to condemn me!'

'But why did you not do this openly?' asked the Colonel. 'Why did you want to do it secretly, like a thief? And he, as far as we know, had not the slightest intention of sharing your final days with you! He didn't even reply to your letters! We're well aware of that as well! But you decided to take him to the West by force, yes, *by force*! And to do this you sent Judy Sanders to see him once again!'

'Listen! This is too stupid!' said Tanya. 'Yes, I brought her here to get married to my grand-nephew,' she went on. (By now she was sitting upright again, her hands intertwined and placed confidently on her knee.) 'But what has force got to do with it? She isn't Rambo, you know! She is a nice girl, and I should have been happy if she and Alexey really had fallen in love with one another. By the way, in the good old days parents always used to arrange matches for their children, there was nothing shameful about it. I thought that if I were to come myself and introduce him to a nice girl, then he could have the choice whether he came back with us or not. I am a well-off person. I have four hotels in Florida and some savings in the bank. My husband and I earned the money through hard work and honest labour. And I considered it right that it should all be passed on to Alexey. I had nobody else left! And to suggest that I intended to carry him off by force is just laughable! How can you remove someone by force from *your* country? I am not a naive young girl, you know!'

'Oh no, you are certainly not a naive young girl,' replied Anisimov. 'Naive young girls do not hire fictitious wives for their grand-nephews. Nor do they send them secretly into areas that are off-limits to foreigners. But then I don't want to be taken for a fool either and have people tell me sob-stories about reunions with their favourite grandsons! Tell me, Mr Stone, how would you have acted if some Russian tourist had come to you in America and, straight after meeting her, her grandson had killed two members of the CIA and then disappeared? Would you have let the tourist go back to Russia? I am certain you wouldn't!'

'Our laws are somewhat different, you know,' said Stone. 'People are allowed to leave our country without having to enter into fictitious marriages . . .'

'Pure propaganda!' said Anisimov, cutting him short.

'In our country this, in your country that! ... *We* have facts! And you just have *words*! This is a much more serious matter than simply the desire of a lonely old woman to carry off her only relation! A murder has been committed, and for us that is the point of departure! Being an accessory to murder is punishable by law in our country. In short, I have put you in the picture and I am now informing you that in the very near future I shall be handing the results of our investigation over to the USSR Chief Prosecutor's office. Pending the prosecutor's decision and possibly the trial, Mrs Tatyana Goehr will forfeit the right of departure from the USSR. That is all for today. I'm sorry but I have other business to attend to! Petrov, stay here for a moment. And you, too, Lieutenant Katunova.'

'Comrade Colonel!' said Stone, getting up from his seat. 'Why all this haste? You must realise yourself that this will cause certain diplomatic complications, so to speak ...'

'I can't help that! It won't be the first time. The law is the law, I'm sorry. Goodbye.'

With a shrug of the shoulders, Stone headed towards the door. Tanya, losing all her fire at one stroke, stayed sitting quite shaken in the armchair. Then she quickly got up and went after Stone. As she walked past the Colonel's desk, she caught the intent glance which he deliberately darted at her from beneath his lowered brows ...

13

Tanya spent the next three days collapsed in her hotel room, relentlessly dragging at cigarettes and downing one cup of coffee after another. Nobody disturbed her apart from Elizabeth, nobody summoned her anywhere, and even Oleg Petrov, always so attentive before, now showed absolutely no interest in why she didn't come downstairs even to have something to eat in the restaurant. On the other hand, Elizabeth exasperated her with her attentions and wild schemes for resisting what she called 'barbaric Soviet despotism'.

'I won't go anywhere without you!' she declared. 'If they won't let the two of us go home together, then I shall stay here and go on hunger strike! And that's not all. I shall go out onto Red Square with a placard. I shall send telegrams to Gorbachev, Reagan and to the United Nations!'

This would begin in the morning, and then Elizabeth would bring her some breakfast, which Tanya would force herself to eat – if only to escape the reproaches of her importunate friend. After that Elizabeth would disappear – most probably to visit Stone at the American Embassy. But Stone would be unable to say anything to cheer her up. 'The KGB reckon on catching Alexey and Judy any day now, and then all will become clear ...' Elizabeth would return to the hotel, purse-lipped, more determined than ever and with yet another new plan of campaign.

'You and I must visit Sakharov!' she announced. 'You explain everything to him in Russian, and he'll understand. And Gorbachev listens to him – he even releases political prisoners at his request!'

On the fourth day, when only twenty-four hours were left until the departure of their holiday group, Tanya was no longer seized with panic and fear, but by the melancholy of complete despair. If the KGB were to arrest Alexey and Judy, nothing would become clear at all. Things would simply become more complicated and confused.

'What do you think?' asked Elizabeth. 'Does Gorbachev's wife have any influence on her husband? Let's try asking for a meeting with her ...'

'Leave me alone, Elizabeth! Go on an excursion or something! Tomorrow is the last day, and you haven't even seen Moscow.'

'But why ... why do you always drive me away when you feel bad? I want to help you after all!'

'I'm sorry, but here you are quite powerless. Tomorrow you will have to leave, but I will be obliged to stay and die in my native land. When it comes down to it, I suppose, it's better than being buried somewhere in Florida ...'

'Don't be so stupid!'

There was a loud knock at the door of their room. The two friends exchanged glances. Elizabeth got to her feet and walked out of the bedroom.

'Hello, Mrs Wollens,' (Tanya could hear Oleg Petrov's voice). 'May I see Mrs Goehr?'

'She is resting,' replied Elizabeth coldly.

'But it's very important. I would like to have a word with her before the excursion.'

'She won't be going. She doesn't feel well ...'

Tanya got up from the bed and rushed into the sitting-room.

'It doesn't matter, my dear. I can speak to Oleg if it is important.' She appeared in the door of the bedroom looked at Oleg. 'Sit down. I am listening ...'

'If it's possible, then ...' He stopped speaking and glanced from one woman to another. 'I'm sorry, Mrs

Wollens, but I must speak with Mrs Goehr alone. Do excuse me . . .'

'Elizabeth, leave us alone, please. Go down to the foyer for a bit. All the others are assembling there for the excursion . . .'

When the door closed behind the offended Mrs Wollens, Oleg sat down in an armchair and looked silently at Tanya, obviously wondering how to begin.

'What is it then, Oleg?' asked Tanya, coming to his aid. 'Do you have new proof of the fact that I was directing the murders? I have never heard anything more absurd in my life!'

'Well, it's not quite so absurd . . .' he drawled pensively. 'You can't even begin to imagine how serious it all is. And dangerous, too, for you.'

'Oleg! Don't try to pull the wool over my eyes!' said Tanya, becoming angry. 'Tell me what you have been sent for!'

Oleg shook his head disapprovingly.

'First of all, nobody has sent me. Secondly, it seems to me that you have, as they say, chosen the fundamentally wrong tactic . . .'

'If you have come here to try and make me confess to an appalling murder, then you are simply wasting your time!' she said, interrupting him.

'There, you see! I haven't said anything yet, but you are already on the boil. That isn't the way to do it,' said Oleg mildly. 'Sit down. *Sit down*! And, please, do try to understand that I am your friend. I have come to help you and not to get into an argument with you about trifles!'

'You? *You* – my friend?' said Tanya in amazement. All the same, she sat down on the settee. 'Somehow I hadn't noticed it before!'

Oleg moved his armchair nearer to the settee and, after a few moments' silence, said quietly:

'I hope that everything I am going to say to you will remain within these four walls . . .'

'Oleg, I am eighty-three years of age and have no need of such warnings!'

'Yes, yes, I know ... and, out of respect for your years, we thought, or rather, I thought that ...' He stopped short.

'You mean that there's a possibility of a defence?' prompted Tanya.

'No,' he replied firmly. 'There is no possibility of any defence at all! You came to take a traitor out of the country and have got mixed up in a murder. How and to what extent is another question. But circumstances are against you! But there is a faint – don't get me wrong: only a faint – hope, but a hope all the same that ...'

He fell silent again, pensively rubbing the bridge of his nose.

'Oleg, don't torture me! I am an old woman. My heart won't be able to take it. *What* hope? Why do you keep on beating about the bush? I understand perfectly that you are just an ordinary pawn in this game. So just tell me why they have sent you here.'

'No!' said Oleg, interrupting her indignantly. 'You're getting everything the wrong way round again! There are no pawns or kings in this game! It's simply that, if the case gets as far as the courts, then the whole thing – solicitors, barristers, legal costs – will set you back an enormous amount of money. And who knows whether it will be of any use? Personally I very much doubt it. In the whole of our legal history there has not yet been a court which has found in favour of a foreign defendant. But, on the other hand, people are the same here as they are anywhere else. And if you are dealing with a person who understands you, then everything can be sorted out quickly and with the minimum of fuss! Without taking things as far as the court and the public prosecutor's office. You are a wealthy individual ... All I ask is that you think carefully before you give your reply!'

Oleg stopped talking, casting his eyes round the room meaningfully.

They wanted money! My God, now she understood all

their idiotic threats! After all, it was so obvious: first drive her into a corner until, out of fear, she was fighting for breath and unable to think straight, and then – demand money! Yes, in the end they were no different from street thieves! . . .

Her first impulse was to burst out laughing in Oleg's face. But she managed to restrain herself and simply continued to stare her new-found friend in the eye. And she saw there a bottomless well of unruffled calm and cynicism.

'Please tell Colonel Anisimov that I have given serious thought to all the accusations levelled against me. And I am willing to cooperate with the investigator at any time convenient to you.'

'Well, there you are, my dear,' said Oleg with some animation. 'That way it will be a lot easier for all concerned.'

Tanya produced a note-pad from her little table and wrote on it in bold letters: 'How much?'

Oleg took a pen from his inside pocket and wrote down '50,000'.

Tanya stared at him in amazement, but said nothing, and quickly wrote: 'Can I draw money on an American cheque in a Moscow bank?'

'No,' he replied with a shake of his head.

'Where can I get money like that in Moscow then?' she wrote.

Oleg stared at her thoughtfully, then transferred his gaze to her fingers before looking her in the eye again and writing:

'Your rings will cover this sum.'

Tanya could see the Colonel's eyes before her, studying her hands. She was choking with indignation. What? Her rings, her and her husband's family jewels which were priceless, would be worn by some KGB colonel's lousy wife! Villains! Scum! . . . But did she have any other choice?

'And shall I be able to fly off tomorrow with the rest of the group?' she wrote, after a pause.

He gave her a nod.

'And how can you guarantee that nobody will detain me at the airport?'

'I will accompany you as far as the steps onto the plane, and there you will give me the rings. But no tricks, because we can hold up the plane's departure ...'

Oleg gave Tanya a meaningful stare.

Tanya twisted the pencil thoughtfully between her fingers, came to a decision and then leaned down towards the writing-pad.

'And what will happen to Alexey and Judy?'

Oleg looked at her carefully and then said in his normal voice:

'Do you know where they are?'

'No,' said Tanya quickly, startled to see the cruel expression which his face had assumed.

'Then don't think about them! They have Article 93 of the Criminal Code waiting for them – premeditated murder with aggravating circumstances. I have heard that even in America people are condemned to death for murdering a police officer, let alone here ...'

Tanya looked at him in horror.

'But do you ... Do you think they'll find them?'

'I don't doubt it,' he said harshly. 'The militia have been alerted right across the country.'

'And what does that mean?' Tanya hissed through her lips.

'That means,' said Oleg as he got to his feet, 'that their photographs will be displayed right across the country. They won't be able to hide for long.'

'But I ... I would like to ... help them somehow, if they should be found. With money ...'

Oleg gave her another searching look, said nothing for a while, but then again asked point-blank:

'Do you know where they are hiding?'

'No, but I thought if it's possible for me, then perhaps ...'

'No, for them it is *im*possible! The best thing that you

can do for them is leave the country as quickly as you can!'

He looked at his watch.

'It's time to go on the excursion! Will you be coming with us?'

He walked to the door.

'I don't know. What is it today?' asked Tanya limply.

'The Moscow Underground. We're going to look at a few stations. Let's go. I think this will be your last visit to Moscow. Why lose a whole day?'

Oleg suddenly came back into the room, picked up the writing-pad, tore out the sheet on which they had been corresponding and set fire to it with his lighter.

14

The metro station Mayakovskaya was softly illuminated by fluorescent lights set in circular niches in the ceiling. A group of American tourists was standing on the platform, admiring the station architecture – its lightness and harmony, the successful combination of geometrical figures on the marble squares of the light-coloured floor with the graceful upward soaring curves of the many steel arches.

The Muscovites rushing past them towards the train cast envious sidelong glances at the exhausted foreigners, some of them slowing down their pace, staring at them with genuine interest and then hurrying on their way. It was about five o'clock in the evening, and the Moscow rush-hour was about to begin...

'Well? Now can you tell me what Oleg was talking to you about?' said Elizabeth, grasping Tanya tightly by the elbow as if afraid that she would run away.

'Nothing in particular. I've already told you that everything is all right! Tomorrow we will be flying home. Me, too.' Tanya was doing her best to smile in an attempt to reassure her friend. There could be no question of telling Elizabeth of the deal she had made with the KGB.

'What's happened then?' asked Elizabeth in horror. 'Have they *found* them?'

'Fortunately not!' The words burst from her lips. 'But that doesn't alter anything,' she quickly added in a more cheerful tone of voice. 'Tomorrow we shall be flying home.'

'And what about Judy?' asked Elizabeth. 'And why have they suddenly decided to let you go?'

Tanya said nothing.

'I know!' said Elizabeth suddenly. 'They're tricking you! They're not going to let you go anywhere, but they want the rest of us to leave without kicking up a fuss. They'll sit us all down in the plane, and then they'll hold you up at the last moment, saying that you've got drugs in your suitcase, or something. Do you understand me? I've seen it on television – that's how they act!'

Tanya gave a sigh.

'Elizabeth, don't talk nonsense ...'

'Vladimir Vladimirovich Mayakovsky!' uttered Oleg triumphantly as he led the whole group towards a tall, bright-coloured statue of the poet in the depths of the station concourse. 'The great Soviet poet! This metro station and the square above it are named in his honour. He was the first poet to sing the praises of the October Revolution ...'

Yes, Tanya could remember this coarse, quarrelsome Futurist poet. At the end of 1918, as a young girl of fifteen, she had even attended a Futurists' evening at the Polytechnical Museum. The tall, young, handsome Mayakovsky was rocking the auditorium with his voice and his frenzied poetry. 'Who with their right is marching? Left foot first now! Left, left!' he seemed to be commanding the whole world with the thunderous Voice of Revolution. Later, at the end of the 1920s, he was in Paris at the same time as Tanya, already in the role of acclaimed Soviet poet and, as she read, had written in one of his poems: 'Oh, to live and die in such a place as Paris! But the homeland that is Moscow still exists!' Then, within a couple of years of returning to Moscow, he blew his brains out. The Russian émigré newspapers wrote that the critics had hounded Mayakovsky, more or less at the behest of Stalin himself, and then that Stalin had posthumously called Mayakovsky the 'best and most talented poet of the epoch'. People said that this was one of Stalin's favourite ploys – he did the same thing to Gorky, Kirov, Ordzhonikidze ...

And now here he was, standing before her – Vladimir Mayakovsky, young, no more than twenty-five years old – almost as she had seen him in 1918, in fact. God, how fickle fate was! This posturing dare-devil of a Futurist who walked around Moscow dressed in a foppish yellow jacket, had become history, a literary classic, and she, that same young girl, who had listened to him spellbound nearly seventy years before, was now standing in front of his memorial! ...

'I'd tear
like a wolf
at bureaucracy.
For mandates
my respect's but the slightest.
To the devil himself
I'd chuck
without mercy
every red-taped paper.
But this ...
I pull out
of my wide trouser-pockets
a priceless cargo's
Bill of Lading.
You now:
read this
and envy,
I'm a citizen
of the Soviet Socialist Union!'

Oleg was declaiming Mayakovsky's celebrated poem, translated into every language in the world. The woman from Chicago, with her eyes closed, swayed gently from side to side in time to the harsh rhythm. One of the tourists was smiling, another quietly tapped his foot. And within distance of the group those very same Soviet people, about whom the poet wrote with such pride, were charging the doors of the underground train, shoving and trampling each other. When Oleg had finished reciting poetry, the Americans began to clap loudly, which caused some surprise and even alarm amongst the Russians scurrying past.

'Our next stop is the Belorussia station,' Oleg announced. 'You must please follow me. Everyone keep together, and don't go off in different directions. It's now the rush hour in Moscow, and you might get pushed about. Although, in general, ours is a hospitable people. Just be careful!'

And then in a loud voice, audible almost across the whole length of the platform, he shouted out in Russian: 'Comrades! Let the foreign tourists through! I appeal to you!'

And the crowd actually did give way a little, moving to either side. The Americans, feeling slightly embarrassed, eyes lowered and mumbling 'Thank you' in all directions, made their way to the edge of the platform through the ranks of sullen, hostile and even suspicious faces and glances. But the doors of the next train had only to open for the whole group of American tourists to be heavily pushed from behind by the enormous crush of Russians. And the Americans, crumpled and squeezed, were simply swept, hurled into the carriage. Someone stumbled, another cried out as his foot was trampled on, one gave a forced smile: 'Just like back home in the good old New York subway! ...'

The solid wave of human bodies forced Tanya and Elizabeth into the train as well and then pushed them apart. Someone rammed against Tanya's shoulder. Hearing no words of apology, she angrily eyed the tall young man dressed in a short, dark overcoat, his hat over his eyebrows and a knitted scarf half covering his face. His eyes flashed insolently. Tanya quickly turned away before she uttered some rude remark. The train moved off. People stood silently, a look of concentration on their faces, pressed up against one another. They smelt of sweat, garlic, cheap eau de Cologne – and their clothes gave off an odour of petrol and turpentine. But it was difficult to condemn them for it – their faces bore the marks of tiredness, the burden of their lives, their arms were weighed down with heavy bags containing potatoes, cucumbers, bread. Tanya looked around for Elizabeth. She was standing not very far away. But as Tanya tried to move towards her, she could suddenly feel that that same lad who had shoved in front of her was blocking her way and not allowing her to move. Tanya raised her eyes in astonishment.

The young man, holding on to the rail with both hands and not looking at Tanya, said quietly almost into her ear: 'Don't move!'

Tanya froze inwardly. What did this mean? Had the KGB sent this man to keep watch on her? But why? After all, she had promised to give them money! Perhaps they had decided to get rid of her after all, to have her killed in a crowd at the hands of some criminal? She looked at the man with fear, fervently trying to think of what to do.

'I have been watching out for you for the past two days. What, don't you recognise me?' he said quietly and lowered his scarf slightly, revealing his face for a moment. Tanya glimpsed a familiar straight nose, thin lips creased in a mocking smile . . .

'It's you . . .' she stammered in alarm, as she recognised Alexey. 'But where's . . . where's Judy?'

She looked about her instinctively.

'No,' said Alexey, with a grin. 'She's a long way away, don't worry.'

'But why . . . why did you kill them?' she whispered almost soundlessly, through her lips.

'There was no other way out. And it was me . . . just me. She had nothing to do with it!'

Tanya shuddered. A feeling of pity rose in her throat.

'Alyosha . . .' was all she could get out. 'But what are you going to do? They'll find you! You must get away!'

He nodded, leaned down towards her ear and said in a quiet voice: 'Can you be in Pakistan in a month's time?'

'Whe-ere?' she said, recoiling from him in amazement. The train was entering the station.

'Let us through! All the American tourists out, please!' announced Oleg's voice loudly to the whole carriage. And then he added in Russian, 'Comrades! Please allow the American tourists to get out!'

'Don't go far,' Tanya whispered to Alexey quickly. 'We need to talk.'

He nodded his head in agreement and moved off behind the American tourists toward the exit. Tanya got off the train and immediately seized Elizabeth by the elbow.

Unlike Mayakovskaya, the concourse of the Belorussia station was executed not in 'style moderne', but with carved ceilings and high reliefs depicting scenes from Belorussian rural life. Oleg was leading his group through the crowd of passengers towards an enormous sculpture of a woman with a sheaf of either plaster or bronze corn in her arms. He was saying as he walked: 'The overall length of the Moscow Metro is 180 kilometres ...'

'Don't scream, and don't look shocked,' ordered Tanya, as she took Elizabeth firmly by the hand. 'I have just been talking to Alexey. Just now, in the carriage ...'

Feeling that Elizabeth, even so, was starting with surprise, she squeezed her elbow even harder: 'Keep quiet! Don't turn your head! We must think of some excuse for getting away from the guided tour! I must talk to him!'

Ahead of them Oleg's voice was intoning:

'The Moscow Metro was opened on May 15th, 1935. The first line was 11.6 kilometres long and was constructed in the record time of three and a half years.'

'Oleg!' Elizabeth's voice suddenly interrupted him loudly. 'I don't feel well ...' The crush has affected me! I always feel unwell when I'm underground. And I have left my tablets in the hotel.' Elizabeth was breathing heavily, pronouncing her words with difficulty.

Tanya was filled with admiration as she followed the transformation of the ever honest and principled Elizabeth into a consummate actress.

'Perhaps I should get into a taxi with her and take her back to the hotel?' said Tanya, embracing Elizabeth solicitously and turning her eyes assiduously away from Oleg who had run up. 'My dear, can you make it as far as a taxi?'

The tourists suddenly leapt into action. Someone ran up, grabbed Elizabeth's hand and began to measure her pulse. One of the women started rooting around in her handbag which doubtless contained every possible drug for every conceivable occasion.

'What is it you take? What is it you take?' she kept on saying insistently to Elizabeth. 'I have got . . .'

'I can't remember . . . I can't remember. In the hotel I've got . . .' Elizabeth mumbled half-fainting, as it seemed, leaning on Tanya with her whole weight.

'I hope you won't object if I take her back to the hotel?' Tanya said to Oleg.

'I'll get a doctor right away. We have doctors in the metro . . .'

'No, no,' protested Elizabeth. 'I won't take Russian medicine! Under no circumstances! I've got my own in the hotel . . .'

'All right, all right. Go back to the hotel. Only I'll make sure you get a seat in a taxi!'

'Thank you,' said Tanya, noticing with amazement that Elizabeth, who was leaning on her, was becoming heavier and heavier. What if her impressionable friend had really been taken ill!

'Ladies and gentlemen,' said Oleg to the group of tourists who had fallen silent. 'I'll just leave you for a moment. Please don't go wandering off! I'll just put these ladies into a taxi, and then I'll be back!'

He took Elizabeth by her other arm and the three of them made their way towards the escalator.

By facing Elizabeth on the same step, Tanya could keep a close eye on who else was coming onto the escalator. Glimpsing at last the tall figure of Alexey, she gave a sigh of relief.

As soon as they stepped out of the metro, the biting, frosty wind made even Oleg wince in his sheepskin coat. The people running past them in the opposite direction dived into the metro. There was a gloomy queue of freezing people waiting at the taxi rank, and no taxis.

'We'll go back indoors,' Tanya said to Oleg. 'When you get a taxi, give us a call. Otherwise she'll have a complete collapse!'

Oleg nodded and went over to the head of the queue to explain that he needed a taxi urgently for a sick American woman. But to judge from the faces of the people standing in the queue, it wasn't obvious that they would be willing to give way for him . . .

When she went back into the metro, Tanya looked around carefully for Alexey. He was standing near to a row of telephone booths. Tanya left Elizabeth and hurried over to him.

'We'll be going by taxi to the hotel in a moment,' she said, talking to him from behind. 'You stand here and I'll come back for you.'

'No, your guide will probably take the taxi driver's number and check up where you went to. Go to the hotel and then after a quarter of an hour or so, walk along to the Central Telegraph Office. Do you know where it is?'

'Yes,' said Tanya. As she turned away from him, she bumped into Elizabeth.

'Why did you come over to us?' whispered Tanya angrily. 'Are you out of your mind? It's enough that I am in danger, let alone you! . . . Let's go, quickly. Oleg is already on his way back . . .'

The taxi driver had probably been alerted about something because he darted a quick, interested look at them and, without a word, started up the car and moved off.

Skirting the monument to Gorky, the taxi drove out onto Gorky Street and joined the flow of cars slowly descending the road. The yardmen were loudly at work, removing snow from the windows. From a small transistor radio lying on the back seat came the breathless patter of a hockey match commentator. Outside the car windows you could see tired, sullen-looking Muscovites hurrying away from work, huddling in queues at the food shops. Here and there in the roadway people would appear with raised arms, probably trying to catch a taxi. People were milling around at the trolleybus stops, and as soon as one arrived, they would all rush towards the door at once, forgetting about the queue . . .

'Tell me!' said Elizabeth, pressing up close to Tanya and whispering in her ear. 'Where is Judy?'

'I don't know,' came the reply. 'Somewhere or other . . .'

Tanya was keeping a very careful eye on the corpulent taxi-driver dressed in high fur cap with ear-flaps.

'But she can't stay in Russia for ever!' said Elizabeth with loud indignation, forgetting all caution,.

The driver looked at them carefully in his mirror.

'Do you speak English?' Tanya said in English, deciding to check.

'What? Me? . . . I do not understand . . .' he said, for some reason mangling the Russian words. And then, after a few moments' silence, he added quietly to himself: 'The swine! He said they spoke Russian!'

Tanya decided not to correct the taxi driver's 'good' opinion of Oleg and only smiled at him.

'What did he say?' asked Elizabeth. 'Can he speak English?'

'He says not. But who can be sure?'

'No, we absolutely must think of something!' said Elizabeth, beginning her furious whispering again. Then suddenly she sat up straight. 'I know! They must escape abroad!'

Tanya looked at her in astonishment. It seemed that

Alexey was more suited to being Elizabeth's grandson than hers, since they both appeared to have equally crazy ideas.

'Yes, they must flee abroad!' Elizabeth continued confidently. 'Cross the frontier in secret! I've read about it in a book. It is possible.' And she pressed her hands excitedly to her breast. Tanya could not stand this melodramatic gesture which always indicated extreme excitement on the part of her friend, often turning into tears.

'In the book, of course, everything took place in East Germany,' she went on, 'But that doesn't matter. I am convinced that it is possible to escape from Russia as well. From a ship, or something ...'

'From what ship?!' asked Tanya in despair. 'Who would allow them to get onto a ship?'

But the next moment something in Alexey and Elizabeth's craziness made her heart beat faster. Alyosha would certainly not have risked simply hanging about in the centre of town for two days to meet her. He probably had a plan ... Ah, but that would be fantastic! But how could she help him?

'How much Soviet money do we have left?' she asked feverishly.

'About three hundred roubles, I think,' Elizabeth replied.

'No, that's not enough,' said Tanya with disappointment. Then she suddenly ordered the driver in Russian. 'Stop! We've arrived.'

Indeed they were drawing up to the Hotel Rossiya.

15

Tanya had already walked up and down past the Central Telegraph Office four times, waiting for Alexey to appear. The wind had died down, but it was still unbearably cold. The tall thermometer on the other side of Gorky Street was showing −19° Celsius. The people walking past cast astonished looks at Tanya: fancy not wearing a hat in such freezing weather! She was cursing herself for forgetting to put on a shawl. Her ears were frozen and in general she felt a conspicuous oddity amongst these Muscovites wrapped up so carefully in their overcoats and synthetic fur hats.

At last, she caught sight of the familiar tall figure. Alexey was walking towards her, his head wrapped in a scarf and slightly lowered. All that was visible was a pair of tensely flashing dark eyes.

He drew level with her and walked on by. Tanya, with her heart beating madly, stopped at the entrance to the pedestrian subway running under Gorky Street and, unable to contain herself, looked round. Alexey was nowhere to be seen. 'They're probably following me!' Tanya said to herself in terror. And yet she had tried to be so careful! She had dashed out of the hotel when there were a lot of people about – all the tourists were coming back for dinner after their various excursions. And when she had been walking up Gorky Street, she had kept a continuous check to make sure she wasn't being tailed. And when she reached the Telegraph Office ... In dismay she went with the rest of the crowd down into the subway, up the steps on the other side and then came to a halt, uncertain what to do next. Someone bumped into her, another shouted, not unkindly, 'Have you gone to sleep, or something? Keep going!' Tanya realised that she was impeding the crowd movement and stepped over towards the window of a gift shop. She peered vacantly at the old fashioned handbags, umbrellas and gloves displayed in it . . .

Next to her in the window Alexey's reflection appeared.

'Follow me,' he said softly.

'Wait a minute,' said Tanya, She wanted to take him by the arm, but she stopped. 'Are we being followed?'

'No, I've checked.'

'Where is there a jeweller's shop around here? The nearest?'

'A couple of blocks away. Why?'

'Take me there!'

'What for?' said Alexey in amazement.

'I'll explain later. Let's go! It's already seven o'clock.'

'But I wanted to say to you . . . I have a plan . . .'

'Fleeing across the border?' she interrupted him impatiently. 'I know. So let's go. Well, come on. I'm following you . . .'

Alexey gave a puzzled shrug and began walking up Gorky Street. Tanya waited a few moments and then set off after him.

After a quarter of an hour's rapid walk through Arts Theatre Lane and Pushkin Street, filled to overflowing with people and cars, Alexey brought her out onto Stoleshnikov Lane which she had known as a child, full now, as then, with shop signs of the most varied kind – from a second-hand fur shop to a patisserie and the big jeweller's shop 'Agate'. But as they approached the shop, Tanya could see a large sign saying 'Closed' on the door, although behind the glass a light was on in the shop's long, narrow premises. Inside, behind the counter, two young female shop assistants were having a lively conversation, putting on fur boots and fur hats. Standing by the door was a shortish old man, already dressed in a dark overcoat with an astrakhan collar. Having lowered the ear-flaps of his fur hat, he was impatiently trying to tie the cords under his chin.

Tanya knocked firmly on the glass door. The old man turned around and gave her a quizzical look. Tanya made signs to him to open the door. Opening it a little, the old man poked through his large aquiline nose which was obviously Semitic.

'Are you a jeweller?' Tanya asked quickly.

'What if I am?' he said with a typically Jewish intonation.

'I want to sell something.'

'The shop is shut. Come back tomorrow.'

He was about to shut the door, but Tanya placed her foot in the crack.

'I can't tomorrow,' she said, staring beseechingly at the old man. 'Who would buy these rings from me?'

Tanya hurriedly removed one glove and stretched her hand towards the old man. He darted a quick glance at the rings and raised his eyes to look at Tanya.

'Who are you?' he said with a different and obviously worried intonation.

'I am ... Why do you need to know? I am ...'

Tanya was on the point of inventing some surname, but she stopped short in fright. Behind the old man there had appeared the corpulent figure of a militiaman dressed in a dark sheepskin coat.

'What's the matter, comrade?' he said in a deep voice. 'Don't hold people up. The shop is already closed.'

'She's come to see me, Vasya,' said the old man all of a sudden, and he opened the door wide and beckoned Tanya inside. 'Come on in.'

Tanya looked around in confusion. Alexey was standing on the other side of the road pretending to be looking at the patisserie window. But reflected in the window were the doors of 'Agate'. Tanya turned back and entered the shop decisively.

After the cold of the street, it seemed to her that she had stepped into a Turkish bath-house. In the long room with counters stretching along the right-hand side it was stuffy and hot. Unbuttoning his overcoat and taking off his fur hat as he went, the old man walked back the length of the shop to a glass booth enclosed on three sides, entered it and sat down. Above the glass hatch was a sign saying 'PURCHASE OF GOLD FROM THE POPULATION'. Tanya went up to the hatch.

'Show them to me,' said the old man, placing a small, black-framed magnifying glass over his left eye.

Tanya, looking anxiously towards the militiaman who had remained by the door, began to take off her rings. At last she passed one over to the old man.

'But that's not the only one. I want to sell this one, and this one ...' And, straining at her fingers, she began to remove all the rings she was wearing.

The old man slowly took one ring after another and, raising them to his eye, examined each of them for a long time through his magnifying glass. Then he dropped the lens into the palm of his hand and looked up at Tanya calmly.

'How much do you need?' he asked tonelessly.

'I want to tell you that this ring here is a very old piece,' said Tanya hurriedly. 'It was made by ...'

'Yury Polyakov who at one time used to work under Fabergé,' said the old man, continuing for her. 'Another similar ring with a Persian sapphire was made by him at the same time for the Tsarina. That one was better, but it was confiscated and is now to be found in the Kremlin, in the Palace of Facets. But this one ... this one used to belong to the Princess Odalevskaya ...'

The old man momentarily stopped for breath and gave Tanya another long, hard look.

'Who are you? How did you come by these rings?'

'I am ... What difference does it make who I am? Are you able to buy it or not?'

Tanya looked at the militiaman once again.

'But this one ...' said the old man, taking one of the rings, 'this one is already much later. It was made by the celebrated Kharkov jeweller, Isaak Kopelevich, and as far as I remember, he made it for the bride of the Kharkov millionaire, Nikolay Goehr in ... Yes, in 1890 it was. He even set in these small diamonds as figures. But you can only see it through a magnifying glass. God, what geniuses they were!'

His face suddenly creased as if her were about to burst into tears, but instead of this his narrow mouth widened, and Tanya could see to her amazement that he was smiling.

'Why do you want to sell them?' he said. 'Why do you want paper instead of these eternal things ...?'

'They'll be taken away from me in any case,' said Tanya, unable to contain herself.

The old man looked at her once again and nodded his head in understanding.

'How much do you need?' he asked quickly.

'How much might they be worth? I haven't the faintest idea!'

'I am asking you how much you *need*. As for these things. They are like the souls of the long departed ... They are priceless. How much?'

'One hundred thousand!' Tanya gasped out.

The old man turned round towards a small metal safe and opened it, without a word.

'See you tomorrow, Boris Izrailovich,' one of the girls shouted loudly from the depths of the shop. The other one gave a wave of the hand and they both left the shop. The militiaman waddled over to the door and closed it.

'Count it,' said the old man, taking out of the safe some thick packets of bank-notes wrapped round with paper bands and placing them on the counter.

Tanya's eyes moved confusedly from the growing heap of money, to her rings, and back again. Only now did the reality hit her that she was about to lose for ever these possessions that were so dear to her heart and from which she had never been parted, even during the most difficult times. She looked at her fingers with their pale stripes instead of rings, and angrily clenched them into a fist.

'Do you have a bag of some kind?' she asked in a harsh voice, trying to get rid of the lump that had formed in her throat.

The old man rummaged around under the counter and gave her a cloth shopping bag.

Tanya, without counting, began throwing the packets of money quickly into the bag, while the old man carried on removing yet more piles of bank notes from the safe, all tied around with narrow paper bands.

At last he stopped and shut the almost empty safe. He looked as Tanya angrily thrust the packets into the bag, and then asked in a quiet voice:

'Tell me, are you Odalevskaya?'

Tanya raised her face. In the old man's eyes she could read genuine compassion.

'Yes, I am the Princess Odalevskaya!' she replied defiantly.

'I knew as much,' said the old man sorrowfully. 'That's why I didn't ask to see your passport.'

'And why should you have needed to see that?' asked Tanya in surprise.

'It's the rules. Yes, I guessed it was you. And people used to say that you had gone abroad,' he went on, thoughtfully chewing at his lips. 'That means that they were wrong. *You* are here, too ...'

His words seemed to contain such a sorrowful undertow that Tanya could not stop herself shouting out: 'No, no! It *is* true! We really did leave. But I have come back here as a tourist ...'

Tanya shoved the last bundle of notes into the bag and suddenly straightened up, as if she had been electrocuted. 'And who ... and who will you sell the rings to?'

'To no one,' replied the old man, pursing his lips. I have bought them for myself. Tomorrow I shall return the shop its money ...'

Tanya felt like going up to this shambling, eagle-nosed old man and kissing him.

'Thank you!' was all she could say.

When she went out onto the street, she caught sight of Alexey. Standing as he had been earlier on the other side of the road, he was obviously freezing to death, even though he was wrapped up in an overcoat, fur hat and warm scarf. Tanya went up to him and said softly:

'Now we need to find a warm, cosy spot.'

Alexey stole a rapid glance at her and at the shopping bag but, saying nothing, set off quickly down the street. At an entrance to one of the buildings, he stopped and looked round – to check whether Tanya could see him, and then he quickly opened the door into the block of flats and went inside. Tanya waited for a few moments and then, after carefully examining the people walking by, ducked into the same doorway.

In the entrance hall a tiny electric light was burning, dimly illuminating a broad marble staircase with a massive wooden bannister. There was a smell of boiled cabbage and mould. The sounds of a child playing on the piano were coming down from above. Alexey was standing in the middle of the first flight of stairs and, with his back leaning against the bannister, was waiting for Tanya. As soon as she entered, he began to climb on up. Fortunately for Tanya, the building only had two storeys, and as soon as they had reached the top landing they stopped.

'This is for you,' said Tanya when she had recovered her breath. And she started taking the bundles of bank notes out of the bag.

'For me? But why?' he said in amazement.

'Well, you are intending to escape across the border, aren't you?' she replied. 'It's to help you bribe the border guards.'

'Bribe the border guards?!' he said with his twisted smile. 'There's no way you can bribe *them*, what are you talking about?'

'Oh, yes you can. If a KGB colonel suggests a way for me to bribe my way out of prison, then ... They can *all* be bought! All you need do is discover how, when and what with! Here, take this. It's only part of your inheritance. There's fifty thousand roubles for you here.'

'*How* much?' exclaimed Alexey in disbelief.

'But I *can't* let you have any more!' she said, not understanding the meaning of his cry. 'I'll have to give the rest in order to get out of this place myself! But thank God for one thing. Because of you I thought of the idea of selling my rings, so at least no KGB creature will get to wear them now! Well, what are you standing there for? Hide the money!'

Alexey obediently undid the buttons of his overcoat, lifted up the bottom of his sweater and began stuffing away the bundles of money underneath this shirt. Tanya feverishly helped him to cram some of the packets up his back. But when he had lowered his sweater again and buttoned up his overcoat, his stomach and back looked unnaturally swollen.

'It won't work,' said Tanya firmly. 'Take your shirt right off. You'll have to wrap them in that.'

Alexey silently threw off his coat, sweater, shirt – and the piles of money scattered all over the floor. Tanya looked pitifully at his thin, naked shoulders. 'Nothing but skin and bone!' she said to herself, remembering her nanny's favourite expression about thin children.

'Alexey!' she said in a trembling voice as she watched him pulling on the rest of his clothes again. 'My God! What's that mark you've got on your back?"'

On his back Alexey had a large deep scar almost the length of his spine.

'Oh, it's nothing at all!' he said, brushing her remark aside and quickly pulling his sweater on over his naked body. 'It's from the wound I got. It was probably one of your shells that got me, I expect. An American one ...'

'And on your shoulder? What sort of tattoo is that? Have you been in jail?'

'Not yet,' he grinned. 'That's my blood group and Rhesus factor ... Everybody who is sent to Afghanistan gets one of these tattoos ...'

'Alyosha,' said Tanya, with a sigh. 'Don't you worry about spending the money, please, either on yourself, or on Judy. And especially not on the border guards. But how were you intending to get into Pakistan without any money?'

'I can't tell you that, I'm sorry,' he said, squatting down and wrapping the money up in his shirt. 'Well, it's just that I've got a friend ... or rather, we were in the army together. He may not be a border guard, but as for money ... well, he likes it too. So it'll come in handy.'

'Alyosha, do look after Judy, I implore you! ...'

As he stood there perfectly still, with his astonished eyes on Tanya, she suddenly glimpsed her brother in him.

'Well, I have after all ... I've done it all for her ...' he said, and his voice had the same intonation which nineteen-year-old Petya had used when talking about his Lena.

'Alyosha! ...' she said, bending down towards him, deeply moved. But interpreting this movement in his own way, he straightened up and said with a laugh:

'But don't you worry. Most likely I'll be returning you this money in a month's time in Pakistan, in Peshawar. Or at least, whatever's left. Will you be able to be there in a month's time?'

'Good heavens, Alyosha! What does the money matter?! Of course, I'll be there. Let's just hope that you'll be there, too.'

'I shall try to,' said Alyosha. And Tanya noticed that his eyes began sparkling recklessly again. 'What date is it now? The 17th of March, right? If we're not in Peshawar by the end of April ... Well, so what! That will mean we've been caught, and you can go back home and say "goodbye" to your fifty thousand roubles!'

That twisted, street-wise, mercenary smile appeared on his face again. But Tanya no longer reacted to it. Stepping right up to him she said in a firm voice:

'Alexey, whatever happens to you, I want you never to forget that you are an Odalevsky, Prince Odalevsky!'

'I'll remember,' he said, suddenly becoming serious. 'I'm remembering it now.'

'And that's not all!' she said, interrupting him sharply. 'I want you to know that you didn't kill the KGB men in vain. You have only settled accounts for the murder of your grandfather and my parents and sisters. They more or less destroyed our whole line, after all!'

Alexey looked her in the eye and said, after a short pause: 'You're not bad for a woman! You're my kind!'

16

The next morning Tanya and Elizabeth were leaving with the rest of the American group by Intourist bus for Sheremetyevo airport. Sitting in the bus next to Tanya in the seat across the gangway were Oleg Petrov and Katunova, and behind Tanya, wearing a short sports jacket, was that same fifty-year-old, roundheaded employee of the 'Tourist Protection Department' who had accompanied Katunova on her visit to Tanya and Elizabeth's room.

'You don't trust me,' Tanya said to Oleg with an excited laugh, clasping her dark-gloved hands until they cracked.

Elizabeth rolled her eyes as a cautionary signal, but was unable to stop her friend, who for some incomprehensible reason had become extremely cheerful. Tanya was openly jeering at Oleg, the gloomily silent Katunova and old roundhead. All the way to the airport, with exaggerated vivacity, she regaled the other dumbfounded tourists with descriptions of how the streets flashing by outside had looked before the Revolution:

'Look on your right, ladies and gentlemen, that is the Petrovsky Park. Can you see that red building in the middle? That was Peter the Great's Palace. Here was where all the Russian tsars used to stay on their way from Petersburg to Moscow to be crowned. And this was where Napoleon fled from the burning Kremlin: "From here, sunk in thought, he viewed the threatening flame", as Pushkin wrote. After the October Revolution the Bolsheviks turned this palace into a firewood store. Or was it a cabbage warehouse?' she said, turning to Oleg.

'I don't know,' he said coldly. 'Now, stop this ...'

'But what's here now?' said Tanya, interrupting him.

'I said, stop this propaganda of yours!' said Oleg, softly but firmly.

'But Mr Petrov,' said one of the tourists in a loud voice, 'we want to know what is there now, in the palace. Is it really a cabbage warehouse?'

'It's not a warehouse at all!' said Katunova, unable to contain herself. 'It's an air academy.'

'An "air" academy. What do you mean – they study the weather?' asked Elizabeth.

'No, it's an air force *engineering* academy,' said Katunova angrily.

'And now look on your left-hand side, ladies and gentlemen,' continued Tanya. 'This was once Khodynka Field where foreign ambassadors used to be ceremonially received ...'

'Cut it out!' Katunova ordered her in Russian.

'But why?' said Tanya, turning towards her with feigned astonishment. 'Will you really arrest me? Bear in mind that now I have something which I could tell the court. A few minor details about the KGB's love of jewellery ...'

But for all her bravado Tanya was inwardly extremely tense. She did not know how Oleg and Katunova would react when they were offered money instead of rings. And this gloomy roundhead of a KGB man was also obviously not accompanying them for nothing. In the event of something happening he must certainly be under orders to ... To do what? Kill her? Arrest her? ...

Yesterday at dinner she had specially put on the sort of evening dress which requires long delicate gloves. Fearing that today Oleg might notice her naked fingers, she had not gone downstairs to breakfast. Poor Elizabeth, who mentally trembled whenever she had to tell a lie, had to explain to everybody yet again that Tanya was not feeling very well and that she had no appetite. But now the moment of decision was approaching. Apart from fear, however, Tanya also felt slight impatience. She was longing to see Oleg and Katunova's faces when she ... It was a pity that the Colonel had not done her the honour of attending this performance in person.

Thanks to the presence of Katunova and the round-headed KGB man, the customs inspection passed off quickly and simply. Tanya and Elizabeth weren't even made to open their suitcases. All the officers did was take their passports, stamp them hurriedly, and wish them a good journey. A minute later they had crossed the official border of the USSR – on the staircase leading to the first floor of Sheremetyevo airport.

Tanya and Elizabeth sat down in the large hall on the first floor to await embarkation. The other tourists were clustering around the souvenir kiosks, buying Russian matryoshkas and tins of caviar ... Tanya and Elizabeth sat there in silence, staring tensely at the bustling crowd. Russia remained there below them – exotic from the outside and an unsolved mystery from within. Although Tanya had managed to glimpse it all the same in Mytishchi and in the office of KGB Colonel Anisimov ... But here, on the first floor of the international airport, there was the façade again – floors covered in soft carpets, deep, comfortable armchairs, kiosks selling caviar, bars selling American cigarettes ...

Judy! Poor girl ... No! She had forbidden herself to think about her! Otherwise she would simply go mad! Or cry out! Or ...

'Attention! We announce boarding of the Pan Am flight for Amsterdam and New York. Passengers are requested ...'

'That's ours!' said Tanya, getting up in excitement.

Oleg, Katunova and the roundheaded KGB man got up as if by command and approached together.

'Mrs Goehr,' said Oleg, touching her sleeve. 'Perhaps we could do it here? ...'

'No,' said Tanya, removing her arm sharply. 'By the aircraft steps, as we agreed! Or are you afraid that they won't let you through?!'

He grinned: 'Well, all right, all right! ... Only wait for the rest of the passengers, so that you are the last.'

'Are you afraid that I won't pay up?! Or that I'll make a public scene?'

'Goehr!' said the roundheaded KGB man, entering the conversation for the first time. 'In my pocket I have a warrant for your arrest! So that ...'

'Ah! but you don't scare me!' said Tanya, doing her best to hide her fear. 'An agreement is an agreement! And I am a princess!'

'What's the problem?' interrupted Elizabeth, unable to understand what they were saying in Russian. 'What do they want, Tanya?'

'Everything is all right, my dear. We are flying home!'

And, straightening her back, Tanya unhurriedly walked off to join the queue waiting to board.

When, by the steps leading to the Pan Am Boeing, she offered Oleg a neatly wrapped package, he could not at first understand what it was.

'It's money,' said Tanya softly, attentively watching the American stewardess on the first step of the ladder. She was dressed only in her short uniform coat and was wincing with the cold.

'What money?' said Oleg in confusion. 'And where are ...'

'The rings?' said Tanya, finishing his sentence. 'I have sold them.'

'What?' said Oleg, choking.

'Just so. What difference does it make? You wanted money? Here you are then. Here is fifty thousand!'

Katunova hurriedly grabbed the parcel from Oleg's hands and began to thrust it back on Tanya: 'Give us the rings! Or I will arrest you on the spot for attempting to give a bribe to a state official!' she hissed angrily.

Tanya quickly took off her gloves.

'I have no rings! Either you take the money, or I will start screaming the whole place down!' And she made a firm grab for the handrails of the steps.

'Tanya,' said Elizabeth, beginning to descend the aircraft steps again, 'what is going on? What's that parcel that they're thrusting on you? I told you so. It's drugs. Help!' she shouted. 'It's a set up!! ...'

Using the momentary confusion on the part of Katunova and her colleagues, Tanya began rapidly climbing the steps. The KGB man went to rush after her, but Oleg grabbed him by the arm.

'What are you doing? Have you gone mad? This isn't Aeroflot! This is Pan Am! These are Americans! They'll cause a big scene!'

'The bitch!' Katunova hissed, clutching the packet of money in her hands.

Without looking back, Tanya continued on up the stairs. The ascent seemed an eternity to her. Her heart was beating madly. Never had she imagined that her whole life would depend on ten wretched stairs! My God, she was fleeing Russia once again! And once again Russia – the Russia that she dreamt of at nights and which never left her even at the happiest moments of her life – that Russia was driving her away again!

In the aircraft cabin Tanya collapsed weakly into the seat next to Elizabeth.

'Ladies and gentlemen,' the stewardess's Boston accent came through over the loudspeaker, 'the crew of this Pan Am Boeing 707 would like to welcome you on board ...'

PART THREE

17

Trundling about on his home-made wooden trolley, legless Nikolay would raise his sharp axe, rear up and bring it crashing down with all his might on the next thick log or stubborn stump. Young, only twenty-two years old and naked to the waist in spite of the frost, he was chopping firewood with a kind of frenzied, mischievous joy. He shouted out at each unsuccessful blow, swore when he couldn't drag the axe out right away if it got stuck in a log, and was audibly happy when a log flew into pieces at the first blow. Steam rose from his shoulders, powerful as with all legless invalids; sweat poured down his broad, red face, and fresh splinters of wood stuck to his hair. On his left shoulder he had a tattoo, like Alexey's . . .

Standing at the door of the house, Judy had been observing him for a long time and was now beginning to feel the cold, even in the leather and sheepskin coat which she had borrowed from Nikolay's wife and thrown over her shoulders. The house which belonged to this strange young couple stood at the edge of a village. But Alexey, when he left for Moscow, had forbidden Judy not only to show herself in the village, but even to walk outside the house. (Nikolay and Liza did not refer to it as a house in fact, but as a hut – in view of the fact that it was a hundred years old.) And only in the evening, when the sun had gone down as it had now, would Judy go out onto the back steps to take a breath of fresh air. After sunset the village of Peshnya would immediately turn in and go to sleep, as apart from Liza and Nikolay there were no young people living there. In fact, the entire economy of the 'Moscow Dawns' collective farm consisted of a single small cowshed, where Liza worked as a milkmaid. In the summer the old *kolkhoz* workers would grow cucumbers in their kitchen-gardens, and the women would gather mushrooms in the forest, taking both sorts of produce to the market in Moscow. Thus they would survive the whole year – on milk, mushrooms and cucumbers . . .

Eventually one of the logs shot right up onto the back porch landing at Judy's feet, and Nikolay noticed her.

'Aha!' he said, shaking his curly head. 'So you've woken up! And quite right, too – you've had quite enough beauty sleep. In any case, some guests have arrived.'

'What guests?'

'Army friends of mine and Alyosha's – Boris and Fedora. We're going to have a binge. They've gone off to fetch Liza from the farm. And there's no need for you to be shy – you're okay! Come on, take off your hat. Go on, take it off,' he shouted threateningly, but as a joke, of course.

Judy pulled off her fur hat, feeling awkward. Two days earlier Liza had removed the plasters from her head, and now it had grown a short stubble of sharp, prickly hair.

'Well, there you are! You look like Joan of Arc,' he said cheerfully and trundled unceremoniously right up to her so that his large, curly head was level with her feet. And then, looking up at her from down below, he grinned. 'Hey, not bad! You're a bit of all right. A smooth pair of legs right up to your knickers!' and burst into laughter when he saw that she was embarrassed.

'Don't you worry,' he said. 'Invalids like me tend to get a bit obsessed with that sort of thing, but I don't go hurling myself at friends' women. Now, if I'd met you before he did, that would have been different! I may not have any legs, but I'm all right as far as being a man is concerned. That's why Liza doesn't leave me,' he said, chortling again. 'Understand?'

Pressing himself up on the wooden blocks which he used to propel himself along, Nikolay manoeuvred his trolley up onto the back porch and, as he shot past Judy, accidentally but painfully drove over her foot. His face immediately darkened, and he snapped out rudely:

'What are you biting your lip for? It hurts then, does it? Well, why don't you say so! What do you want to feel sorry for us cripples for? We should be thrown on the rubbish-tip like bags of shit, shouldn't we!' And with that he sped angrily off the porch into the kitchen. From outside on the other side of the fence came the sound of a car driving up, followed by the screeching of brakes and someone banging impatiently on the horn. Nikolay hurtled out of the kitchen, flew down the three steps of the porch on his trolley, clattered onto the frozen ground and zoomed off to the gate to open it. Painted in all kinds of wild colours, like a carriage on the New York subway, an old pick-up rolled into the courtyard. Sitting at the wheel was a frail-looking young man with a thin face, sunken cheeks and long, straight, ash-blond hair almost down to his shoulders. When he jumped down from the cab, you could see that he was dressed in jeans and an enormous jacket five times too big for him. Sticking out of the pockets of his jacket were the necks of vodka bottles. Emerging from the truck at the same time were Nikolay's wife Liza – large, red-cheeked and dressed in a sleeveless, padded jacket, felt boots and woollen shawl – and a tall, dark-haired young man in a military pea-jacket and with a gentle, almost girlish face which looked as if it had never yet been shaved. His left hand was holding a guitar while he kept his other in the pocket of his jacket. Judy thought she had already seen these faces somewhere before, but she couldn't remember where. Then it suddenly dawned on her – from the photographs in the room!

'So here you are! So here you are!' shouted Nikolay cheerfully as he shut the gate and trundled across to them. 'Well, make your acquaintance, Judy. Here are two more Afghan war heroes! This is Boris, otherwise known as "the

Performer" – our former regimental songleader and joker,' he said, pointing to the frail-looking one with the long blond hair and the crazy jacket. 'As a reward for his banter our sergeant major, known as "the Rat", knocked out eighteen of his teeth with the butt of his rifle. And this is Fedora. According to his passport his name is Fedor, but we all call him Fedora – because he has a feminine kind of gentleness. Fedora, come and meet Alyosha's girl! Don't be afraid! She doesn't bite ...'

'Oh, come on, that's enough ...' muttered the tall lad with the gentle face, warily looking up at Judy through his long, downy eyelashes, his cheeks bright pink. 'Hello ...'

Judy stretched her hand out towards him, which made Fedor blush even more. He put his guitar clumsily down on the porch and offered Judy his left hand: 'Fedor ...'

Only now did Judy register that the right-hand sleeve of his jacket was quite empty and tucked deep into his pocket.

A few minutes later the guests were sitting down at table – Boris 'the Performer' in his sweater, and Fedor in his army blouse minus epaulettes. Beneath the unbuttoned collar a thin, steel chain was visible. Liza was busying herself in the kitchen – frying potatoes in an enormous frying pan and managing to set the table at the same time with plates, glasses, sauerkraut and home-pickled cucumbers. Judy wanted to help her, but Nikolay grabbed her imperiously by the arm and made her sit down at the table.

'Sit down,' he ordered. 'She'll manage it by herself. You talk to the guests. We've got visitors, damn it! Heavy metal performers, no less! Don't you understand me? It's as if you've just arrived from Mars, or somewhere! Don't you have heavy metal in the Baltic states, or what? You know what hard rock is, don't you? You don't? Ah well, you'll find out later! ...'

From the moment the guests had appeared, Nikolay had been excitedly speeding round the table on his wooden trolley, its ball-bearings rattling noisily over the unpainted wooden floor, talking incessantly, hurtling over to the stove, throwing firewood into it, fanning the flames of what was already a roaring fire, and returning to the table once again . . .

'There, you see, boys, what beautiful women we have in our country,' said Nikolay. 'Alyosha is no fool! He's managed to grab a Joan of Arc for himself in the Baltic states. Or perhaps it wasn't in the Baltic states. You can't work out whether she and Alyosha aren't pulling the wool over our eyes. Well, anyway – you can talk to her yourselves. Boris, what are you keeping so quiet for? I can understand Fedora saying nothing. He's a virgin, after all, only just weaned from his mother's tit, but you're no virgin, are you! I know you've got no teeth, but that doesn't matter! Now if you'd left another part of your anatomy in Afghanistan, that wouldn't please the girls so much, would it . . .' And Nikolay threw back his curly head and burst into peals of laughter.

'And did you bring *your* little knob back with you safe and sound? Or did it get rubbed off among all the nurses in the military hospital?' interrupted Boris at last with an angry growl, moving his empty mouth with difficulty.

'See what I mean?' said Nikolay, turning towards Judy. 'You hear how he mumbles? He can't pronounce half the letters in the alphabet. But just you wait for him to put his teeth in and start singing. You'll soon start to rock. Now don't you get angry with me, Boris! I'm just crazy with delight that you've rolled up. It's so depressing here, can you imagine? Sitting all by yourself in this hole. Liza away at work for days on end. Thank God that Alyosha and Judy arrived. Though she's ill all the time and doesn't leave her room. And there's something wrong with Alyosha too. He's not the Alyosha we used to know! He was a live-wire then! But now he snaps at you like some great wolf. And what's he got to complain about? He came home safe and sound, his arms and legs all in one piece. He ought to be glad. Just look at Fedora, after all! He's got no arm, but he still manages a smile. What are you smiling at now, Fedora?!'

Fedora really had been smiling all this time, looking lovingly at his friends. Even Nikolay's coarse bantering had not darkened his pure features.

'Nothing in particular!' he replied. 'I simply feel happy. It's as if we had never parted. You are rude as always – in order to give yourself courage! It's funny!' he said in a shy, deep voice, stealing a glance at Judy. 'You don't happen to sing by any chance, do you, Miss ... I'm sorry, I don't know your surname ...'

'No, why do you ask?'

'For goodness sake just call her Judy!' interrupted Nikolay. 'She is Alyosha's girl, after all!'

'We've got a group, you see, and we need a female singer,' said Fedor softly, taking no notice of Nikolay. 'And, after all, we're not really professionals ...'

'Ha! Not professionals, eh?' said Nikolay, interrupting again. 'They've only been invited from Saratov to perform in Moscow, haven't they, and he says they're not professionals!'

'Not to Moscow itself, but near Moscow,' said Fedor. 'We're giving a concert tomorrow in Podolsk. Would you like to come?'

Liza came into the room, rosy-cheeked and animated. Her hands were occupied with the large frying pan full of potatoes. Boris hurriedly cleared some room on the table.

'Well, boys, grab what you can, and I'll fry up some mushrooms as well,' she said in a loud, slightly sing-song voice, as she placed the pan down on the table.

Liza was about twenty. She carried her stocky, well-developed body in a slow, purposeful way, keeping her large muscular legs wide apart. A bulky, cotton flower-print dress hugged her ample bosom and half covered her knees in their knitted woollen stockings. Her grey felt boots slid noiselessly over the floor. As she was walking past Nikolay, she suddenly lifted him off the trolley, hoisted him under her arm and planted him down on a chair at the table. The men fell silent. Then, having done her duty, she rushed off back to the kitchen.

'Well, boys! Let's get stuck in!' said Nikolay in an even louder voice, blushing but trying to play down the awkwardness of the situation. He filled the cut glasses with vodka and was the first to grab hold of one.

'To our little gathering!' he said.

'Perhaps we ought to wait for Liza?' Fedor suggested.

'She'll soon catch up! Forward, boys!' said Nikolay, emptying his glass at one go, making a wry face and grinding his clenched teeth loudly.

Boris and Fedor also drank theirs. Nobody touched the food.

'If you don't drink up,' said Nikolay, turning to Judy, 'you'll be doing us a mortal insult. It's not every day I have guests like these! Drink, I tell you, drink!'

Judy raised the glass obediently to her lips, took a small sip and put the glass back down on the table.

Nikolay naturally began to protest.

'Is that any way to drink? Who taught you, for God's sake?! I'm sure it wasn't Alyosha! He's a great expert in this matter himself! But then *we* don't exactly drag our feet, either! Let's down another one, lads!'

Only after they had emptied the first bottle did the conversation begin to get going. Liza was already sitting down with the others, propping her ruddy cheek on her hand.

Boris had been demobbed later than Nikolay, and he was now reporting on events, mumbling with his toothless mouth.

'Kovalchuk from the first platoon was killed near Kandahar. Sashka Golovin from the signals platoon is a lucky bastard – he had three fingers blown off by a mine when we were clearing a road in Kunduz district. Vaska Belov from our group was still there when I got demobbed …'

'And what happened to the Rat? Is he still torturing new recruits?' asked Nikolay. The vodka seemed to have had no effect on him except that his face was covered with large droplets of sweat and his fair hair had darkened, sticking to his forehead and temples in tiny ringlets.

'Where else would he go, anyway? Once or twice people tried to shoot him in the back, but he's got nine lives, the filthy tom cat. Nothing but light scratches.'

'What do you mean: "people" tried to shoot him?' grinned Nikolay. 'It was you, I bet . . .'

'No. If it had been me, I wouldn't have missed,' Boris replied.

'He fed the Rat on his own teeth, you know,' said Fedor.

'How do you mean?' asked Nikolay in amazement.

'Well, you remember how the Rat eats,' mumbled Boris. 'He doesn't chew anything, just swallows it down whole. Well, I scattered my teeth in his millet porridge. He swallowed the lot – all eighteen. And an hour later, he's in the military hospital with violent stomach spasms. The doctors gave him an X-ray and almost went crazy – they thought that he had swallowed his own teeth . . .'

'Listen, boys, there's one thing I don't understand,' the tipsy Liza's melodious voice rang out when they had all finished laughing. 'Why don't these partisans give in? After all, think how many of our lads have died already!'

'Yes, I reckon 100,000 of our men at the very least have been killed or maimed there so far,' said Boris. 'But as for the Afghans, it must be more than a million . . .'

'More than a million!' said Liza in horror. 'And they still don't surrender! All the same, they won't defeat us! The Germans couldn't beat us, so why should these Afghans!'

'You just shut up, Lizaveta!' said Nikolay, thumping his fist angrily on the table. 'You don't know your arse from your elbow! The Germans came to *us*, whereas we are the ones who have come to *them* and burn their villages to the ground! Like the facists! We're the ones who wipe out their children with gas and napalm! Do you understand the difference?! We're to them what Hitler was to us . . .'

'What are you getting so hot under the collar for, Nikolay?' Boris began to say reluctantly, without raising his head from his plate. 'We were soldiers. We were ordered to burn the villages, so we burnt them. If it hadn't been us, then others would have come. The Americans.'

'Why the Americans?' said Judy in surprise.

'*Because*, that's all!' said Boris stobbornly. 'The Americans were intending to set up military bases in Afghanistan. Right under our noses! But we got in there first. We couldn't have let ourselves be placed under threat, after all!'

'Now why are you giving a fucking political lecture?!' said Nikolay flying into a rage. 'You're surely not going to come out with that whingeing "Keep quiet, keep quiet" rubbish! Why are you afraid of telling yourself the truth! Not that propaganda shit they fed us on in the army – I mean what is *really* going on! Are you afraid? But that's what we've got *glasnost* for now! ...'

'Calm down,' said Liza, giving Nikolay an affectionate hug. 'You're so drunk you're beginning to go over the top!'

'Hang on, Liza,' he said, extricating himself from his wife's embrace. 'Boris, you just tell me what it is you sing about at your concerts. It's a pity I haven't got any legs, or else I'd have gone to listen myself! If it's just a load of crap about love and roses, then what's the point of this fucking *glasnost*?! No, Boris, you just look the truth in the face! Gorbachev himself wants an end to this war, only he doesn't know how to do it! Just leaving would be too much like losing face. All those Czechs and Poles would take it as weakness! But honestly – who is it needs this war now anyway? And what have the bloody Americans got to do with it? Have you seen them there? No? Me, neither! But my legs are there! And his arm! And your teeth! And for fucking what? For Afghan Communism? Well, our own can go and fuck itself for all I care! ... And they've bought me off! For my two legs they gave me two thousand roubles compensation in special certificates, so that I could buy myself this house and not plague them any more . . .!'

Fedor was quietly rocking from side to side on his chair, Boris was looking gloomily down at his half-empty plate. His ash-blond hair was hanging loose; unhealthy red patches had appeared on his pale, sunken cheeks.

Liza stood there with her hands on her hips and stared pityingly at Nikolay, who had flown completely off the handle.

'And how much pension do you receive?' Fedor asked Nikolay softly.

'The same as you do – forty roubles!' said Nikolay, getting worked up again. 'Now come on, Fedor! Instead of sitting there saying hardly anything, you tell me what I dragged Communism into that Afghan shithouse for! So that at the age of twenty-two I could be legless and get a pension of forty roubles a month? For Communism?! Not bloody likely! If I didn't have Liza, could I really live on forty roubles? A cripple, bugger it, without either leg! Okay, today I've got Lizaveta with me, but tomorrow she'll meet a normal, healthy guy and – bye bye, Nikolay! And what will I do? Peg out from starvation? Sing songs up and down railway carriages? Songs about my "international heroism"!? And if I should ever have children, what heroic act shall I tell them I performed? Shooting up half a dozen Afghan villages with a machine-gun – that's fucking heroism for you! Driving an armoured car all over those vineyards that they've taken centuries to grow, that's heroism for you! Somehow I don't seem to hear any songs on the radio about that kind of heroism! Perhaps you'll sing us one! No, Yury Shalygin was right when he told them all to go to fucking hell! He'd had enough of this fucking "heroism" and went off to England! . . .'

'Nikolay, you really have gone over the top,' said Fedor gently. 'What are you coming out with this nonsense for? Yuri Shalygin passed over to the other world a long time, God rest his soul . . .'

With this Fedor crossed himself and got up from the

table. He started walking up and down the room in agitation, stooping slightly, as if afraid of hitting his head against the wooden ceiling.

'But that's where you're wrong, dear boy,' uttered Nikolay with a triumphant grin. 'Yurka is alive! And he's in London at the moment! The rebels sent him there – Alyosha told me so! ...'

As they heard this, Boris and Fedor looked at each other, as if wanting to say something. But Nikolay carried on excitedly.

'And all we suckers get to hear about at political indoctrination lectures are Americans, military bases, Zionists, the Chinese! ...'

'Come on, boys, what are you all getting so worked up about?' remonstrated Liza loudly. 'Can't you sit down and talk to each other like civilised people? Drink vodka, have a bite to eat and sing some decent songs? You're always going on about this damned war! And as for you, Boris, why are you so fed up? You've brought your guitar with you, after all. Why don't you sing us something to raise our spirits?'

'You know, Nikolay,' Boris said suddenly in a soft voice as if he hadn't heard Liza's request, 'it's true what you said about love and roses. I'm scared to sing about Afghanistan somehow ...'

'But we used to sing together there,' said Nikolay with a smile, in a more conciliatory voice.

Liza hastily left the room and came back holding the guitar which Fedor had brought. She presented it to Boris and asked him affectionately once again:

'Go on, play us something. Do you know "Snowball Berry Red"?'

'No, I can't remember it ...' said Boris, pensively strumming the strings. 'How could that happen? Yurka Shalygin in London? ...'

'Come on, Boris, let's sing our song, the one we used to sing together in the army ...' and, calming down, Nikolay sank limply back into his chair. 'As for Shalygin ... Wait for Alyosha to come. He'll tell you.'

Boris, bending over the guitar, began to tune the strings.

Liza took some framed army pictures down off the wall and sat next to Judy.

'Look what they were like when they were younger. Boys, come and look at yourselves as you used to be!'

On the black and white amateur snaps, Judy could now easily recognise not only Alexey, but Nikolay, close-cropped and youthful-looking, Boris, with his short stature, and Fedor, with his delicate features.

'And here is Shalygin,' said Fedor, pointing to a lad with a snub nose and prominent cheek bones. 'And this is Sergey Sukhar. He was older than all of us. He was drafted when he was a research student. And this is our driver Pavel Yegorov ...'

Sukhar had a delicate, elongated sort of face, while Pavel Yegorov, who was smiling in the driver's seat of the armoured troop-carrier, had chubby cheeks and looked almost like a boy.

'And here are my legs!' Nikolay, poking his thumb at his legs on the photo. 'Just look what legs I used to have. Two of them!' he shouted.

'Now that's enough from you,' said Liza, giving him a soft poke with her elbow. 'So you had legs. You'll grow some new ones!'

'Oh yes!' said Nikilay, beginning to get worked up again. 'And where will they come from?'

'You'll see,' she replied. 'We'll have a son, and he'll have your legs.'

'Okay, okay ...' said Nikolay, immediately calming down again. The first chords sounded quietly from the guitar. They had a clear, stark rhythm, and at the first sounds of it, Nikolay shook his curly head and began singing in an unexpectedly quiet, gentle and sorrowful voice:

'Speaking through tears he said to her
"I must leave you,
Just for a while, so wait for me here and
Don't grieve you!"'

Fedor looked at his friend and, blushing slightly, joined in with his deep, low voice:

'The soldier left, but he never saw the spring again
And so returned back home in a metal coffin plain.
His mother weeps, his father shadow-like stands still.
How many have returned whose hearts never will.'

Boris wasn't singing, just accompanying, his head bent low over the finger-board of the guitar.

'How many have returned, who life never tasted,
In metal coffins plain. How many lives are wasted.'

'What a surprise!' exclaimed Alexey, red-faced with cold and smiling in the doorway. 'Fedora! Boris! This is marvellous! I was wondering what the car was outside, striped like a zebra! I thought I'd come in quietly, like a partisan ...'

Throwing his rucksack off his shoulders, he gave Fedor a bear-hug and frowned when he felt the empty right sleeve of his soldier's blouse.

'So they caught you, too, the sons of bitches! ... Well, Boris, I hope that you're all complete, at least?'

'Almost,' mumbled Boris through his toothless mouth and took up a boxer's stance opposite Alexey. 'Well, will you let me lay into you, like I used to? Eh?'

Small and puny, he was almost two heads shorter than Alexey.

'Go on, then, punch away!' said Alexey goodnaturedly and stuck out his chest a little. Boris thumped his fist into his chest for all he was worth – so hard that you could hear it echo.

'Good!' said Boris, satisfied. 'Now let's hug each other!'

'But what are you mumbling for? Where are your teeth?'

'I've got them here,' said Boris, pulling a small plastic box from his pocket and opening it like a snuff-box. It contained two dentures. 'I use these for concerts,' Boris grinned. 'I put them in when I sing ...'

After removing his coat, Alexey sat down at the table not taking his beaming eyes off his friends.

'Well, tell me about what you've been doing,' he said. 'Fedora, when did you get demobbed?'

'In August. We were being brought up to attack Yattabad, but in the pass our armoured car got blown up. Many of us were done for – including Valka Yerokhin and Fima Kaplun. But you wouldn't have known them, because they were transferred to us from No. 4 Company in place of you and Shalygin.'

Fedor fell silent. He looked around at his friends and smiled. 'But Boris and I met Kashchenko. He came to our concert in Kazan. He was wearing a hat and tie.'

'He was a son of a bitch, that Kashchenko!' declared Alexey spitefully. 'Him, and Zhebatko, and Durov! They were all fucking squealers!'

'How do you mean?' asked Fedor.

'Oh, it doesn't matter. Let's forget it ...' said Alexey, brushing the question aside.

'Well, Zhebatko always was a squealer,' agreed Boris. 'And Kashchenko became a big wheel in the Komsomol. But as for saying that Durov was, too ...'

'Durov turned informer, too. Still, enough of that!' said Alexey. 'But what about Sergey Sukhar? Does anyone know anything about him? Is he still in Dushanbe?'

'Not just him, but Pavel Yegorov is there as well. I've had a letter from him.'

Fedor put his left hand into the right-hand pocket of his blouse and extracted a worn sheet of paper torn from a school exercise book and covered in large handwriting.

'Let me have a look,' demanded Alexey, taking the letter from him and immediately beginning to read.

'What does it say?' Nikolay asked Fedor.

'Nothing in particular. Pavel's got a job as a driver. He stayed on for additional service, and is driving lorries to Afghanistan. He's dicing with death, the fool! If you ask me, he's ferrying copies of the Koran for Sukhar on the sly. Or hashish . . .'

'Isn't there any address?' asked Alexey, turning the letter around in his hands.

'I left the envelope at home, in Saratov. When I get back, I could send it to you . . .'

'It's all right. It doesn't matter,' said Alexey, as he gave the letter back to Fedor.

'Well, boys, I am really glad to see you. But I've no more time just now. She and I must push off.'

Alexey filled his plate with vinaigrette salad and hurriedly began to bolt the food down, hardly bothering to chew it.

'What do you mean: "push off"?!' said Nikolay indignantly. 'It's pitch black outside!'

'That doesn't matter. Business, old man! I need to get somewhere very urgently!' And Alexey darted a quick glance at Judy who had so far not said one word.

'But you *can't*! I won't let you go anywhere!' Nikolay persisted. 'The boys have only just arrived. It's so long since we've seen each other, and you want to push off!'

'Go on. Go and get your things together,' Alexey ordered Judy curtly, paying no attention to Nikolay.

Judy stood up and went off to her room. A little while later Alexey followed her in and shut the door firmly behind him.

'Did you see Tanya?' she asked impatiently.

'Yes,' he replied quietly. 'Are you ready? We must go.'

'To Moscow?' she said joyfully.

'No. A bit further away than that. Let's go, and I'll tell you on the way.'

'What did she say to you? What's happening to them?'

'Let's go. We don't have time now!'

'Why? What are you in such a hurry for?'

'The militia have started up a nationwide search for us. Our photographs are stuck up on walls everywhere. Even here, at the railway station. Someone from the village could see them any time. We must run for it. Where is your jacket?'

'Out there, in the corridor,' whispered Judy, her voice weak with agitation. 'What do you mean: "nationwide search"?'

'I mean that the militia throughout the whole country have been ordered to look for us as dangerous criminals. There are more photographs of us in the country than there are of Lenin! And you don't look bad on them, either. A real doll!'

'But where are we going?'

'Let's leave right now. I'll tell you on the way.'

When the two of them came out of the room, Alexey's friends were seated silently around the table.

'Well, then. You're off?' said Nikolay, with an angry, set smile.

'Yes, Nikolay,' Alexey replied, going up to him and placing his hand affectionately on his shoulder. 'Thanks for everything. I'm sorry it's turned out this way. I've spoilt your party, you might say. But that's how things happen sometimes. Take this for your hospitality at any rate.'

He took a tightly wrapped bundle of new notes from his pocket and offered them to the astonished Nikolay.

'What are you doing?' wailed Liza fearfully. 'Have you robbed a bank, or something?'

'No, of course not! I've met a rich relation of mine. Here, take it. Don't be afraid! It's not stolen money!'

'I welcomed you as a brother, and you, you ...' cried Nikolay angrily and turned away. 'You know where you can go with your money, don't you?'

'Stop it, Nikolay!' said Alexey gently. 'I know what things are like for you and Liza on the collective farm with only cucumbers and potatoes to live on! But I've actually got some money! That's why I'm offering it to you as a brother! You shared the last of what you had with me, and I'm doing the same for you!'

Alexey put the money down on the table, went over to Liza, embraced her, kissed her three times on the cheek and, taking Judy firmly by the hand, turned towards his friends.

'I don't know whether we'll get to meet again, boys, but farewell for now ... It's good that I managed to see you all, after all. That means I'm bound to be successful!'

He stretched his hand towards Fedor to say goodbye, but Fedor did not take it. Instead he looked over towards Boris and said in a demanding voice:

'Well??'

'I suppose we'll have to mention it,' said Boris obscurely and sighed.

'What are you talking about?' Alexey asked suspiciously and frowned.

'Alexey,' said Fedor, suddenly getting up from his seat. 'Can I have a few words with you?'

Alexey looked anxiously at Boris, at Nikolay, at the door leading to the kitchen where Fedor had disappeared and then, not without hesitation, marched after him.

Fedor was standing in the kitchen, pensively stroking his cheek with his left hand. Alexey stood suspiciously a few steps away, his right hand in the pocket of his short jacket.

'Listen, Alyosha,' began Fedor quietly. 'Have you got into this mess because of Yurka Shalygin?'

'Into what mess?'

'Look, don't try and kid me!' begged Fedor gently. 'I'm not Zhebatko, you know. Boris and I saw the photographs of you at the petrol station. We couldn't *not* look. And when Nikolay said that Yurka was alive and living in London, we just put two and two together. In Saratov as well, we have both been called in by the KGB and asked about your friendship with Shalygin ...'

'Well?!'

'Well nothing. We didn't split. We said that we'd all been friendly with him. We were all in the same platoon, after all ... But the long and the short of it is that you and she' – here Fedor nodded to the other room where Judy had remained – 'can go nowhere now either by train, or by plane, or by bus. So why don't you come along with us? Tomorrow we're doing a gig in Podolsk, and then we're off to Saratov. I don't know where you intend to hole up, but in my opinion the best place would be with Sukhar in Dushanbe – you've made the right decision there. We won't be able to take you to Dushanbe, of course, it's three thousand kilometres away, but we'll be able to get you well away from the Moscow region, at least ...'

Alexey removed his hand from his pocket and gave a sigh of relief.

'What are you doing?'

'Forgive me, old mate,' said Alexey, wiping the sweat from his forehead. 'I'm a sod! I was keeping my revolver at the ready in my pocket. Even my hand has got sweaty. I thought that the two of you would try to take me. Whereas in fact you're fucking godsends ...'

'Oh, Alyosha!' said Fedor in an aggrieved voice. 'What a sinner! You can't even mention God without swearing!'

'So have you become a believer, then?' said Alexey in amazement.

'Yes, I have,' said Fedor calmly. 'Who was it kept you and me from dying in Afghanistan, if not God?'

18

It was pure, unadulterated hard rock. Judy had never heard such a deafening sound from a group even in America. Boris and Fedor were unrecognisable. In black leather trousers and a jacket thick with metal studs, Boris was hurling himself about the stage with his electric guitar, shrieking the lyrics into the microphone, flinging himself to his knees and springing up again, leaping into the air, twisting and contorting...

'Babe, you really let me down,
You gave me the runaround.
Keep your fella. Go to hell.
I'll find me another girl.
Take her home and get unwound.
Drink myself into the ground!
Drink myself into the ground...'

'Lame Dog' consisted of six musicians including Fedor who was their manager. They were all geared up in identical black leather studded jackets and straining to force the loudest possible sound from their instruments, amplified to even greater effect by the two enormous loudspeakers at either side of the stage. But it wasn't the performers who struck Judy so much as the audience – fifteen- and sixteen-year-olds rhythmically chanting and screaming in time to the heavy metal. Judy had never dreamt that here in Russia teenagers could form such an ecstatic crowd, gyrating to the rhythms of a rock concert, throwing their arms wildly into the air and screaming – just the same as her old high-school friends in Madison, Alabama. Though at least in Alabama even the open-air concerts had been warm. This outdoor heavy metal concert was taking place in March, with the winter temperature at 20 below! Even so, Boris was dripping with perspiration. Fedor was sweating, too, as he pounded the organ with his left hand (and making a fair job of it, much to Judy's surprise). The other four members of 'Lame Dog' were a lot younger than Boris and Fedor, seventeen at the most. The lyrics of their songs were somewhat primitive – 'a lot of crap about love and roses' as Nikolay had put it the day before. But who bothers about the words of rock songs anyway? The five hundred teenagers crammed into this leisure park concert arena, in the town of Podolsk just outside Moscow, had come to scream to the sounds, dance to the rhythm and roar their approval at the end of each song. Half a dozen militiamen were standing next to a couple of police cars a little way away, casually observing a concert which would have been unimaginable in the USSR until very recently. Positioned behind the wooden wing of the stage, Judy just couldn't make up her mind what to keep her eye on – the stage itself with the diminutive but wildly energetic Boris and the rest of the group, or the exhilarated Russian teenagers and the impassive militiamen stationed behind them. As a precaution, Alexey had stayed behind in the musician's pick-up truck which was parked in the snow at the back of the wooden staging . . .

'Listen now,
People,
I'm telling you, yeah,
When you see two lovers in the summer's heat
On a bench in a park or a tree-lined street,
When you see two lovers
Walk the other way!
Don't spoil their day! . . .'

chanted Boris, half-sobbing, half-singing.

There was now a short interval, and Boris spent five minutes silently sitting in the pick-up with his eyes closed. Then he took a few gulps of vodka straight from the bottle, wincing from the pain in his gums, put his two dentures back in his mouth and said to Alexey:

'Okay, okay, fine! But I really wish you'd come out and listen to the next number ...'

'I can hear everything perfectly well from here,' murmured Alexey gloomily. 'You're going to ruin your throat, you know. You used to have a real voice, and now here you are just screeching and caterwauling!'

'Well then, I'm going to sing just for *you.* Personally!' smiled Boris, enigmatically. 'Come on! You won't forget it ...'

'I can't, can I? The cops are out there. Will it be over soon?'

'I'm pretty sure it will!' said Boris with another mysterious grin. 'Well, what is life without a few risks here and there!' And with that he abruptly opened up his suitcase, burrowed about in it and extracted a small package which he then proceeded to unwrap. It contained two medals – 'For Valour' and an Order of the Red Star. Under the astonished gaze of Alexey, Fedor and the other musicians, he carefully pinned them on the front of his leather jacket and said: 'Okay, guys! I'm going to sing on my own now. You're just going to keep quiet.'

'What are you going to sing?' asked Fedor anxiously.

'A new song. You don't know it. Come on, let's get going!' And Boris climbed resolutely out of the truck.

The audience greeted him with a frenzied roar.

'We want more, we want more! Rock on Boris, rock on Boris! Go for it, go for it ...'

Boris stood on the stage, pale, calm and with his head bowed. He waited for the noise of the crowd to die down. Then he struck a gentle chord on his guitar and equally softly spoke into the microphone.

'I'm now going to sing you a new song of mine ...'

'Go for it, go for it! . . .' responded the crowd with excitement.

'Calm down a bit,' Boris told them quietly. 'Nobody has ever heard this song before. It's dedicated to my old friend Nikolay, who . . . Well, you'll see from the song . . .'

Boris, experienced performer that he was, softly strummed the guitar strings a few times to get the audience into the mood that he needed. And then he began to sing sadly and quietly in a totally different style from the earlier hard rock.

'We all lost something in Afghanistan.
One friend lost his legs, another his arm.
My teeth were all shattered.
But none of it mattered.
They can't shoot away your soul!
Afghanista-aan,
Afghanista-aan!
They can't shoot away your soul!

You can live without teeth in Afghanistan.
You can live without legs and your right arm.
The medals you've got
Show the world that you've not
Lost your soul, lost your soul on the way.
Afghanista-aan,
Afghanista-aan!
Lost your soul, lost your soul on the way!'

The audience was listening in silence, bewildered and suspicious. Boris was almost imperceptibly increasing the volume and accelerating the rhythm of the song.

'In the year two thousand they'll send from Kabul
A huge zinc coffin completely full
Of arms, legs and teeth,
Hundred thousand apiece,
And two hundred thousand souls.

Afghanista-aan,
Afghanista-aan!
And two hundred thousand souls!'

'I look in the coffin. My soul is not there!
I rush to my friends and ask them where
It sank to the floor
Like a drunken whore!
Where did my soul go to sleep?
Afghanista-aan,
Afghanista-aan!
Where did my soul go to sleep?'

By now, Boris had gradually developed the rhythm into strict march time, and was half-singing, half-shouting the words as a harsh recitative.

'In the coffin you find an official form.
It tells you your duty you did perform –
Regimental best
Along with the rest.
But it doesn't mention your soul!
Afghanista-aan,
Afghanista-aan!
But it doesn't mention your soul!'

Suddenly, Boris shifted the martial rhythm into hard rock and carried on singing, to the enthusiastic roar of the audience.

'We all lost something in Afghanistan.
One friend lost his legs, another his arm.
Will you do the same?
And who will you blame
When you find you've lost your soul?
Afghanista-aan,
Afghanista-aan!
When you find you've lost your soul?'

Boris finished the song with a short, sharp chord, but the audience carried on chanting and shouting: 'Afghanista-aan! Afghanista-aan! More! More! More! More!'

The other members of the group pounded out the rhythm of the song together with the audience, but Boris stood silently on stage, his face ashen and ravaged, his guitar lowered to the floor. Judy stood in utter amazement in the wings. Was it really possible to hear such a song in Russia? In a country, according to everything she had heard and read, that was completely under the control of the Party, the KGB, the police and censorship? She followed Boris's gaze above the heads of the screaming audience and suddenly realised what he was staring at – the militiamen who were still standing quite impassively in exactly the same place beside their cars. And then she realised – Boris was waiting to be arrested. His whole appearance, his staring eyes, the droop of his body, his hunched shoulders, the rigidly lowered arms all seemed to say: no, no, I'm not a hero! I just blurted something out in the heat of the moment – the truth about my soul! So you'd better come and get me. Come and arrest me . . .

But the militiamen just carried on stamping their feet quite indifferently on the snow beside their cars.

'They're not going to arrest you!' Judy felt like shouting at Boris. Well, how could they after all? In full view of this wildly enthusiastic, screaming audience? The teenagers would have torn them limb from limb!

Boris suddenly seemed to realise this himself.

'So now we return to our usual repertoire,' he said into the microphone with a smile.

'We want Afghanistan! We want Afghanistan! . . .' shouted the fans.

Seeing that the crowd would not be convinced by words, Boris signalled to the rest of the group and struck his guitar strings forcefully. A new rock number exploded over the audience and drowned the few remaining voices still shouting for the Afghanistan song. Instead, everyone was swept into another love song, and in a few moments the scene was exactly as it had been at the beginning of the concert – the same hard rock, the same excited screams from the audience, the same gyrating and swaying and waving of arms in time to the music.

Judy was just about to return to the pick-up when a sudden, violent movement began at the back of the crowd. Fans scattered in all directions, rushing off into the sidepaths of the dark, snow-covered park. Judy looked anxiously towards the militiamen, but they weren't the cause. In fact they were getting back into their two police cars. The doors slammed shut and the cars drove off. The cry grew louder and louder, echoing around the rapidly emptying concert arena:

'*Lyubers! Lyubers!* The *Lyubers* are coming!'*

Then, in the distance, Judy saw a vast, dark mass of youths advancing along the central avenue of the park. The tightly-packed mob were swarming towards the concert arena. There were at least two hundred of them, many brandishing short steel rods or chains and wearing knitted ski-caps. They smoothly divided to either side as the two police cars drove straight on past them towards the exit, and as soon as the cars had disappeared through the park gates, they charged forward with a frenzied cry. Some headed straight for the stage, others chased after members of the audience who were fleeing in all directions.

No, it wasn't a fight. It was mass robbery with violence.

Judy had experienced innumerable surprises that evening, and the latest was that hardly any of the five hundred fans who were being attacked were fighting back at these *Lyubers*. The gang were hurling their victims to the snow; laying into them viciously and mercilessly with their steel rods, chains and fists; grabbing money from their pockets and tearing watches from their wrists;

*Gangs of nationalistic youths named after their place of origin, the town of Lyubertsy near Moscow *Tr.*

stripping off not just their fur hats, which they stuffed down the fronts of their own coats, but all the rest of the clothes of some of the boys and girls. The *Lyubers* laughed raucously as they tore up the clothes, and whistled loudly after their naked victims as they fled in terror...

Only the leading contingent of *Lyubers* – about forty square-shouldered louts – didn't bother with robbing anyone. They were forcing their way towards the stage through the crowd like a battering-ram, not so much pushing people to one side as simply heaving over any people standing in their path and trampling them underfoot.

The performance had been abandoned, of course. Judy could see Boris, Fedor and the other musicians looking fearfully round at the wedge of *Lyubers* advancing towards them through the crowd. They quickly gathered together their simple but heavy equipment – amplifier, organ, loudspeakers, drum-kit – and dragged them off behind the stage.

'Quick! Get to the van!' Boris shouted as he rushed past Judy. She started to run after him, suddenly realising that she was threatened with the same danger as everyone else.

When they saw that the performers were about to get away, the *Lyubers* began really to hurl themselves at the stage, shouting, swearing, and sending anyone flying who got in their way. But they still hadn't quite reached the stage and as the pick-up was only a few steps away, Judy was sure that she, Boris and the others would be able to avoid any violence. However, as they emerged from the wings and jumped down the back of the stage, they saw that another group of *Lyubers* had run into the narrow space between the stage and the truck to head them off. The youths were mockingly waving their chains and steel rods in the air. Even if Boris and the others had dropped all their equipment and run unencumbered, they would not have made it. Somebody brought Fedor down with a vicious blow from a long steel rod, while another hefty *Lyuber* rushed straight at Judy. She saw a young face with its white smile, a raised hand clutching a short chain. She didn't even have time to shout out or scream. All she could do was instinctively raise her hands over her head, trying to protect it from the inevitable blow.

Then a deafening shot followed by another made everybody freeze, attackers and victims. Judy threw herself to the ground and, raising her head slightly, saw Alexey. He was standing at the open door of the pick-up with a revolver in each hand. A third shot raised a shower of snow and earth right by the feet of the hulking brute who had stopped two steps away from Judy, his hand with its short steel chain still frozen above her head.

'Right! Now listen, you fucking *Lyubers*!' screamed Alexey, white as a sheet but with a kind of intoxicated excitement. 'Make the slightest move and I'll blow your brains out!' Then he added to Boris, Judy and the others: 'Come on, quick! Get in the truck! See to Fedor, someone!'

Boris and one of the other members of the group lifted the blood-soaked Fedor up from the ground and dragged him over to the truck. The others gathered the equipment together. As Judy climbed into the truck, some of the other *Lyubers* who had been charging towards the stage through the arena, suddenly appeared at the back of the stage. Keeping one revolver aimed at the first group of attackers, Alexey abruptly jerked the other in the direction of the new arrivals and pressed the trigger.

'Freeze, you bastards!' he shouted after the shot had rung out. 'You're not in Lyubertsy now, damn you! Who's got the guts to risk a bullet, eh? Come on then!'

None of them moved.

'Well, there you go!' said Alexey with satisfaction. 'Take the wheel, Boris. And if any of you lot so much as touch the truck, you're dead! And as for you,' he snarled, turning to the youth who had laid into Fedor with his steel rod, 'Come here! Come on, move it, you bastard, or I'll shoot you on the spot!'

The youth, who couldn't have been more than sixteen, edged gingerly towards Alexey.

'Closer!' commanded Alexey. Now that all his friends had piled into the truck he felt more secure – they were safe behind him, protected by his two revolvers.

'Closer, closer,' Alexey barked again at the sixteen-year-old. 'Do you know who you hit, you little runt? Well, go on, tell me! Do you know, then?'

'Yeah ... er, yeah, I know ...' muttered the boy uncertainly, staring at the muzzle of the revolver pointing straight at him.

'Well, who is he then?' asked Alexey.

'Heavy metal singer ...'

'So why did you do it?'

'Shouldn't play fucking American rock, should he?' the boy spoke up with sudden defiance. 'This is Russia, not America!'

'So that's it, then? You wanted to kill him for a bit of music, eh?' said Alexey, suddenly jerking his revolver at another *Lyuber* who was quietly trying to sneak round behind him. The youth froze immediately and took a step back. Alexey continued his conversation.

'Just for a bit of music, eh?'

'Yeah! ...'

'And it was for a bastard like you that he lost his arm in Afghanistan, was it? You knew about that, did you?'

'So why does he spread Western influences in Russia, then?'

'You're a bloody moron, you are! "Western influences"? Arseholes! You've been reading too much KGB shit! I could smash your stupid, snotty-nosed little face in! I just don't want to get myself dirty, right?'

Alexey swung round onto the running board of the truck and shouted to Boris who was already at the wheel: 'Okay, let's move it!' adding for the benefit of the *Lyubers* who were now standing in a semi-circle: 'I'm telling you again! If any of you lay so much as a finger on this truck, I'll blow your brains out, I bloody swear I will!'

Boris started up his painted truck and moved off. Alexey bent down to the open door and spoke to the others who were sitting inside cradling the blood-covered Fedor: 'How is he then?'

'It's his shoulder,' someone replied. 'That bastard broke his collar bone!'

The pick-up, with Alexey clinging to the running-board but still armed, sped down the dark central avenue of the park. The remains of the recent bloody massacre lay on either side – torn pieces of clothing, felt boots, women's footwear, bloodstains on the snow....

When they came to the park gates, Boris shouted out: 'Where do we go now?'

'The hospital, where do you think! "Where do we go now", indeed!' mimicked Alexey. Then he climbed down into the truck and closed the door.

'But the militia will get you there!' shouted Boris, swerving the truck round into a dark, snow-covered street.

'Just get on with it!'

'Alexey, you really ought to switch to a taxi ...' murmured Fedor's soft voice. His eyes remained closed. The blow from the steel rod had caught him across the right shoulder. Hanging out from his torn and blood-stained leather jacket was a small crucifix on a thin steel chain.

Alexey carefully placed the crucifix on Fedor's chest and bent over him.

'We will switch to a taxi, don't you worry ...'

'A taxi's the best thing ...' whispered Fedor again and added, 'Come here, bend down closer ...'

Alexey knelt down beside him. Fedor opened his eyes and said in such a quiet voice that neither Judy nor any of the others could hear:

'I know about the promise you made to Ulima ...'

'You know? How the hell ...' Alexey uttered loudly in amazement.

'Sshh ... I ... I promised her the same thing ...'

'You?! You mean to say you went with her after me?'

'Come on. Take it easy. Don't shout! Yes, okay, I did. But that's not the point,' mumbled Fedor in an agony of strained composure, 'The point is that I was in hospital with some of the pilots who transported Afghan children into the Soviet Union. And they told me where they had taken them. In 1982 and 1983 they went to a boarding-school near Alma Ata, in 1984 to somewhere near Perm, and in 1985 to near Khabarovsk. Ulima's boy was taken away in 1984, so that means he's in Perm, only I haven't any arms at all now, so what can I do about it?!' finished Fedor with an agonised smile.

'So ... that means you and I are ... "kith and kin", so to speak!' murmured Alexey, twisting his mouth into a spiteful grin. 'And who slept with her after you, then? She was a prostitute ...'

'Hang on!' exhorted Fedor, patiently and almost inaudibly. He closed his eyes and winced with pain every time the truck hit a bump on the uneven road. 'Hang on ... She was no prostitute! Quite the opposite if anything. Do you believe in fate? Just think – you slept with her, you got wounded, but you stayed alive. I went with her, I got wounded, and I could have been killed again just now, but I'm still alive. Something saved us, didn't it? And do you know what it was? The fact that she prays for us! Well, we promised to get her son back, didn't we? God is even protecting you from the KGB – because of her prayers! ...'

Fedor opened his eyes again and looked straight at Alexey.

'A taxi! A taxi!' Boris suddenly shouted gleefully from the wheel. He had spotted the familiar green 'For Hire' light ahead.

'Drive straight to the hospital!' ordered Alexey.

'No,' said Fedor. 'You're going away. And I shall pray for you. The prayers of the sick get there quicker you know,' he added with a barely perceptible smile from his bloodless lips.

Boris stopped the truck at a taxi-rank and shouted to the driver who was stamping his feet beside his taxi:

'Hey, where's the nearest hospital?'

'Go on! Off you go!' whispered Fedor to Alexey, and with obvious effort, raised his left arm and slowly made the sign of the cross over him.

19

'Wake up! Wake up! It's already five thirty!' said Judy, shaking Alexey by the shoulder.

He opened his eyes and looked at her uncomprehendingly.

'You asked me to wake you at 5.10! I've been trying to wake you up for twenty minutes already! Come on! Get up!'

'Uh-uh ...' murmured Alexey, dropping off to sleep again.

The train began to reverberate with a heavy rumbling of wheels and the brakes gave an earsplitting screech. Slowly, like a sick, lumbering animal, it came to a halt. All was quiet apart from the loud snoring of the elderly man on the top bunk who had joined them late the evening before. There were two narrow sets of bunks along either side of the compartment, which was cramped and with very little air to breathe.

With a single movement, Judy pulled the blanket off Alexey. But he was asleep fully dressed and did not react. Finally, losing her temper altogether, she grabbed him by the shoulders, pulled him towards her and pushed him down onto the floor. There was a muffled bang.

'Fucking hell! What are you doing? Have you gone stark, staring mad, or something?!' he moaned and was left sitting on the floor in confusion, rubbing his bruised side.

'The train's stopped. You asked me to ...' Judy began. But Alexey did not allow her to finish. He jumped up and rushed into the corridor.

A few moments later he reappeared.

'Quick! Get dressed! We're getting off.'

He hastily threw on his own coat, grabbed their rucksack and walked out of the compartment.

Judy followed him.

The dimly-lit corridor was deserted. All the doors in the carriage were closed apart from the steward's compartment at the very end of the corridor from which a thin yellow light emerged. There was a pungent smell of bleach coming from the lavatory.

'Where are you going?' the steward asked in surprise. He was a young lad of Eastern extraction with a big nose. 'I've already told you: this is Perm. Your tickets are to Sverdlovsk. Go back and get some sleep, mate!'

'No, we've changed our minds,' said Alexey. He offered his hand to Judy and helped her jump down off the carriage step.

'Hm! that's people for you!' the steward carried on. 'Still a day's journey away from Sverdlovsk, and they get off the train!'

Without stopping, Alexey dragged Judy along the platform.

'What time is it?' he asked.

'Twenty minutes till six,' said Judy, who could never remember how to say the time correctly in Russian and always made mistakes. Usually Alexey laughed at this and often asked the time when there was no need. But now he did not even smile. 'Why have we got off here?' she asked.

'Because we have to. I've got business in this town,' he replied, still holding her by the hand and squeezing her fingers painfully.

Judy looked miserably round the empty platform. The few passengers to get off the train were dragging their belongings towards the station building. It was cold, there was a heavy smell of burning coal, and thick grey clouds of smoke arose from the steam engine.

For six days they had been changing from train to

train. They would always get on late in the evening and alight before dawn. Alexey explained that by doing this there was less risk of their meeting the railway militia who often patrolled the carriages and might identify them at any moment.

But the chances of their being recognised from the photographs pinned up at stations on the 'Wanted Criminals' boards were extremely small. Apart from the photographs of them, there were a dozen or so others displayed. And the hordes of people were so preoccupied with their own business that they passed by with complete indifference and never even paused to look at the features of criminals being sought nationwide. But even if someone did look, they would have to look carefully and – even more difficult – memorise the faces that were printed on poor-quality yellow paper of the kind used in the USA for wrapping-paper. So that recognising Alexey and Judy from those photographs would have been almost impossible. It was only with great difficulty that Judy could recognise herself. The photograph had been enlarged from the one in her passport. Looking down at her from the stand was a clean, young, attractive, long-haired American girl in a thin blouse; her eyes were neatly done with eye-shadow and she had a smile that revealed strong, gleaming white teeth ... Whereas now she couldn't even remember the last time she had cleaned her teeth. She was standing in front of the photo-display wearing felt boots and some kind of ghastly men's jacket, head shaven beneath her scarf and with sunken and unmade-up eyes – Cinderella before the portrait of the Princess! And recognising Alexey was even more difficult – he had ceased shaving and had quickly grown a short stubbly beard and moustache.

But apart from that, they were surrounded by thousands and thousands of people also wandering around the country – young couples, demobbed soldiers, workers, people between jobs, drifters; either rushing to earn money in Siberia or else rushing to escape from Siberia.

Wearing quilted jackets, bodywarmers, army canvas jackets, heavy overcoats or nylon coats, and smelling of sweat, onion, garlic and vodka fumes. In the trains people ate hard-boiled eggs, pork fat and sour bread and drank vodka or cheap Algerian red wine, commonly referred to as 'ink'. Half of them – men as well as women – had mouths full of metal teeth – caused by lack of vitamins. From here, several hundred kilometres away, even Moscow with its more or less decently dressed inhabitants seemed to be a distant planet, almost like Western civilisation. It's amazing, thought Judy, how this wretched, impoverished, half-starving country, with its standard of living somewhere in the sixteenth century, had managed to subjugate half the world! And if half the world really is subordinate to it, then how come the country is so poor? Byzantium, Rome, Great Britain, during the heyday of their empires were all monstrously rich. But as for these people ... Why are we in America afraid of them?

'Let's go, let's go!' said Alexey, tearing her away from the contemplation of her own picture. He was constantly on the alert, and imagined that they were being pursued wherever they were.

Judy was on her last legs. The poverty-stricken, alien life all around had started by surprising her, but then it had begun to get on her nerves – the dirt, the lack of toilet paper, the food – heavy, foul-tasting and of dubious freshness, the water that smelt of iron and chlorine. During the day they kept warm and caught up with sleep in cinemas, and ate terrible food in various low dives. The sticky, sour-tasting black bread, the bluish sterilized kefir, the potatoes and pies (fried, of course, not in butter or margarine but in machine oil) – all this gave Judy a constant bad taste in her mouth, heartburn and a bloated stomach ... But the main thing was her own filthiness, the railway engine soot on her body, up her nose and in her eyes – all this fatigued her even more than the fitful sleep and hasty changes from one train to another. She began to be haunted by the same recurrent dream: she would be with her mother in Alabama, in a swimming pool, and next to her, floating on a tray, would be a large, delicious-smelling hamburger, and she could hear someone singing: 'Help yourself, help yourself, help yourself to a slice of pizza!' Why a hamburger should always accompany the tune of a pizza advertisement, Judy did not know.

During the day she would stare at Alexey with amazement. Their slovenly, nomadic life seemed to have no effect on him at all. A beard and moustache had altered his face almost to the point of non-recognition, making him look older, gloomier – almost like a character out of Dostoyevsky. He was more pensive, talked little, hardly looked at her, and she had the impression he regarded her as a millstone round his neck.

The first day, when he had told her about his meeting in Moscow with Tanya Goehr, Judy had taken heart. She had stopped crying, and new hope had restored her former determination and self-confidence. Now that they had money, perhaps they really would be able to bribe somebody and escape across the border. But why was Alexey behaving so strangely?! It was something to do with Perm – a place almost as far away as Siberia! Alexey kept prevaricating; he was keeping her in the dark about something. But why? Whenever she tried asking him about it, he said nothing; all he did was roll his eyes . . .

'Alexey, I've already told you! I need to have a wash!' she said and stopped.

They were standing in the large, dimly-lit hall of Perm railway station. beneath the high windows on either side were rows of wooden benches completely filled with sleeping people, suitcases, sacks, large wicker baskets. The window ledges were also filled with countless grey knapsacks, sleeping children, unwashed and unshaven passengers waiting for their trains. The air was full of tobacco smoke, and gloomy-looking, overtired people were milling about. By the wall with the closed ticket counters people were asleep on the floor or on their bundles and suitcases, sleeping in relays so as not to lose their place in the queue ...

In the middle of the hall, surrounded by pillars heavily chained together, was an enormous fig tree with tough green leaves.

Judy had already become used to Russian railway stations. She was not frightened by the shameless stares of unshaven, sloppily-dressed men. She would simply avert her gaze, turn away from the particularly importunate ones, and hold on more tightly to Alexey.

'I know, I know!' said Alexey impatiently. 'But first of all we must have a bite to eat. And then we'll look for a public baths.'

They stood outside the glass doors of the station restaurant, and Alexey gave the bronze handle a despairing turn. The restaurant was shut.

'They don't open till eight, the swine!' he murmured angrily, reading the sign on the door. 'Even when you've got money, you can't get anything to eat! Perhaps the buffet will have something ...'

Turning back the other way, he looked carefully all around him and moved off towards the other end of the hall. Judy followed him.

There was a queue of people clustered beside the long counter of the buffet. Alexey deposited Judy at the end of it and moved off towards the head of the queue. Elbowing his way forward, he settled himself next to a young man who looked old for his age and was wearing a crumpled soldier's greatcoat which no doubt served him both as a blanket and pillow on his long journey.

'Are you an Afghan?' Alexey said softly to the soldier.

He nodded.

'Me, too. I was wounded in the Lohar valley ...'

'Hey, push off!' A tough-looking fellow in a high fur hat immediately accosted Alexey. 'We know your type! Come on, just push off!'

'Where did you spring from, old man?' said Alexey,

smiling peaceably. 'Can't you see I've met an old mate of mine? Can't we even have a chat?'

'We know your sort of "chats"! You're queue-jumping! ...' said the man defiantly and moved right up to where Alexey was standing. 'Push off, or else!'

'Okay, okay! Keep your hair on!' said Alexey quietly. 'No need to make a fuss! I'm going ...'

He thrust a five-rouble note into the soldier's hand and moved away.

Ten minutes or so later the soldier came over to them and, with a smile, offered them two plates with a couple of glasses of tea and something to eat.

'There was bugger all to get – only boiled eggs. But there was some tinned fish as well, cod in tomato sauce. Watch out for the tea, it's scalding hot.'

'Thanks, mate,' said Alexey, taking the plates from him and offering one to Judy.

With difficulty she bit off part of the shelled egg and began chewing it listlessly. She stared at Alexey, amazed that he could devour bread, eggs and mouthfuls of tinned fish at this early hour.

'Why did we get off here?' she asked.

'I need to go somewhere,' he snapped.

'And what then?' she said, taking a gulp of almost unsweetened tea.

'Then we'll see,' he replied, as laconic as ever.

'Perhaps you'd like to tell me why we are travelling in completely the opposite direction from the border!' she said, losing her temper.

'Don't shout!' he replied, looking at her angrily. 'If I succeed in doing what I've got planned, then ...'

'Then *what*?'

'Then I'll know exactly where we're going! And that's enough questions. I'm damned if I know for certain myself!'

He drank his tea in one swig and wiped his mouth with his hand.

'And when are we going to go to the baths?'

'We can look for one straightaway. Why aren't you eating anything?'

'Because I don't want to,' she pouted and peevishly put the piece of black bread back on to the plate.

Alex wrapped up the remains of the bread in a piece of paper and stuffed it into his pocket.

'Let's go. And do up the buttons of your coat! That's all we need, for you to get a cold!'

When they went out into the street, it was already beginning to get light. On the square by the station, behind piles of snow, stood an empty trolleybus with iced-up windows. Alexey and Judy quickly boarded it and sat down near the door.

'Hey, you two!' the driver called to them. 'Who's going to pay then? Pushkin?!'

'I'll pay, don't worry,' said Alexey, going over to the automatic pay box. He dropped ten kopecks in and then turned towards the driver. 'Where's your nearest public baths, then?'

'Public baths? Sit down, and I'll tell you when to get off. It's on Razin Street.'

'Is that very far from here?'

'About five stops. Sit down. I won't forget.'

Alexey went back to Judy, but instead of sitting next to her he sat down one seat away. She felt offended. Why did he keep his distance all the time, she wondered. Even when he took her by the hand, a kind of shudder always seemed to cross his face. 'God, the sooner I get away from this country the better!' she thought.

The automatic doors didn't close completely – some ice on the bottom step prevented it – so there was a gale blowing through the crack. Skirting the short, stumpy memorial to Lenin, the trolleybus lurched away from Station Square and slowly trundled up a snow-covered street. They sailed past five-storey buildings with lights burning here and there, the occasional tree, lonely passers-by, and tall drifts of grey, ice-crusted snow.

A street or so later a pack of stray dogs bounded past.

Stopping by a huge snowdrift next to a grocery shop, they began to dig wildly in the snow in search of food. One of them suddenly rushed at a little boy walking along the pavement with a school satchel over his back and a half-eaten pie in his hand. The dog jumped up, snatched the pie and immediately swallowed it whole. The boy burst into tears. Judy looked back at him miserably ... 'Okay, guys! Time to get off,' shouted the driver. 'Razin Street.'

Alexey moved towards the front exit. The driver began to give directions. 'Walk straight on to where there is a chemist's shop. Turn the corner, and a couple of blocks further on you'll come to the baths.'

'Thanks, pa,' said Alexey, as he jumped down the steps. Without turning round to look at Judy, he marched off down the street.

They found the ramshackle, two-storey building immediately. The wooden sign 'Public Baths' was split down the middle.

Standing in the half-lit, damp corridor behind the wooden barrier leading to the changing rooms was a tiny plump old woman dressed in a long dark skirt and a plush jacket. She looked at them carefully as they entered.

'Are you open already, ma?' said Alexey offering her a three-rouble note and nodding in Judy's direction. 'She wants to give herself a wash. Is that all right?'

'Why not, for heaven's sake? Of course she can,' mumbled the old woman with her toothless mouth. 'We are open from six in the morning. That'll be seventy-five kopecks.'

'And do you have a towel? I'll pay for it.'

'We're not supposed to as a rule, but I've got my own,' said the old woman with a cunning smile. 'For a rouble I can let you share it.'

'Do that, ma! Do that!'

The old woman counted out the change and offered it to Alexey.

'There's no need, ma. Keep it yourself, and have a drink on me,' he said, pushing away her hand with the money. 'You'd better go and show her how to use the facilities here.'

'I can do that, of course I can!' said the old woman, bustling about happily and emerging from behind her barrier.

She took Judy down a narrow, dark corridor, opened a door marked 'Women's Baths', and led her into a spacious, dimly-lit room with long wooden benches along the walls. Above the benches were metal hooks with women's clothes.

'You get undressed here, my dear,' she said. 'And then you go through that door over there. You'll see the tubs when you go through. Have you got any soap? Or a loofah?'

'No, I don't need anything. Except for hot water,' said Judy, gasping slightly because of the heavy, moist atmosphere.

'But how can you manage without soap? Here's a piece for you,' said the old woman, offering her a big bar of dark brown soap that smelt like dog's pee. 'What are you turning your nose up for?! It's good stuff. It'll wash you as good as new. It doesn't matter that somebody's already used it. You don't get germs on soap!'

Judy took the cracked piece of soap with somebody's dried black hair stuck in it, turned it around in her hand and gingerly put it down on one side.

'Thank you,' she forced herself to say.

The old woman sat down silently on a bench and looked on sympathetically as Judy got undressed.

'How many years did you serve then? About five?' she said.

'Served where?' Judy asked in surprise.

'You know what I mean! In the camps! You weren't at a health resort, after all!'

Judy stared at her in amazement. 'I haven't been in any camp. What makes you think I have?'

'Come off it! I can see perfectly well – you're nothing but skin and bone. You look all right in the face, but your body's much too thin. You only saw people looking like that in the war. And she says she hasn't been in prison!' grinned the old woman with obvious disbelief. 'And where did you get your head shaved, then? No flesh on her, nothing but bones, and she says she hasn't been to jail!'

Judy turned away from her bashfully. Hanging up her underclothes on a metal hook, she headed into the shower-room.

The heavy, moist, hot air hit her in the face. Thick clouds of vapour hung motionless in the boiling hot steam-room. Judy could make things out only with great difficulty, and she looked around her in confusion.

There were only two showers, and both were occupied by fat women all covered in soap. A naked, short-legged, droopy-breasted woman, bent double with a full bowl of water, walked past. Putting the bowl down on a wooden bench, she washed her long sparse hair and dipped her head into the water. A handful of other women were doing the same thing over bowls next to her, silently and single-mindedly washing their hair, emptying the dirty water away next to them and returning to the taps for more.

Streams of soapy water were flowing over the warm concrete floor, and empty tin tubs were floating about in them. Huge drops of water accumulated on the grey walls and dropped down from the ceiling.

Overcoming her disgust, Judy lifted up a bowl which had floated to a halt not far from her and went over to the queue at the taps. A thin trickle was emerging from the cold water tap, while a thick stream of boiling water came out of the other. Rinsing her bowl with boiling water and somehow managing to mix some cold water in with the hot, Judy emptied the water over herself with immense satisfaction and closed her eyes in bliss.

She kept on taking more and more water, pouring it over her head and her breasts, when she suddenly noticed the other women had stopped and were staring at her. Feeling embarrassed, she smiled at them and filled her bowl once again.

'What were you in prison for?' a fat woman aged about fifty demanded. Her dye-stained yellow hair was tied in a scraggy knot above her forehead. 'Was it thieving or prostitution?'

'I haven't been in prison,' asserted Judy, smiling at all of them again. This time, however, her smile looked somewhat pathetic, as if she were facing a jury.

'Yes, she's a thief!' said the short-legged woman with the sagging breasts. I've had a look at her underwear. Her knickers and bra have all got foreign labels!'

'Or else she's a dissident,' suggested a tall brunette sporting a single gold tooth. 'Gorbachev's let them all out, and now they're spreading AIDS about, whoring with foreigners!'

'I don't understand what you are talking about!' Judy mumbled in confusion.

'She doesn't understand!' said a dyed blonde, putting her hands on her hips. 'Did you see that? Trying to play the innocent!'

'My sister got robbed a couple of days ago!' said the short-legged woman. 'Cleaned her right out they did! And all the militia can do is spread their hands and say that a new group of dissidents have just been released!'

'Yesterday a twelve-year-old girl got raped in the entrance next to ours!' came a shout from the other end of the steam-room. The woman was aged about forty with round hips and covered all over in soap. 'They let those filthy scum out, and we're afraid even to let our children go to school!'

'What do you want from me?!' stammered Judy. Thoroughly confused, she backed away towards the doors and away from the naked women standing around her. 'I haven't robbed anyone! I haven't been in prison anywhere!'

'What's the point of talking to her, eh, girls? She'll be gone in a minute, and so will our underclothes! If the militia can't sort them out, we'll have to do it ourselves!'

And with that the woman with the sagging breasts

jumped towards Judy and gave her a shove in the shoulder.

Judy recoiled in fright, threw her bowl on the floor and rushed for the exit. The woman began to scream wildly. Someone's nails pressed into her hand and began to force her back. Pushing away the heavy, moist bodies that were falling upon her, Judy managed to tear free and rush into the changing room. The women hurled themselves after her, shrieking.

They brought her down on the cold slippery floor, and the fat dyed blonde fell plump on top of her with her damp pendulous breasts. A bony woman with freckles smacked Judy round the face as she twisted and turned, and somebody else gave her a nasty kick in the thigh.

'Clear off, you bitches!' a voice suddenly shouted above their heads. His pale face distorted, Alexey rushed at the screaming mass of naked female bodies. He grabbed hold of someone and threw her against the wall. Then, with his hands slipping, he began wildly digging about in the frenzied scrum, trying to reach Judy who was lying underneath.

'Oh! A man! A man, girls! Quick! Hide!' Screaming, they all scattered in different directions. The frightened old woman in charge of the baths vanished into the corridor.

A few moments later everyone had disappeared.

'Get up. Can you manage?' asked Alexey, helping Judy up from the floor. He sat her carefully on one of the wooden benches and threw somebody's towel over her shoulders.

Judy was trembling, head hunched over her knees and pressing herself tightly into a ball.

'Have they hurt you? Are your legs and arms all right?'

'Yes, I think so,' she replied quietly, trying to stop her body trembling. 'Why did they do that to me? What have I ever done to them? Why did they decide that I must have been in prison?'

'That's the kind of town this is,' he replied. 'The

countryside is full of camps around here. They're not to blame. When they let the convicts out, many of them spend the first few days or weeks hanging around the town. And the local people have become brutalised. They carry out their own justice.'

Judy leapt up, threw her arms around him and squeezed against him with her moist naked body.

'I can't stand it any more,' she cried. 'I'm afraid! I want to go home!'

She could feel him tense up. Clumsily he raised his arms and tried to stroke her shoulders.

'I know,' he said in a muffled voice, as if trying to force himself. 'I know everything. We'll try to do something about it. But first of all I have to carry out my promise.'

'What promise?' she said. He was attempting to extricate himself, but she clung to him even tighter.

'I made a promise ... to a girl ... in Afghanistan,' he said, trying to prise her fingers away from his neck. 'And I must carry it out.'

'But what is it? What must you do?' she demanded, trying to ignore his attempts to get free.

'Our people took her child away and brought him here. I must make an effort to find him.'

'Her child?!' she said, recoiling and looking him carefully in the eye. 'Is it your child?'

'No. But I promised her. And she is waiting. I *have* to do it.'

'But what will we do with him?'

'I must take him to her.'

'In Afghanistan?! But there's a war going on there!'

'Well, so what? His mother is there! He must go home!'

Judy felt suddenly embarrassed at her nakedness and hurriedly reached for her clothes. Alexey turned away.

'So, we'll be going to Afghanistan?' she said, putting her underclothes on over her wet body. 'But you said Tanya would be waiting for us in Pakistan!'

'Well, we can't get straight to Pakistan in any case,' he

said. 'But we can try to do it by way of Afghanistan. If we bring this girl – this woman – her son, then she will help us make contact with the rebels. And that way we can get through to Pakistan. This boy will be a kind of safe conduct for us, once we get there ... And in any case, as I say, we don't have a border with Pakistan. So whatever we do, we'll have to go through Afghanistan.'

'Why didn't you tell me anything about this boy before?'

'I wasn't certain myself. But now I've made up my mind – it's our only way out.'

Judy went up to him and looked him carefully up and down: 'Is this woman called ... Ulima?'

Suddenly the door from the corridor burst open and in marched a militiaman in a fur coat tightly belted around his corpulent stomach.

'What's going on here?' he said in a domineering voice. 'A man in the women's baths? Show me your papers!'

Alexey walked slowly over to him.

'Officer, you're too late! There's been a riot here! They nearly killed this girl here! I had to intervene to calm them down!'

'What do you mean "a riot"? Don't spin me any hard-done-by yarns like that! Show me your papers! And that applies to you, comrade!'

'What are you getting so upset about, officer?' said Alexey. 'Just because there was a bit of shouting, you immediately start demanding our papers! We're perfectly ordinary folk.' Alexey smiled beseechingly. 'Let us go.'

'I said: show me your papers! If you haven't got any, we'll go down to the militia station and sort it out there. Come on, girl, out you go! And, no tricks, unless you want to earn yourself a new prison term!'

'Why do we have to go to the militia station, officer?' asked Alexey, walking right up to the militiaman. 'You want to see our papers. Well, here they are!' And with that, he suddenly thrust his hand into his pocket and produced a revolver, ramming it into the militiaman's fat stomach. 'Just one squeak out of you, you bastard, and I'll fill you full of holes. Turn to face the wall, and don't make me have that sin on my conscience! Marusya, tie his hands up with something,' he ordered Judy. 'Here's a towel!'

The militiaman's fat arms scarcely met behind his back. But Judy with trembling hands managed somehow or other to bind them together. Large beads of sweat caused by the heat and fear stood out on the militiaman's face. Some woman peeped out of the shower room, but as soon as she saw Alexey holding a pistol, she cried out and rushed back in.

'I wouldn't play jokes if I were you, lad!' said the militiaman. 'You'll be caught in no time at all, and you know what'll happen to you for attacking a representative of the authorities?!'

'Shut up, officer! You and I have already had our chat. I've got enough facing me already without you sticking your oar in! Sit down!'

Alexey quickly knotted a wet towel around the militiaman's hands. Then he removed his holster-belt, tied the militiaman's ankle to the wooden bench using the belt, and stuffed somebody's outsize bra into his mouth. Then, a little more calmly, he removed the pistol from the holster, unloaded it, dropped the bullets in his own pocket, and threw the revolver into a corner.

'Marusya, are you ready?' he said to Judy, who was hurriedly putting on her felt boots and jacket.

Together they dashed out into the corridor. It was quiet and empty. As they approached the outside door, they caught sight of a small, dark blue militia van on the street outside. Standing next to it was a tall militiaman in a short sheepskin coat together with the old bath attendant in a woollen shawl.

Alexey dashed back inside. Running past the doors marked 'Men's' and 'Women's' baths he stopped outside the toilet. Opening the door, he saw it had no window, so he ran on down to the last door at the end of the corridor

– the boiler-room. Judy ran after him. He opened the door and pushed her inside ahead of him.

They were immersed in a dry, smoky heat. There was a loud spluttering sound coming from the reddish flame in the oven. Thick pipes stretched away from the boiler beneath the ceiling; and over to the right behind a mountain of coal was a narrow, dusty window. Alexey clambered up the coal heap to reach it and looked out. The window overlooked the yard at the back. Rotten wooden barrels, old tyres and lumps of iron lay scattered all over the compacted snow.

Alexey forced the window frame in towards himself. Heavily, and with a cracking sound, it gave way, dried paint and pieces of wood scattering everywhere. He lifted Judy up on to the windowsill and pushed her forward. She jumped down, slipped awkwardly and fell flat on her face into the snow.

'Are you all right?' asked Alexey after jumping down himself and standing next to her. 'You haven't sprained your ankle, have you? Get up! We have no time to lose!'

The tiny cluttered yard was completely closed by high buildings. There were various doors all tightly secured from the other side, and try as he might, pulling at them with all his strength or hurling his whole body against them, none of them would open. But at last one of them did give way with a great creaking sound, and they rushed into a dark, musty smelling corridor. In front of them they could see a thin band of light gleaming under a front door.

They went up to the door. Alexey slowly opened it a little and peeked out. The militia van was about ten yards away from them on the left. The old bath-house keeper, wrapped in her big woollen shawl, was standing next to it, alone this time.

Alexey grabbed Judy by the hand and they dashed out into the street, running to one side of the old woman.

'There they are!' she shrieked. 'Stop them! Stop them!'

Alexey looked back. The militiaman had dashed out of the bath house.

'Stop!' he shouted, 'Or I'll shoot! Stop!'

Alexey and Judy turned the corner. Alexey looked feverishly around, wondering where they could hide. Without letting go of Judy's hand, he ran across the broad avenue, deftly manoeuvring between the moving traffic. They ran into the entrance of some building or other and hid behind the door.

The militia van sped up to the crossroads with its siren full on and then suddenly stopped, as if lying wait.

Breathing heavily, Judy and Alexey waited in silence.

'He's calling for help on the car radio,' Alexey whispered. 'Any moment and they'll have the whole area sealed off!'

The traffic lights turned to red, and several cars came to a halt, blocking off the militia van.

'Do you see that lorry there?' said Alexey, pointing to the vehicle closest to them, a tip-up lorry with builder's rubble in the back of it. 'Quick, let's make for that!'

Bending down, the two of them rushed up to the cab of the lorry. Alexey quickly opened it and pointed his gun at the dumbfounded driver.

'Don't say a word! Do you see that dick standing over there? We need to get away from him!' With that he bundled Judy up into the cab and made her crouch down on the floor. Hunching himself up, Alexey squatted down beside her, while still keeping the driver covered. 'Let's move, friend, it's green! If you get us through, I'll make you a rich man. Only no tricks, okay? I've got nothing to lose – you'll take the first bullet, and I'll take the second!'

The lorry moved off, motor roaring. Judy, afraid even to breathe, kept staring at the driver. With his eyes focussed intently ahead of him, the driver shot them an occasional inquisitive glance. He seemed not to be scared at all. Quite the opposite, his thick red lips widened into a smile.

'Don't worry, lad, we'll give them the slip!' he said confidently. 'So what was going on? Were they trying to nick you? I only got out myself a year ago! So what camp were you in?'

'I haven't been in camp, friend! Not yet, anyway! Have any more of them arrived yet?'

'I'll say! Don't get up yet, whatever you do! There are still more of them coming. Two Volgas – and some on motorbikes, too! You should just see the commotion you've caused! We'll just turn the corner and then ...'

The driver made a sharp turn, giving Judy a slight bump on the head. They drove into a narrow, deserted street.

'Listen, mate, do you know of any boarding-school for foreign kids around here?' asked Alexey, still crouching.

'The one in Vakhrushi, you mean? For Afghan children? Or the one for Palestinians in Korytny Posyolok?' asked the driver. 'You're okay to get up now. There's no more fuzz around.'

'The one in Vakhrushi, it must be. So what have you got around here – an international settlement or something?' Alexey said with a grin. He cautiously raised himself a little and put away his gun. 'I don't know ... Afghans, Palestinians!'

'Yes, we're bringing up Communists for the whole world, I suppose,' said the driver, also with a smile. 'And when they grow up, they'll give the capitalists what for! So it's Vakhrushi you want?'

'Exactly! Will you take us there? I'll pay you!'

'Well, you've promised me a fair bit already, you know! And Vakhrushi is thirty kilometres away!'

'Here, take this,' said Alexey, offering him a hundred-rouble note. 'That's on account. If you take us there, I'll give you as much again. How about it?'

The fellow hid the money in his inside pocket and scratched the back of his head. 'Do you really need to go there straightaway? I've got to unload this lot, you see. It's not very far away ...'

'No! Either you take us there now, or else ...' replied Alexey in a harsh voice.

'Okay!' came the reply, and the driver struck the steering wheel with his hands. 'If we must, we must. It normally takes me a month to make two hundred roubles. Now I can earn it all at one go. Only let's agree on one thing – you tell me a few yarns while we're on the road, so I don't get too bored.'

The truck emerged into a quiet street in the suburbs. Judy sat down in the passenger seat, pulled off her scarf and stretched to look in the driving mirror.

The driver's eyes sparkled at her with curiosity. He said nothing, but then burst into peals of laughter.

'What's up with you?' Alexey asked darkly.

'It's a real hoot!' he said, still laughing. 'It's so funny! Like in a film! The gun, the fuzz, the girlfriend with the shaven head! If you tried telling anyone, they wouldn't believe you! And you say you've never been in prison!'

Alexey looked at the chortling driver, then at Judy, and finally burst out laughing himself. Quietly to begin with, and then louder and louder.

Judy didn't quite get it at first, and looked first at one, then at the other, and then she too found herself beginning to smile.

20

'I know everybody says that they got jailed for nothing,' the driver said. 'I've heard people say it myself, and haven't believed them. But the woman who nobbled me I really only did see for the first time in the militia station. Someone had raped her and robbed her in the main entrance to a block of flats, not very far from where I live. A big, strapping woman she was, with an arse like a barrel. I would have run a mile! Why the bitch testified against me, I don't know. I think the investigator must have made her do it. They don't like it when they have unsolved crimes on their books. It means they don't get their bonus payments! And they dug up some little girl as well to give evidence against me. She'd seen me grab hold of the woman and drag her into the entrance. She was only tiny, but God could she lie! And she reckoned she could remember my jacket, and my face, and how I threatened the woman with a knife. And I was over the other side of the town at the time! This all took place in Pskov. I'd just returned after being demobbed and was as happy as a sandboy. I'd managed to get a good job, buy some decent clothes, and a girlfriend had appeared on the scene. My mother, of course, was already getting ready for the wedding. And then, there you are – they grabbed me right outside the house, twisted my arms behind my back, gave me a couple of punches in the gut and carted me straight off to jail.'

The driver fell silent, peering angrily ahead at the churned-up road with its frozen potholes.

There wasn't much room in the cab, and every time there was a jolt, Judy was thrown against Alexey's hard shoulder. Sometimes she grabbed hold of him in fright to prevent herself from being tossed in the air.

Outside there was a low, lustreless grey sky barely lit by the wan, glacial sun that looked like the remnant of a bar of soap. Beneath them stretched a snow-covered wasteland with stumps of trees sticking up here and there, logs, felled and half-decayed trees, railway sleepers. It seemed as if the snow were only covering up the remains of some awful disaster – a forest fire or a hurricane. And stretching away into the depths of the snow, to the circle of forests on the horizon, were the pock-marked ruts of old roads and fresh roads, and of things that weren't roads at all, but simply duck-boarded furrows in the snow. The occasional charred tree trunk sticking up out of the snow lent this landscape a prehistoric, even Martian look. A few dozen rickety wooden crosses marked out a graveyard . . .

'What's happened here?' asked Judy. 'A fire?'

'Timber felling . . .' said the driver.

The further they drove from the city, the more the snow-covered wastelands of this 'timber felling' were interrupted by high blind fences with barbed wire strung out on top and long grey wooden barracks behind them. At the corners of these fenced-off areas were wooden watch-towers manned by guards with sub-machine guns.

'There's my little camp for you!' said the driver, nodding towards one of them. 'Two years and six months of my life – gone just like that! Until they turned up the real rapist!'

'Prison!' Judy thought to herself with a shudder. Her hands went cold with fear, and she involuntarily drew closer to Alexey. But he turned his head towards her in surprise and moved further away, as if her proximity was unpleasant to him. 'Why is he taking me here? What child is this that we're looking for, for God's sake?! What kind of madness is this?!'

Blocking the road ahead of them, an enormous tip-up

lorry was doing a lumbering U-turn. They came to a halt.

Stretching out to the left of them, with mountains of pipes, concrete blocks and cable drums scattered all over the place, was a building site. Tall iron and concrete piles were sticking up out of the foundation trench. Drawn up on the side of the road were several lorries loaded with large paper cement bags. Chains of people stretched back from each lorry. One after the other, at equal intervals, bending low under the weight, they would drag the cement bags off on their backs towards the building site. All were wearing identical clothing – dark-coloured padded body warmers, quilted trousers, enormous patched felt boots. Their heads were wrapped in scarves.

'They're women!' shouted Judy. 'Why are they carrying such heavy loads?'

'Women!' said the driver with a contemptuous smile. 'They're not women, darling! They're female convicts!'

'How do you mean?' asked Judy, as she turned her eyes towards a group of men wearing white sheepskin coats and carrying sub-machine guns. They were standing at a slight distance and observing the women carefully. Some of them were holding dogs on leads, their moist tongues hanging out.

'Have you just dropped in from Mars, or something?' said the driver in amazement. 'You must know what I'm talking about! . . .'

'And why are they . . .?' Judy began, but Alexey gave her a dig in the ribs and she fell silent. She could not take her eyes off the monstrous scene, however.

'Listen,' said Alexey, obviously wanting to change the subject. 'Why did you stay around here, instead of going back home to Pskov?'

'Well, why do you think, man?' said the driver excitedly. He put his foot down and they moved off down the road which was now clear. 'I swore to myself that I would find that woman! And my mother knows me only too well. She gathered her things together and rushed over here, weeping and begging me on bended knees. "Let's stay here," she says. "If you go back there, you'll end up in jail again, for sure." Well, I looked at her crying and calmed down a bit. She's right, I thought. What's the point in digging your own grave? So we stayed. Mother exchanged flats. For somewhere smaller, it's true, but never mind,' he said, squinting at Judy. 'We get by. The only thing is, I'm still looking for a girlfriend. All the girls here are crazy, somehow. Most of them gather together in the "Permian Sunsets" restaurant, or in the "Central" – there aren't any others. They get pissed as newts and hang on the men's necks of their own accord. You won't believe this, but the city's got nearly a million inhabitants and there's nowhere for anybody to go! It'll be a hundred years before any of your so-called *glasnost* reaches here! Anyway, this *glasnost* is damn-all use to me! All I want to do is meet a nice girl somewhere and spend a bit of time with her. But where? At the House of Culture? They're all drunk out of their minds there as well, even before the dancing begins! Women go in for drinking even more than men now. Don't get me wrong, I'm not against people having a drink, but for young girls aged fifteen or sixteen to be sprawling about on the stairs absolutcly plastered is too much! What do you think, my pretty one?'

'Yes, you're right, I suppose,' said Judy absent-mindedly. She was tensely watching the column of men moving along the road, all identically dressed in filthy coarse overcoats, brown ersatz felt boots and quilted caps with ear flaps. 'Who are these?' she asked.

'Convicts!' he spat out, scarcely reducing speed. 'They're driving them back to work.'

The endless column of exhausted convicts was moving slowly down the slippery, icy road. Accompanying them on each side, holding their sub-machine guns against their chests and shouting loudly, were the escorts with their dogs. As if at a single command, the grey faces of the camp inmates all turned at once in the direction of the lorry as it passed by. Seeing a woman's face at the window, one of them gave a loud whistle, and you could hear dirty remarks, shouts and hoots. Dozens of eyes gleamed with excitement and pale frozen lips parted in a smile.

Judy shrank back into the seat.

'Come on, put your foot down!' ordered Alexey.

The driver obediently increased his speed and they overtook the column of convicts, only to draw level immediately with one coming in the opposite direction. These turned off the road towards a long embankment where three or four hundred convicts were dragging sleepers and rails and banging metal dowels into the sleepers with sledge-hammers – they were building a narrow-gauge railway line. Both the convicts who were already at work and the new arrivals seemed strangely stunted pygmies. 'They're just young teenagers!' Judy suddenly realised. Beneath the pulled-down caps one could see the thin faces of fourteen- or fifteen-year-old boys, grey-blue from cold.

Obviously Alexey too didn't feel quite himself at this scene.

'Fucking hell!' he said nervously. 'How much further is it to Vakhrushi?'

'This *is* Vakhrushi,' smiled the driver. 'It's a famous place.'

'Famous for what?' asked Alexey, on his guard.

'Famous for its swamps,' replied the driver, no longer smiling. 'If you're thrown into the camp at Vakhrushi, you might as well admit that it's curtains for you! They cut peat here. And they still use spades and pick-axes to this day. Spend two springs here and you're a dead man. You might as well be given the death sentence at the outset . . .'

Judy felt herself trembling with fear. Until now fear for her own life had to some extent concealed what was going on around her: only the sight of dirt and poverty, and the absence of ordinary comforts had made her shudder. But now her entire being revolted against the terrible things she had seen around her, and she was quite unable to comprehend them.

How could these people live like that? What kind of embittered soul did you have to possess in order to force your own women and children to do hard labour like that – with sledge-hammers in the snow in such freezing temperatures! They may have committed some crime or other, but all the same, they were people, your own Russian people, *their* sisters and children! Even Hitler, even the slave-owners of Rome didn't do that to their people! ...

The lorry drove into a settlement of pitiful wooden huts and chipped breeze-block houses and slowly drove along the narrow lanes. Ten minutes or so later they stopped at a tall, blind fence. Sticking up behind it was a four-storey building made of brick. The gate in the fence was also blind, made of fresh, yellow planks. To the left of it was a door, also closed.

'Well, here's your boarding-school!' said the driver. '"Sunshine", it's called ...'

Alexey thrust his hand into his pocket, produced another hundred-rouble note and offered it to the driver.

'Perhaps you could wait for us for an hour or so?' he said. 'Then I'll pay you as much again ...'

'No, I can't,' said the driver. 'They'll give me the sack. As it is, I'm taking a risk ...'

'Okay, then. As you like,' said Alexey, opening the door and pushing Judy towards it. 'Let's go.'

Judy did her best to smile at the driver. 'Thank you,' she said, and jumped down off the step onto the hard, frozen ground. Alexey jumped down after her and threw his rucksack over his shoulder.

'See you again!' the driver shouted to them cheerfully. 'But watch out for the fuzz! They're real sods around here!'

With a roar the lorry swung around and sped away down the deserted road. A shroud of snow twisted in its wake. A tiny, shaggy-haired dog bounded out of one of the courtyards and barked after it loudly.

Alexey walked slowly along the fence, occasionally testing the tightly nailed planks with his hands. Noticing a rubbish bin by the side of the road, he went over to it, overturned it and rolled it towards the fence.

'Take hold of the rucksack,' he said to Judy and, climbing up onto the bin, grabbed hold of the top of the fence.

'There's barbed wire on the other side as well,' he said, jumping down and giving the rubbish bin an angry kick.

'Listen,' said Judy hurriedly. 'There's no need. What do you want this boy for, anyway? Let's head straight for the border. We've got enough money ...'

'Belt up!' he snapped rudely and made his way towards the boarding-school entrance.

'But why?' asked Judy, grabbing him by the sleeve. 'Haven't you had enough with killing the KGB men? There will be police all round the place ... They'll be bound to catch us!'

'I said that I had to. Okay?' said Alexey, pulling his arm away and walking on. But he hadn't taken a step before Judy's pale face appeared in front of him again, and she said 'But I won't let you! ...'

Alexey's eyes narrowed in an unpleasant way, and his cheek-bones stood out sharply.

'Well, go on! Hit me!' Judy shouted contemptuously, trying to stifle her fear. 'Hit me! Well, what is it? Can't you do it? You slave! But then you're all slaves here! Cowardly slaves! Slaves! Slaves! ... How can you stand to live here?!' And Judy couldn't hold back any more – she burst into tears. At last she had found the word to define them! That was why they all had such lustreless eyes, such impassive faces, the constant tension of enmity, of hatred towards everything and everybody! They were masochistic slaves who wanted slavery for everyone! ...

Alexey stood next to her as she cried and sobbed like a child, repeating in English over and over again:

'You're slaves! Nothing but bloody slaves!'

'You're just crying out of pity for us,' he said pensively, and with his hard fingers he began carefully to wipe away her tears. 'But there's no need to feel sorry for us, you know! We should all be gathered up in a single sack, and someone should tie a big stone to it and then ...'

He fell silent. Then, as if something in him had broken, he began to mutter indistinctly: 'She was only twelve. And one of our soldiers had raped her. She gave birth when she was thirteen. A boy. And six months later the child was taken away from her and brought here.' He nodded in the direction of the fence. 'I got to know her later, when she was already fifteen ...'

Judy had calmed down. She looked in amazement at his face with its stubbly, sunken cheeks and with tiny icicles on the dark, almost black moustache. For perhaps the first time he now had a relaxed and kindly expression. He walked away from her and leant his back wearily against the wall.

'By that time she hadn't seen her boy for eighteen months,' he said, raising his eyes to look at Judy. 'So there you are. I promised her that I would find her son. But then I got shell-shocked. I was put into hospital, and then I got a job ... But I had made her a promise, you understand?!'

'Do you ... love her?' asked Judy softly.

'Yes, I did love her ...' replied Alexey, turning his suddenly convulsed face away from her for a moment. Turning round again, he said hurriedly: 'Listen, if you're afraid to do it, then I'll go by myself. And you wait here ... But I have to do it, you see? So as not to be a slave, as you put it!'

'But how will you get him away from here?' Judy asked miserably.

'I'll use money to do it! We've got fifty thousand, after all! For money like that you could buy the whole school! Lock, stock and barrel!'

Judy looked at him silently. Then, turning away, she headed resolutely towards the school gates. 'Come on,' she said, 'Let's go!'

She gave a loud knock at the door to the left of the gate.

There was no reply.

Then she gave the door a hefty shove and it opened wide with no trouble at all. There was nobody guarding it, and only an empty courtyard on the other side in front of the four-storey building. Standing on the left hand side of the building outside a side entrance was a covered lorry. Two young lads in blue overalls were unloading milk churns from the lorry and rolling them into a wide open door.

The two of them crossed the yard, and Alexey opened the heavy spring-loaded door of the school.

The spacious entrance hall was adorned with a huge portrait of Lenin and a banner saying 'Long Live Friendship Between the Peoples of the World!' Immediately opposite the entrance was an office. Sitting inside was a wizened and wiry little man of about fifty-five wearing an old army service jacket without epaulettes. In front of him was a glass of tea and some food on a plate. He raised his eyes to look at them as they entered, and wiped his mouth with the palm of his hand.

'What do you want then?' he asked suspiciously.

'Well, pa, I'm looking for a particular boy,' said Alexey with a smile, 'I want to find out if he's here.'

'Have you got permission from the Town Council?' said the man, leaning his hands on his desk in an authoritative way.

'Well, no. I only want to take a look at him, that's all. Why bother to . . .'

'It's not allowed!' said the man, interrupting him and moving his plate of food to himself.

'Well, who's in charge here? I want to have a few words . . .'

'I'm in charge here! And if I say it's not allowed, that means it's not allowed! Away with you!'

He got up from his chair again, stumped noisily around the desk on his wooden leg and moved threateningly towards Alexey.

'Keep your hair on, pa!' said Alexey, peering past the man into the depths of the corridor. 'What's going on at the moment? Is it lunchtime?'

'I said clear off! It isn't any of your business what's going on here at the moment! Go away! And what's your name? If you're not careful, I'll call someone in authority and they'll talk to you rather differently!'

At the far end of the corridor leading off the entrance-hall one of the doors opened and pairs of children aged six or seven began appearing, holding each other by the hand. The boys all had identical crew-cuts, while the girls all had straight dark hair just covering their ears. The boys were wearing warm grey flannel jackets with high collars, and the girls had dresses of the same material. Stepping silently in their felt boots, the children walked along the corridor towards the staircase at the end. It was odd to see such quiet children – as if they weren't children at all, but old folk in a geriatric home. A tall fat woman in a wide skirt and a black man's jacket walked along at their side. She kept a careful eye on them, occasionally shouting out in a dry, irritable voice:

'Ramsur, hold Fatima by the hand! Maksud, don't turn your head round! Hey, you at the front: keep in line!'

The children trembled with fear and lined up obediently.

'Listen, mate!' Alexey said in a hurried whisper. 'Here's fifty roubles for you. Don't make a fuss! All I want to do is have a look at him! We've come from a long way away, and it's only for one day!'

The man's eyes gleamed as he saw the note with the portrait of Lenin that was being offered.

'But why do you need to see them?' he asked uncertainly. 'They're all as black as the ace of spaces, after all! Or did you have an affair with someone?'

'Yes, you've got it right, dad! I was on station in Afghanistan, and you know yourself ... So I'm terribly anxious to catch a glimpse of him. He's my flesh and blood, after all, and I've never seen him before ...'

'Well, lad, I'd like to help you, but I don't really know how to. Unauthorized persons aren't supposed to be here at all. How will you find your one, anyway? They give all of them different names here.'

'Well then, pa, just tell me who it is looks after all the paperwork here.' So saying, Alexey extracted another fifty-rouble note, folded it carefully into the first one, and waved them before the eyes of the custodian. The man went almost crazy at the sight of such money. 'All you've got to do is tell,' Alexey said. 'And if something goes wrong, you can swear blind that I forced my way in or climbed in through a window ...'

'At the end of the corridor over there you'll find the Personnel Department,' the man said. 'That's where all the papers to do with the children are kept. Valentina Terentyevna is in charge. But she's a really ruthless old hag!' said the man, still looking at the money and shaking his head in disbelief. 'You'd better not try offering her any money! She'd call the militia immediately! And to tell you the truth, lad, I'm pretty scared of her myself. She'd give me the sack in no time at all! And then what would I do? I've got a sick wife at home.'

And with a great effort he tore his eyes away from the money.

'Don't worry, dad!' said Alexey, thrusting the money into his pocket, and gave him a trusting slap on the shoulder. 'I'll be as quiet as can be ... And if something should happen, pa, then it's got nothing to do with you. I won't give you away, come what may! I give you my word as a soldier!'

And with that he quickly moved off down the corridor.

When they opened the door marked 'Personnel Department', they found a small, desiccated-looking woman with short grey hair combed smoothly back. She turned quickly to look at them. She was standing next to an open book case, arranging books on it. Lying on her desk was a heap of files containing documents.

'Who are you then?' she said in a loud voice that was used to being obeyed.

'We're from the ... City Education Department. Come

to do a check!' said Alexey, closing the door quickly behind Judy. Seeing the key protruding from the lock, he gave it two turns.

The women looked at them in amazement.

'From the Education Department? And carrying rucksacks?! And why have you locked the door?!'

'Because that's how it's got to be!' said Alexey, going up to her and taking her cautiously by the arm. 'Don't you worry about anything! Sit down in your chair. I don't want to have to use this thing' – he produced his gun from his pocket – 'but if I have to . . . Well, you don't need me to tell you! . . .'

'Who are you?' said the old woman. She shrank inside the large leather armchair into which Alexey had pushed her. 'And what do you want?'

'I need to know the whereabouts of a certain child. A boy. He was removed from Afghanistan almost two years ago. He was brought out of Afghanistan in December 1984, to be exact.'

'And how do you know that he was brought here?' asked the old woman, beginning to recover her wits. 'There are other boarding-schools where children from Afghanistan are taken.'

'I know. The pilot who used to fly these children out told me. But look, why don't we reach a peaceful understanding?'

Alexey sat down on a chair in front of the old woman, then produced from his rucksack a bundle of notes tied up tightly with a paper band and put it down on the desk in front of her.

'There are a thousand roubles there,' he said. 'You let me have the child, and the money is yours.'

'You swine!' said the old woman contemptuously.

Alexey put his hand silently into his rucksack and extracted a second wad of notes and placed it next to the first.

'Two thousand.'

The old woman said nothing, and stared at him with hatred.

He then produced two more bundles of notes.

'Four thousand! You've never even held such money in your hands before!'

The old woman suddenly jerked her grey head forward and spat loudly in Alexey's face.

He started back and jumped up, his face distorted with anger, and swung up his hand with the pistol.

'No!!' Judy screamed and rushed over towards him. But Alexey had come to his senses himself. He lowered his arm and wiped his face, his lips trembling with anger.

'You b-b-bitch! You Party whore!' he shouted.

He strode towards the window and with one movement tore down the heavy old curtains hanging from a rickety wooden pelmet. There was a gentle shower of plaster. The old woman got up from the armchair.

'What are you doing, you criminal? You are destroying public property!'

'Button your lip, fascist!' said Alexey, pushing the old woman back into the armchair. He then grabbed some papers from the desk, crushed them in his fist and stuffed them into her mouth. 'I'll give you "public property", you bitch! You've been destroying it yourself for the last seventy years!' – And with that he began to wind one of the curtains around the old woman.

She tried to mumble something, twisting and turning about, but he swaddled her, legs and all, into a tight cocoon. Then he yanked out the telephone wire and used it to tie her to the armchair.

Only after all this did he pause for breath. He looked around him, went over to a high wooden cupboard and opened it. Stacked neatly on shelves were rows and rows of slender, numbered files. Alexey took out a few of them, and quickly leafed through one ... then a second ... then a third, and then flung them all away angrily.

'Let me give you a hand ...' said Judy, going over to him.

'Look at the kind of thing they do here, the bitches!' he said, showing her one of the open files – the case history of one of the children along with a photograph. 'Not content with altering their names, they give them all new dates of birth – either May 1st or November 7th! Workers' holidays, in other words! How will we ever find anything here?!'

He looked round helplessly at the shelves of files.

On the very top shelf at one end was a thick copy book in a brown calico cover. Judy stood on tiptoe, lifted down the book and opened it. There on the first page in an even calligraphic script was written: 'SUNSHINE BOARDING-SCHOOL: REGISTER OF NEW ARRIVALS. Perm Regional Education Department.'

'That's more like it! ...' said Alexey, becoming interested.

Somebody knocked quietly at the door and then pulled on the handle.

'Valentina Terentyevna!' said a timid female voice. 'What's happening? Have you fallen asleep? Your lunch has been on the table for ages. It'll get cold! Valentina Terentyevna, are you there? We've already put the children to bed, and we're waiting for you.'

Alexey and Judy froze and looked at the old woman in the armchair.

But although she was trying to move, she was swaddled too firmly. All the same, Alexey went over to her and pressed his hand over her mouth which was already gagged with paper.

On the other side of the locked door someone turned the handle and gave another knock. But receiving no reply, they slowly went away again.

All this time Judy had been leafing through the 'Register of New Arrivals'. Each page contained the date of arrival of a new group of children and columns headed: 'Arrival's number', 'New name', 'Weight', 'Approximate age' and 'Personal file number'.

Alexey came over to join her.

'They measure the children's weight like so many cattle!' Alexey gave a bitter smile. 'All the rest they invent themselves. Go on to November 1984. Just look at these names! Half of the boys are called Nazym, like Nazym Khikmet! ... Wait a minute!' He stopped her at the page headed '21st November'. 'Her boy was taken from her in November, though the exact date, of course, I can't remember. So let's see ... "Approximate age"' – Alexey moved his finger down the relevant column. 'There you are! Six months!' He moved his finger down to the name and then swore. 'Damn! It's a girl! We must keep on looking ...'

'There's another one aged six months,' said Judy, pointing to the bottom of the page, 'and there's one aged seven months. The first is called Nazym, and the second – Muslim.'

'Muslim is in honour of the singer Muslim Magomayev. See if there are any more in November.'

Judy turned over the page. The next entry was dated January 3rd 1985.

'So there you are,' said Alexey. 'What are their personal file numbers?'

'8411 oblique 19 is Nazym's,' Judy dictated, and Alexey immediately located the relevant file on the shelf. '8411 oblique 27 is Muslim's.'

Alexey got down the second file, opened the two of them and then angrily slapped them against his knee.

'It's a dead duck!' he said.

'What do you mean?' asked Judy.

'Well, just look,' and he opened both files again and showed her the photographs of the children. They were of infants in arms with their tiny, wrinkled faces and short little bodies. 'How can you recognise anyone from these? They're three years old by now! That's it! Let's go! Although, hang on a moment ...'

Alexey rushed over to the old woman's desk, took a metal rubbish bin out from under it, and raked all the papers off her desk into it. Then he used a match to set light to a whole matchbox. It flared up instantly and he threw it into the bin. The papers caught fire with a dry red flame. Then Alexey hurled the telephone off the desk into the flame, as well as the fan with its plastic casing and blades, a plastic paperweight and all the plastic biros, together with the plastic tumbler in which they were standing.

'What are you doing?' Judy asked, terrified as she watched Alexey drag the flaming bin over to the door.

'Don't worry!' he said, placing the bin about a yard away from the door. 'Plastic takes a long time to burn, but the main thing is that it makes a lot of smoke and gives out a really good smell!'

And indeed the plastic of the telephone, the paperweight and all the rest was gradually catching fire and, as it did so, began to give off the most appalling stench and clouds of black, sooty smoke.

'And now let's go, quickly,!' commanded Alexey, grabbing a wooden chair with his left hand. With his right, he turned the key in the door, took it out and cautiously pushed open the door.

The door opened onto an empty corridor with not a soul about. Judy and Alexey stepped out of the office. Then, jamming the foot of the chair in the door handle and holding it there, Alexey began to close the door. As soon as there was no more room for his hand to reach past the door, he quickly slammed it shut so that the tilting chair wedged the door from the other side. Smoke was creeping out from underneath. Locking the door from the outside, Alexey rushed along to the old watchman who at that moment had looked out from the entrance hall down the corridor.

'Listen, dad, where's the fire alarm? Terentyevna's papers have caught fire ...'

'The panel's over there in the wall! You'll see the button!' said the watchman, beginning to rush around in fright. 'Come on, let me do it! although maybe not. I'd better run along and take a look ...'

'No, pa, don't you go rushing into fires with your wooden leg!' said Alexey, pressing the button. 'They'll sort it out without you!'

A siren began to wail loudly throughout the building. Frightened women appeared from several rooms.

'What's happened? Is it a fire?! Where? ... We're on fire!!' they screamed, looking around in confusion.

'It's down there, in the far room!' said Alexey, rushing up to them. 'Quick! Help!'

Everybody rushed along to the door of the Personnel Department and started banging on it. They tried to open it, each one pulling on the door-handle in turn. But the door was shut tight, and more and more smoke and fumes were escaping from under it with a terrible smell.

Alexey and Judy slipped off unnoticed down the corridor and went up the stairs to the next floor. The siren's loud wail resounded throughout the building, drowning out the cries of the teachers, nurses, cleaners and cooks who came running from all directions.

From the door marked 'Director' there appeared a very stout woman in a light-coloured dress with an artificial rose on her bosom and straw-coloured dyed hair fluffed up high.

'I order you to cease panicking!' she shouted slightly breathlessly and waved a piece of paper about – probably instructions on what to do in case of fire. 'We'll carry out everything according to plan! First of all, lead the children outside! All of them! Right away! And you, Darya, run for the fire-hose!'

A few women were already running from the end of the the corridor, unrolling the long fire-hose as they did so. Somebody else was trying unsuccessfully to open the rusty valve of a fire extinguisher. But the door of the Personnel Department remained as firmly shut as before, and black, acrid smoke continued to pour from under it. Standing next to it was the distraught old watchman. The door-handle had been pulled right off the door, and he stood there helplessly turning it over and over in his hands.

Running up the stairs to the first floor, Judy and Alexey found themselves in a long corridor with a large number of doors off it. Some of them stood open, and frightened children were running out of others. Everywhere you could hear the sound of their loud crying and screaming. A skinny, oriental-looking girl of about fifteen ran past. Alexey stopped her.

'Where are the three-year-olds?' he asked.

'What?' she said, not understanding – or perhaps she could not hear him properly over the wail of the siren.

'What room are the three-year-old children kept in?'

'On the second floor ... room number thirty-four,' she said, understanding at last. She spoke with an accent and rolled her black protruding eyes in fear.

'Are you from Afghanistan?' Alexey said mistrustfully.

'Yes ... But what's on fire?'

'Something down below,' said Alexey with a vague wave of the hand, and ran on up to the second floor. Judy, taking several steps at a time, rushed after him. The door of room 34 was open. From inside came the heart-rending screams of two-, three- and four-year-old children, terrified by the wailing siren. Some of them were sitting on the narrow iron bedsteads; others were lying down, with blankets pulled up to their chins, while others ran around the room, shouting 'Bombs! Bombs!' Alexey and Judy stopped in confusion at the sight of about thirty pairs of frightened black eyes fixed upon them. Then suddenly:

'Papa! Papa!!' Children began to scream from all sides, launching themselves at Alexey. 'Papa! Babá!!'

Alexey involuntarily backed away, but Judy's heart melted at the sight – a dozen orphaned children throwing themselves at the first dark-haired stranger they saw in the hope that he was their father! Meanwhile they continued flocking around him, grabbing hold of his arms and legs and wailing: 'Papa! Babá!'

'Quiet!' Alexey shouted at last, regaining his senses. 'Quiet!'

And when the children had fallen silent, he went on: 'I can't be the father of every one of you!'

'Quite right!' said Judy, faintly grasping the idea behind his words. And stepping forward she said loudly:

'Nazym! Which one of you is Nazym?'

Several boys jumped down barefoot from their bunks and ran towards her.

'You're not Nazym!' a little girl shouted at one of them. 'You're Manukher!'

The impostor said something in Afghani and hurled himself at the girl.

Judy turned towards Alexey. He was examining the boys who had rushed up to him, and then he shook his head.

'God alone knows!' he said. 'Not one of them looks like her!'

Then, turning to the others, he shouted: 'Muslim! Which one of you is Muslim?'

Two boys from different ends of the room quickly jumped down from their bunks.

'Papa! Babá!' they shouted and rushed towards Alexey, grabbing hold of his legs with their tiny hands. One of them had light hair which set off his swarthy little face with its dark eyes. 'Papa! Babá!' he wailed, choking with tears.

'This is the one!' Alexey shouted excitedly. 'He's fair-haired! Ulima said he had fair hair, like his father! Muslim, where's your coat?'

Then he bent down to the second boy and said: 'I'm sorry, I can't take you with me as well . . .'

'I knowed you would come,' said the fair-haired boy, smiling through his tears. 'My coat is in the cupboard. Are you going to take me away? . . .'

Alexey tried to go over to the wall-cupboard, but the boy clung tightly to his leg, as if rooted to it.

'Bring something warm for him!' he shouted to Judy as he lifted the child in his arms and ran out of the room. In the doorway he collided with the same dark-faced fifteen-year-old girl he had stopped in the corridor a couple of minutes earlier. She flew into the room, glanced fleetingly at Alexey as he ran out and in a strict voice she shouted something to the children in Afghani. They began to remove their clothes from the ends of the beds and quickly dressed. The girl rushed immediately to help a few of them. The others were calling to her from all sides:

'Fatima, help me! No, me! Fatima! Muslim's father has come to get him! Fatima, I've done a wee-wee in my trousers ... Is it us bombing the Russians? ...'

Judy ran over to the wooden cupboard, divided into narrow compartments each with a door and stretching the length of one wall. She opened the first that came to hand, took a child's coat and hat off the peg, and grabbed a pair of black felt boots from underneath the bottom shelf. Seeing a pile of neatly folded vests, pants and shirts at the top of the cupboard, she grabbed them too, then raced quickly out of the room.

The corridor was already filled with screaming, hastily dressed children. The siren still howled deafeningly. Ahead of her Judy caught sight of Alexey with a rucksack over his shoulder. He had Muslim by the hand and was moving quickly forward through the crush. Judy tried to catch him up, but more and more children were emerging from the rooms, panic-stricken at the sound of the siren and the general commotion. They kept on screaming 'Bombs!', bumping into each other, fighting, shouting and getting in each other's way.

The ground floor was even more crowded. The door of the Personnel Department door was still shut. The old watchman and another young fellow in dark-blue overalls were trying to break in with axes. They had already managed to pierce a small hole, through which acrid black smoke was pouring. Meanwhile a few women stood at the ready next to them with a pump and a hissing fire-extinguisher.

'It looks as if something serious has caught fire there!' thought Judy. 'And what about the old woman?! Don't tell me ... Oh God, not another killing!'

Alexey and Muslim were waiting for Judy behind the stairs next to a side entrance. They pressed themselves against the wall, allowing the children to run out and past them.

'Let's go!' said Alexey. He grabbed Muslim's coat from Judy and, without putting it on properly, just wrapped the boy up in it and quickly stepped outside.

Clutching the child's things to her breast, Judy rushed out after them. She was surrounded by the sound of children crying and shouting, the noise of feet and the wailing of the siren.

The school gates were open wide, and frightened, angry teachers were trying to calm the half-dressed children who had been led outside. They shouted at them, grabbed them by the scruff of the neck like kittens and shook them roughly and unceremoniously. But even the ones they managed to lay hands on only remained silent for a second.

Carrying Muslim in his arms, Alexey rushed over to the lorry which the two lads had recently finished unloading. One of them they had caught a glimpse of just now – he had been standing in the door of the Personnel Department. But the other one was nowhere to be seen. Alexey opened the cab door, shoved the quiet Muslim onto the seat and sat down at the wheel. Judy got in on the other side. Alexey turned the ignition key: the starter motor whirred, but the engine would not fire. He tried again, pressing down the accelerator as far as he could, but all he got from the starter was a strained whining sound.

'Hey you! What do you think you're doing?' shouted the young lad in blue overalls who suddenly appeared from the side door. 'Clear off out of our lorry!'

Alexey paid no attention to him and tried as before to get the lorry started. 'Shut your eyes and lie down!' he said quietly to Muslim.

Meanwhile the lad in overalls had jerked open the door.

'I thought I told you to clear off?!' he shouted, grabbing Alexey by the sleeve.

'Shut your face!' Alexey screamed at him. 'Can't you see? This boy needs to go to hospital urgently! He's nearly dead from carbon monoxide poisoning!'

'To hospital?' said the lad, looking doubtfully at the half-dressed Muslim who was lying with his eyes closed on Judy's lap.

'Come on!' Alexey shouted. 'It's on Terentyevna's orders! What's your name?'

'Stepan ...' said the lad in surprise.

'That's right. "Take Stepan's lorry!" she said, "and rush him to the hospital!"'

Alexey's face looked serious. 'Check whether he's still breathing!' he shouted to Judy.

'But Valentina Teren ...' Stepan began as he saw Judy bending apprehensively over the boy.

'Do you want to go to prison or something, you idiot?!' Alexey shouted, and anger distorted his already far from benign expression. 'He could snuff it any minute! How do we get this old banger started?'

'Hang on a minute. You need to crank it,' said the lad, pulling the crank handle from beneath the seat. Slamming the door, he went round to the bonnet, inserted the handle and gave it a sharp turn. The engine started immediately.

'Thanks, old man,' said Alexey, poking his head out of the window. 'You've saved someone's life, so to speak ...'

'Let me drive!' said the lad, raising his arm to open the door. But instead of waiting, Alexey drove away past him. Sounding the horn, he roared out through the open gate into the street, frightening the children and teachers gathered there.

Outside he turned left and put his foot on the accelerator. With its load of empty milk churns rattling loudly, the lorry sped away from the boarding-school. Coming towards them from the other direction with its siren sounding was a fire engine. Alarmed by the siren, hastily-dressed people rushed to their front gates and out onto the street.

Alexey turned the corner and drove to the edge of the settlement, looking round constantly to see whether they were being followed. The empty milk churns continued to rattle and roll around the back of the lorry. Outside, the rows of squat snow-covered huts got fewer and fewer. At last they drove out of the village into the snowy fields. Calmer now and looking around less and less, Alexey headed towards the forest.

'Listen,' said Judy, unable to contain herself any longer. 'That old woman ... What do you think? Will she have suffocated?'

Alexey turned to look at her, and after a pause said: 'Cats like that have nine lives! But you were great! I thought that you would chicken out, instead of which you ...'

'Why should I have chickened out?' said Judy in surprise. 'I've done karate. Only for a few months, admittedly, but all the same ...'

'Karate?' said Alexey with a doubtful smile.

'Yes, for self-defence. A lot of women take it up back home ...'

'So it's true that you have criminals roaming the streets?'

'What do they do in your country then – fly through the air?'

Alexey burst out laughing. 'If they're like you and me,' he said consolingly, 'then they mainly drive around in stolen lorries!'

The lorry reached the edge of the forest. When they were a fair way in, Alexey turned off at the first crossroad onto an old duck-boarded track, and then across onto another road.

Judy could sense that his mood had changed. Although his face looked as tense as it had done earlier, his intonation was less sharp than before. He cast frequent affectionate glances at Muslim who with quiet excitement bounced up and down at each bump in the road. Alexey took the boy's hand and placed it on the steering wheel. Muslim immediately grasped it with all his strength.

'That's right!' said Alexey. 'You've got a good grip. You must eat a lot of porridge!'

"No-o-o!' said Muslim, laughing and turning his curly head. 'I hate porridge! Aunt Natasha tells me off 'cos I don't eat it!'

'And why don't you eat it?'

''Cos I don't want to. I like meat!'

'Quite right! That's a man's food.'

Stretching along the road (if that was the word for this ice-covered, bumpy, rutted, pot holed forest cutting) were two walls of snow-covered fir trees, pines and cedars. Occasionally these walls would break as they drove past abandoned timber clearances with half-uprooted stumps, felled trees and the remains of conifers sticking through the snow. Every now and then they also met empty or loaded lorries going in the other direction, and tip-up trucks or trailers loaded with timber.

Alexey would then lean forward suspiciously and grip the wheel tightly with both hands, as if he was about to be rammed. But everything turned out all right, and the vehicles would speed on by.

Suddenly Alexey turned off the road down a cutting which headed off into the thick of the forest. After driving down it a little way, he stopped.

'We need to switch to another vehicle. I'll run back to the road and flag someone down. You two stay here. I'll not switch off the engine, just in case ...'

'I want to go too,' said Muslim, with a sudden whimper. 'Don't want to stay with her!'

'Why not?' said Alexey, stroking his head.

'Don't want to! Want to go with you!'

'But I'll be back in a moment. I'll just stop some passing car, and then we'll be off again,' said Alexey, trying gently to persuade him. 'And she's nice ... she won't hurt you ...'

'No-o-o! I don't want her! I want to go with you! She's horrible! My mummy's dead and now you're with *her*! She is not nice!'

'Who told you your mummy's dead?' Alexey asked in a trembling voice.

'Vera Viktorovna. She said our mothers got killed by the rebels. And our fathers. But I knowed you're not dead! Fatima teached me how to pray, and I asked Allah to send you back. Don't want nothing else! Don't want her! Just want you! ...'

Muslim flung his arms round Alexey's neck and hugged him tightly with his whole body. 'Papa! Don't leave me any more! Papa!'

Alexey embraced the boy silently, his stubbly cheek rubbing against the boy's silky hair.

'Don't worry, I won't leave you!' he whispered, scarcely audibly.

Judy watched with amazement. How gentle and affectionate he could be! So why was he always so sharp and rude with her? ...

'Listen to me, Muslim,' said Alexey, extricating himself and looking him in the eye. 'If you want to be with me, then you must do what I say. We don't have the time to argue! I have to go and stop another lorry so that we can carry on with our journey. And you must wait for me here ...'

'Why do we need another lorry?' the boy asked softly.

'Because ... you may be taken away from me! And so that we are not found, I have to change lorries.'

Alexey opened the cab door. 'Sit here and wait for me.'

Judy moved into Alexey's seat at the wheel. Muslim knelt on the other seat and pressed his face up against the window. From there he could see Alexey disappearing down the cutting, and he remained like that for about half an hour until, at last, a small lorry covered in a tarpaulin drove up to them.

'He's coming! He's coming! Papa's coming!' shouted Muslim, jumping joyfully up and down on the seat.

And, sure enough, Alexey climbed out of the lorry together with a red-cheeked young soldier who was carrying a thick coil of rope. The soldier and Alexey said something to each other, smiled in the direction of Judy who was sitting at the wheel, and then went over to the bonnet of the lorry. Then, as Alexey stepped behind the soldier's back, Judy realised immediately what was about to happen. She threw open the door in alarm and was about to shout out. But she did not have time: Alexey had already struck the back of the soldier's neck with his fist; the soldier started up with a jerk, raised his hands to his head and fell down.

'What ever did you have to do that for?!' said Judy. She jumped down onto the snow in horror. 'Did you have to kill someone else?! Haven't you killed enough people already?! You swine! ...'

'Cool it!' said Alexey, giving her a good-humoured smile. 'He and I came to an agreement. He asked me to himself. I gave him five hundred roubles, and he pocketed them. And he told me to hit him, but not too hard ...'

Alexey dragged the soldier's unconscious body into the cab of the lorry.

'Help me lift him up!' he said. 'What are you goggling at him for?! Don't you believe me? He'll have to have an excuse, and this way no one will smell a rat when he says someone clobbered him and then drove his truck away! Come on! Get hold of his legs. Wait a minute. I'll help Muslim down first ...'

They dragged the soldier up into the cab and placed him on his side across the seat.

'He's promised to lie there for five hours,' said Alexey, tying the soldier's hands and feet loosely with the thick rope. 'Not even Gorbachev earns one hundred roubles an hour! And we'll have covered a good distance in that lorry of his in five hours! ...'

The soldier was beginning to groan slightly, without regaining consciousness.

'Come on! Get into the other truck!' Alexey ordered.

A minute later they were already speeding along the track. After a few kilometers they emerged from the forest onto a tolerable dirt road and Alexey was able to put his foot down to almost full throttle. Bouncing over the pot-holes, the lorry rushed along and sent clouds of powdery snow behind it. Muslim laughed happily, pressing up close to Alexey and grasping the wheel with both hands. Alexey meanwhile whistled as though urging on a team of horses and made inarticulate warlike noises.

'Where are we heading now?' Judy asked sadly, unable to share in their joy.

'Don't worry!' said Alexey, suddenly placing his hand on her knee. 'We'll get through! With a girl like you around, there's no doubt about it!'

Then, slightly embarrassed, he snatched his hand away again and said hurriedly 'And now we've got a general with us too! There's no stopping us now! Am I right, General Muslim?!'

The boy laughed happily.

Alexey's sudden gesture – and even more so his embarrassment – sent a wave of warmth down Judy's spine. She turned her blushing face away to look out of the window and, surprised at her own unsuspected feelings, stared blankly at the monotonous winter landscape flashing past outside.

PART FOUR

21

The bazaar in Dushanbe, the capital of Soviet Tadzhikistan, had its long and noisy rows of stalls set up right in the middle of the town. People dressed in quilted oriental robes and multi-coloured dresses bustled noisily among the huge chaotic mountains of tomatoes, cucumbers, dried apricots, persimmons, grapes, peaches, cherries and melons.

The men were wearing bright skull-caps, the women either black yashmaks or brightly dyed kerchiefs. Customers would often squat down, suspiciously feeling or smelling the vegetables and fruit. They haggled furiously, objected in loud guttural accents to the prices, or else they simply smiled contemptuously.

Mounted on a high pillar in the middle of the bazaar, the funnels of four loudspeakers pointed in various directions and broadcast some dirge-like Eastern melody at full volume. A stout young Tadzhik woman with narrow dyed black eyebrows was sitting on the ground beneath this column, her legs bent at the knees and spread wide open, revealing two enormous thighs. In front of her was a hearth of white-hot coals with a squat tripod on which was placed a cast-iron cylindrical vessel with a wide opening at the top and hollow inside. Lying next to it was a pile of moist dough covered with a wet cloth. She would tear off a lump of the dough, smack it loudly up against her thigh, throw it into the air, smack it against herself on the other side, then turn it over again and slap it on her thigh once more. After a dozen or so such operations the piece of dough would turn into a damp, flat cake and the Tadzhik woman would throw it deftly into the metal cylinder, keeping it pressed against the edge of the red-hot hollow area inside. A few moments later, with a lightning movement, she would retrieve the hot cake all cooked and ready from the vessel and offer it to the next customer, who would eat it on the spot – with goat's cheese, water-melon or grapes. The Tadzhik woman would push the rouble payment into her bosom, pull off a new piece of dough and slap it against her thigh. The cakes were selling quickly, and there was a queue of people in front of her.

Judy and Alexey held Muslim tightly by the hand while he chewed away at some Turkish delight. They stopped in front of an enormous cauldron full of pilau. Thick aromatic steam was rising from the cauldron. Standing next to it was a Tadzhik with a desiccated, wrinkled face. Using a greasy iron spoon he would ladle a pile of rice into the pilau, using his fingers to adjust any stray rice gains. Pensively he smoothed out the rouble notes that he was given and then bent down to see to the cauldron once again.

'Would you like to try some?' Alexey asked Judy.

'*I* would!' shouted Muslim insistently.

Judy shrugged her shoulders uncertainly. A couple of hours earlier they had eaten in some *chaikhana*,* and Judy was still having to swallow greasy spittle and cope with indigestion from the highly seasoned meat and noodle stew she had eaten.

Alexey took some pilau from the Tadzhik and gave it to Muslim. Like a real Asiatic, he thrust three fingers into the hot rice and after stuffing his mouth full, began turning this way and that, looking all around him with avid enthusiasm. Here in the bazaar he was like a wolf cub who has finally escaped back into his own environment. Muslim darted this way and that, yelping and squealing,

*A Tadzhik teahouse – *Tr.*

asking to try everything, and they had to keep a firm grip in order not to lose him. 'What's this?' 'What's that?' 'Is this food too?' he kept on saying, pointing to persimmons, grapes, melons, pomegranates, dried apricots, and peppers. He had never even suspected the existence of such an array of fruit and vegetables while he had been at the 'Sunshine' boarding-school!

Judy was examining with interest the women dressed in their bright flowery dresses. Their dark faces with black dyed eyebrows were fixed and submissive. Their backs were completely straight, since on their heads they carried heavy wickerwork baskets full of purchases as they glided swiftly along after their unencumbered husbands. From time to time the latter would self-importantly come to a halt, choose some goods, haggle long and rhetorically with the merchants, drink a glass of hot green tea if it was offered, and then move on. And the women moved silently behind them, carrying their heavy loads on their heads. Just occasionally, instead of women, the men would be followed by donkeys almost as submissive and laden with panniers.

Despite the fact that there were so many people milling around, nobody hurried. The rhythm of both merchants and customers was leisurely and reflected an inherently oriental awareness of the immobility of time. Nobody paid any attention to a couple of young people walking along with a child.

At long last, Judy could feel her sense of fear had abandoned her. She stopped looking around apprehensively and shuddering at any unexpected noise behind her. And she ceased to cast her eye anxiously over every man who passed, suspecting him of being a KGB agent.

They had taken almost a week to reach Dushanbe, changing trains all the time just as they had before. But now, with a sleepy whingeing child, it was much more difficult to jump out each morning at an unfamiliar railway station and then spend all day hanging about the cinemas in search of warmth and eating hurriedly in cheap cafeterias. Although life at the boarding-school had made Muslim older than his years, he would still get tired and play up, refusing to eat anything apart from cutlets, bread and milk. But Alexey was amazingly patient and affectionate with him, especially when it was a question of getting him something to eat. Not one cafeteria, nor even the restaurants, had milk on the menu, and in the shops there were enormous queues for milk. All the same, Alexey would pay the waitresses and counter-girls ten roubles for each glass of it, so Muslim always had his milk. In turn, the child idolized him – although, come to think of it, he would have idolized him even without the milk. There was no question of telling the boy that Alexey was not his real father – the revelation would simply have killed him . . .

After journeying across practically half of Russia, Judy discovered to her astonishment that even her vague ideas about the poverty of this country, which were based on reading American newspapers, were very far from the truth.

All the State-owned shops were empty. Their long dusty shelves contained nothing but tins of cheap fish and aubergine pâté, together with packets of macaroni. Limp cabbages covered with black pockmarks were piled directly on the floor. The empty shelves marked 'Bread' were stacked with packets of hardened salt. It was somewhat better in the cooperative shops, which belonged, as Alexey explained, not to the State, but to cooperatives made up of several collective farms. These shops had one or two sorts of smoked sausage on sale as well as butter and sometimes meat, or even ordinary sausages. Here they sold sweets, sugar, flour, rice, buckwheat, but all at a price three or even four times higher than prices for the same products in State shops. 'But do your collective farms really produce chocolates?' Judy asked Alexey on one occasion. 'These co-ops are a pure fiction,' he grinned. 'They've nothing to do with the collective farm system – apart from the prices, of course. Old Gorby is afraid to raise prices officially, as the people would rebel. That's why the State shops selling at standard prices have got nothing in them, and yet the cooperative shops are not his responsibility. In fact, it's all a load of eye-wash, of course. They are *all* State shops ...'

Looking in at a haberdashery shop one day, Judy spent a long time fingering the enormous pairs of knitted women's underclothes. They were all the same faded green colour. Even the largest woman would have found them reaching down to her knees, where they were threaded with thick, tough elastic! The bras were also unbelievably big and of the same antediluvian fashion! Judy put them down in despair, deciding that she would carry on as she had been. She had one set of underclothes, the ones she had arrived in from New York, and every night she rinsed them in the toilet in the train before going to sleep. They did not have time to dry properly in the berth overnight, so she would put them on damp and they would dry on her ...

But once the train had got clear of the Siberian March snows, it sped them swiftly towards the south, to Central Asia, towards the April spring which had arrived early this year in Tadzhikistan. Dushanbe greeted them with a hot, almost summer sun, the fragrance of flowering Lombardy poplars, dry dust and a chain of mountains cutting off the horizon, the high Pamirs, sharp-pointed like the teeth of a saw, and white from never-melting glaciers. And as if to contrast with the cold, faded, leaden grey of Siberia, everything here was hot, bright, multi-coloured, like the glaze of the clay pottery glittering in the sun and occupying several very long rows of stalls in the bazaar. God! What pottery that was – worthy of a poem! The most improbable colours – crimson reds, penetrating blues, deep greens, violets, white – merged miraculously in capricious patterns on clay pitchers, dishes, vases, teapots, goblets, cups, pots, tea-bowls ... This whole miracle of folk art, honed by centuries of ceramic craftsmanship, was standing and lying simply on the ground – hundreds upon hundreds, in rows. And in the same place, seated by their wares, were the potters, working at their primitive wooden work benches, each of them using his foot to turn a wheel. And under their hands, the damp clay would spread out on the wheel, coming to life as a pot-bellied jug or a flat dish ...

'Hey, youngsters!' said a dirty-looking gypsy with a large golden ear ring in one ear who had been dogging Judy and Alexey. 'Want to have your fortunes told? Or smoke some grass? ...'

Alexey paid no attention to him. But then he turned round suddenly to him and asked him quietly:

'Do you know Sukhar?'

The gypsy gave Alexey a suspicious look.

'I know everybody here. And who are you?'

'A friend of his. If you take me to him, you'll get three roubles!'

'Huh, you must be joking! Who would give away his friend for three roubles?! You must take me for a real fool!'

And with that the gypsy turned around contemptuously and walked away.

'Hey, I'll give you a ten-rouble note!' Alexey shouted after him, but the gypsy shrugged his shoulder scornfully and disappeared in the crowd.

'If you don't want to tell me then I'll find him myself!' said Alexey, and moved on.

Two dark-complexioned, narrow-eyed young girls in torn flowery dresses rushed up to him.

'Give us a rouble!' demanded one of them, a girl aged about thirteen with pigtails plaited in tiny twists. The other one was running along beside her with hand outstretched.

'Do you know Sukhar? I've got a meeting with him, but I can't find him!' said Alexey, taking some money out of his pocket and looking at the girls expectantly.

'Yes, he's in the meat stalls! That's where his place is!' said the girl, stretching her hand out for the money.

Alexey gave her a rouble and another to her silent companion. Lifting Muslim up on to his shoulders, he began to walk quickly towards the meat stalls.

The dressed carcasses of sheep, hung up on large metal hooks, slowly swung in the sun and oozed large droplets of yellow fat. Yellowish-white sheep's tails turned inside out to reveal the fat, and lifeless sheep's heads with grey films over their wide-open eyes were laid out on the counters. Heaped up next to them were mountains of chopped-up, dark-looking meat, eggs, and wickerwork boxes with live and dead chickens whose heads customers could choose to have cut off on the counters, there and then. There was a smell of blood and decay, and large green flies swarmed thickly over the sheep's carcasses and got in the eyes of the donkeys who hid behind the stalls in the shade of the dusty poplar trees. The grey aprons of the meatsellers were covered with enormous brown stains, the varied shades of blood quite dazzling to the eyes.

Elbowing his way through the customers, Alexey stopped near a squat-looking Tadzhik in a black skull-cap, selling fermented mare's milk.

'Fresh *koumiss*! Ice-cold *koumiss*!' the Tadzhik shouted in Russian in a piping, almost feminine voice.

'I want some *koumiss*!' Muslim announced.

'Do you even know what it is?' laughed Alexey, but he took the boy off his shoulders, set him on the ground and said to the Tadzhik:

'Pour us some out.'

'Rouble the glass!' said the Tadzhik and dipped a narrow cut-glass container into the tall milk churn. 'Marvellous *koumiss*!' he shouted. 'We milked her at five this morning, so it's quite fresh!'

'Would you like some?' said Alexey, turning to Judy.

'What is it?'

'*Koumiss* – you know, mare's milk. It's really thirst-quenching.'

'No . . .' said Judy, turning away in disgust.

Alexey and Muslim downed a glass each, and the boy

immediately said: 'Oi! That tastes good! More! ...'

'Isn't Sukhar here today?' Alexey asked with an air of indifference as he settled up with the Tadzhik.

That latter quickly flashed two narrow slit-eyes at him.

'Who are you?' he asked sharply.

'A friend of his ... We agreed to meet, but he's not here.'

'I know nothing,' said the Tadzhik, turning away.

'Look, there's nothing to be afraid of! I'm not a cop! I'm his friend!'

The Tadzhik pretended not to hear, and began once again shouting, 'Fresh *koumiss*! Ice-cold *koumiss*! ...'

Two young lads wearing trousers and shirts but with skull-caps on their wiry black hair closed in on Alexey from either side. A knife blade flashed in the hand of one of them.

Judy screamed in fright. But Alexey took her calmly by the hand and stared at the lads intently.

'Who are you?' said one of them, prodding the blade sharply into Alexey's side.

'I'm looking for Sukhar,' said Alexey. The muscles in his cheeks clenched, and Judy felt him squeeze her hand tightly.

'Tell me who you are,' said the lad, shaking him slightly by the shoulder.

'He and I were in the army together. Put that knife away!'

'Why are you wandering around the bazaar like an evil spirit and frightening people?'

'I've already told you! I'm looking for Sukhar! Tell him that Alyosha Odalevsky is here.'

The two lads exchanged glances but said nothing.

With a nod towards Judy and the child, one of them asked: 'Who's this, then? Your wife?'

'Yes,' replied Alexey without a moment's hesitation. 'Tell Sukhar that Alyosha Odalevsky is looking for him ...'

'Let's go!' said the lad, prodding Alexey forward with

his knife. 'You and I can tell him ourselves! But not here! And don't think of running away. We'll catch you up! ...'

He hid the knife and moved off after Alexey. Judy hurriedly followed them. Realising that something serious was happening, Muslim went quiet and walked along next to Judy, clutching her hand.

They turned off behind the meat stalls and found themselves in a wide courtyard filled with lorries, cars and donkeys. A few men in long quilted robes were sitting on the bare ground next to their donkeys and camels, lazily sipping hot tea from bowls and smoking hookahs. There was the sickly sweet smell of hashish in the air. The smokers looked at them nonchalantly as they passed by, and spat leisurely upon the ground.

Opening a narrow door bearing the sign '*Chaikhana*', the lads pushed Alexey forward into a smoke-filled room crammed full of men. Here the smell of hashish was heavy and persistent. One of the lads pushed Alexey into some side corridor, turned to Judy and said harshly: 'You stay here!'

'No!' said Alexey, turning towards him. 'They're coming with me!'

'She stays here!' said the lad, moving towards him menacingly. 'And you walk on! We'll soon see whose friend you are!'

'I said that I won't go anywhere without them!' said Alexey, rushing to Judy's side. But then he suddenly gave a loud groan, clutched his stomach and bent double. Standing next to him and smiling contemptuously, the second lad was unclenching his fist.

Judy dashed towards Alexey. Terrified at seeing him desperately gasping for air, she threw both arms around him and tried to shield him from a second blow. Alexey struggled angrily in her arms, turning his face away, flushed now and with tears in his eyes.

The lad who had struck Alexey suddenly gave a loud cry, and Judy caught sight of him trying to tear his arm away from Muslim who had sunk his teeth into it. But

Muslim had him in a mortal grip, and the second lad went to aid his friend.

'Don't you lay a finger on him!' screamed Judy, beside herself with anger. And without noticing it, she carried on shouting in English: 'Damn you! Don't touch him! You bloody shit!' And, lifting her left leg up sharp and high, she kicked the lad on the chin with her boot. He keeled over onto his back, like a rag doll. Judy turned abruptly towards the other one – in a karate stance with her legs bent slightly at the knees and placed wide apart, the palms of her hands held out straight. Then she saw standing next to the lad a tall thin blond fellow aged about thirty with a neatly clipped fair beard and moustache. He had a narrow face with a high forehead and his long curly hair was held in place by a thin sweat band, like a hippy or a rock star.

Leaning on a stick with an elegant silver handle, the fair-haired man, limping slightly on his left leg, went over to Judy.

'How did such a marvellous American accent turn up in our parts?' he smiled.

'Sergey!' said Alexey, straightening up with difficulty. 'She's with me! Muslim, come here!'

The boy ran quickly over to him and clutched at his leg. Alexey lifted him up into his arms.

The fair-haired man turned towards Alexey and scrutinized him silently, obviously not recognising him.

'What, don't you know me?' said Alexey, still trying to regain his breath. 'It's me, Alyosha Odalevsky! Army Number 29627 ...'

'Alexey?!' said the blond fellow, raising his light-coloured brows. 'What are you disguised like this for? A beard and a moustache? Your own mother wouldn't have recognised you! Well, how are you doing? And is this karate lady with you? Who is she?'

'It's his wife,' said one of the lads, holding on to his arm which had been well bitten by Muslim.

'His wife? So you've got married? To an American?'

said Sergey, not ceasing to stare at Judy.

'I'll tell you everything! Come on, let's go somewhere ... to mark our reunion!'

'Why go somewhere?' said Sergey, leaning on his stick and opening a door leading to the back of the *chaikhana*. 'Let's go to my place! I've got everything there!'

They walked through another room filled with Tadzhiks sitting on low platforms deeply wrapped up in some sort of board-game. They were obviously playing for high stakes – lying next to each board were piles of notes. Two shapely Tadzhik women wearing crimson dresses and brightly-coloured baggy cotton trousers drawn in at the ankle with embroidered ribbons were silently carrying small squat teapots around the players, pouring green tea into the tea-bowls and filling the sugar-bowls with fine-grained sugar.

The fair-haired man walked across the room with a confident proprietorial air, and the Tadzhik waitress lowered her eyes and made way for him.

Opening a narrow door, Sergey courteously let Alexey, Judy and Muslim through into a large softly-lit room. Covering the floor was an enormous luxurious carpet, each of its corners scattered with cushions embroidered with flowers. Next to the far wall was a cumbersome old-fashioned writing desk with carved legs and a brass desk-set on its green baize. To one side of it was a bar of similar old-fashioned design with a refrigerator built into it.

Sergey went over to the bar and opened it. Inside was a battery of bottles with non-Russian labels familiar to Judy.

'What would the lady prefer? Whisky, scotch, vodka? Or some good Georgian wine? You still won't exchange anything for vodka, Alyosha, or has that changed?' Smiling hospitably, he offered them tall thin glasses.

When they had all taken their first swallow, Sergey looked questioningly at Alexey.

'Well, tell me all about it, old boy! What brings you to our parts? And when did you take time to produce the wee one? Before you entered the army, eh? But I'm sorry:

what's your name?' he said to Judy. He had been casting curious appraising glances at her all the time, and seemed to be chatting with Alexey out of necessity.

'Judy,' she replied, feeling that his scrutiny of her was not unpleasant. The whisky was going to her head slightly, and her long-forgotten feminine coquetry suddenly re-emerged with unexpected strength. She liked staring Sergey straight in the eye, smiling at him, listening to his soft, low voice.

'I've come to visit you on business, Sergey!' said Alexey suddenly, as if angry about something. 'You've expanded a fair bit here, I see – hashish, gambling. Did you get all the money from importing copies of the Koran?'

'Well, I can see you haven't changed, old boy!' said Sergey, smiling good-naturedly at Alexey. 'You still call a spade a spade! I'm a war invalid, I get a pension! What do you mean, Korans? Are you drunk already, or something?' Sergey looked lingeringly at Judy once again.

'Come off it, Sergey! What are you trying to pull the wool over my eyes for?! And there's no need to be afraid of her! Anyway, the point is that we need to get into Afghanistan somehow! And from there – into Pakistan!'

'I see. So you've decided to abandon this motherland of ours ...' said Sergey seemingly not even surprised. 'But why do you have to choose such a ridiculous way to do it? After all, you could do it legally. You are an American, Judy, aren't you?'

'Yes ...'

'Where from, if it's not a secret?'

'New York.'

'There, you see, old chap! It's so simple! Your wife is an American, so all you have to do is to visit the American embassy, then our Visa and Registration Department, give in your papers and Bob's your uncle! ... Or won't they let you out for some reason?'

'Yes, but she's *not* my wife, you see!' Alexey rasped out impatiently. 'If it was as simple as you imagine it to be, I shouldn't have trailed out here all the way from Moscow!

There's a search on for us! We could get put away for life! I've knocked off two KGB men! Our photos are displayed everywhere! There's no way she can stay here. And there's my American great-aunt waiting to meet us in Pakistan – and only one way to get through to her – via Afghanistan!'

'Things are never simple with you, Alexey! One thing at a time! First things first! So she's not your wife?' said Sergey, turning to look with renewed interest at Judy. 'Whose is the boy then? Why did you knock off the cops? And what American aunt is this? Take me through it step by step!'

And so with many digressions and looking discontentedly at Judy, who did not lower her gaze during Sergey's now frankly immodest scrutinies of her, Alexey began to tell their confused and complicated story.

Twenty minutes or so later, having finally worked out what it was all about, Sergey burst into loud laughter.

'Well, old boy, you've certainly cheered me up! There's a story for you! You couldn't invent something like that, even if you wanted to! And you – a prince?! Well, that for my money, brother, is the neatest joke I've ever heard. *You* – a prince! Ha ha ha! Here I am with a grandfather who was a roofmender and a mother who worked as a bookkeeper during the Siege of Leningrad, yet I know four languages! And I very nearly wrote a doctoral dissertation on the Neolithic Period! Meanwhile, you with your savage boarding-school education turn out to be a prince! It's like a joke! You – a prince! Although, if you think about it, returning a child to its mother is the action of a prince! Ha ha ha!'

Sergey was sitting on the only soft armchair in the room. Judy and Alexey had settled themselves on the floor amongst the cushions. Muslim, having eaten his fill of pilau, fruits and Turkish delight in the bazaar, had fallen asleep long ago, his head buried in a mountain of cushions.

'I need your help!' said Alexey, staring resentfully at his laughing friend.

'I realise! I know! But how can I help you, old man? After all, it's only in spy novels that people can cross borders just like that! You and I know what the Afghan Mojahedin are like, don't we, old lad? Just let them find out that you've fought against them and they'll blow your brains out, no questions asked! And a few other things, besides!'

Sergey got up out of the armchair, limped over to the writing desk and removed a small metal box from the lower drawer.

'Would you like some? It's cocaine. Of the purest quality! You can rely on the opinion of an expert.'

And he sprinkled a little of the white powder onto a glass plate.

'No, thank you,' Judy smiled. For some reason this self-assured, handsome man suddenly struck her as unpleasant. Whether it was because he was laughing so contemptuously at Alexey, or because his looks had become completely shameless, she did not know. She had wanted a gentle flirtation which committed her to nothing. But as soon as he had found out that she was not Alexey's wife, Sergey's eyes had started gleaming with strong and obvious desire.

Alexey got up willingly and walked over to the desk. Leaning over the plate, he snorted the powder in deeply several times. Sergey meanwhile took a tiny pinch between his delicate white fingers and began to rub it into his gums.

Soon the eyes of both of them began to shine and their lips curled up in blissful smiles.

'But why do you have to go over there?' said Sergey, lounging in his armchair again and smoothing his fair curly beard with the palm of his hand. 'Why risk your lives? Stay here! I promise you, it'll be as good here as in New York. Or even better! If you should want a swimming pool, we can have one built right in your house. Do you know, old boy, how many people there are hiding here already? Whether from the army or the courts? And there are stories worse than yours! Of course, as far as having people to talk to here is concerned, it is rather tedious, but you get used to it! Think how much of a Leningrader I was, but I've grown accustomed to it!'

'But why didn't you go back to Leningrad?' said Alexey, stretching out on the floor with his hands behind his head.

'Well, what would I have done there? Burrowed about in the Neolithic Period again during the days and read Samizdat and listened to *Voice of America* at night? No, old boy. After Afghanistan my convictions changed very sharply. Let other idiots mess about as dissidents trying to force human rights out of the Kremlin! I've developed the taste for a different kind of life. You need to live finely and in comfort. And not spend your time squeezing out human rights for yourself and then going to prison for them. Instead of that simply *buy* them. Freedom of movement? As much and as often as you like? Just give a couple of thousand roubles to the City Committee secretary, a couple of thousand more to the KGB, and I can go on a tourist trip to New York – like some cotton-grower who's been commended for his output, or a Hero of Labour! Everything in our country is bought and sold, just like in America – you know yourself.

'All the same,' drawled Sergey, turning the silver handle of his walking-stick pensively in his hand, 'I did make a trip to Leningrad ... to bury my mother. But I arrived a day too late, and she died in hospital. The bastards hadn't even informed her that I'd been wounded. There were no letters and so, poor soul, she'd already said goodbye to me! She started going to church just before she died – a Communist like her! Those "heroic actions" which you and I performed in Afghanistan have made a lot of people think differently about things!'

'Well, that certainly applies to you!' Alexey said lazily from down on the floor. 'And you don't keep any of our old army photographs on the wall ...'

Sergey looked at him, was silent for a while, then, as if

shaking off his pensive mood, looked cheerfully at Judy.

'Well,' he asked her, 'do you like this Soviet way of life of ours? Though I can imagine your answer! I'm sure you think of us as savages! Poverty, dirt, squalor! Am I right?'

'No, why should you think that? ...' said Judy in embarrassment. In fact, that *was* more or less what she thought of Russia, but for some reason she didn't want to admit it to Sergey. 'People are the same everywhere ...' she went on.

'Ah, but that I don't believe!' he countered. 'And you don't need to feel awkward with me! I've just told you what I myself think about our great and enigmatic Russian people! We're lazy and we're barbaric! Twentieth-century civilization has scarcely touched us. The Bill of Rights is more of a secret here than the atom bomb. But if you like I can introduce you to some really interesting people. To the real people invisibly running this juggernaut known as the Union of Soviet Socialist Republics! There's the head of the local militia, for example. He gets a regular wage from me every month. But who am I? Small fry!'

'Forgive me, but I would like to.... Do you have a shower?'

'But of course! Forgive me for not mentioning it earlier! It hadn't occurred to me that you had just got off the train ... I can imagine how difficult it must have been for you wandering about the country all this time.'

Sergey jumped up from his armchair quickly, went over to the writing table and picked up the telephone.

'I have nothing like that organised here. This is my – how do you say? – "office". But we can go straight away to my house, where you can relax and take a shower. And then we'll think up something interesting – along the lines of the degenerate West!'

After speaking a few fragmentary phrases of Tadzhik into the phone, he headed towards the door.

'But Sergey, how about Afghanistan?' said Alexey, stopping him. 'Will you help us?'

'We'll talk about it, old man! We'll talk about it! But you can see for yourself, the lady is tired. Let's go, Judy. If you'll permit me I shall take you by the arm.'

And squeezing her elbow possessively with his dry, cold fingers, Sergey led her out of the room. Alexey came along behind him, holding the sleeping Muslim in his arms.

22

In delight Judy turned over onto her stomach and buried her face in the pillow. The matt silk sheet flowed softly over her outstretched naked body and cooled her after the hot bath. She had almost forgotten the sweet feeling of nakedness, the slightly intoxicating lightness of being clean.

From his 'office' Sergey had driven them to the outskirts of the city, to a large stone-built house, similarly filled with carpets and furnished simply but elegantly. You could feel that its owner had a liking for light coloured antique furniture and large amounts of free space.

The dining-room table was set for four, but Judy said no to dinner and asked immediately if she could use the shower. Alexey said that he was tired, and Sergey showed them their bedrooms, one for each of them, even for Muslim, and then disappeared off somewhere himself, saying that he had business to conduct.

Even while she was still in the bathroom, Judy thought she would fall asleep as soon as her head touched the pillow. But now, as she tossed about from side to side, she realised that she didn't want to sleep, so she got up and wandered around the room. Her feet sunk pleasantly in the soft white carpet decorated with an intricate oriental pattern. She stopped and stared with interest at an enormous handwoven tapestry hanging over the head of the bed. On it was depicted a love scene. A dark-haired muscular man and a naked woman of ample frame with luxuriant fair curls were joined in a kiss as they fondled each other's secret places. And flying around them amid brightly-coloured flowers were birds of paradise of the most brilliant turquoise.

The room was large and nearly bare of furniture. Apart from a wide low bed and a squat pouffe of embossed white leather standing next to it, there was nothing in the room at all. On the wall opposite the bed was an enormous oval mirror in a heavy gilt frame, in which the whole room was reflected.

Judy went over to the window and moved the heavy, light-coloured curtain.

The whole courtyard, surrounded by a high stone wall, was covered with light pink marble. In the centre was a large circular swimming pool, filled with water. Along the sides were long low benches with little tables. In the middle of the courtyard stood an enormous oak tree beneath which the breeze gently swayed a large white swing. Behind the wall was a row of deep green poplars, and beyond them there gently rose the yellow-brown mountains.

'Well, how do you like it?' Judy suddenly heard Sergey's voice behind her.

She squealed at the unexpectedness of it and threw herself under the sheet on the bed.

'Forgive me for entering without knocking,' said Sergey, closing the door behind him and limping over to Judy. 'I was sure that you were asleep. Is everything all right for you here?'

'Yes, thank you,' said Judy with a smile, and pulling the sheet right up to her shoulders. 'Everything is marvellous!'

'But why are you so scared?' he asked, coming closer and sitting next to her on the bed. 'I thought that only Russian women were so stupidly shy. But about American women I had read completely the opposite. You must be the exception!'

He took her hand.

'You must already have realised that I like you,' he said.

'But this house ... is it yours?' she asked, not knowing what to say.

'Yes,' he replied, raising her fingers to his lips and beginning to kiss them.

'And do you live here alone?'

'Sometimes ...' he said. Without taking his lips away from her fingers, he began with his other hand to feel her shoulder.

Judy shivered slightly at his touch. Long-forgotten desire suddenly rushed to her head and took her breath away. She pressed the slipping sheet more tightly to her breast.

'Would you like something to drink?' asked Sergey, moving his fingers over her cheek, her lips, her chin.

'No. Or rather, yes. Whisky, please.'

'What beautiful lips you have,' he said. And these high, pale cheekbones. Admit it. Have men often told you that you are exceptionally beautiful?'

'No, they haven't said that to me. And, in any case, I should still like to have some whisky. Perhaps you could wait for me in the dining-room or in the courtyard. I'll get dressed and come down to you.'

'Why bother to get dressed?' he said. 'Lie down on the bed. We'll have it brought to us!'

And with that he reluctantly let go of her hand, got up from the bed and went over to the door. He shouted something into the corridor in Tadzhik and came back to the bed once more.

A few moments later a tall Tadzhik girl about fourteen years old and wearing a skull-cap, a long flowery dress and baggy cotton trousers appeared silently in the room. She wheeled in a trolley with a couple of glasses and bottles of several different kinds including even tonic water. There was crushed ice in a silver bucket. Next to it, in a tall bowl also made of silver, was an array of fruit – apples, peaches, bunches of large amber-coloured grapes.

The girl wheeled the trolley over to the bed and, without raising her eyes, left the room again.

'I didn't know that there were servants in Communist Russia!' said Judy with a smile, watching as Sergey unhurriedly placed ice in the glasses.

'In Communist Russia there is everything!' he said, offering her a glass of whisky and sitting down next to her on the bed again without touching his own glass. 'Though not for everyone, admittedly ... But then in America not everyone has everything, do they?' he said with a slight smile. 'I think that the only people who have everything there are those who have understood the essence of life.'

'And what is it, the essence of life? Tell me,' said Judy, smiling.

'Enjoyment! But then it's not up to me, a Russian savage, to explain that to you, a visitor from another planet! The whole difference between your society and ours is the fact that with you everything is arranged so that people can enjoy life today, here and now. Whereas with us that will be possible only in some distant future ...'

'And you don't want to wait?'

Sergey gave her a careful look, picked his glass up from the table and took a couple of gulps.

'No, I don't want to wait ...' he said, bending over to kiss her feet through the sheet, then travelling further and further up her tense body.

Judy wanted to push him away, but she could feel that this self-confident bantam-cock had a certain power over her. Whether she was afraid of him, or whether ... she was simply starved of male affection, she did not know.

Reaching her pubis, he suddenly pressed her thighs with his hands and, panting and whispering, tried to push his head even deeper in between her legs.

'Don't do that! Don't!' said Judy. She pushed Sergey away, but felt dizzy with the desire that suddenly gripped her. Another minute and she felt she would weakly relax her legs, seize Sergey's large head with its soft, downy hair and press her lips to his.

As if reading her thoughts, he suddenly raised his flushed face to hers. He forced her back by the hair and, opening his mouth, seized her lips vehemently with his own. Judy cried out in pain.

He kissed her long and greedily. Throwing the sheet onto the floor, he slipped his hands over her naked body, then, kneading her breast with his hand, forced the firm fingers of his other hand in between her legs.

Unable to control herself any longer, Judy began to press his fingers further into herself, her whole body moving up and down in rhythm. Everything began to swim before her eyes; her hands involuntarily squeezed Sergey's shoulders; a muffled moan sprang up from somewhere near her stomach and moved convulsively into her mouth which was enclosed in a kiss. A few moments later, moving her head crazily from side to side, she gave a loud cry, and a violent wave of ecstasy almost made her black out. Sergey moved away from her and got up.

'And that's only the beginning, little girl! The main thing is still to come!'

And he began slowly unbuttoning his shirt. This revealed the same tattoo on his left shoulder as Alexey and Nikolay had. Dropping his trousers and underpants onto the floor, he said: 'I knew that you wanted me. Almost as much as I want you ...'

He sat next to her on the bed and took a few swallows from his glass of whisky. He looked attentively at her outstretched, motionless body.

'Ah! what a figure you have! And what breasts! Like those of a little girl ...' and he moved his fingers slowly over her nipples, down past her stomach and slightly twisted her pubic hair. 'Stand up! I want to look at you!'

Judy shook her head with weariness. The last thing she wanted to do now was get up and demonstrate her figure. How marvellous it would be if he now simply got up and went and left her in peace. Her aversion towards him suddenly made her feel sick, and his tawdry admiration of her body was repulsive.

Sergey bent down and touched her breasts several times with his moist lips. She shuddered and moved away. He gazed at her thoughtfully, and a cruel spiteful look flashed in his eyes.

'What's wrong?' he asked.

'I'm tired,' said Judy, turning away from him.

'But I'm not!' said Sergey grasping her firmly by the chin and turning her towards him. 'I'm not tired at all! And I want you even more now than I did earlier!'

'But I don't want to! Please go away! What happened just now was a mistake! I didn't want it!'

Judy turned her face away again. 'Oh, please, please! Go away!'

Sergey grabbed her violently by the arms and, pressing down on her with the whole weight of his body, began to kiss her lips, even though they were distorted with pain and repulsion.

'Stop playing that kind of game with me!' he whispered hoarsely. 'I don't like people joking with me like that!'

'Leave me alone! Go away!' Judy could feel his hard knee painfully forcing its way between her legs. Her hands, firmly pressed against the bed by Sergey's fingers, had gone numb. It was difficult for her to breathe as his moist body pressed down on her breast and stomach.

Relaxing for a moment and submissively offering her lips to be kissed, Judy suddenly gave Sergey a sharp kick in the chest and jumped to her feet. Before he had time to realize what was happening, she grabbed a whisky bottle off the table and brought it down on his head. Fragments of glass flew over the bed and carpet, Sergey's fair hair was immediately covered in blood and, with a final spasm, he froze lifeless on the bed.

'Oh my God!' Judy whispered to herself in English. Terrified, she tried to get dressed, but was unable to put her feet in the right side of her knickers. 'I've killed him! Oh, my God! ...'

A red stain was spreading from Sergey's head over the pillow and the silk sheet.

Dashing out into the corridor, Judy rushed over to the room opposite and opened the door.

Alexey was asleep on a wide, low ottoman, his legs splayed wide and his head thrown back. The room was in semi-darkness, and the thick, dark curtains in front of the large window were shifting slightly.

Judy ran up to Alexey and tugged at his shoulder.

'Wake up, Alexey, wake up!'

He moved his dry lips slightly and, without opening his eyes, smiled.

'Is it you? I knew that you would come ...' he said, placing his hands on her shoulders and, still half asleep, pulling her towards him. 'At last! Come to me! Don't be afraid ...'

'Alexey! Wake up! I've killed him! We need to get away! ...'

But Alexey, neither listening, nor hearing, was gently stroking her hair and her shoulders which were trembling from weeping.

'Why are you crying?' he asked. 'Don't be afraid. If you don't want to, we won't do it.' He tenderly brought her face to his and touched her lips with his own dry lips.

Responding with a short kiss and moving the palm of her hand over his stubbly cheeks, Judy, still weeping, said to him again:

'Alexey, wake up! We must get away! I've killed him!'

'Who?' he said, opening one eye mockingly. 'What are you crying for? Who have you killed?'

'Sergey.'

'Oh yes!' he said just as cheerfully. 'And with what?'

Without waiting for an answer, he moved her head towards him. Clumsily, almost like a boy, he pressed his slightly open lips against her mouth, moving his trembling fingers up and down her back in a tender caress.

'With a bottle!' said Judy, moving away from him in amazement. What was this? The usual attraction a man has for a woman's warmth when he awakes from sleep, or ...? But after all, during the whole time of their long journey, not once had he tried to get close to her. On the contrary, he had avoided even looking at her, and only in extreme situations, at moments of danger, had he taken her by the hand ... But she had no time to worry about such details now.

'Alexey! We must get away! Wake up!'

'I'm not asleep!' said Alexey, reluctantly sitting up in bed. 'Calm down! Well, what's happened?'

'I've killed him! I've smashed a bottle over his head! There's blood everywhere ... A lot of blood!' And she began to cry again.

'You have killed Sukhar?!' he said, appearing not at all worried. 'But why?!'

'I was in my room. He came in. And ... well ... and ...'

'And he began pestering you, right?'

'Yes.'

'The bastard! I knew he was a shit, but not with his own friends! Where is he?'

Alexey got up angrily off the bed, threw on his shirt and, turning away, began to button up his trousers.

'Come on! Show me!' he said.

When they went into the room, Sergey had already regained consciousness. He was half sitting, half lying on the bed, leaning his elbow on the bloodstained pillar and, supporting his head with both hands, was groaning softly. Next to him, on the sheet, two giant blood stains had run together. Closing the door behind him, Alexey quickly went up to him. Bending down slightly, he examined the wound on his head. Judy had stopped apprehensively by the door.

'Well, old man, I think you got off lightly with a small fright! Your skull's all right – only a skin wound!'

'Call somebody!' begged Sergey, his face distorted with pain. 'I need a doctor! They'll know who to phone!'

'We can deal with this ourselves!' said Alexey, taking Sergey under the arms and dragging him up against the head of the bed.

'Have you gone crazy, or something? Go and call someone! I've lost a bucketful of blood! And if you don't want to, I'll do it myself . . .'

Sergey opened his mouth in order to shout, but Alexey immediately grabbed him by the shoulders.

'I'll hurt you, if you start to scream! So now you're going after other people's women! Haven't you got enough of your own?'

Sergey pursed his lips together gloomily and said nothing. Alexey tore a strip off the sheet and tied it around his damaged head.

'He says he's lost blood! Well, I'll give you some of mine – we've got the same blood group! . . . And now let's get down to business! When does Pavel Yegorov fly off?'

Sergey leant back against the bedhead, gave Alexey a dark look and then transferred his gaze to Judy. Suddenly he gave a mocking smile.

'You're both crazy! You just can't seem to do things like ordinary people! You always have to make some kind of fuck-up!'

He bent over towards the drinks trolley, but fell back groaning onto the bedhead again.

'Get me something to drink,' he moaned.

Alexey poured some water into a glass, gave it to Sergey, and poured himself out half a glass of whisky. Then, turning to Judy, he said: 'Do you want one, too?'

She shook her head.

'So why set off all these fireworks around yourselves?' said Sergey. 'The militia looking for you all over the country! Photographs of you hung up everywhere! Any dog in the street would recognize you! It's essential to do things quietly and rationally. But you . . .'

Sergey fell silent, took a small sip from his glass, then looked sarcastically at Alexey as he swallowed half a glassful at one go.

'See that! Now who would down whisky like that?!' he said. 'It's not vodka, you know. It needs to be drunk delicately, without hurrying . . .'

'Now, you listen to me, teacher! I think I've already given you enough warning. Just stop giving your lectures here! Why are you treating me like some greenhorn? Or do you want to make yourself look big in front of her?'

Alexey nodded towards Judy who was sitting exhausted on the floor and carried on:

'Listen, Sergey, I'm asking you as a human being – please put me in touch with Pavel Yegorov! I know that he stayed on for additional service and is an army driver here, ferrying provisions to our units in Afghanistan. Is that right? Yes or no?'

Alexey shook Sergey insistently by the shoulders again.

'Well, yes ... That's right,' said Sergey with obvious unwillingness, fastidiously removing Alexey's hands from his shoulders. 'How do you know?'

'I just do, that's all. But what are you mucking me about for? Fuck it! I've come here all the way from Moscow! All over the country I've been hiding from the cops, like the lowest of the low! I thought to myself: well, who will help me out, if not my ex-army buddies? And yet the first thing that you sodding do is go after my woman! And as soon as I want to talk about business, all you do is bugger off!'

Alexey's face was red and his eyes flashed malevolently. As he became more and more worked up, he thumped his fist again and again on the bed near where Sergey was sitting. At every blow Sergey winced and clapped his hand to his bandaged head.

'Look, don't get so worked up, Alexey!' he pleaded. 'How was I to know that she was your woman?! Did you tell me that? Or did she? I spent some time observing you. You didn't look at each other, you seemed like strangers. Perhaps this is some new-fangled form of love? Anyway, to cut a long story short, I misunderstood the situation.'

Sergey ran his tongue over his parched lips and took another swallow from his glass.

'But as for helping you out, old man, what you're proposing is fantastically risky! For everybody! If they find you in Pavel's truck, it'd be immediate court martial for him, you know yourself, and then the firing squad! And in any case, apart from that, he ...'

'What?' Alexey asked sharply.

'You wouldn't recognise him!' Sergey said slowly, reluctantly.

'I wouldn't recognise you, either. When I got badly hit, the whole platoon rushed to the hospital to give me blood. Whereas now ...'

'Yes, I know. We all change ...' said Sergey.

'Sergey!' said Alexey, suddenly changing his tone of voice. Then he added quietly, as if through a supreme effort: 'I'm *begging* you! Not for myself ... but for her and the boy! And then, I'm not asking you to do it for nothing. I'll pay you! Ten thousand roubles ...'

Sergey raised his eyes in astonishment.

'Now I didn't know that you were capable of asking for something in a civilised way! Your princely blood is stronger than your Soviet upbringing, I can see that!'

'Don't mess about!' said Alexey with embarrassment. 'Tell me how to make contact with Pavel. I know that he brings you drugs from Afghanistan.'

'Ah, Alexey! And you call yourself a prince! Now, who talks about such things out loud? I take delivery of merchandise, old man, and not something that could be defined with such a crude word! It's the decaying West which has drugs! Whereas we ...'

Alexey ground his teeth together angrily.

'All right, Alexey,' said Sergey, 'I'll help you. But if you end up with a noose around your neck, then don't start blaming me in the next world for not trying to dissuade you!'

Sergey lowered his feet to the floor and tried to stand.

'I'll get on the phone to my boys right away,' he said. 'and they'll take you somewhere to get photographed for the passports. If I order them today, they'll be ready in a couple of days. Each passport will set you back three thousand ...'

'Why do we need papers?' asked Alexey, helping him to stand up.

'Well, you really don't know a thing! We're two hundred kilometres off the frontier here, and there are patrols everywhere! Have you forgotten, or what? When you get your passports, we'll travel to Parkhar. There's a supply base there from which lorry convoys make their way into Afghanistan.'

Wrapped in the sheet and supported from the side by Alexey, Sergey moved towards the door.

'I'll be going with you, too,' he said. I have to prove to you that I haven't changed as much as you think. And my apologies to the lady!' He stopped in front of Judy. 'There was something about you I didn't understand, it seems ... Which is hardly surprising, I suppose – you are from another civilization, and so on! As for me, Alexey, I do need to see a doctor now. I have a respect for medicine, you know ... Why didn't you tell me right away that you would pay?! That alters the whole thing, you know ... I use a different ethical code with my clients. But tell me, if it's not a secret, where did you get the hundred thousand from? Did you rob a bank?'

23

The slightly shabby Soviet passports were ready. Judy looked with curiosity at her altered face and unusually short hair, like the style of some fashion model. She was reading at the same time, trying to learn off by heart the handwritten details of her new name, UVAROVA, Lina Donatovna; place of residence – the city of Pskov, Michurin Street, No. 22; place of birth – Vilnius, Lithuanian Soviet Socialist Republic; spouse – Uvarov, Yury Nikolayevich, son – Uvarov, Mikhail, born 1984. Vilnius was chosen so that her Lithuanian descent would explain why she had a slight accent when speaking Russian . . .

But for three days now Sergey had been putting off their departure for Parkhar, saying either that he had a headache, or that he had urgent business, and he would disappear from the house for long periods. Judy and Alexey remained there alone with Muslim, if you didn't count the two young Tadzhik girls who would appear first thing in the morning, cook breakfast, lunch and dinner in the kitchen and discreetly clear up the house, before disappearing without trace towards evening.

Judy and Alexey would spend hours lounging about in the courtyard, sunbathing, catching up on lost sleep, laughing at the antics of the quickly tanning Muslim. The boy ran around all the time and never seemed to get tired. He was getting increasingly attached to them and kept running up to Judy more and more, burying his head in her lap and calling her 'mama'. To her surprise she discovered that she found this pleasant. But on the whole, the boy spent nearly all his time with Alexey who was teaching him to swim. And he did so with such assiduity that you would have thought they were going to have to swim across the border and not go in the lorry of Alexey's old army friend. However, paying attention to the boy obviously helped Alexey avoid direct contact with Judy . . .

As for the incident between Judy and Sergey on the day of their arrival, nobody ever mentioned it. Everyone pretended that nothing had happened. When Muslim was asleep, Alexey would become gloomy and self-absorbed, as before; Sergey was excessively chatty and polite, demonstrating his 'other ethical code'; and Judy, as she observed them, would shut herself off. In the evenings they tried to entertain themselves by watching television, but each evening all three channels – two local ones and the national network from Moscow – kept showing Gorbachev's speeches at various conferences, political meetings and gatherings. Gorbachev went on interminably, for two or sometimes three hours at a time, about 'glasnost', economics, 'perestroika', discipline at work and increasing the productivity of labour. Judy thought to herself that if the US president were to keep droning on for a couple of hours every day about the same thing, then after a month he would be transferred from the White House to a lunatic asylum. Then, after Gorbachev's speeches, there were endless tedious documentary programmes on the same subjects – 'perestroika', 'glasnost', the productivity of labour and so on . . . But after everything Judy had seen during her wanderings, she could no longer imagine how anything in this country could be 'restructured'.

'Do you believe in this "perestroika"?' she asked Sergey one day. As he listened to Gorbachev holding forth, he had been smiling condescendingly.

'Have you been to Italy?' he asked.

'Yes, with my father, when I was a child,' she replied, surprised at his question. 'But why do you ask?'

'And did you get to see the Leaning Tower of Pisa?'

'Yes, we even stood at the top of it . . .'

'Well, that's what our economy is like – the Leaning Tower of Pisa. All the experts have been screaming for the last three hundred years that if the Tower isn't rebuilt immediately, it will come crashing down. But however loudly they scream, people are afraid to touch the thing. Because as soon as people do start to rebuild it, the Tower really will collapse. Meanwhile, it's still standing – by some miracle! And it's the same with our economy. That's why Gorbachev spends so long talking, trying to convince himself. As for doing something serious – not on your life! He's afraid to!'

After switching off the television, they all went to their rooms and, like friendly acquaintances, wished each other goodnight. During the night Judy would toss and turn, unable to sleep, and listened eagerly to the slightest noise, almost physically forcing herself not to rush into Alexey's bedroom. In the morning she would stare attentively into his face, trying to discern the slightest sign that he might have been similarly tortured, but she could find nothing and would turn away feeling hurt.

This morning, when they met as usual at breakfast, Sergey suddenly announced definitely that they would be leaving in a few hours' time. And he drove off in his light blue Moskvich, telling them all to be ready by one o'clock in the afternoon.

There was nothing to gather together, and after changing into the Hungarian bathing costume which Sergey had 'obtained' for her three days earlier, Judy went out into the courtyard. Alexey was already lying there, drying off after bathing in the pool. His long body, in close-fitting swimming trunks and slightly pink, was stretched limply on the marble floor. His eyes were closed. Judy, with a shiver, went into the water.

The pool was about eight metres in length. After swimming several times from end to end, Judy stopped, puffing and panting. How weak she had become! In the pool at New York University, which was much bigger than this one, she used to do ten lengths and never feel tired. After splashing about a little, she got out of the water and lay down next to Alexey. It was still cool, but the hot Central Asian sun immediately warmed her body which was dripping with water. Looking around, she noticed Muslim playing enthusiastically on the swing beneath the shady oak tree. She lay down limply on her stomach and closed her eyes.

'Do you think that we really will be leaving today?' she asked Alexey after a few moments' silence.

'I don't know,' he replied without moving.

'And what kind of place is this Parkhar? Have you been there?'

'No,' he replied coldly. 'We'll see when we get there.'

'Have I woken you up? Were you asleep?'

'No.'

'Why are you so....' But Judy broke off, feeling hurt again.

Why was he so grumpy when he spoke to her? When she had run to him afraid that she had killed Sergey, why had he been so gentle with her, and now so abrupt and estranged? But was this something she could ask him about? He would simply laugh or make some rude remark! Well, so what? If he didn't want to talk to her, he didn't have to! What was he to her anyway? Just let her get away from this terrible country, and she would forget about him altogether!

'Listen. I've been wanting to ask you,' Alexey suddenly said very loudly, without opening his eyes. 'You don't have to reply, if you don't want to, of course. But ... do you have anybody close? ...'

'Yes, my mother, my sister ...'

'No, I don't mean that! I mean a man ... a boyfriend ...?'

'Oh, *that's* what you mean!' she said. 'Yes, I do.'

'Aaah! ... I thought so!'

She could not work out whether he said this with relief, or disappointment.

'But things are difficult between him and me,' she went

on quickly, as if wanting to correct her mistake. 'We have almost broken up.'

'Yes, I see! I see perfectly! There's no need to carry on!'

'But why do you ask?' said Judy, feeling her heart beginning to thump.

'Just out of interest,' he replied lazily. 'I hardly know anything about you, after all. And then, that time you came to me ... Ah well, that was all nonsense!'

'What do you mean? Carry on!' she said impatiently.

Alexey opened his eyes and looked at her.

Only now did Judy notice how much he had changed.

His thick, dark beard was neatly trimmed, his face looked older and more expressive, his hair had grown noticeably longer and fell down onto his shoulders in straight wet locks, and this really did make him resemble those pictures of Russian princes which arose in her imagination when she had studied Russian nineteenth-century literature. And although he wasn't at all the kind of man who normally appealed to her, he did radiate a kind of strength, and this strength attracted her.

He looked at her in silence, as if trying to solve some difficult and unpleasant problem. Their faces were close, and Judy even thought that she could feel his warm breath on her cheek. She was certain that in a moment or two he would say something important to her, something she very much wanted to hear. A wave of tenderness and desire suddenly passed through her sun-warmed body and made her feel slightly light-headed. But Alexey said nothing. He turned away from her and placed his arms beneath his head. Judy realised that she would have to make the first move herself. A moment later she suddenly thought: but why should I? And immediately laughed inwardly to herself: why, because she wanted to! And had done for a long time.

She drew up closer to him and began moving her hand gently over his damp hair, digging into his hot shoulders slightly with her fingers. His shoulder muscles contracted, but Alexey did not move. Judy raised herself slightly, pressed her breasts under the damp swimming costume closer to him, and touched his burning hot shoulders with her lips.

He turned abruptly over onto his side, grabbed her roughly by the hand and rolled sharply onto his back, so that she found herself on top of him. Smiling, she moved her lips towards his face and then froze. Looking at her were two angry eyes, and Alexey's lips had turned pale and were tightly pressed together.

'What's wrong?' she could scarcely breathe out.

Alexey did not simply throw her, but literally shook her off himself down onto the hard marble and moved away. Then he suddenly sat up.

'You just stop that!' he cried hoarsely. 'Stop that, okay?'

'Stop what?' she said, sitting opposite him and rubbing the wrist he had so roughly grabbed to throw her off him.

Without replying, Alexey got to his feet and stepped quickly across to the swimming pool. Only now, for the first time, could Judy get a view of his naked back: running almost the whole length of his spine was a deep, dark, claret-coloured scar dotted with small marks – the signs of surgical stitches. Without looking around, Alexey took a running jump into the pool. Judy looked at him swimming, lifting his arms up high into the air and raising fountains of water around him. After pondering a little, she also entered the water.

They swam at a distance from one another, as if afraid of getting close. Raising her head out of the water, Judy sometimes caught his tense gaze upon her. But he would hurriedly avert his eyes, and she would also plunge her hot face back into the water once more. Damn! What was wrong with him? They must sort out once and for all what it was between them! She could feel that he wanted her, after all, so what was all this game-playing about?! Sergey was right: they fought shy of each other almost as if they were afraid of burning themselves! . . .

The found themselves next to each other and without saying a word both swam over to the side of the pool. When she had stopped, Judy turned her wet face resolutely towards him:

'I want to ask you something,' she said. 'When I ran to you from Sergey, you were asleep ... and in your sleep you decided that I was her! Am I right?'

'Who?' he said, holding onto the side with one hand and running the other one uncertainly over his wet hair.

'Your ... Afghan woman!' she shouted.

Alexey said nothing for a long time. His eyes suddenly looked shifty. He smoothed his wet beard several times, and then said softly:

'No, I knew it was you.'

'So, you wanted me. Am I right?'

'Yes ...' he said, yet more softly.

'And what about now?'

'I've already asked you to cut it out!' he said, drawing close to her, his eyes narrowing angrily. It seemed to Judy that he wanted to strike her. 'Well, go on! Tell me! How much did my great-aunt promise to pay you?! Go on! How much will you make from me if I fall for you?!'

'You cretin!' she screamed. With the back of her wet hand she struck him in the face as hard as she could and, losing her balance, fell headlong into the water. Surfacing again and spitting out water, she swam quickly to the other end of the pool. Muslim came running from the swing to head her off. Pale in the face and furious, he had some kind of stick in his hand.

'I'll kill you! I'll kill you!' he screamed as he ran.

Alexey swam vigorously across the pool, caught Judy up, jumped up out of the pool and grabbed the boy in his arms. But Muslim tore himself away and was screaming hysterically:

'She hit you! She hit you! I'll kill her! I told you she was bad! I told you ...'

Judy got out of the water and walked past them towards the house.

'Tart! Whore! Bitch!' Muslim shouted after her from Alexey's arms, summoning up all the swear words he had had time to pick up at the boarding-school.

Alexey suddenly smacked him in the mouth with his fingers.

'Shut up! I was the one who offended her. Not the other way round! I'm to blame. Judy, forgive me, do you hear?'

But without turning round she walked quickly towards the house.

The side-gate creaked open, and Sergey walked into the courtyard. He looked excited.

'Well, guys, let's take to our horses. Into the shower quickly, a quick bite before we leave and then – farewell great and mighty Russia!'

The blood began to beat joyfully in Judy's temples. 'Just as soon as ever possible!' she thought feverishly. Sensing the men's stares, she ran lightly and easily into the house.

Sergey whistled after her in admiration.

'My, what a figure she's got! Like a goddess! You've certainly been lucky there, Prince!'

Through the open gate Alexey could see Sergey's light blue Moskvich. Two boys in skull-caps – the ones who had come up to Alexey with a knife in the bazaar and then beat him up – were dragging two enormous heavy suitcases outside.

'And what's that?' asked Alexey suspiciously.

'Nothing to worry about, old boy. That's your luggage. Pavel knows what to do with it. You can put your own clobber in on top in a minute ...'

'Wait a minute! What's in them?' he repeated insistently.

'It's clothes, that's all. What did you think? Do you think I'm smuggling cartridges into Afghanistan, or something? Or do you think they'll give me merchandise in exchange for Soviet roubles? It's clothing. If we get searched on the way, you can say that it's yours. That's all. One favour for another. Where are your medals?'

'What medals?'

'The ones you got for serving in Afghanistan ... What medals, indeed!'

'You're crazy. I told you how we got away. Do you think I had time to pack my medals?'

'You can wear mine.'

'On my shirt? Medals? What for?'

'I told you, you can wear mine. And there's an end to it,' he said firmly.

24

Sergey's light blue Moskvich with fishing tackle tied onto the roof slowly climbed up the narrow mountain road. Its puny motor roared laboriously, as it almost literally hugged the sharp reddish stone of the high perpendicular cliff on their right. To the left, a couple of yards from the car, was a precipice. Beyond it there opened up an almost biblical landscape – a green valley lit by the bright southern sun and the gentle lower slopes of windswept mountains, covered with stunted vegetation, tough dog roses, dwarf plum trees and apricots ... In the valley itself apple orchards alternated with cotton fields, vineyards, tiny villages. But all of this was already far down below and was almost indistinguishable in the heat haze, through which green hills scattered with motley patches of spring poppies protruded like the humps of a camel. Grazing their flocks of sheep on the grassy slopes of these hills were Tadzhik shepherds, seated upright on their donkeys or walking along next to them holding long sticks. And this whole picture exuded a feeling of Old Testament peace and calm, of the rightness of the world as it was in the beginning – before capitalism, socialism, Leninism, terrorism, IBM, television, the price index, Japanese microchip dumping and before the struggle to fulfil one's socialist obligations and to reduce the state deficit ...

'Peace encompasses the world and with it my soul,' declaimed Sergey and then added: 'They're not my words, you know. They belong to the ancient Moslem poet Rumi. The Tadzhiks are just about one of the oldest nations in the world. Perhaps even older then the Jews. And somehow even before the birth of Christ, they all managed to live for centuries without NATO, SEATO, the Warsaw Pact and all the rest!'

He grinned, as if he had read Judy's thoughts. 'And they didn't live at all badly, believe you me! And they managed without any Pierre Cardin, Karl Marx, Michael Jackson or Margaret Thatcher. A Madonna, they did have, it's true – but that wasn't the singer! ...'

Going downhill Sergey drove fast but carefully. Alexey and Muslim were sitting next to him on the front seat. But Alexey constantly had to call the boy to order, as he kept on trying to grab the steering wheel, or pull at the medals 'For Bravery' and 'For Service in Battle' pinned to Alexey's shirt. At other times the boy laughed with excitement when their Moskvich came literally within an inch of colliding with a car coming in the opposite direction, or with a camel ridden by a Tadzhik.

They were heading south through the Darvaz mountains to the Pamirs. The sun was high above their heads. Judy's head began to spin from the frequent, sudden turns in the road. She tried not to look at the twisting road surface whenever it broke off into a precipice. At the most dangerous spots, large stones were placed by the side of the road as a warning to be extra careful. Down below in the gaps between the rocks, mountain streams were foaming – hurtling down the mountain with such speed that they brought large stones with them. Where the mountains receded slightly from the rivers, there were green fields huddling, tiny settlements and villages. Domestic goats, climbing up the twisted trunks of old mulberry trees, would be eating the green foliage ... And next to them – across the fields and mountain slopes, mulberry and apricot groves, villages and crags – strode enormous electricity pylons. Balanced on their sagging wires were the same turquoise 'birds of paradise' which Judy had seen in the tapestry in Sergey's house ...

Frightening some hens who rushed out from under its wheels, the car turned a sudden sharp corner and burst onto the dusty street of a mountain settlement. The low windowless adobe huts were surrounded by a fence made of pressed dung on the other side of which coloured washing was hung on lines to dry, tanned and dark-eyed children ran about barefoot, apricots were drying out on mats, and women knelt and used long narrow sticks to fluff up grey camel hair.... After nearly running down a brood of turkey chicks taking a dust-bath – which caused another gale of laughter from Muslim – Sergey sped through the village and immediately braked sharply. The road ahead of them was shut off by a lowered barrier. Next to it stood a small wooden hut with a faded cloth banner saying 'STRENGTHEN THE BROTHERHOOD OF THE SOVIET PEOPLES!'

Judy instinctively ducked back against the seat and looked anxiously at Sergey and Alexey.

'They're going to check our papers,' said Sergey. 'Let me do the talking. And remember, Judy, no smiling, and look them straight in the eye!'

They stopped by the barrier. For a long time nobody appeared from the hut. Alexey wanted to sound the horn, but Sergey grabbed hold of his hand.

'There's no need to. They can see us. We are loyal subjects – let's wait ...'

Finally, walking slowly out of the hut and buttoning up his wide belt as he did so, there appeared a middle-aged sergeant major of the border service.

Without a word he took the passports proffered by Sergey, leafed through them and then asked coldly: 'Where are you travelling to?'

'To the river Kyzylsa, to catch trout.'

The sergeant looked at Alexey and Muslim, and then transferred his eyes to Judy.

'What, have you come here all the way from Russia just to catch trout?' he asked.

'He's an old army friend of mine, Comrade Sergeant,'

said Sergey. 'At Nangarhar he rescued me with a broken leg from right under the noses of the partisans. He carried me in his arms even though we were under fire. I've only just now persuaded them to visit me. So I want to show them all there is to see hereabouts. And you know yourself, the Kyzylsa is fantastically beautiful, and as for the trout . . .'

Sergey spread his arms out wide.

'Why, last year I caught one this size! I know certain places there . . . Do you smoke, Comrade Sergeant? Help yourself!'

He offered the sergeant a packet of Kazbek *papirosy*.

'I don't smoke!' the sergeant rapped out and then said to Alexey: 'Show me your left shoulder!'

Alexey unbuttoned his shirt, revealing the tattoo on his left shoulder. The sergeant's expression softened visibly.

'Uncle, are you a real border guard?' Muslim shouted at the sergeant enthusiastically. 'But where's your dog?'

The sergeant didn't answer him and returned the passports to Sergey.

'Will you be long on the Kyzylsa?'

'I think we'll be on our way back by tomorrow evening.'

'The border is quite close by, comrades. So have a good time, but be careful. No camp fires or binges! Are you taking any vodka with you?'

'One bottle as per quota. And that's for drinking with the fish soup, to celebrate our meeting . . .'

'Okay. Only keep everything quiet and civilised. And no poaching!'

Without a smile the sergeant enunciated these learnt-off phrases with great precision, while slowly and carefully inspecting each of them in turn.

'Good heavens, Comrade Sergeant,' Sergey said, starting up the car. 'We're family people. Why should we start any fires, let alone do any poaching? All we want to do is a bit of quiet fishing and then drive back home. May we go now, Comrade Sergeant?'

The sergeant looked at him silently, nodded and went back into the hut.

During this conversation Judy, following Sergey's instructions, had been looking the sergeant straight in the eye. The most difficult thing of all was preventing herself from smiling. But Sergey had warned her before that Russians very rarely smile at representatives of authority, and that it can only arouse unnecessary suspicions. And now, for the first time, she realised that not smiling at somebody you met was just as unpleasant as wearing someone else's clothing . . .

About four hours later they had covered no more than a hundred kilometres of the mountain roads and successfully negotiated three more check-points. Worn to a frazzle, they finally began the descent into the valley and into the shadow of the mountains which cut off the setting sun. The little town of Parkhar, rolling in orchards, lay before them. As they entered it, they passed a *chaikhana* with an enormous vertical wheel with ducts that drew up water from an irrigation canal and poured it back down – for coolness.

'Be prepared!' said Sergey, looking at Judy meaningfully in the driving mirror. 'In Parkhar there are patrols at every step! At any moment they could demand to see our passports again. So no panicking, Lina Donatovna! And as for you, Prince, shall we fortify ourselves first, or go straight to Pavel's?!' He obviously liked to call Alexey 'prince', emphasising the word with a mocking intonation. This obviously angered Alexey, but there was nothing he could do about it.

'Let's go straight to Pavel's!' he said coldly. 'We can have a bite to eat at his place.'

The dark evening, saturated with the sharp smells of the south, slowly enveloped the border town of Parkhar. On the narrow cobble-stoned streets, beneath the crowns of Lombardy poplars and plane trees, a few sparse street lights were flickering on. Sitting outside their narrow clay houses and leaning against the walls were desiccated-looking grey-bearded old men wearing skull-caps and pink-coloured robes, with hookahs and amber beads in their hands. In spite of the heat they were wearing long, thickly knitted coloured socks. There were dogs running around, cats wandered about unhurriedly, and there was a smell of spices, apple orchards, warm dust, scorched grass and hashish. A little girl aged about twelve was walking along from an irrigation canal, carrying a yoke on her shoulders with two bucketfuls of water. Somewhere in the distance a donkey was braying in a high, sharp tenor.

'These Moslems are real devils!' Sergey was saying cheerfully, as he drove the dust-covered car. 'Their religion forbids them to drink vodka, so they smoke grass! All quiet and civilised. While all we Russians want is vodka! By the bucket, preferably . . .'

A little while later they stopped outside a two-storeyed wooden house with carved shutters and a high-stepped porch. The building contrasted sharply with all the low clay houses surrounding it. Indeed, even in Russia it would have been difficult to find such a grotesque, folksy looking structure with its pale blue colour and bright red wooden mouldings in the shape of cockerels, firebirds and other mythical creatures.

'This is where Pavel lives!' said Sergey, getting out of the car. 'Now don't be surprised at anything! There's no accounting, as they say, for taste!'

A huge brown mongrel leapt out from round the corner of the house and, rattling its chain, began to bark hoarsely. Muslim rushed over to Alexey in fear.

'Don't be scared,' said Sergey. 'It's tied up. I must say, though, it's a fearsome beast! A mixture of Alsatian and wolf. It's even attacked Pavel once or twice.'

Sergey lifted up a stone from the ground and threw it up at the front door.

The dog tried to break away from its chain, barking angrily and baring its salivating fangs. The door to the house finally opened and on the threshold appeared a puny-looking figure in long dark shorts and with a tattoo on the left shoulder identical to Alexey's, Nikolay's and Sergey's.

'What do you want?' he shouted.

'Pavel, it's me!' said Sergey. 'Call your beast off!'

'And who's that with you?' asked Pavel, standing motionless at the top of the steps.

'Come down and see for yourself! And shut that creature up!' Sergey shouted irritably.

'Pavel, it's me, Alyosha Odalevsky!' said Alexey, taking a step forward.

'Alyosha?' asked Pavel suspiciously advancing towards them. As he approached, the more his face – full-cheeked and almost boyish as on the army photographs – brightened up, and the last few steps he actually ran, throwing his arms around Alexey and crying for joy:

'Alyosha! What brings you here?! Alyosha, it really is you! Come on, let's go into the house! All of us! And who's this – your wife? Alyosha, damn it, who would have believed it!! Look, I'll calm this creature down and you go on in!'

Pavel grabbed the dog by the collar and dragged it back into the yard. The dog kept on trying to escape his grip, growling and snarling, squinting its blood-shot eyes at the guests.

They entered the house. After a small dark entrance hall came a light room crammed with furniture and a television blaring away at full volume. The owner obviously had no clearly defined sense of taste: a tall, carved antique sideboard stood cheek by jowl with a modern divan upholstered in dark, cherry-coloured velvet and blue plush armchairs. Next to some cupboards rose the different coloured shades of three antique standard lamps. Stretching along the wall was a highly-polished bookcase filled with crystal vases, fruit bowls, cheap china statuettes and army photographs, each one under glass, in a thin metal frame. (Judy now knew everyone in these photographs apart from Shalygin, with his snub-nose and high cheekbones.) In the corner was a wooden bar, obviously home-made.

'Sit down! Sit down!' said Sergey cheerfully. 'And don't be surprised at anything. Our Pavel is an odd chap! I'll switch off the television, shall I? . . .'

'What do you mean: an odd chap?' said Pavel smiling, 'What are you blethering on about, Sukhar! You'd do better to open the sideboard and get them all something to drink! Meanwhile, I'll go and put on some trousers . . .'

He disappeared into the next room. Sergey went over to the bar and looked inside.

'Sideboard, indeed!' he said, mimicking Pavel sarcastically. 'Now what can a Soviet person keep in a bar that he calls a sideboard? Vodka, naturally! And wine! No, but just look at this! The lad's got more money than he knows what to fucking do with, and yet he drinks cheap wine! How can he drink such filthy stuff?!'

Sergey turned to Judy and Alexey holding a large, dark-coloured bottle in his hand.

'I advise you to try a little of this, Judy! You'll never forget the wonderful taste of the fruit and berry paint-stripper they call "Gift of the Sun"! If, of course, you survive!'

He put the bottle down on the table.

'Alyosha! Alyosha! My greatest friend!' Pavel was humming, as he came out of the room. He was now wearing tight jeans and a white T-shirt emblazoned with the smiling face of Mickey Mouse. When she saw that, Judy burst into laughter, as though she was also meeting an old friend.

'What?' said Pavel, turning to look at Sergey in surprise. 'Have you been talking a load of nonsense about me again?!'

'No! He's got nothing to do with it!' spluttered Judy, continuing to laugh. 'It's just that . . . seeing Mickey Mouse out here! It's nice, that's all!'

'Mickey who?' said Pavel in confusion and looked at Alexey. 'What's all this double-Dutch she's speaking?'

'I'm not speaking double-Dutch!' said Judy. 'It's the picture you're wearing! What, don't you know who

Mickey Mouse is?! I saw it, and it made me laugh!'

Pavel looked at his T-shirt, then at Judy. Then he turned to look at Alexey and, still not understanding what she was talking about, decided not to ask any more about it. Instead, he smiled broadly at his friend and sat next to him on the divan.

'Alyosha, you swine! Why didn't you let me know you were coming? I would have arranged such a welcoming party! But as things stand ... I can't even have a proper drink with you! The thing is that tomorrow morning I'm off on a mission. Ah well, that's life!'

And he shook his head with its shock of hair miserably.

Pavel had a round face with chubby cheeks, like a girl. His small, close-set eyes sparkled with happiness and good humour, and the smile never left his full and slightly cracked lips. It was obvious that he was genuinely pleased about Alexey's visit. Muslim, like a puppy, immediately detected the good nature in Pavel and climbed up on his lap straightaway, examining Mickey Mouse with great curiosity.

Judy sat opposite them in an armchair.

'Are you going away for long?' Alexey asked casually.

'For a week at the very least,' he replied. 'How long will you be here for? But what are we blethering on without a drink for?! Sergey, get us some glasses and we'll have a drink! I can down a couple with you at least! What a meeting! What a meeting! But perhaps you want something to eat? I'll have a look to see what I've got.'

Pavel lifted Muslim off his knees and dashed off busily into the kitchen.

The others looked at each other in silence.

'Well, how do you find him?' Sergey asked softly.

'No different, really,' Alexey replied just as quietly. 'So what is there to notice?'

'I don't want to say anything. You'll realise why yourself. And as for your business, you'd better talk to him about that yourself. He's got it in for me as it is, though God knows why.'

Sergey put the glass down on the table and lowered himself limply into the armchair.

Left to his own devices for a moment, Muslim tugged at the long wire of one of the standard lamps. The lamp fell onto the floor with a crash, breaking its ceramic support. Alexey grabbed hold of the boy who had burst into tears with fright. Pavel rushed from the kitchen.

'What happened?' he shouted. 'Ah! that!' he said when he saw the broken lamp, and gave a light wave of the hand. 'That doesn't matter! Don't cry, son. I can buy a hundred more like that! The only thing is that there's nowhere to put them!'

He quickly gathered up the broken fragments and hurled them, together with the lamp itself, into another room.

'I'm not too well off for food, guys. I'm away tomorrow, so I'd already cleaned things out. All I've got left is tinned meat, but I can soon fry up a bit of potato.'

He turned to Judy: 'Could you give me a hand?' he said. 'And by the way, what's your name?'

'Judy' she smiled.

'What did you say?' he asked in surprise. 'I've never heard of such a name in my life!'

'She's an American, Pavel,' said Sergey with a grin. 'You've never met a live American before, I daresay!'

'And I suppose you've spent your whole life eating off the same plate with them!' Pavel snapped. 'Anyway, you may be an American, but do you know how to fry potatoes?'

'Possibly ...' said Judy, showing willing and going off with him into the kitchen.

A couple of hours later, as a result of non-stop sitting at the table and consuming a large portion of potatoes and fatty meat, Judy could scarcely keep her eyes open. Alexey had tried several times to steer the conversation with Pavel round to crossing the border, but the latter was so excited that he scarcely listened to what the others were saying. Pavel drank three full tumblers of fortified wine, ate scarcely anything and spent all his time reminiscing loudly and at length about their army days. Carried away by his memories, he saw himself as Alexey's closest mate without whom life now was not worth living.

'When I went back to my home village, old mate, I felt so depressed,' he said. 'I lived there for a few months and then decided to bugger off. I couldn't stand the quietness of the place! I became quite ill! I used to dream of our boys going into battle, helicopters droning above us, everything around us on fire, and us going on and on in those armoured vehicles! I nearly hanged myself there, it was so quiet, can you believe? No, I think that we need to go back in time. It's become my whole life! I can't live without it!'

'Well, everyone, I've heard all this before!' said Sergey, stretching and getting up out of his armchair. 'He's off his rocker, our Pavel. That's my diagnosis! What normal person would want to head back into that hell? And as if that isn't risky enough, he ferries merchandise in for me, only because that makes it all the more dangerous! And he goes first in the convoy so he can play heads or tails with the mines! Well, okay, I'm off to bed . . .'

When the door had closed behind him, Pavel turned to Alexey and said in a fervent whisper:

'You can see that I'm not crazy, can't you, Alyosha?! You've got to understand me. Although I don't really understand myself. I carry shells and contraband in the same lorry. Sometimes I work for the Soviet authorities, sometimes for Sukhar, sometimes for the Mojahedin. I get mixed up myself. But you should just take a look at what's going on in Tadzhikistan. It's slave-owning Communism! They're all part of a mafia, from top to bottom. The Central Committee secretaries take millions in bribes and live like lords. Have you ever wondered why Gorbachev can't bring the war to an end? Do you think it's because the Afghan Communists are dearer to him than his own soldiers? Not a bit of it! It's because the General Staff won't let him. And why won't they let him? Because they're all on the make, that's why! You can't imagine how much swag our generals have taken out of Afghanistan! Carpets, silk, gold brocade, glazed pottery, antique silver, diamonds! Nobody see it – apart from us drivers, that is. We have to transport the stuff – trunkfuls of it!'

Pavel got to his feet and began to walk nervously up and down the room.

He was short in stature, rather puny-looking with stooping shoulders, but he took broad, heavy strides. When he reached the wall, he turned abruptly and walked the other way, rumpling his hair. Then he suddenly stopped as though remembering something, and stared intently at Alexey.

'Hey! I'll show you something now, and you'll groan!' he said. 'You remember Yurka Shalygin? You and he used to be buddies, after all, and go AWOL to that village ... Now, what was it called? Where that Ulima of yours used to live. Oh, I'm sorry I'm talking about this while she's here!' (he nodded in Judy's direction) 'but water under the bridge! Anyway, to cut a long story short: you thought that Yurka was killed. Am I right? Well, take a look at this!'

And he went to the home-made bar, bent down and, tensing all his muscles, lifted it up a little and moved it away from the wall. He produced a Finnish flick-knife from his pocket, lifted one of the wooden slats at the back of the bar with it, stuck his hand in the gap and extracted a bundle of newspapers tied around with string. He untied the string with his teeth, opened the top newspaper and placed it triumphantly on the table in front of Alexey. It was the same issue of *Pravda* that the KGB man had shown him in Mytishchi, in the office of the Party secretary at his factory. Alexey immediately recognised it from the headline: THE RUSSIAN SOLDIER – VICTIM OF THE SOVIET COMMUNIST PARTY'S CRIMINAL POLICIES.

'Just read this bit, this bit here!' said Pavel, exultant and almost shouting. He turned the page and poked his finger at another large headline: 'There it is! Read that!'

'I've already read it,' said Alexey.

'You've already read it??!' said Pavel, so amazed that he forgot to close his mouth. 'Where??!'

'In a certain place. And that's why I've come to see you.'

'Did you already know that Yurka's still alive?!'

'Where can I sleep?' asked Judy, getting up and feeling that if she were to stay up one more minute, she would fall asleep right in the chair.

'In the same room as the boy!' said Pavel, rushing to show her into a tiny, dark bedroom. There were two beds there, a wide three-leaved mirror and a few chairs. Everything was higgledy-piggledy as if all the furniture had been put there in a hurry and simply left anywhere.

Without bothering to get undressed, Judy lay down on the bed and fell asleep immediately.

She woke up at the sound of loud conversation in the room next door. She recognised the voices of Alexey and Pavel. Turning over on her other side, she tried to get to sleep again. But despite the black southern night outside, she was unable: Pavel and Alexey were talking too loudly on the other side of the wall.

'When we were fighting, I used to think that there was nothing worse than mountains!' Pavel was saying. 'I grew up on the Volga, after all, and there's not a hint of any mountains there. Though there were hills galore, of course! We used to toboggan down them in winter. And when I landed in Afghanistan and saw the rebels picking our lads off from the mountains with their guns, I came to hate those mountains with ferocious hatred. But now ... Now I can't live without them!' Pavel's voice rang out stridently.

'When we're putting our convoy of lorries together,' he continued, 'nobody gets *ordered* to drive at the head of it. The boys draw lots – because the leading lorry always gets the first mine, and the first bullet! The lads get really frightened, the greenhorns! I'm the only one doing extra service. Driving after the petrol tanker is dangerous, too – if it blows up, the lorries following it go up as well, as sure as eggs is eggs – you'll get blown to smithereens! But I'm not afraid! Do you understand me, Alyosha?! I can feel it in my bones that not a bloody thing is going to happen to me! I've already been in several ambushes, and I've been all right. It's as if I've got a charmed life!'

'Touch wood, you idiot! Three times! And don't go on about it so much!' said Alexey, telling his friend off good-naturedly. He said nothing else for a moment and then added: 'And generally, Pavel, well – you've risked your life. You've proved to yourself that you're not some cowardly shit, that you're worth something. But now call it a day. Push off, while you're still in one piece. If you don't want to go back to your village, then move to some town, in Siberia, say, and start living like a normal human being! You can get a job as a driver anywhere.'

'Ah, Alyosha, but don't you understand? Well, after all this how can I simply go and live in some town and go to fucking work?! I'd go crackers right away!'

'Well, what will happen when the war comes to an end? It can't go on indefinitely, after all. What will you do then?'

'Well, that's not going to happen all that quickly! Our boys can't leave here with their tails between their legs! But the Afghans are a strong people, they won't make any concession, they'll fight on until the end.' Pavel paused and gave an appreciative whistle. 'Phew! You've seen how they fight yourself! Using guns against tanks! Although they do business with me, they look at me as though I were a pile of shit. Quite right, too. Who am I in their eyes? A fence, that's all! One arse on two stools! You can see the kind of house I've built for myself out of this bloody trade. Sukhar may be a shit, but he's not mean – he pays well. But I live by myself, like a wolf. There's a Tadzhik woman who sometimes comes, the local chemist ...'

'But Pavel,' Alexey interrupted, 'you still haven't said whether you'll take us with you on the trip?'

'Oh, Alyosha, I really don't want to! God knows what'll happen! You don't know what you're asking!'

Everything went quiet for a moment. There was the sound of a tumbler being placed down on the glass table and of somebody pacing heavily from corner to corner.

'My number's up in this country, anyway!' said Alexey. 'Well, I might manage to keep out of their way for a year of two. But then they'd catch me and I'd get it in the neck,' he said pensively. 'But this way, at least I'd achieve something: I'd get the kid back to his mother and the American girl on her way back home to America.'

'What about yourself? Couldn't you go to America?'

'God alone knows! I'm completely mixed up ...' Alexey spat out unwillingly.

'You mean you've fallen for the American girl? And what about her?'

Judy lifted her head off the pillow listening tensely for Alexey's answer.

'What about her?' he said, laughing mirthlessly. 'Well, she's an American, brother, what do you expect? I'm damned if I can make her out! All I want to do is send her home in one piece! However you look at it, it's only because of me that she's landed up in this mess! As for me – well, I don't know. America's a frightening place, too. A foreign country. Perhaps, I might manage to run Yurka Shalygin to ground and join up with him. If you help me ...'

'Okay ... Damn it, let's go! I'm lucky, after all – which means we'll get through! Only how are we actually going to pull it off? Let's say I pick you up at the Chikmansk turn-off – I could have a flat tyre so as to fall behind the convoy. But three days in the back of a lorry – how will the littl'un cope with it! It would be okay for the two of you – just don't eat anything and you won't need to go. But what about the boy? He's bound at least to need the potty ...'

'Sergey has got hold of some sleeping tablets for him . . .'

'Sukhar works out everything in advance, just like a scientist! He consulted the doctor, I daresay . . .'

Judy pressed her eyes tightly closed. She had lost the urge to sleep. Alexey's words still rang in her ears and for some reason she suddenly felt so frivolous that she rolled over and over onto her front and back again several times, hiding her face in the pillow, so as to muffle the laughter that came from deep inside her.

25

Holding his rucksack on his knees, Alexey undid it and began to get out bundles of money.

'Count it!' he told Sergey gloomily.

'Don't worry,' said Sergey cheerfully, 'I can tell just by looking how many notes there are in a bundle! By the way, you owe me another couple of thousand for the boy's birth certificate. It's cheaper because it comes without photographs.'

Alexey gave him a dark look but said nothing and produced another couple of thousand. The two men were in a dense wild rose thicket about five yards away from the Chikmansk turn-off which Pavel had mentioned to Alexey the previous night. Muslim, who had been given a quarter of a sleeping tablet about an hour before, was sleeping soundly on one of the two enormous suitcases filled with clothes – Sergey's contraband goods.

Because of the thick bushes you could only see the mountain road if you stood right up. Just now at dawn the road was empty apart from Sergey's blue Moskvich standing at right angles to the rock with its hood up for show and screwdrivers and spanners scattered on the ground. To any passing driver this would look like an ordinary break-down in the middle of the country. But during the twenty minutes that they had spent here nobody had come down the road. Beyond the Chikmansk pass the closed-off frontier zone began, and nobody apart from soldiers would drive that way.

'Pavel refused any money, of course?!' suggested Sergey.

'I didn't even talk to him about money,' replied Alexey.

'That's what I was telling you. The guy's off his rocker. Still, there's something mystical about it. For the last eight months he's come out of all sorts of scrapes – completely unscathed! Not even a scratch!'

'Touch wood!' said Alexey scornfully.

Sergey did so rapidly, and then carefully packed the bundles of money into his attaché-case, smiling broadly at Judy.

'Well, farewell, my American lady! Forgive me again if I got things wrong. It's a Russian custom that we ought to kiss three times before parting ...'

'Pack it in!' interrupted Alexey rudely.

'Oh, Prince! And you would spoil a moment like this! Okay, mate! What are you getting so worked up about?! I was only joking! I won't kiss her after all! And I won't kiss you either! See you sometime, mate! Enjoy the West! I'd go myself ... Only I haven't got a princess of a grandmother waiting for me there! Oh yes! I nearly forgot. Take off the medals! ...'

And he unpinned the medals from Alexey's shirt himself.

'You know what the Afghans would do to you if they saw these medals, don't you?! By the way, if you still have any money left, would you like me to look after it for you? They don't go a bomb on our roubles in the West ...'

Alexey stood there in gloomy silence.

'No? Well, all right. It's your affair! See you!'

With that, Sergey slapped Alexey on the shoulder and, without turning round, he limped over to his car, swinging his attaché-case and leaning slightly on his stick. Throwing the case into the car, he gathered all the spanners and screwdrivers off the ground, slammed the hood shut and got into the car. Accelerating hard, he swung the Moskvich around on the narrow road and, sticking his left hand out of the window to wave farewell, headed quickly off to the north. A minute or so later the clouds of dust behind him subsided, and the road became empty once again.

Without looking at each other Alexey and Judy sat down silently on the second suitcase. Alexey took off his shirt and placed it over the back of Muslim's neck as he slept – the sun had already risen high in the sky and was hot on the boy's head. For the whole time since Judy had slapped Alexey in the swimming pool, they had contrived not to say a single word to one another. Besides, they had not been left alone with each other for a moment since then. But now, after what Judy had inadvertently heard that night …

'Alexey …' she said in as gentle a voice as possible.

'Well, what now?!' he interrupted rudely without turning to look at her. 'Only three more days to go, and then you'll be rid of me! Be patient!'

'No, wait …' she said, paying no attention to his coarse tone of voice, and stretched her hand towards him, wanting to touch his.

But her gesture was interrupted by a muffled rumbling in the distance, which got louder.

'They're coming!' whispered Alexey.

'Where?' asked Judy. She tried to sit up a little, but Alexey grabbed her by the arm. 'Stay down!' he said.

Judy apprehensively lowered herself to the ground again, and Alexey cupped the palms of his hands around Muslim's ears. But it was clearly unnecessary – the boy was sleeping serenely, although the roar of the approaching column of lorries was getting louder and closer.

Finally, slowly and ponderously, the first tarpaulin-covered Ural lorry drove close past them. Behind it came another … and another … and another. They were spaced equally apart, their powerful engines wheezing heavily and the windscreens of their high cabs flashing in the sunlight.

'Seven … eight … nine …' Judy was counting, and

then suddenly thought to herself in terror: 'They're not going to stop! Pavel has tricked us – he'll drive right past!'

But, as if it had heard her, the penultimate lorry suddenly turned sharply off the road and stopped on the tiny space by the rocks where Sergey's Moskvich had been standing shortly before. The leading lorries had disappeared around the bend and continued down the road, but the lorry bringing up the rear also came to a halt. A young driver, his army blouse unbuttoned, jumped down from the cab and ran over to where Pavel, similarly clad, was already placing a jack under the back axle of his lorry.

'What's the problem?' Alexey and Judy heard the rear lorry driver ask anxiously.

'What did you say?' Pavel roared at him. 'You were driving right behind me and didn't see! Blockhead! I've driven over a nail! Where do they pick new recruits up! Would you notice if I'd gone over the cliff?!'

Pavel was rapidly unscrewing the nuts on his burst tyre with an enormous wrench.

'Well, there was so much dust that I couldn't see a thing,' said the other driver, justifying himself. 'Do you need any help?'

'Dust my foot! Push off! Go on! Go on! I'll catch you up and bring up the rear. Well?! What are you hanging about for?!'

'As you like ...' said the driver, taking offence, and went back to his own lorry.

'Bloody recruits! ...' said Pavel, still swearing loudly even though the young driver could no longer hear him – he had climbed back into the cab of his lorry, started up the engine and, steering carefully to avoid Pavel, rolled off down the road.

As soon as the lorry had disappeared round the bend, Pavel turned away from his burst tyre and shouted cheerfully.

'Hey, Alyosha! Come on out then, quick!'

Alexey lifted up Muslim in his arms and ran quickly over to the back of the lorry. Judy grabbed hold of his rucksack and took hold of the handles of the two suitcases, but she realised immediately that she would not be able lift even one of them.

'Oi! Mickey Mouse! What are you doing?' said Pavel, his face appearing out of the bushes.

'It's the suitcases ...'

'Leave the suitcases! They're not your concern! Just get up into the back!'

And Pavel leapt over to the suitcases, grabbed one by the handle, hoisted the other one onto his shoulder and rushed towards the lorry. Judy, bending double for no reason, ran alongside him.

Alexey, who was already in the back of the lorry, took the suitcase from Pavel's shoulder and shoved it right in under the awning. Judy grabbed the side of the lorry and climbed up. In her excitement and haste she could not get her foot up onto the high running-board, and it was only when Alexey heaved her up that she managed to roll her stomach over the metal side and clamber up to join him. He pushed her into a narrow gap between the awning and some wooden boxes, hurriedly took the second suitcase from Pavel and then lowered the tarpaulin flaps of the awning.

With scarcely any time to adjust to the darkness, Judy looked around her. In front of her was a wall of heavy flat boxes with yellow metal bands. Printed on them in thick black letters was the word EXPLOSIVE. The back of the lorry was crammed full of these boxes almost to the roof of the canvas awning. It was impossible to see how there was room there for one person, let alone three. Muslim was lying on the floor in the tiny space between the boxes and the tail-board. This was where the suitcases were. Alexey was standing with his back to the boxes, his face touching the canvas, and Judy could see that, perhaps for the first time in the whole of their adventures, he was at a loss as to what to do.

Outside Pavel continued to tinker about with the wheel, whistling cheerfully to himself. At last there was a loud crash – he had obviously managed to remove the damaged wheel. Then Pavel started straining and grunting as he put on the spare wheel, and a minute later the back of the lorry settled down as he lowered the jack.

Judy was already soaking with sweat because of the stuffiness when one of the canvas flaps suddenly opened and Pavel appeared.

'Hey, what are you standing there for?! he asked in amazement. 'Oh, yes! I forgot to tell you! Crawl forward over the boxes, and your compartment is there waiting for you. It's not luxurious, but you'll survive! I had to give the loaders a crate of vodka to leave the space. I told them I had a lot of merchandise to transport. They usually get something from me, so it's not the first time! Oh, but wait a minute! I nearly forgot!'

He disappeared, returning a few moments later holding a bag.

'Hang on to this!' he said. 'It contains chocolate for the boy, some water and vitamins. I got them through my chemist friend. Only don't drink much water. Just wet your whistles and it'll pass!'

'Thanks, Pavel, said Alexey. 'How much do I owe you?'

'Are you crazy, or something?' said Pavel indignantly. 'In the next world we'll settle up! Go on! In you get, idiot! My name's not Sukhar!'

He jumped up into the back of the lorry, lifted the suitcases on to the crates, shoving them into the narrow space between the boxes and the roof, where Alexey was already sprawled out. Alexey immediately crawled away, pushing the suitcases in front of him. Then there was a crash as the suitcases fell down from a height onto the floor of the lorry, and Alexey's face appeared.

'Fantastic compartment, mate!' he said joyfully, all wet with sweat. 'Let me have the boy!'

Pavel carefully passed him Muslim who was perspiring in his sleep. Then Pavel jumped out of the back and rushed round to the cab.

Judy was still crawling forward over the crates, shoving Alexey's rucksack and Pavel's bag ahead of her, scraping her back against the hard roof of the awning and her stomach against the thick, rough ropes holding the crates together, when suddenly the lorry's engine roared. There was an abrupt jerk and they moved off. She was shaken about on top of the crates until Alexey offered her his hands and she finally fell head over heels into a spacious niche in between the crates and the back of the cab. She didn't hurt herself, however, and if she did cry out, it was only for joy. It was all so simple. There really was a whole compartment there! There was no room to stretch right out on the floor, but sitting and standing were possible, and Muslim was sleeping peacefully on the suitcase. What an amazing fellow he was, this Pavel! She felt like planting a kiss right on his chubby cheeks!

Alexey touched her tentatively on the shoulder.

'What happened? Did you hurt yourself?'

Sitting down on the floor, Judy said nothing and waited to see what he would do next.

'Did you knock yourself?' he said, bending down to her apprehensively.

Judy sat up a little, placed her arms around his neck and drew him towards her, intending to kiss him. Alexey fell on top of her in surprise, but immediately started back and straightened up. Judy gave a loud laugh.

'Quiet!' he said. 'You'll wake up the boy!'

'You must be joking!' she replied, continuing to laugh. 'If he can sleep with the lorry jolting about like this, do you really think he'll wake up with me laughing?'

Falling silent, she got up, moved over to Alexey and felt for his hand.

'Aren't you happy that we're on our way?' she said.

'There's nothing to be happy about ...' he answered after a pause.

'Why?'

'*Because*! ...' he replied sharply and retrieved his hand. 'Do you know what's in these crates?' he went on.

'What? Bullets, I expect ...'

'Bullets, my eye! They're howitzer shells! One burst from a partisan machine-gun, and there'll be nothing left of us. Nice work Pavel's got! Oh well, let's settle ourselves down.'

He leant over, swaying with the lorry's jolting, opened one of Sergey's suitcases and began to drag various articles of clothing from it – men's jackets, sweaters, trousers. The 'compartment' began to smell immediately of moth-balls and stale old clothing – so strongly, in fact, that Muslim even sneezed in his sleep.

'That's Sukhar for you, the bastard!' Alexey swore to himself in a fit of temper. 'He makes money from shit! Buying up rags like this in a second-hand shop! They'd fall apart after one month's wearing!'

He shook half the clothes out of the suitcase and loosened up the rest with his hand, making it into a kind of cradle. Then he carefully transferred Muslim to the case and sat down by it, motioning Judy to the clothes lying next to him which he had thrown out of the case.

'Go on, sit down,' he said. 'I won't bite.'

Judy sat down.

It was becoming very stuffy. Judy unbuttoned her warm knitted jacket, took it off, and moving up close to Alexey, leant her head on his shoulder. He did not move.

'Are you afraid of dying?' she asked.

He said nothing for a long time, but then carefully ran his hand over her head.

'Don't panic now!' he said. 'This is the biggest risk we've taken so far. But I remember the way you gave that bloke a good kick in the teeth in the *chaikhana*! My little karate expert! By the way,' he went on, putting his arm around her shoulders, 'about that ... Forgive me for ... hell, all the rubbish I said that time at the swimming pool ... It was just a pretence ...'

Judy ran her fingers over the tattoo on his shoulder.

'What's this?' she asked. 'Why do you all ...'

'It gives my blood group and rhesus factor. All of us get marked like that ...'

'Kiss me ...'

Alexey touched her hair lightly with his lips and moved away.

'No! Not like that!' she said, hurt.

But he carried on stroking her short hair, occasionally touching her cheek and neck with the palm of his hand.

'Please, *kiss me*!' she said, jerking her head emphatically. 'It's stupid to think that you might soon be meeting your Ulima! And what if we die? You said yourself: one round would be enough! *Kiss me*!'

And without waiting for him to make the move, she pressed her lips to his mouth. Alexey squeezed her shoulders painfully. Without tearing his lips away, he slowly leant back against the second suitcase and drew Judy towards him.

Suddenly there was a loud rustling noise. A tiny covered aperture opened in the front wall of the canvas which they had not noticed before in the semi-darkness.

Alexey and Judy started away from each other in fright.

A fresh breeze came in through the aperture, and on the other side they could see the back of Pavel's head indistinctly looming in the cab.

'Well, are you still alive?' he shouted, half turning round, with one hand on the wheel and holding open the flapping canvas window with the other. 'Breathe in a bit of fresh air, or otherwise you'll suffocate in there. If there's any danger, I'll close it. Have you worked out what's in the crates yet, Alyosha! I'm not leading the column this trip though. I'll take care of you! How's the boy! Is he still asleep?'

Ahead of them through the windscreen the whole column of lorries could be seen slowly ascending the steep road to the next Pamir pass. And even further away were the high mountain peaks with their snow caps.

26

They had been driving for three days and were now inside Afghan territory. Just before the border, at the river Pyandzh, the convoy of lorries had been joined by an armed escort – a column of ten T-80 tanks with two armoured cars at the front manned by sappers and another two at the rear with sub-machine guns. At the head of the whole column was a mine clearance vehicle for dealing with plastic mines. During the day two MI-6 reconnaissance helicopters would be circling constantly over the column. The helicopter pilots maintained a careful observation of the surrounding cliffs, on the look-out for sudden gas attacks. The sappers exhausted their drivers with constant orders to stop. At the first suspicious sign – a stone on the dusty road, the tracks of a donkey or a mountain-goat or even their droppings – the whole column would grind to a halt while one of the sappers took his boots off, crept gingerly ahead in a cat-like way on his bare feet and probed for mines with his hand-held detector.

In the evening, when dusk descended rapidly on the mountains around them, the roar of the tanks, the lorries and the helicopters would die away, and the convoy would halt for the night with the sub-machine-gunners forming a tight cordon around them. Escaping through that was inconceivable, and in any case where would they escape to? All around them were wild, steep rock-faces, mountain ridges without any vegetation, sun-scorched stony plateaux. The nights were altogether the most dangerous and agonizing time for Alexey and Judy. During the day, in spite of the heat and the burning sun which they could feel through the canvas awning, they could at least breathe fresh air through the tiny canvas window which Pavel would open. Above the roaring of the engines they could chat, move about, massage each other's stiff limbs. During the day they could also allow Muslim to stay awake and move about at least for a few hours, and Alexey even managed to do a few exercises with him. The boy was putting up with all the inconveniences of the journey, in particular his meagre ration of chocolate, quite stoically, but he was constantly asking for a drink. Alexey tried teaching him only to moisten his mouth with water, but this did not help – as soon as he was given a bottle or flask of water, Muslim would drink from it quickly and greedily and they did not have the heart to take it away from him. So then Alexey taught him to pee in the rags that Sergey had sent with them in the suit-cases. He would then stuff the urine-sodden clothes into the gap between the canvas roof and the crates with the howitzer shells. These clothes would quickly dry out with the sun and wind, and they did not smell.

'Where are we going!' Muslim would ask.

On the third day of the journey Alexey made up his mind to tell the boy the truth – putting it off any longer was pointless.

'We're going home to your mama, Muslim,' he said, holding the boy on his lap just as Muslim was about to fall asleep, having been given the regular quarter sleeping tablet. 'They lied to all of you in the school where you were. Your mama is alive, she's waiting for you. Her name is Ulima. Remember it. She loves you very much and can't wait for you to get home.'

'You're not fibbing?' said Muslim, half asleep.

'I'm not fibbing.'

'Say: I swear by Mohammed!'

'I swear.'

'I believe you. And do you believe in Allah?'

'How can I put it ...?' said Alexey with difficulty. 'I also grew up in a boarding-school, like you. Our teachers taught us *not* to believe. Either in God, or in Allah. There was only one boy whose parents had believed in God and had taught him to do the same. But they had died, and he was living in the boarding-school. He would pray quietly to himself under his blanket so that no one could see him. But we used to beat him. And we beat him hard and used to throw him out onto the snow without any clothes on. That wasn't right. I feel ashamed of it now ... So you carry on believing!'

'But our school is better!' said Muslim with a smile. 'Everybody believes in Allah. Only we don't tell the teachers. 'Cos they want us to believe in Lenin. And not in Allah. One teacher found out that we were praying to Allah and said to us: "Children, anybody that wants sweets, pray to Allah and ask him to put them under your pillow in the morning." We all prayed, and I asked Allah for meat. But he didn't give me any. He didn't give anybody anything. And she says: "You see, children! There *is* no Allah! But now you pray to Lenin and ask him for some." We all did, and I asked for meat again. And in the morning everybody had sweets under their pillows, me too. He's stupid, that Lenin! I had asked him for meat! We all swore at him. We'd all asked for meat, and he'd left us sweets!'

'The bitches! ...' Alexey swore softly to himself, through his teeth. 'You see?!' he said to Judy. 'Some teachers!'

'And who taught you to believe in Allah?' Judy asked Muslim.

'Fatima ...' answered the boy, shutting his sleepy eyes. 'The big children teached the little ones to believe in Allah ...'

'Muslim ...' said Alexey, giving the boy a little shake on his knees. 'Wait a minute, don't go to sleep. Your mama Ulima didn't call you Muslim ...'

'I know,' said the boy, interrupting him. 'It was them

who thought up names like that for us. But only the big children know what their mummies called them. I don't.'

'Your mama called you Akhram. That's a good name.'

'Akhram ...' Muslim said slowly, drawing out the word as though testing out his new name and altering the 'k' to 'kh' in the Afghan manner. 'Akhram! Did you think of that?'

'No,' replied Alexey. 'Your mama Ulima thought of the name for you when you were born. Your grandad was called that, too. Remember: if anything should happen to us, your mama Ulima lives in the Lohar Valley, in the village of Tapbil. Tapbil – can you remember that?'

'Course I can. Tapbil means swapping,' and the boy said something in Afghan which included the word 'tapbil', and immediately translated it: 'I'm swapping bread for a chop!'

'But now for the most important thing, Akhram. I would wish very much for you to be my son and for me to be your father. I swear by Mohammed! But it isn't like that. Your own father died in battle ...'

'No!' the boy screamed in spite of his sleepiness. '*You* are my father. You are babá,' and he threw his arms around Alexey's neck.

Judy could feel tears streaming down her cheeks.

'Akhram ...' said Alexey, stroking the boy on the head. 'We are already travelling over your country. This is Afghanistan, do you understand? I promised your mama that I would bring you back to her. And I have almost done so. Remember: if anything should happen to us, and you remain alive – your mama Ulima lives in the village of Tapbil ...'

'I remember, babá,' whispered the boy, almost asleep. 'I remember ...'

Alexey placed him carefully in the open suitcase with the clothes. Judy wiped her tear-stained face with her dirty hand ...

But that night ... At night they had to sit in their dark hole between the crates, hiding like mice, wrapped up well in advance in whatever warm things they could find in Sergey's suitcases – in the mountains at night it would get very cold. In the total silence and darkness, beneath a scattering of large southern stars, the slightest rustle could be heard from a long way away. In this tense and hostile night the only sound would be the occasional noise of the sunbaked rock-face splitting in the cold, and whenever that distant cracking sound was heard the guards would call to each other anxiously. In order to keep warm, the guards would walk constantly up and down the column of lorries and, whenever their steps drew closer to Pavel's lorry, Alexey and Judy even tried to stop breathing. The only sound then would be the carefree snoring of Pavel asleep in the seat in the cab . . .

But on that third night, when it was already long past midnight, Alexey and Judy, who were dozing uncomfortably in each other's arms, were suddenly wakened by a loud scream from the boy.

'Mama! Mama!' Muslim was calling in his sleep.

Alexey pressed his hand over the boy's mouth, turning him over onto his side. The boy carried on sleeping quietly and never woke, but the hurried steps of the sentry could be heard approaching the lorry.

Alexey and Judy froze. Alexey carefully removed two pistols from the rucksack and placed one of them in Judy's hand. They held their breath.

The young lieutenant in charge of the sentries almost ran up to their lorry and jerked open the door of the cab where Pavel was asleep.

'What's going on?' he said nervously. Pavel raised his sleepy face from the seat.

'What *is* going on?' asked Pavel blankly and grabbed his sub-machine gun.

'Who was it shouting out "mama" here?'

'Well, me, I expect. In my sleep . . .'

'What, in a child's voice?'

'Well, it can happen,' he said, coughing, as if to clear his throat. 'And what voice do you cry out "mama" in in your sleep?!'

'God knows! I'm not sure ...' said the lieutenant, calming down. 'I thought somebody might be cutting your throat ...'

'Cutting my throat!' mimicked Pavel, making the seat creak loudly on purpose and raising his voice. He carried on speaking without a break. 'Cut my throat – well, that'd take some bloody doing! Good bloody reason you've found for waking me up! So he doesn't like my mama! Just you carry on with your fucking guard duty, and don't come waking me up any more! I've got to drive this bloody thing tomorrow while you're snoozing away in your old rattle-trap! Go on! Bugger off and let me get some shut-eye! ...'

'Okay, you get to sleep. Only don't swear at officers! Do you want to go to the glasshouse?!'

'But I'm not swearing. "Bugger" is for elegance, you might say.'

And Pavel put his sub-machine gun down on the floor of the cab.

'Okay, carry on sleeping then, you elegant bugger!' the lieutenant mimicked Pavel petulantly. He slammed shut the door of the lorry and marched off, his boots crunching loudly on the sharp stones of the road.

Alexey and Judy leant their heads back simultaneously against the crates of shells and, closing their eyes, quietly let their breath out. From the cab they could hear the grumbling voice of Pavel who was lying down to sleep again:

'Now you're not even allowed to call your mother's name in your sleep, the sods! ...'

Suddenly there was the sharp whistle of a flying mortar shell. And at the same moment a deafening explosion shook the earth and the mountains. The lorry shook so hard that Alexey and Judy crashed their heads against the canvas roof and the boy was thrown out of the suitcase.

Then there came a second explosion – even closer. The crates with the shells were leaning over dangerously, ripping their supporting ropes. One of them broke completely and whipped Judy violently round the neck, but she did not even notice it. All around them was the deafening roar of sub-machine-gun and machine-gun bursts, bombs were exploding, and the leading lorry stuffed with shells disintegrated with a terrible explosion. The mountains, from where the Mojahedin were firing at the column with mortars and grenade-throwers, amplified the explosion at least tenfold with booming echoes. Muslim had woken up and was screaming in terror. The Soviet tanks and machine-guns were firing blindly at random at the rock-faces around them. In his armoured vehicle the major in command of the escort was shouting something into the microphone of his walkie-talkie. Pavel was hurled out of the cab. Jumping wildly to his feet, he ran around to the back of the lorry, yelling:

'Get out, Alyosha! Get out! This is all because I didn't take the leading position. Get, out, damn it! We'll get blown up!'

'A knife! Give me a knife!' Alexey yelled from inside the lorry, trying to tear open the canvas with his nails and teeth. But because of all the shooting and explosions they could not hear each other.

The next explosion shook the lorry so violently that the top crate of several that had broken free ripped the canvas awning with its sharp corner, while the remaining crates slipped down pinning Alexey, Judy and the screaming child against the inside of the lorry.

Sticking his hands through the hole in the canvas, Alexey tugged upwards with all his strength. The canvas made a cracking sound, as it tore. A hole appeared. Cold air, mixed up with the smell of burnt gun-powder, hit them in the face. Around them machine-guns were banging out tracer-bullets, the two tanks as yet undamaged were firing deafeningly, the other eight were on fire, and the figure of a man with clothes on fire somersaulted out of one of them, his mouth wide open in a scream.

'Catch the boy!' Alexey shouted at Pavel who was standing below, and hurled Muslim towards him.

Pavel fell on his back with the boy on top of him as he caught him. Alexey jumped out of the lorry and screamed at Judy: 'Jump! Jump!'

But she, deafened by the explosions and by fear, was stuck helplessly on the top.

'For fuck's sake, jump!' shouted Alexey. He leapt up, grabbed her by the sleeve of her jacket and literally tore her down. She came crashing from above and knocked Alexey off his feet.

'Come on, run!' he said, jumping to his feet immediately, the whites of his eyes flashing. Grabbing Muslim up into his arms, he bent down and ran off with him away from the road and behind some rocks, shouting: 'Follow me! Judy, Pavel, follow me, for God's sake!'

Judy ran after him, unable to think of anything else and afraid only of losing sight of him in the darkness. Beneath her feet the earth was shaking from the explosions, tracer-bullets were outlining the sky with their bright dotted lines. The smell of burning and the crushed stone obstructed her breathing, and chunks of blown-up earth were raining down on her head, back and shoulders. Pavel ran after them, but suddenly stopped.

'I've left my machine-gun behind!' he shouted and ran back to the lorry.

'Come back!' Alexey yelled at him at the top of his voice from behind some large boulders.

'I shan't be a moment! You don't bloody realise! I've got a charmed life!' Pavel shouted cheerfully as he ran, intoxicated with the danger.

He dived into the cab, grabbed hold of his machine-gun, a cartridge pouch, and an army kit-bag with food and clothing. And started to run back, without even bothering to bend down.

'Red Alert!' he chuckled as he went, whirling the kit-bag around over his head.

But at that moment another bomb scored a direct hit on the lorry. The savage explosion blended earth and sky, threw Pavel up like a rag doll and enveloped him in a hail of burning earth, crates of exploding howitzer shells and fragments of the vehicle.

'Bloody hell! Pavel!!' Alexey shouted, and thumped his fist as hard as he could against the boulder. 'Pav-e-el! . . .' he groaned, his voice disappearing in a thin, piteous descant, while he himself continued to look fixedly at the place where, only a second before, laughing and waving his kit-bag around, Sergeant Pavel Yegorov of the Soviet Army had been running. In that place now was an enormous crater, a great hole with shells still exploding in it, the earth and remains of the lorry still burning. And around them mortar shells were still exploding, machine-guns still chattering coldly and spitefully, continuing the battle against the invisible Afghan partisans, concealed behind the rock face.

Judy tugged at Alexey's shoulder. 'Let's run ! . . .' she said.

But he did not hear her.

'Please. Alyosha! Let's run for it! . . .'

He turned his face – dirty, bearded, with distant, whitish-looking eyes – slowly and mechanically towards her. This was the first time since the moment they had first met in the workers' hostel in Mytishchi that she had called him Alyosha. And although at this second he could remember nothing, nor connect anything in his mind, nonetheless this word did seem to restore him to reality.

'Yes, yes . . .' he said uncomprehendingly. Then suddenly, as though regaining consciousness, he shouted out: 'Yes, let's run! Follow me! But where's Muslim?!'

The boy, stunned by the explosion, was lying silently at his feet, with his mouth agape and his eyes wide open with fear.

Alexey lifted him up into his arms, holding him firmly, pressing him tight against himself like a wounded limb, and the boy immediately squeezed his arms around his neck and only then burst into tears again:

'Papa! . . . Babá! . . . Run! . . . Please! . . .'

But Alexey was already doing precisely that – into the

dark, between the rocks, bending low, holding the boy with one arm, and using the other to feel his way through the sharp stones and boulders ahead of him. Seen from the side he resembled at this moment some beast, an orang-outang, say, fleeing from danger with its cub.

'Follow me, Judy! Follow me! ... Quickly! Quickly! ...'

Judy was running – stumbling, falling, leaping. Alexey's voice ahead of her and the roar of explosions behind her were urging her on, but her strength was exhausted and her breathing jerky.

'Come on! Quickly, Judy! Quickly!' Alexey was calling. Through some heightened animal instinct he could find ways in between the dark rocks, managing not to step into fissures, or stumble on loose stones. They had already run a fair distance, so that the noise of fighting and explosions became less, and occasionally disappeared completely behind the huge rocks. But Alexey did not stop, and only looked round at her from time to time, shouting: 'Come on, Judy! Quickly now!'

She fell over, crying. Her strength was finished.

He ran on a few more steps, looked around, saw that she was lying on the ground, and bounded back to her.

'Get up!' he said, pulling her by the sleeve of her jacket. 'Get up! ...'

'I can't ... I can't ...'

'Get up! We must keep going! You don't know what's about to happen!'

And he grabbed hold of her by her sleeve and dragged her bodily along behind him. It was not with the strength of his muscles, but with his veins, nerves and heightened awareness of danger still ahead that he managed to carry the boy along and drag Judy with him over the earth and rocks as well. She, like a puppy, could only cross the rocks on her bloodstained hands and knees. Screaming out with pain in a mixture of Russian and English:

'Let me go! Let me go! Leave me! Please!! ...'

But he refused to let her go. She decided he had simply

taken leave of his senses. This thought terrified her even more than the horror she had just lived through and, with strength from she knew not where, she suddenly lunged to one side – like a person drowning at the bottom of the sea who makes one final, semi-conscious dash for life. Tearing herself away from Alexey's hand, she rolled away to one side, jumped up onto her knees, stretched out her blood-stained hands in front of her and screamed out, snarling like a wild animal:

'Don't come near me! Leave me!!'

A loud droning sound in the sky made them both turn their heads.

'They're coming!' Alexey yelled. 'I said they would! Follow me, Judy!'

With enormous bounds he rushed towards a large crevice in the rocks. Judy, not yet understanding what was about to happen, but realising that Alexey had not gone mad after all, ran after him. Looking in bewilderment and fear up at the sky where the heavy drone was becoming louder and louder, Alexey dived into the cleft in the rock, left the boy there, literally tearing him away from his chest, jumped out again towards Judy, and grabbed her by the hand.

'Down there!' he said, pushing her into the crevice. 'That's all! Freeze! It's our lot! ... Well, the Soviets, I mean! Now it'll really start! You've seen nothing yet!'

And he dragged Muslim further into the cleft and sat down himself, exhausted, his lips trembling with fatigue.

'Come over here more! ...' he called weakly to Judy.

She crept over to him on all fours.

And at that moment, behind her back, through the entrance to the crevice, the dark sky was suddenly lit up with a bright, unnatural, luminescent silver light.

'They've p-put up f-flares, the b-bastards!' Alexey stammered hoarsely. 'Well, hang on now, Muslim! ...' And once again he pressed the sobbing child tightly to his chest.

With the dropping of the flares, the Soviet airforce had

bathed the mountains in a shining, eerie light almost as bright as day.

And then it began.

Judy had never seen anything like it even in Frank Coppola's film *Apocalypse Now*. Heavily droning bombers dived steeply and dropped their bombs on the rocks surrounding the column of lorries under attack. After them, helicopters in battle formation would dive in even closer to the ground and strafe the rocks with napalm, incendiary bombs and machine-gun fire. In the ensuing explosions and fire, everything beneath the dead white sky was in flames – the earth, the stones, the rock-faces.

Judy was praying soundlessly with her dry, black lips. But she knew that they would not come out of this alive. Neither she, nor Alexey, nor Muslim, nor the Afghan partisans. Surviving a hell like this was impossible.

27

Half of the next day they spent sleeping. But this was not the refreshing sleep of people who are simply tired. It was deep oblivion, a dead swoon. Like that of a seagull wounded in a gale, falling like a stone onto a saving shore and lying there inertly, stunned – a ball of tortured feathers, washed and dragged about over the sand by the tide's foaming waves . . .

In this oblivion of sleep Judy's body could feel that something was disturbing it – now scratching, now tickling her cheek. With a slow-motion gesture, her hand tried unconsciously and instinctively to shake this thing from her neck. But a few minutes later the same scratching and tickling feeling would be felt on her shoulder. Her body was ordering her eyes to open. The pupils of her eyes squinted down at her shoulder. And at the same moment her brain awoke and commanded her body to freeze.

Crawling slowly over her shoulder, as large as the palm of her hand, was a scorpion.

Spell-bound and with bated breath Judy followed its leisurely movement with her eyes. Lying deeply asleep next to her was Alexey with Muslim in his arms. And outside, beyond the cleft in the rock, a new spring day was shining. Floating high in the sky above the mountains were fleecy white clouds and a blindingly clear sun. A slight breeze was stirring the sparse but clean grass on the steep mountain slopes, the claret-coloured petals of mountain poppies, the tiny, greenish-white flowers of edelweiss. In the clinically transparent air large white butterflies were flying about and cicadas were chirring. Lizards slid nimbly over the warm rocks. The world was continuing to live as if nothing had taken place the previous night – as if the firing, the explosions, the deaths, the living hell – simply had not happened. As if the blood, the burning human bodies, the pieces of human flesh flying through the air had not existed. A sun-filled, life-giving, translucent spring day hung above the world.

The scorpion was slowly crawling over Judy's body – from one shoulder, across her neck to the other shoulder. It stopped at a vein pulsating on her neck, examined it attentively, crawled over it in a business-like manner and continued on its way. On the other shoulder it was obviously bewildered by a deep scratch covered with congealed blood and dirt. It decided to crawl around it and, having done so, as slowly and deliberately as ever, it dropped off Judy's body onto the ground.

At the same instant Judy jumped up with a piercing scream, a scream loud enough to wake a dead man from his grave.

Alexey jumped wildly to his feet.

'What's wrong?!' he shouted.

Judy continued to scream hysterically, pressing her back right up against the wall of the crevice and pointing at the scorpion crawling over the ground.

Alexey bent down and picked the scorpion up by its high grey back.

'But it's only a scorpion ...' he said, in obvious bewilderment.

'Yes, yes! I know! A scorpion!!' screamed Judy in tears.

Alexey shrugged his shoulders in puzzlement, went over to the entrance to the crevice and hurled the creature far away over the rocks. Then he stretched himself, scratched his side and looked around in astonishment – Judy was sitting on the ground next to the wall and weeping. She was completely hysterical – tears flowing uncontrollably, nose running, shoulders shaking. Everything that she had experienced the night before, and everything that she had lived through during her journeyings around Russia was now coming out in this fit of crying.

Alexey went up to her, squatted down next to her and began to stroke her head.

'Come on ... It's all right ... It was only a scorpion, after all ...' he was saying gently. 'Go on ... you just cry ... you just cry ...'

Muslim also woke up at last, sat up, rubbed his sleepy eyes with his dirty little fists and then stared at Judy in amazement. This three-year-old boy, having lived in a Soviet boarding-school, was already older than his years in any case, and in this one night had grown up twice as much again. A new sorrowful expression, unlike that of a child, had appeared on his face.

'I can't stand it ... I can't stand it any more ...' Judy was saying, swaying to and fro as she wept.

'Have you been hitting her?' Muslim asked Alexey sternly.

When they emerged from the crevice, their attention was caught by a large vulture with a long, bald neck which was swooping in a smooth, steep semi-circle down below them, as it descended to the mountain road. Extending its long feet with crooked talons, the vulture swooped down on the precise place where the column of lorries had halted the previous night.

Only a few hours earlier, during the fighting, in the darkness of the night, Alexey and Judy had thought that they had fled a long way from the road, perhaps as much as a kilometre. Now, in the daytime, it turned out that the place where the fighting had happened was only a couple of hundred metres away. But now there was no road there, or lorries, or tanks. Huge torn craters gaped open in the riven earth, strewn with rocks from cliffs blown up in the bombing, burnt-out remains of lorries, and the warped and fused-together fragments of tank armour-plating and steel caterpillar tracks. Huge vultures were hopping about this graveyard, using their beaks to extract gobbets of human flesh from under rocks and burnt out metal. 'Hunting' alongside the vultures were grey-brown jackals with bristly muzzles. One of the jackals, straining with all four paws, was using its teeth to drag a human leg in a charred boot from under an overturned tank turret. A yard or so away from it yet another vulture had its claws fastened on the blackened remains of a tank driver, pulling lumps of flesh from his stomach and swallowing them whole.

'Fuck you!' groaned Alexey and, seizing a heavy stone from the ground, hurled it down towards them with all his might.

But neither the vultures nor the jackals displayed the slightest reaction. Only the vulture nearest where the stone fell jumped unwillingly to one side, holding an enormous piece of flesh in its beak. Stepping on it with its bony claws, it began tearing at the meat with its beak.

'What are they eating? People?' asked Muslim.

'Come on, let's get away from here!' said Alexey, grabbing him by the hand and, without turning around again, he started to stride off down the dry mountain slope.

Judy went after them.

'Where are we going to?' asked the boy, as he walked along.

'I don't know,' Alexey replied nervously. 'Downwards. There will be water there . . .'

Only a person who had never been in real mountains thinks that walking downhill is easy – you just go down, and that is all there is to it! Judy discovered very quickly that descending a stony, windswept mountain slope is probably more difficult than climbing up one. And almost certainly more dangerous. The force of inertia and your apparent lightness carry you down, pulling you, forcing you to run, but the slightest false step and you risk either not being able to stop, or – in the event that you can – you simply fall backwards with a thud and, back and bottom furrowing the scree, you hold firm to the dangerous slope in that way.

Alexey taught them not to go straight down the slope, but to descend like a snake, side on to it, placing your feet not straight in front of you, but edgewise to each other. And not to plump your feet straight down, but to bend slightly on the ball of your feet, like skiers, to give yourself buoyancy. And to fall on your side before you start to slide downhill unable to stop ... Muslim found this easy. It came naturally to him, as if he had not only been born in Afghanistan, but had grown up in these very mountains. But for himself and Judy Alexey broke off two sticks – branches from the very first tree they came across, sticking up out of the rocks all alone. He gave one stick to Judy and showed her how to use it – not leaning on it, but using it to brake herself against the earth, holding onto it like an oar.

The sun beat down mercilessly on their uncovered heads. Surrounding them as far as the eye could see were mountains. Into the fathomless and already cloudless sky they raised their pointed peaks, covered with layered crowns of glaciers and snow. The dry heat seemed to have driven away every living thing – even the birds, lizards and butterflies. That a war might be taking place here was completely incomprehensible, as was the fact that people could live here at all.

But Alexey was continually raising his head to the sky, scouring the horizon.

'I think that I may have gone slightly deaf after the fighting last night,' he said to Muslim and Judy, when they were sitting down to regain their breath in the shade of some boulders. 'If you hear anything in the sky, hide straightaway. Straightaway! Our helicopters won't go away leaving us alive ...'

He fell silent for a moment, and then added: 'Yes, that's how we fight! We finish off our own men, anything to stop the Afghans getting hold of their weapons. Come on! Let's go!'

And he got to his feet.

'I want something to drink.' whimpered Muslim.

'Come on ...' repeated Alexey.

An hour later Judy happened to rest her hand by chance against the edge of some enormous boulder. Detecting something unusual, she examined her hand in surprise and immediately called to Alexey:

'Alyosha!'

Her hand was damp. The rock which she had touched was moist.

Alexey immediately began to scramble up and around the giant rock. It was a grey granite boulder about the size of Madison Garden.

'Come here!' he called from above. 'Come here! There's water!'

Judy and Muslim climbed joyfully up and around the boulder, on their hands and knees.

It was not a spring or a stream. What Alexey had called water turned out to be a thin film of moisture, oozing down from the glaciers on the mountain top above. But they were glad even of this. Sprawling on the moist, uneven stone, they absorbed this moisture into their clothes and licked it with their tongues, like dogs. They carried on doing this for a long time, for what seemed almost an eternity. After quenching his thirst at last, Alexey turned over blissfully so as to moisten his back as well.

Suddenly he froze.

Standing at the top edge of the boulder and pointing their Soviet Kalashnikovs at them were three bearded men, a couple dressed in the Afghan style and one in a Soviet service jacket without epaulettes, but all wearing identical grey turbans on their heads.

'Judy ...' whispered Alexey softly, under his breath. There was something in his muffled voice which made her look up immediately. And before she had realised who these men were, Alexey had said to her just as quietly:

'Speak only in English ... Say something now!'

Judy looked in terror at the guns pointing at them.

'Say something!' Alexey ordered softly.

'Don't shoot! Don't shoot!' Judy shouted out in English as loudly as she could, and carried on: 'I am American! I am American! Don't shoot!'

The partisans began to talk about something in loud voices. One of them, with a short black beard, climbed quickly and easily down over the rock and, pointing his gun at Alexey and Judy once again, walked in a circle around them.

'American?' he said with interest.

'Yes, American!' Judy replied straightaway, lifting her head off the ground slightly.

'American!' shouted the partisan and added something else in Afghani for the benefit of his friends above. They started to laugh.

He gestured to Alexey and Judy to get to their feet. They stood up and raised their hands. Then suddenly Muslim went up to the partisan and, raising his smiling face, began to say something in Afghan. The man stared at the boy in amazement and then began to ask him something hurriedly. Muslim turned to Alexey and Judy in excitement and said proudly:

'They're the ones who blew up the Russian tanks! They have been following us for a long time, and we didn't even notice them!'

After searching Alexey and Judy and finding no weapons on them, the partisan motioned them to walk on ahead. The three Afghans and Muslim walked behind them, talking animatedly. Muslim, his piping voice almost choking with excitement, was telling them something and answering their short, guttural questions.

For some reason they led them upwards, and not down. After half an hour's climb up steep paths between the rocks and boulders almost invisible to the eye, they brought them to a cleft in the rock almost identical to the one in which they had hidden themselves the night before. About a dozen or so more partisans came out of the crevice to meet them. A fairly young Afghan wearing an astrakhan fur cap, with a short dagger in his belt and dressed like most of the others in wide trousers and dark waistcoat above a long linen shirt, listened carefully to what the first three had to tell him. Then he spoke to Muslim about something, turned to Judy and asked her in English:

'Who are you?'

The others all fell silent. Judy realised that he was their commander.

'I am an American! And we need to get to Pakistan!' she began to say impulsively, afraid that she might be stopped. 'Please!'

'And who is he?' said the Afghan, nodding in Alexey's direction.

'He is my fiancé! The two of us need to get to Pakistan! If you help us, you will get a lot of money!'

'I am asking you who he is! A Russian?' the Afghan asked again coldly.

'Yes, he's a Russian. We were running away from the KGB!'

'Why is this child with you? Where did you get him from?'

He spoke English very well apart from his 'r's' which were too resonant and rolled.

'We are taking him back to his mother. She is an Afghan. He was taken away to Russia when he was only six months old. We want to give him back to her.'

The Afghan carefully turned his eyes away from Judy to look at Alexey, and then addressed Judy again.

'How do you know the woman to whom you are taking the child?'

'We . . .' mumbled Judy. 'We . . .'

'Tell the truth!' he said. 'We will check everything!'

Then he turned suddenly to Alexey and asked him point-blank in Russian: 'Did you fight here?'

'Yes,' Alexey replied.

'With what troops?'

'With the motorized infantry.'

'How come you know his mother?' he went on, nodding towards Muslim.

'Our unit was stationed near the village of Tapbil in the Lohar valley. That's when we got to know each other,' said Alexey, looking the Afghan darkly in the eye.

'Why do you wish to give her her child back?'

'Because ... she asked me to.'

'Is it your child?' said the partisan, staring intently at Alexey.

'No.'

'You're lying!' the Afghan shouted suddenly and struck him violently in the face. 'Haven't you got enough women of your own?! Bastard!!'

Judy screamed and rushed towards Alexey who had gone pale and was biting his lips. He removed her hand roughly and rubbed his lip which had begun to bleed.

'Don't hit him! He's my father!' screamed Muslim in a mixture of Russian and Afghan and grabbing the partisan by the sleeve. 'Don't hit him!'

'I am not lying,' said Alexey quietly. 'You can check.' 'His father was Vasily Batkov who deserted to you in the Lohar valley and converted to Islam. He died in 1984, blown up by a mine ...'

'I shall check it,' said the Afghan calmly. 'I shall check.'

Then he gave some order in Afghan. Two of the partisans tore Muslim away from him.

'He is not lying!' said Judy, forgetting herself in her fear. She ran up to the commander and also grabbed hold of his sleeve. 'He is not lying! Believe me, it is not his son! ... Ask his mother! ...'

The commander jerked his arm away in repugnance.

Muslim tore himself from the arms of the Afghan who was holding him, rushed over to Alexey and threw his arms tightly around his knees, shouting:

'Don't touch him! He is good! Don't touch him!'

The commander looked at the boy and at Alexey in silence. Blood from his lacerated lip was oozing down

Alexey's dark beard.

'You can see for yourself,' said Judy. 'The boy is fair-haired, and he is dark. It's not his child, I swear!'

'Tonight we shall descend,' said the commander at last and motioned them in the direction of the crevice in the rocks.

The partisans pushed Alexey roughly into the fissure with Judy and the boy behind him. Inside it was shady and cool. There were two donkeys lying on the earth, and next to them were light machine-guns, three light mortars, some Kalashnikov sub-machine-guns and some ammunition belts. Some felt blankets were laid out next to the wall, and lying motionless on one of them was a partisan, either wounded or already dead from his wounds, and next to him a leather water bottle and the remains of an interrupted meal – some goat's cheese and bread . . .

The partisan who entered the crevice last suddenly shouted something out.

'Keep absolutely still!' ordered the commander in Russian.

Everybody froze – the partisans as well as Judy and Alexey.

Now, in the silence, you could clearly make out the drone of rapidly approaching helicopters.

The Soviet 'flying tanks' or MI-24 helicopters were hugging the mountains, on the look-out, like vultures, for prey.

The Afghan commander issued a curt, guttural order to his men and nodded towards a hole in the depths of the fissure. They quickly loaded the grenade-throwers and mortars onto the two donkeys, transferred the wounded man to a home-made stretcher and headed towards the hole. The commander pushed Alexey and Judy along in their direction, keeping Muslim next to him. Judy could not believe that the heavily laden donkeys would actually manage to push their way through the dark, narrow hole. But the Afghans forced them through. After that, Judy and Alexey found themselves in a long, dark but wide passage or tunnel, what the locals called a *kiriz*. It descended steeply and coming from the bottom of it you could hear the trickling of water. These were the underground tunnels of an irrigation system which the Afghans had built up over the centuries. In the summer, when the glaciers in the mountains began to melt, the water in these tunnels would gradually rise and swell, pouring down into the valleys towards the vineyards – vineyards which no longer existed, having been beaten into dust by eight long years of war. But mother nature had no knowledge of this, of course, and continued to hurl the streams of water down, and this water would wash with it mines and fragments of shells from the red and yellow Afghan soil, as well as the remains of burnt-out, blown-up armoured troop-carriers and the bones and skulls of Russian and Afghan dead . . .

Frozen with cold, slipping in the icy water that trickled along the bottom of the dark *kiriz*, and surrounded by their captors, Judy and Alexey walked through the subterranean kingdom of the spirits of Afghan Mojahedin.

Circling around above them, above the mountains, were Soviet MI-24 helicopters, whose pilots could see below them nothing but jagged cliffs, dry, hard and dead.

28

In the mornings, at sunrise, the sound of the *muezzin* calling people to prayer could be heard loudly in the settlement. The tiny mosque had been smashed by Soviet bombing as had a dozen or so of the larger houses, and this was probably why the Afghans prayed in the mornings not at the mosque, but on the flat roofs of their tiny, low, clay houses. Although, perhaps, praying on their roofs to the rising sun had been their ritual even when they did have a mosque. Spreading their highly coloured rugs, they would kneel down on them and, placing their hands on their knees, bow down to the east, crying out the first syllables of their prayer and singing in thin voices:

Allah O Akbar!
Allah O Akbar!
Ashakhadu anna la ilala illa-llab ...
Ashakhadu anna la ilala illa-llab ...
Ashakhadu anna Mokhamed rasula-llab ...

This was how each new day would begin – hot, dusty, and long. Outside the rickety wooden door of the clay and dung live-stock shed where Alexey and Judy had already been held for three weeks, there were hens scratching around, goats grazing, donkeys wandering about swishing their tails. Sometimes a noisy band of children would run past, or women would appear in their voluminous coloured dresses and veils. The house – if you could call a windowless clay hovel a house – where Judy and Alexey's shed was situated belonged to God knows whom – most probably the partisan commander. But nobody lived in the house. Or, at any rate, nobody spent the night there. Sometimes during the day, and more often at night, old Afghan men would turn up there, accompanied by donkeys loaded with crates of cartridges, mines, or other weapons. The crates would bear Soviet, American, German and heaven knows what other markings, even Israeli ones. The old men would swiftly unload the boxes and carry them into the house, returning a few days later, again at night, to carry them out, load them back onto donkeys, and disappear with them into the night.

There was always some old man standing guard outside this house-cum-ammunition store. It was also part of his duty to keep an eye on the prisoners and once a day to give them something to eat and drink – bread, green tea and dried apricots. But to call this old man a sentry would have been an exaggeration. Leaving his weapon in the shade of the house, he would spend the whole day engaged in domestic tasks – feeding the hens, milking the goats, beating off the donkeys pestering the old she-ass, drinking tea with dried apricots, cleaning out the irrigation ditch, praying. The next day a different old man would put in an appearance, doing the same things with equal diligence.

The prisoners' 'captivity' was also a fairly relative phenomenon. The doors to their shed were locked neither during the day, nor at night. They could wander about the yard, sunbathe or help the guard in his uncomplicated labours. Alexey found it fairly easy to pick up the subtleties of rural life, and even learnt how to milk goats, but most often he would help whichever guard it was to clear the irrigation ditch of weeds and silt. Alexey and Judy were forbidden to go outside the courtyard, however – at the slightest attempt to go out onto the street they would hear the guard's guttural shout behind them. They could have run away from this 'prison' a long time before, of course – during the night. But where would they have run to? Going back to the Russians was absurd. And finding their way through to Pakistan without the

Afghans' help – unthinkable . . .

True, every now and then lines of Afghan refugees from settlements destroyed by Soviet bombing-raids would wander eastward through the village at night, heading in the direction of Pakistan. They were exhausted and ragged old men and women, younger women and children, weakened by hunger, rickets and pneumonia. Those adults who had a little more strength would carry wounded, wasted children in their arms. How many of them would survive these marches towards Pakistan – through mountains where the temperature would drop to zero Celsius each night and where in daytime the unfortunate refugees would be prey to Soviet helicopters? But the Afghans would not have taken Alexey and Judy with them, even on foot like this. All the same, whenever they heard the sound of refugees tramping through the village at night, Judy and Alexey would rush over to the fence in the hope that one of them might turn out to be Ulima . . .

But Ulima never came.

Alexey and Judy blindly awaited their fate. The partisan commander had disappeared along with his detachment and Muslim the day after they had arrived in the settlement. But the partisans were hardly likely to have set off for the Lohar valley, in a different part of Afghanistan, in order to find the village of Tapbil, and to check Alexey's testimony. Most likely they had gone off on new operations against the Russians, and the boy had been sent off down some partisan chain of contacts to Tapbil to look for his mother. But trying to ascertain any of this from the old sentries was impossible – none of them spoke any English or Russian. The only thing left to do was wait. Wait until Muslim had found Ulima, and for Ulima somehow or other to make her way back here or at least convey to the partisan commander that Alexey was not Muslim's father. But what if Muslim did not find Ulima! Or what if Ulima did not want or was unable to make her way here? Or what if the commander and his small band of partisans should be killed during one of their operations?

In order not to think about all these 'ifs', Judy was trying to learn some Afghan. Through signs and gestures and mimicry she was extracting from the taciturn old guards more and more new words, denoting simple ideas: woman was 'khanum', man was 'mart', money was 'paisa', thank you was 'tashakur', goodbye was 'khuda khafer', son was 'macha', what is your name? was 'nash shuma chis' . . .

They would sleep on a thin layer of straw strewn on the earthen floor. Although during the first days of their imprisonment there they would diligently sweep out the shed and bring in fresh straw from the donkeys' stall, the earth, steeped in donkeys' urine, smelt disgusting and sickening at any time of day or night. At night it would get cold, and Alexey would squeeze Judy tightly to him trying to keep her warm. Sex, in the neighbourhood of copulating donkeys, brought them no joy or pleasure at all, and they forgot about it. They learnt to sleep in each other's arms without sexual desire, like brother and sister. Sometimes they would be woken up in the middle of the night by the drone of helicopters. The helicopters would be heading east, and then return. Alexey explained that the Soviets were laying ambushes for the caravans returning with weapons from Pakistan. Sometimes it seemed to Judy that this was how it had always been, that she had spent the whole of her life in this animal shed, and that New York University, her mother in Alabama, none of these had existed or, if they had, then in another life or in her dreams . . .

At the end of the third week or at the very beginning of the fourth (they had lost exact count of the days), they were woken up one moonlit night by the sound of a vehicle. Into the courtyard drove either a pick-up, or a small lorry of prehistoric date, dirty, with the paint peeling, and its roof cut right off. In the moonlight you could see jagged round holes in its sides, obviously caused by bullets or shrapnel. It had no number plate, of course, and one headlight had come away from its socket and was hanging down on a cable. The back of this pick-up or lorry was crammed full with light-weight boxes of some kind, obviously not ammunition or weapons – the handful of old men who had run up to it were easily able to pick up two or even three of them at a time and carry them quickly into the house. The well-proportioned, lean figure of the partisan commander flashed in between the lorry and the house, accompanied by some other tall individual in a turban, and disappeared through the doorway. Then from the depths of the cab the tiny figure of a child jumped out and rushed headlong towards the shed where Alexey and Judy were. They both recognized Muslim immediately. One of the old men tried to stop him, but Muslim dived right through the old man's legs, and the latter, weighed down by three crates bearing red crescents and some foreign inscription, spat in the boy's direction and carried the boxes into the house.

Alexey walked out of the shed towards Muslim, and the boy ran straight up, into his arms.

'Papa, there's no mama! There's no Tapbil! Tapbil has been burnt! The Russians bombed it! They killed mama! They killed everyone! ...'

Alexey sank down onto the ground with the boy, as if collapsed. Hugging Muslim close, he was swaying with him from side to side.

'Don't cry, babá, don't cry ...' Muslim was saying. 'We killed a lot of Russians, too. Not these Mojahedin, but others!'

Judy leant back against the wall, horror-struck. If Muslim's mother and all the inhabitants of her village had been killed, then there was no way that Alexey could ever prove to anyone that he was not Muslim's father. Especially as the boy persistently called him 'papa' ...

The lean partisan commander came out of the house and headed towards their shed. Striding along next to him was the man in the turban, aged about thirty and wearing the same kind of wide linen shirt as do the majority of Afghans. Only his beard looked somewhat fairer in colour at close quarters than those of the locals. The commander was saying something to him in Afghan as they walked across. At last they halted in front of Alexey and Judy.

'Hi! Are you American?' the one with the fair beard said to Judy in English. He was smiling for some reason. Judy immediately realised, from his even white teeth and the smile accompanying his 'Hi!', that he was American himself.

'Yes,' she said, overjoyed. 'I'm American. And who are you?'

'Well, I'll tell you that later on. But for the time being ... they have brought me here to check out whether you are American or not. How I'm supposed to do it I haven't the faintest idea! You've got no papers, I suppose? ...'

'Of course not,' she grinned.

The American looked at her carefully, then transferred his gaze to Alexey and Muslim, then to the commander standing there impassively, and finally back to Judy again.

'Where were you born?' he went on.

'In Boston. But my parents moved to Madison, Alabama when I was four years of age,' she said hurriedly. 'What do they intend doing to us?'

'That depends on whether you are an American or not,' he said to her with an encouraging smile. 'Where did you go to school?'

'I finished high school in Madison. And then I studied for two years at New York University ...'

'You went to college in New York? That makes it a lot easier! I got my Ph.D. at Columbia. And how did you land up here?'

'Didn't they tell you?' she said, nodding in the direction of the commander.

'They told me that they had captured a Russian soldier accompanied by an Afghan boy and a woman who keeps on screaming that she's American. Now that's a wild combination, right? So tell me your story. Only before you start, tell me what you would really like to eat right now.'

'Me? ...' said Judy in confusion. 'The thing I'd really like is a hamburger or ... pizza with pepperoni! But why do you ask?'

'She's an American,' he said to the commander.

'How do you know?' he replied suspiciously.

'Because I dream of eating a hamburger as well. I'm sick of your goat's cheese and your green tea. Besides, she has an Alabama accent.'

'Well, she could have been taught that in a KGB training school,' the commander countered suspiciously.

Making use of their conversation, Judy turned to Alexey, who was still sitting on the ground, and explained everything to him joyfully:

'He's an American! They've brought him here to check out whether I'm an American as well ...'

'I see!' Alexey nodded coldly. 'Well, I hope you haven't forgotten anything about that marvellous America of yours!'

Judy stopped laughing and, looking the American straight in the eye, began to tell her story.

She went on for about twenty minutes, getting things mixed up occasionally and interrupted from time to time by questions from the American. The partisan commander, whose knowledge of English did not allow him to follow Judy's flow of words and her slang expressions, went away, taking Muslim with him. After this Judy felt herself more at ease and continued with her story at even greater speed.

When she had reached the end, Michael – that was his name – gave a whistle of admiration and said: 'Well, that's some story for you! And do you really think that this old woman, his great-aunt, will come to collect you from Pakistan?'

'She's there already!' said Judy with conviction. 'What date is it today?'

'The 21st of April.'

'The 21st of April?!' Judy exclaimed. 'Why, she'll have been there for a long time already, looking for us in the Afghan refugee camps. But how to find her, I have no idea.'

'Well, that's easy. Through the American consulate in Pakistan.'

'But who are you? Can I find out now? A representative of our government with the Afghan partisans, or something?'

'You must be joking!' said Michael. 'Our government doesn't have any official representatives with the Mojahedin, and the White House is categorically against American citizens visiting Afghanistan! No, I'm a private individual, and I'm here at my own risk. It's just that I did my Ph.D. on Persian poetry, and the rest is to do with my love of adventure.'

He smiled.

'In any case,' he went on, 'none of that is important. I'll go and talk to the commander right away. I think everything is going to be all right . . .'

And off he went.

Judy rushed over to where Alexey was still sitting and threw herself at him, tickling him and squealing with joy: 'We're going home! We're going home!'

Then she kissed him.

Alexey gave way to her joy or, at least, pretended to, doing nothing to spoil her enthusiasm, trying only to protect himself from her tickling.

'They're coming back!' he said suddenly, hearing footsteps.

Michael, accompanied by two more Afghan partisans, was walking across the courtyard from the unloaded lorry in their direction. The commander was not with them.

'Well, what's happening?' said Judy, rushing towards Michael.

'We're heading for Pakistan immediately. Do you have any things?' he said, with an awkward smile. 'Hurry up, because you don't have time to say goodbye.'

‘What do you mean: to say goodbye?!’ said Judy, looking at Michael in amazement.

‘He’s not going with us,’ said Michael, nodding towards Alexey.

‘What do you mean: he’s not going with us?! Why not?’

‘That’s what they’ve decided. Until he can prove that this boy is not his son, he’ll have to remain here . . .’

‘But they’ve destroyed the village by bombing! The boy’s mother has died! How *can* he prove anything! But they could carry out a blood test!’

‘Don’t make me laugh! What blood test! Here?!’

‘I won’t go anywhere without him!’ cried Judy and grabbed Michael by the arm. ‘Please, *beg* them! He has told them the truth. They’ve *got* to let him go! This boy isn’t his son!’

Michael gently disentangled his arm and said to her softly: ‘Look, there’s nothing I can do! I tried, but . . . And, after all, the boy does keep on calling him ‘father’. How do you know that he didn’t rape some Afghan woman, when he was on service here! The Afghans are a stubborn race at the best of times, and when it is a question of revenge for the loss of someone’s honour! . . . They won’t let him go! You’ve been unlucky, in fact. There are seven big partisan armies in Afghanistan, and some of them even have representatives in Europe and Washington. You could have tried to reach an agreement with them. But you have been taken prisoner by some small detachment, which submits to nobody. Apart from Allah, of course. There are hundreds of other groups like this . . .’

‘What’s he saying?’ said Alexey, butting into the conversation.

Judy turned to look at him in confusion.

‘He’s saying . . . They won’t let you go! Until they sort out who the boy belongs to!’

‘But what about you? Will they let you go?’

‘Me? . . .’ Judy turned sharply towards Michael and

said in English: 'I am staying with him. I won't go alone!'

'But are they letting you go?' Alexey persisted.

'No, I'm not going anywhere without you!' she said.

'Listen to me, Judy,' said Michael. 'Dawn will be here at any moment. I shall be off in five minutes' time. If you should decide to come with us, then there is a seat for you in the car. Make up your mind!'

He went off again, but the two partisans who had accompanied him remained.

'You *have* to go!' said Alexey softly.

'No!' Judy replied firmly. 'I am staying here with you!'

'Don't be stupid! You can't be of any help to me. And there's no point in the two of us dying!'

'No!' screamed Judy, about to get hysterical. 'Why did you have to take the boy? I told you! I told you!! ...'

'Shut your mouth, you idiot!' he said, abruptly interrupting her. He had turned quite pale. If it were not for the two Afghans standing near them, he might have struck her. 'I *want* you to go!' he went on. 'I don't *need* you!'

'You're lying, you fool!' she said. 'You need me now more than you ever did before!'

He grabbed her roughly by the shoulders, shook her and stared into her eyes.

'You *will* go!' he said calmly. 'You wanted to earn money from me. My aunt will pay you. *Go*!'

'No, that won't work, you cretin! That won't work!' she screamed into his face. 'I love you! I *love* you! Idiot! Idiot!'

She wanted to embrace him, but he pushed her away, and suddenly shouted over to the commander who had just come out of the house with Michael.

'Hey, you! Come here!' he said.

Amazed by this rude shout, the commander looked around, thinking that Alexey was calling not him, but somebody else.

'No, it's you! It's you I'm talking to!' Alexey shouted at him, waving his hand. 'Come over here! Come on!'

He sat down on the ground and removed his left boot.

The commander and Michael came up to him in bewilderment.

'Give me your knife!' Alexey said to the commander as rudely as ever, without getting up from the ground. 'Well, go on! There's nothing to worry about! I won't cut anybody's throat!'

The commander took his short dagger from its leather case and gave it to Alexey.

Alexey drove the edge of the blade forcibly into the thick double sole of his boot and gave the handle a sharp turn. The outer sole flew off along with some nails. Underneath it was a carefully folded piece of paper. Alexey carefully unfolded it. It was the first page of that edition of *Pravda* which Alexey had been shown by Pavel Yegorov in his house in Parkhar. Alexey offered it to the commander.

'What's this? *Pravda*?' he asked in surprise.

'Yes, it's a copy of *Pravda*, only this one tells you the real "truth",' Alexey replied. 'Go on, read it!'

Alexey poked his thumb at the headline and read it out himself. '"Russian soldiers – victims of the Soviet Communist Party's criminal policies." Well, have you ever read this paper? Hundreds of copies are dropped on Soviet bases . . .'

'No, but I've heard about it,' said the commander, bringing the paper up close to his eyes with interest. In the moonlight it was possible to read, if not the text, then at least the headlines.

Alexey stood up.

'This newspaper is produced by a friend of mine,' he said, turning the sheet over and pointing to the surname of the author of an article entitled 'Pass this on to my beloved.' 'That's his name – Yury Tverdysh. Only that's a pseudonym. His real name is Yury Shalygin. When you kill me, find him and give him this newspaper. Tell him that Alyosha Odalevsky asked for him to be told that the KGB is after him. Can you remember? Alyosha Odalevsky – that's me. By the way, he knew the boy's mother. He can confirm that he is not my son.'

'And now – take her away,' he went on, nodding towards Judy. Then, with a sudden lunge he pressed the tip of the dagger against his own stomach. 'Take her away, or I'll disembowel myself!'

PART FIVE

29

The Sufi arrived in the camp on a donkey. The enormous camp for Afghan refugees, one of the dozens of such camps in the Peshawar valley not far from the Afghan border, differed from an ordinary Afghan settlement only by virtue of its huge size and also because the people did not live here in clay huts, but in shanties made of old crates and plywood nailed together, in tents, or simply under canvas awnings. But their everyday life was the same as in any Afghan settlement. There were emaciated chickens running around all over the place, goats lurking about on the look-out for a patch of grass not yet trampled down, donkeys braying, children fighting or playing games, women at hearths preparing meals from the sparse rations distributed by the Red Crescent or other missionary organisations.

In anticipation of the arrival of the Sufi, who to the Afghan Moslems was as influential a figure as the Lyubavitcher Rabbi to Orthodox Jews in America, Tanya Goehr, Elizabeth and Judy had been working in the Catholic missionary hospital, which was housed in four large white marquees with red crescents on the roof. Most active of all was Elizabeth. Although she knew not a single word of Afghani, she managed to chat for hours on end to the stream of wounded, burnt or gassed children constantly arriving from Afghanistan, treating them not so much with medicine, as with her tender-hearted chatter. She would sing them simple children's songs, or rock in her arms the orphaned babies with suppurating wounds caused by napalm, or poison-gas. Sometimes she would bring tears to the eyes even of shell-shocked teenagers.

Tanya was bursting to travel and meet the Sufi who was touring the refugee camps on the occasion of the Moslem spring observance of Ramadan. But Michael kept on restraining her. 'Don't be in a hurry,' he would say. 'The Moslems don't like hurrying. Let him come here and see the work you are doing ...'

The Sufi entered the camp on a donkey accompanied by a small entourage. He was about sixty-five years old, of strong but not tall build, and had a black beard. Nothing, apart from his turban embroidered with gold thread, distinguished his clothes from the clothes of any other Afghan old man. But around his donkey there was the same hubbub as greeted the Pope's arrival in Paraguay or Venezuela. Women wearing black veils were screaming and wailing, while some were tearing their hair and scratching their faces in ecstasy. One could understand the reason why, of course. Fate had deprived them of their country, their land, their dwellings, their husbands, relatives, livestock, as well as maiming their children, and their sorrow found an outlet in their lamentation. Always uncomplaining, silent and submissive, once a year these women were able to raise their cries to Allah so that he – through the Sufi – should hear their grief.

The Sufi was moving slowly, surrounded by the screaming crowd of women. He was uttering a loud prayer, endowing the general clamour with the rhythm of a recitative.

Then, when it was already midday, he visited the hospital, as was natural. In the hospital each bed with a wounded child had a plate of cakes placed next to it. These were the gifts not of the Catholic mission, but of those same women who had been tearing their hair during the Sufi's ceremonial progress during the morning. They had managed to save a quantity of flour from their meagre missionary rations and baked pies for the holiday with dried apricots, raisins and nuts for the wounded children, both their own and those of others . . .

The Sufi walked slowly around the children lying on the beds; naked because of the heat and with their wounds uncovered. Most of them were children injured by 'butterflies' – bombs made in the shape of toy butterflies which the Soviet helicopters would drop. The Sufi placed his hand on the head of each child in turn, saying a few quiet words as he did so.

Then he sat down on a rug laid out on the earthen floor and began to pray. As the prayers went on, his voice grew stronger and louder, but neither his austere-looking face nor his voice contained any sign of tears. Michael softly translated the words of the prayer to the doctors and nurses who were standing to one side, but even without his translation it was possible to understand what the Sufi was asking of Allah. He was not begging Allah to heal the wounded children. Nor was he requesting him to save the dying. He was asking for one thing only – that the Russians be punished. That their children, grandchildren and great-grandchildren should be visited with the same wounds, that their houses and land should be burnt with the same napalm, that their rivers and wells should also be poisoned. The children repeated all together more and more loudly his guttural words after him. Looking at their burnt childish bodies, which no amount of ointments and medicines seemed able to heal, the suppurating flesh of their open wounds, their maimed faces, arms, stomachs, legs, it was difficult not to join in this prayer, it was difficult to remember the Christian doctrine of forgiveness. Elizabeth repeated the words of the prayer in a whisper, understanding not the words themselves, but their sense . . .

Observing the Sufi's desiccated, black-bearded and austere face and listening to his terrible prayer, Tanya realised that it was absurd to ask this man to show mercy to some Russian prisoner.

As the Sufi was leaving the hospital marquee, Michael said a few words to him softly in Afghani and nodded towards Tanya, Judy and Elizabeth who were standing near him, dressed in the dark garments worn by all missionary women and with white kerchiefs on their heads, decorated with the red crescent. The Sufi gave him a monosyllabic reply and walked outside.

'He will receive you!' said Michael, turning joyfully to Tanya. 'This evening . . .'

That evening they went to the Sufi's tent, erected over wooden flooring nailed together hurriedly by some of the old men. The Sufi was seated on a wide carpet, his legs crossed in the Moslem fashion. He motioned them to be seated. Tanya, Judy and Elizabeth sat down awkwardly on the carpet. Michael sat next to them, crossing his legs, too, in the Afghan manner. Very briefly he outlined to the Sufi in Afghani the substance of Tanya's request. The Sufi answered him softly and calmly.

'What did he say? Translate it word for word!' Tanya said to Michael insistently.

'He said that they are not terrorists and do not sell their prisoners. They will give them scot-free to anybody apart from the Russians. They will send them to any Western country which is willing to take them. But this particular soldier, your grandson, got a young Afghan girl with child. Allah does not forgive rapists, not even Moslem ones!'

'Translate this to him word for word,' said Tanya. 'Alexey is not a rapist. More than that – he rescued the boy from a Soviet boarding-school. If he had been a rapist he would not have brought the boy back into Afghanistan, but would have escaped by some other route. Through Finland, for example. But I don't want to argue, nor to beg him for anything. What I am proposing is a simple business deal. If they kill Alexey, it will do no good to anyone. But if they let me have Alexey and the boy, then I will open another hospital here, using my own money. Either here, or in another refugee camp. The doctors here are saving hundreds of Afghan children.'

Michael translated her words diligently.

The Sufi stared piercingly into her eyes, and uttered a few words in response.

'Allah does not forgive sins for money,' Michael translated.

'Tell him that I would not be giving this money for a hospital to atone for Alexey's sin. There *was* no sin. I would give this money for a hospital so that they should not curse the entire Russian people. It is not the Russian people killing their children. It is the Kremlin killing them, the Communists. Let them curse the Communists – Russian, non-Russian, it doesn't matter. The hospital which I'll open will be a hospital run by the Russian Orthodox mission. And it will not be financed by my money alone. I shall give the first three hundred thousand for the founding of a fund. The remaining money I'll collect from the Russian emigration in the West. There are more than two million of us *non-Communist* Russians in the West. And as for *Slavs* in the West, there are twenty million! We have our own newspapers, our own stocks and shares, even our own banks ... Translate it word for word!'

Michael did so. The Sufi asked him a question.

'He is asking why you wish to have this boy, if he is not your grandson's son?'

'Because the child has neither father, nor mother, and I do not want him to end up in my hospital without legs or arms. My grandson rescued him from a Soviet boarding-school, and I want to complete his salvation – by saving him from Soviet bombs!'

'Bravo!' said Michael approvingly and translated her answer for the Sufi.

The Sufi looked at Tanya carefully once again and said something to Michael.

'He wishes to know why he should believe you. What if you were to get your grandson back and were immediately to forget about the hospital?'

'I am a Russian princess!' said Tanya proudly. 'Under my government, that is to say when the Tsar was ruling,

Russia and Afghanistan were good neighbours. But if my word is not sufficient for him, then I can write out the first cheque. A payment in advance – for fifty thousand dollars ...'

Tanya put her hand into the wide pocket of her black missionary dress and extracted her cheque-book.

'Wait a moment,' Michael said to her and translated what she had said for the Sufi.

The Sufi with a short gesture of his fingers commanded her to put her cheque-book away and for the first time during their discussion almost smiled – more with his eyes than with his lips, which were concealed by his moustache and beard. He spent some time saying something to Michael.

'What is it he's saying?' Tanya interrupted impatiently.

'He is saying that if you really do open such a hospital, he will cease to curse all Russians, and will curse only Russian Communists. He says that if all Russians were like you ... In a word, we can go!' said Michael joyfully. 'You will get your grandson back!'

'And the child?' asked Tanya, remaining seated.

'And the child as well! ... Let's go! If you are such a great philanthropist, perhaps you would like to adopt me as your son as well?!'

30

'Unfortunately, Mrs Goehr, we are unable to let your grand-nephew enter the United States,' the American Assistant Consul in Pakistan was announcing to Tanya. 'He is a criminal who has murdered two men. That they were KGB officers does not matter ...'

He was very young, this Assistant Consul – no more than thirty. He was wearing a good-quality Italian grey pin-stripe, a gleaming white shirt, a fashionable and immaculately-tied cherry-coloured tie with a gold tie-pin. On his slender, well-manicured fingers he had a wedding ring and a signet ring, around his wrist he had a dark-coloured watch which showed not only the time, but also his pulse-rate. His office was spotlessly clean with an air-conditioner functioning noiselessly. The only objects on his desk were a telephone, a desk-set with three sharply chiselled pencils, a miniature American flag and a bronze statuette of the Statue of Liberty. Even the most fastidious glance would have found nothing to carp at in this glossy young diplomat. Outside the window of his clinically clean office the wind was stirring the heavy American flag hanging down from the consulate building. Beyond it you could see the modern buildings of new Islamabad, the capital of Pakistan.

'In that case I wish to see the Consul himself,' Tanya replied.

'It's no use, Mrs Goehr. According to our immigration laws, terrorists and persons with a criminal past have no right of entry into our country. We have enough criminals of our own, as you know.'

Judy's heart sank. After all that she and Alexey had been through, who would have guessed that they would stumble up against the leaden barrier of the law – and in the consulate of her own country! At the threshold of her own home! ...

'Do you have any more questions?' asked the Assistant Consul, obviously giving her to understand that the audience was at an end.

But Tanya made no move in her armchair.

'As soon as my grand-nephew arrives here from Afghanistan, he will marry Miss Judy Sanders. She is a US citizen – and he, as her husband ...'

'That won't alter anything,' interrupted the Assistant Consul contemptuously. 'How can we be certain that it will not be a fictitious marriage with the purpose of bringing into our country one more immigrant who wishes to get around the quota and the law? That was why Miss Sanders flew with you to Moscow – to conclude a fictitious marriage with your grand-nephew while there. It does her no credit.'

'But this will be a genuine marriage,' said Judy.

'I have no doubt,' said the official with patent sarcasm. 'But even if it really is a genuine marriage and you were to have ten children by Mr Odalevsky, it would not cancel out the fact that he has murdered two Soviet officers.'

Yes, it looked as if the young diplomat with the cold grey eyes knew the law pretty well!

'Are there any more questions?' he said again, baldly indicating that there was nothing more to talk about.

Tanya gripped the elbow-rests of her chair with her fingers, which still bore the marks of the rings which had remained in Russia. Then, in spite of the Assistant Consul's desire to be rid of her and Judy, she opened her handbag, took out her cigarettes and lighter, lit one up and emitting a cloud of smoke, gazed at the Assistant Consul through the haze. Judy remembered that that was just how she had sized her up during their first conversation in New York.

The Assistant Consul winced at the smoke, but said nothing. There was no ashtray on his desk, and he, of course, was a non-smoker.

'But you do understand, Mr ... I'm sorry, what was your name?'

'My name is Steven Vincent Rapp, Junior ...' the official replied icily.

'You do understand, Steve, that tomorrow or, at worst, the day after I can be in Washington,' Tanya said unhurriedly, taking another deep drag on the cigarette. She was obviously weighing things up in her mind, as people do at an auction before making a decisive bid. 'There, in Washington, I shall hire a lawyer. A good lawyer, with contacts in the Immigration Office. And in a few months' time I shall have both my grand-nephew and the little boy in the United States. It will cost me about twenty thousand dollars. Well – perhaps forty thousand ...'

She took another drag at her cigarette and after a pause said simply, as if in passing: 'Which half of the money would you like in order to spare me all this nonsense?' And, looking away from the Assistant Consul, holding the hand with the cigarette suspended in the air, she looked around for somewhere to shake off the ash.

Mr Steven Vincent Rapp, Junior got to his feet. With his beautiful well-manicured fingers he did up the bottom button of the jacket of his splendid Italian suit.

'Mrs Goehr! You know where you are. This is not the KGB. We do not accept bribes here. Goodbye, Mrs Goehr!'

Tanya realised that she had made a wrong move, but she was not used to giving up. Or at least – not so easily.

'But who said anything about a "bribe"?' she said with a smile, not getting up from her chair. 'I am offering you a deal. You help me to arrange the papers so that my grand-nephew and the boy can fly to the US in a week's time. I will then give you the best room in my Miami Beach hotel for the rest of your life. You can travel there with your family or with your girlfriend whenever you like, at no cost to yourself. How about it?'

Finally she shook the ash into the container with the pencils.

Mr Rapp, Junior followed this gesture with his eyes and then said quietly, without looking up. 'I am sorry, it is impossible. Your papers have already been to the Immigration Office. There is nothing I can do. I'm sorry ...'

Tanya got up and Judy followed her example.

'I'll give you till tomorrow to think about it, Steve,' said Tanya, as she headed for the door. 'I'll give you a ring from the airport. Goodbye.'

Judy opened the door to allow Tanya to go out first.

'Mrs Goehr ...' a voice said behind them.

They both looked round.

'You couldn't wait a little longer?' said Mr Rapp, Junior, for some reason opening up the drawer in his desk and glancing into it. Most probably he was trying to avoid eye-contact with Tanya and Judy. 'I should like to discuss a few details about your grand-nephew's life with you by yourself ...'

'Run along, Judy,' said Tanya, giving her a victory glance. 'Wait for me in the entrance hall ...'

When the door had closed behind Judy, Mr Steven Vincent Rapp, Junior produced from the bottom drawer of his desk a white china ashtray with a coloured picture of the White House and put it down on the desk.

'I think that we do have one possibility ...' he said, raising his incorruptible grey eyes towards Tanya.

31

They were flying from Islamabad to Peshawar on a tiny ten-seater passenger aircraft, on hard aluminium seats surrounded by Pakistani peasants with wicker-work baskets, bags, sacks. But never, not even in the biggest airliner, had Tanya felt as comfortable, light and at ease as she did buffeted about by every air-pocket in the squeaky wagon of a plane belonging to the Pakistan airline, PIA. Her heart was flying far higher than the tiny plane, her soul was singing. 'I did it!' she said to herself exultantly in English. 'I did it!' During the last thirty years of her life in America she had often found herself even thinking in English at times, but had immediately caught herself up, forcing her brain to switch back to Russian again. It would be the last straw for her, a Russian princess, to forget how to speak Russian.

But today was a special case. 'I did it!' sounded so much stronger, pithier and to the point than the Russian equivalent. 'I did it in spite of everything!' she thought. 'So it may have cost me ten times as much as I had anticipated, so I may have lost my family heirlooms, my priceless rings, but to make up for it the life still remaining to me will be filled with meaning, with great deeds and with a big new family. In return for all the trials of my life, for all the horrors, difficulties and misfortunes which I have gone through because of that accursed Bolshevik Revolution in 1917, God has now given me all at one go a grand-nephew, a marvellous grand-niece whom I myself – myself – chose to be his wife, and I even have a great-grand-nephew! What more could an old woman aged eighty-three dream of?! What is mere money compared with wealth like that?!'

Rejoicing, Tanya stole a sideways glance at Judy. 'My darling, golden girl!' she thought. 'I was not mistaken in you. I could feel it straightaway in my heart of hearts, that very first time I saw you in McDonald's on 97th Street! But my God, the things you have had to go through, and how you have changed over these last few months! You have grown up, lost weight, and only your eyes have stayed the same. But never mind! Soon everything in your life will change again, everything! You've no idea what the Russian Princess Tatyana Stepanovna Goehr-Odalevskaya is capable of doing! Of course, Alexey will need time to adapt to America, and he still has to learn English and choose a profession. Prince Odalevsky shouldn't have to earn his living as a common metal-worker after all! But there are good language schools – the Berlitz, for example. And there are universities. And even if the two of them, Alexey and Judy, should both wish to go to university, then I will pay for them, and buy them a house ... Or rather, no! Let them study in Princeton, or New York, or Yale, and I will look after Muslim in Florida ... That terrible New York climate is no good for a child, after all. Florida, the sun – that's what the boy needs!'

The aeroplane came into land, crashing its wheels against the earthen runway so hard that all the passengers were thrown back in their seats and the wicker-work baskets rolled all over the ribbed aluminium floor.

Raising a cloud of red dust, the plane taxied over to the dilapidated and diminutive clay shed which went by the name of 'airport' here. There were donkeys wandering around the 'airport', camels sprawling about, Afghans and Pakistanis sitting on the ground wearily awaiting their flights beneath the scorching sun.

Judy and Tanya got off the plane down a three-runged metal ladder and glimpsed Elizabeth and Muslim amongst the Pakistanis loaded down with their simple goods and chattels heading towards the plane. Elizabeth was holding the boy firmly by the hand.

'Muslim! But where is Alexey?' shouted Judy, freezing from a sudden terrible premonition long before Elizabeth and Muslim reached them.

'Don't worry, he's alive,' said Elizabeth curtly, as she arrived. 'He's gone away, that's all.'

Elizabeth's lips were lightly pressed, like those of a belligerent child.

'Gone away where?' asked Judy in bewilderment.

'Nobody knows. He's simply gone, that's all. And after all we have done for him . . .'

'But *when* did he go? Just now? When he was already here?'

'No. Ask *him*,' she said, nodding towards the boy. 'He'll tell you.'

Judy quickly squatted down by the boy and grabbed him by the hand, clenched in a tight fist.

'Muslim, darling, where is Alexey?' she asked in Russian.

'He went away with Uncle Yura Shalygin. Uncle Yura came to the village. He talked to the commander lots and lots, had a big argument, he collected papa, and they went away. They took some papers for the Russian soldiers. Babá wrote you a letter . . .'

Muslim unclenched his little fist and gave Judy a scrap of paper.

It was a piece of the newspaper *Pravda*, and written across the article entitled 'Pass this on to my beloved' in large bold handwriting were the words:

'DEAR JUDY! DEAR "GRANDMOTHER"! I LOVE YOU. ALEXEY.'

EPILOGUE

A moonless night hung over Afghanistan. In the midst of this night, somewhere a very long way away, beyond the mountains, there were occasional flashes of light – either from fighting or from widespread fire.

But here, along the mountain road where the figures of two men walked, accompanied by a donkey loaded down with panniers, it was completely quiet. The only thing to be heard was the clip-clopping of the donkey's hooves on the stones and the quiet sound of Alexey's voice. He was saying:

'Pavel Yegorov died before my very eyes ... Nikolay is a legless invalid. On forty roubles' pension ... Fedora and Boris are in Saratov. During the day they work in a cooperative, riveting metal buttons. And then, in the evening, they sing on stage – heavy metal. Fedora has lost his right arm, Boris has no teeth. Rat, the sergeant, knocked them all out. Sergey Sukhar has become very rich and lives in Dushanbe. He deals in drugs, that is until they get him. They'll do it all right, and he'll go to jail ... Who else was there in our platoon? You and me. That was the seven of us ... Want to smoke?'

They stopped and lit up cigarettes.

In the sky above their heads shone the large Afghan stars. It was still more than a year before the Soviet troops would begin to be withdrawn from Afghanistan.